Kelex

The A**hole Series

BLUE SAFFIRE

Perceptive Illusions Publishing, Inc.
Bay Shore, New York

Blue Saffire/Preceptive Illusions Publishing, Inc.
PO Box 5253
Bay Shore, NY 11706
www.BlueSaffire.com

Publisher's Note: This is a work of fiction. Names, characters, places, and incidents are a product of the author's imagination. Locales and public names are sometimes used for atmospheric purposes. Any resemblance to actual people, living or dead, or to businesses, companies, events, institutions, or locales is completely coincidental.

Ordering Information:
Quantity sales. Special discounts are available on quantity purchases by corporations, associations, and others. For details, contact the "Special Sales Department" at the address above.

Cover Designed by Covers by Combs www.coversbycombs.com

Kelex: The A**hole Club Series/ Blue Saffire. -- 1st ed.
ISBN 978-1-941924-23-5

Never dull your shine because someone else can't shine as brightly. That's not a you problem.

—BLUE SAFFIRE

CHAPTER ONE

Out of Jail Free

Pit

It's happening. That part of how my brain works that I can never explain to anyone. As everyone crowds the back room of my bar while we wait for Kelex to arrive, each person recounts that day from fourteen years ago—not just that night, but the day. Now that we know Ox and Lex are involved, I think that's important.

It begins. I can't help it.

I watch Ox's lips as they move, I hear the words coming from his mouth, but I'm leaving my body as I take it all in. Instead of sitting with him, Uncle Blake and the rest of the crew, I'm on that track.

Things I didn't know I took in that night come back to me. I see Ox talking to one of the officers as he looks toward me in the back seat of the squad car. Lex is there too. In the distance, she's standing next to a charger and bike while wringing her hands.

My phone buzzes and I'm snapped back into the room. I pull it out to see I have a text. I grunt and nod at the message. I figured as much.

"We ended the night as newlyweds," Ox says.

"And you?" I say to Lex.

She's the last one before I get to Kelex when he arrives. It's here. What I'm looking for is here within this circle. No one is here I don't trust. Not even their other halves.

Uncle Blake is here because he was the one who insisted it was time we do this. Shawna is on her way here because my instincts tell me she's not excluded from this, especially not now.

That text just confirmed what I've suspected for a while now. However, my reach has only begun to get to the answers I needed there. Things have never been what they seemed around here.

"I woke that morning so excited. Ant and I were to meet at the courthouse. After my shower, I stepped out and could hear my father roaring at someone on the phone.

"I rolled my eyes and ignored it that day. It was nothing new and I wanted to stay focused on my wedding day," Lex starts.

I take a sip of my water as she continues. While I listen, Uncle Blake moves to look at his watch, then his phone, grabbing my attention. My focus homes in on him, it all seems nonchalant, but I know better.

I begin to float from the room again. This time, I'm in a room playing with Ox. We're little, back when our father was alive.

The first thing to grab my attention as I focus on the room is the Black guy. His voice has a smooth cadence about it. He's talking to my father, Uncle Blake, and Marvin Jennings.

That's when it clicks. This is Lester Smith, Lex's dad. I remember him.

"I have all we need to take them down. We need to make a move soon. If we don't, I'm going to lose my hold on Vander.

"Things won't be as easy for us. We won't be untouchable," he said the last part toward Uncle Blake.

"You do this, Nicky. It changes everything. It won't matter if we're untouchable," Uncle Blake said.

"That's easy for you to say. We're taking all the risk. We've lost the most," Lester said.

"I'm sorry about Willow and your wife, but someone has to think with a level head here."

"You've seen how they're turning on me. How they're making plays against the founders. What will happen if we don't make a power play and stop them?"

Uncle Blake sighed. *"I think Basil is right. We allow this to play out. Don't rock the boat, Nicky. Give it some time, Lester. I'll steer this ship right. You'll be back on top in no time."*

"Meanwhile, you haven't lost anything and this divide is happening because of you," Lester seethed.

"Because of me? It has nothing to do with me. This started long before—"

"Enough," my father barked. *"I'm bringing them down, Blake. All of them."*

The door to the room opened and my mother walked in with another woman. I go to zone in on the woman and the room loses focus.

"After we married, I went home to get a few things to spend the night with Ant. We had plans to meet that night on the cliff," Lex's voice pulls my attention.

I'm back in the bar, present and in my body, but my focus is on Uncle Blake. This motherfucker. He knows. He's figured out how my mind works.

The one thing I never explained to Skittles about how I think is how I catalog information. It's one of the reasons I'm able to remember so much. I chunk things down and compartmentalize them for future use.

One spark and I can pull an entire thread. It's like linking a web together. Nothing is forgotten, and at the right time, I can connect all the dots.

Now the question is, has he known all along? I get the feeling this is what he's been counting on, but did he mean for this to happen—to use Josh to trigger me? A part of me wouldn't put it past him.

Kelex

I step out of the back seat of the car Blake Knight sent for me and frown as I see I'm being dropped off at Fuck Off. The last thing I need is a bar. A drink or two, yes.

To be in a bar, not so much. I'm barely containing my temper as it is. Even a single hour behind bars for the murder of that bastard is too much. Unfortunately, I was there for three.

Someone murdered my father and they're trying to frame me. I hated his guts, but if I had done this, it would have been much cleaner. Besides, I have too much to live for to do something like this here.

Up until a few days ago, everything had finally been going right. I have a family to think about. I would never have jeopardized any of that for Ulysses Kylix.

"And someone knows that," I mutter to myself. "If any of my family is harmed, someone *is* going to die by my hands. That's a promise."

"Yo," Pit calls as he steps out of the bar. "You good?"

"Do I look like I'm good? Tell me you know something."

"For once, Vander is silent. Although, I want to talk to you. I have some questions."

"Fuck," I grind out. I just want my bed and the woman who has become my calm. The last thing I want is to be interrogated again. "Come on. Let's get this shit over with. I'm only doing this because I know you. You're going to figure this out."

"You can bank on that, but I need everyone to come clean. I want it all."

"What do you mean by that?" I ask as we walk through the bar headed for the back room.

There's no way he can know what I've actually done. There's only one person with that information. I school my features because I know I created that situation and I've handled it. The one person who knows is the only one who can bury me with that truth.

Pit continues saving me from my thoughts. "It dawned on me tonight Blake has figured out how my brain works. He's been purposely drip-feeding me the information.

"He understands that at some point, I'm going to put all the pieces together. However, I don't think he has all the pieces himself," I reply.

"Then who does?"

"We do. The assholes. We've had them all along."

"Okay, so what do you think you need to hear?"

"I need to hear everyone's truth. How that night happened for them. That's where the tie is. We're bigger than Vander. This is bigger than Vander. I just need to hear that night from everyone's point of view."

"So you need me to relive it?"

"I'm sorry to ask this of you, but I need you to go back. While we were waiting for you to get out, everyone else told me about their experience from the start of that day. Deacon, Tak, Luke, Skittles, even Ox and Lex.

"Now, I need to hear it from you. My brain will grab the pieces from there."

"All right. If this will help you figure out what the hell is going on before I lose everything, fine. Let's get this over with."

This isn't the only shit I have to get in check. However, I know to keep one lid closed, I need to get a handle on the one about to blow. We stop outside the private back room.

Pit turns to look at me. We lock gazes as his asks the one question I knew would come up. I'm not about to explain myself, but I understand his concern. I respect it.

"I'm not playing games with her. At first, she was doing me a solid—keeping me sane—while I was a shoulder to lean on. There was no way we could know this was going to happen. Now that it has, I'm sort of glad. She's my alibi," I say to his unspoken words.

Deep down, I know that's bullshit. She may be my alibi, but this goes deeper than that. It always has. I've just been in a battle with who I am and what I want.

"I already know this. I think you should be the one to talk to Skittles. This is going to hurt her feelings."

"I'll handle it. Come on, the sooner I tell you what happened, you all will know there was no way I could've done this."

He places a hand on my shoulder and gives it a gentle squeeze. "We all already know you didn't do this. Now we're going to prove it and find out who did. I'm not allowing you to go down over this."

"Thanks."

CHAPTER TWO

What I Heard

Kelex

Fourteen years ago...

My phone buzzes on my desk as I put the finishing touches on my paper. I pick it up and find a text from Seth. There's a race tonight.

I toss the phone back down. I'm not in the mood for slumming it at a drag race tonight. My stomach growls, reminding me I got up and went straight to work on this pile of homework.

I've been putting my assignments off to do a few modeling gigs and audition for a few films. I'd do anything to avoid the family business. I glance in the mirror at my newly dyed-blond mane.

Yeah, I really would do anything. Cutting off and bleaching away my dark locks has watered down my strong Greek features. Funny part is, I've been getting way more work as a blond.

Which is why I'm so behind with my schoolwork. It's not like I have to work hard for my grades. I barely study or anything. I get A's for breathing. It's a perk of being a Kylix.

I'm not complaining in the least. There's nothing money can't buy, at least not for my family.

I stand and stretch. I guess it's time to shower and eat. Cracking my neck, I head into the bathroom.

I make it through my shower and dress. Once dressed in a fresh Polo shirt and blue jeans, I jog downstairs, heading for the kitchen.

Voices inside my father's study grab my attention. I come to a stop to listen, hoping he's not meddling in my life again. We bump heads consistently.

"Why am I here, Ulysses?"

"You have a problem. A problem that's placed you around a valuable player. You scratch my back... I'll make your problem go away," my father says smoothly.

"Are you kidding me? Everyone who gets involved with you ends up dead."

"Your life is over anyway if you don't find someone to pull a few strings for you. That kid may find the legal loophole you need, but he can't save your ass from what's coming.

"Vander has spoken. You're out. This time for good. You're going to take the fall for the Castro's. Not a single one of them will go down, but you..."

The person sighs. "What do you think I can do?"

"Why are my father-in-law and Blake Knight interested in the kid? What does this mean for my son?"

"You know better than I do. I had no idea Blake was interested at all."

"He is. You have to watch everything that family does closely. You should've learned that a long time ago. You wouldn't be where you are if you did," my dad bites out.

The guy huffs. "I'm sure. Anyway, the elites are about to shake things up. Things are divided. Have been since I was outed. Too many cooks in the kitchen. As you said, my family has been one of eight erased from the main table.

"That bitch got her wish. I don't know anything else. There are only five of the thirteen families left, now that Kylix and Nikolaou count as one. I still don't know how you pulled that off."

"If you're lucky, I might reveal that truth."

"Not sure I want that luck," the guy murmurs. "Anyway, I think they're about to make a move, but I don't know how he fits. The kid is smart. He's different. He doesn't answer to anyone and he—"

My phone rings, cutting his words off. I rush to silence it and move from the door before someone comes out and finds me. I'm seething. I don't want shit to do with this Vander-Bridge Lake bullshit.

Pappoús promised this would be my decision, but my father is hell-bent on forcing me into this life. He's lost his mind. There's no way I'm going through with this and becoming his puppet.

"Hello," I answer the call.

"Ah, you're back with us commoners. Wish I could run off with movie stars and live the life," Jeff, my best friend taunts in my ear.

I release a breath and chuckle. "I offered for you to come with me. Fuck you."

"Yeah, yeah. I know you love me, but I'm not that desperate. I don't need you flying me out."

"Whatever, what do you want, asshole?" I snort.

"You getting into that race tonight? It's a nice pot. Not that you need it," he says.

My thoughts go back to what I just overheard. I work my jaw. Needing to blow off some steam, I change my mind about tonight. The cash will pay for my next vacation. Cabo is calling my name.

I've been messing around with one of the models I started out with. Phoebe Argyros. If she's lucky, I might take her along.

"Yeah, I'll be there."

"What's up with you? Maybe you should sit this one out."

"Nothing new. Same bullshit, new day," I reply.

"Your plate is overrun with the fruits of life. Sounds like some tasty shit to me. Not everyone can have rose-smelling shit, so I say it's a good day."

"Then you eat it. See you later."

***

"You want to talk about it?" Jeff asks as we wait for all the drivers to arrive for this race.

We're both posted up against my ride as the party around the track comes to life. There's something different in the air tonight. I've asked myself several times why I'm even out here.

"No, not really. Although I know you're going to stay up my ass until I do."

"As long as it doesn't stink, I'll stick my nose in it."

I turn to glare at him. "Why are we friends?"

"My father and your father are connected to the same shit. I took pity on you when they forced us to play with each other. You've been my bestie since. Come on, sweetheart, tell Daddy what's the matter," he says and pokes out his lip.

I frown as I think of that day all those years ago. It was the same day I found out the kind of savage my father is and the life he thought he was going to force me into. I blink away the memory of all the blood and the dying man moaning for mercy and his life.

Shaking my head clear, I focus back on Jeff. "You're an ass."

"Maybe, but I'm your ass. What's up?"

"I overheard my father talking to someone about all this Vander bullshit," I say low enough for only him to hear.

"Okay."

"I'm still not doing it. If he wants control of Vander, he'll have to earn it on his own."

"What's so bad about having it all? You're being offered a chance to take over a city and the town connected to it. So what if it's covered in blood? I know you're capable of doing this. Why piss it all away?"

"Because it's bullshit and I don't want the blood on my hands. Listen to you. You sound like him. People aren't things for us to step on like some fucking gods.

"There isn't enough money in the world for me to agree to be like him. I'll earn my own way if I have to. I don't need that life," I seethe.

"Calm down. God forbid life gets any easier for you. Besides, that pretty face is going to open the world to you as it is. You can't have your cake and eat it too."

"Fuck off. Walk a mile in my shoes, then talk shit to me."

"Hell, if I walked in your shoes, I'd take the promotion. I'd want it all. I'd be the one running this shit and they'd all bow down to me."

I snort. "And if it all turned out to be a load of shit?"

"If I couldn't run it all, I'd burn it all down."

I stop and look at Jeff. I mean, really look at him. There's something in the way he says it that strikes differently. It's not the first time I've heard him say something like it. He can be a bit of a spoiled asshole.

He smiles at me and laughs it off. "Bro, there's a race to be had. Forget all that shit," he croons and pats my cheek. "Look, there's some ass over there I want to get in. I'll be back before the flag is down."

"Yeah, right, have at it."

I sit on the hood of my car with my arms folded across my chest. I look off in the direction Jeff just took off in. However, the crowd is so heavy tonight I can't see where he disappeared to.

He won't be back. Instead of searching for him, I lock in and focus on the race ahead. I look around at the other drivers. While this is a sport to me, some of these guys need the money.

No matter what, I'm here to have a good time, but I'm never a loser. I always come out on top. A good race and a pretty face in my passenger seat at the end is a total win for me. Someone's face is going to be in my mattress by the end of the night.

I need to fuck away the bullshit in my life. A crime boss, me? My father has lost his Greek mind. Even with control over all of Vander and Bridge Lake, I'm not interested.

"Don't even bring your ass over here. You're nowhere near pretty enough for me to fuck you," I scoff at the skinny chick about to try to throw herself at me. "Not happening."

The smile on her pale face crumbles. "Asshole."

"Still not fucking you." I shrug.

Don't get me wrong, I love girls of all colors, shapes, and sizes. This one, however, looks like she's trying to fuck her way to a check. That's not attractive to me and never has been.

I might have overlooked her too-big ears if she didn't have that hungry look in her eyes. Ignoring Thirsty Girl and her friends, I do another pass of the crowd. I tilt my head when my eyes land on the new girl.

She's cute with a nice body. Now her, I wouldn't mind having in my bed. Her car is sweet too.

I wonder if she can handle that thing. Maybe after I spank her ass out here on the track, I'll take her home and spank her ass in my bed too. Her eyes lock on mine and she gives me a shy smile.

Oh yeah, I'm fucking.

The model face strikes again. It's always good to be a Kylix. Our family is known for the money and the stellar looks. Although my father loathes me using my face to make money— he loathes it until it's convenient for his bragging.

I lean back on my car and savor the energy buzzing around us. This shit gets my blood pumping. I love the thrill.

All that bullshit from this morning is forgotten. If they've found someone to replace me, I hope they succeed. Fuck my father and his greedy ass. I pray it all blows up in his face.

Pitman's fuck buddy Abby storms by in her too-tight skirt and heels. Looks like they've had another fight. Maybe I can fuck with his head and throw him off his game.

He's the only one I'm concerned with tonight. I'd much rather gain thirty grand than lose five. This purse will be higher than most. These guys are high-stakes drivers.

They don't get behind the wheel for less than a five-hundred-dollar buy-in. Tonight isn't the highest buy-in I've ever had, but it's not the cheapest either.

I saunter past Pitman and his Viper. "Better have my cash, Pitman."

"Fuck you," he barks out and flips me the bird.

I hold my belly and laugh. I love fucking with his grumpy ass. I know he doesn't like me because of my family's money.

Fuck him.

I keep walking and turn to look at the biggest spoiled brat out here. Seth, the organizer of these races. Our families are familiar enough. They're connected. You would have to be to run this caliber of race.

Although they're not as connected as mine. Grayson's can't move the type of shit Kylix's can. While Seth can run these races under the radar and pull in some cash, I could shut these races down permanently and make it like they never existed.

However, rumor has it Seth's dad will have his head if he finds out about them. The old man has his eyes on politics, which means he needs the favor of Vander's elite. That's not going to happen. Even if it were, Seth's bullshit stands to get in the way of that.

"Selfish bastard," I mutter.

I guess we have something in common because I'm talking to us both. I'm also not willing to go through with my father's wishes so he can advance. No matter if I know this is what I've been groomed for since my first solo trip to Greece for the summer. It's the same Greek pride my father and I share that won't allow me to bend.

I squint at the guy in the hoodie who approaches Seth.

"Fuck," I grunt.

We don't need another entry into this race. I know Jeff isn't coming back, so I don't have to worry about him. Yes, the pot will grow, but that's one more unknown stacked against me, taking the fun out of the win.

I'll have to actually focus. I dip my brows more when Jeremy walks over to them. Something about the guy in the hoodie's body language sets my nerves on end. Jeremy seems to make him nervous.

Seth pulls the guy into a hug and nods as he says something to him. They pull apart and Seth pats the side of the dude's head before turning back to Jeremy. Jeremey gestures toward someone in the crowd.

I go to follow his motion with my gaze, but tires screech, pulling my attention away from their exchange. By the time I turn back to their group, Jeremy is gone and so is the guy in the hoodie. Frustrated, I have no idea what Jeremy gestured to.

Whatever they were up to, I missed it. Seth better not be playing any funny shit with the payout. His ass better have my fucking money when this is over.

"All right, all right," Seth calls out as I make it back to my car. "Let's get this party started. I got studying and shit to get to."

The crowd cheers and drivers start to get into their cars. I'm almost in my car when Jeremy opens his ooze-spewing mouth.

"She's not racing with us. She has no business out here," he growls.

This guy loves to hear himself talk. No one else has a problem with her racing. As long as she can pay for her spot, I don't give a shit.

"Doesn't matter either way. Your ass is still going to lose," I scoff loud enough for everyone to hear.

"Fuck off, pretty boy. No one's talking to you," Jeremy replies.

I don't give two shits about any of these guys. Heck, I don't like a single one of them, but Jeremy, he's a piece of shit—reckless, greedy, and self-centered. I always keep my eyes on him when he's racing. Honestly, he should be banned from them.

Fucking dick.

"Well, I'm talking to you," Pitman says, coming around his car. "Shut the fuck up and get in your car."

"Hey! All of you can shut the fuck up and let your engines do the talking for you," Luke calls out.

Pitman doesn't get far before that pussy Jeremy jumps into his car. Damn, I thought this was about to make my night worthwhile. I had my money on Pitman.

Dude's around my height and built solid. That would've been some ass whipping. We start to file toward the starting line.

Like I said, I don't trust Jeremy, so I pull up next to the new girl. I turn to look into her car and give her one of my megawatt smiles. She tips an imaginary hat at me.

Oh yeah, a chick with personality is so sexy to me. I bite my lip and wink at her. Hope there're no hard feelings after I take her cash. The others line up, but my focus is on Gorgeous one car over.

She looks straight ahead, giving me a chance to take in her profile. Those lips are going to be fun to get to know. The car to my right revs its engine, causing me to grin and turn for our signal.

"Seth, you need some better talent, bro," I murmur to myself and roll my eyes at the little show these two put on. "Will you drop the fucking flags already?"

Finally, they put us all out of our misery. The sound of tires squealing fills the air and clouds of smoke rise behind us. I'm filled with a charge of adrenaline.

"*Woo-hoo*," I call out as I take off.

The purr of the engine beneath me matches the hammering of my heart. I love this shit. For now, we're all riding easy.

I turn up my music, tasting victory on its way. Two cars drop back while the rest of us pull forward. I'm a showman. I like my wins to look good.

I back off the gas a bit before I go for it. That's how I see the shit Jeremy gets ready to pull. He swerves right for the girl's car when she pulls up on Pitman's ass.

I don't know what makes me do it, but I smash my foot on the gas. My car darts between Jeremy's and the pink-and-black Aston Martin. I stop breathing when he slams into my driver's side door and my car flips into the air.

"Holy shit."

The sound of my car hitting the asphalt once jars me from my shock as the windows blow out and glass flies everywhere. However, the car flips again and again, landing the third time on its head. It happens so fast, yet somehow in slow motion.

I'm dazed as I look out of the smashed windshield. I can see the pink-and-black car facing in one direction with the back dented in. The front of Jeremy's black car is facing the other way and it's smashed in completely. It catches on fire right in front of my eyes.

He's a few yards away, but I still don't want to be near if it blows. It's going to blow. I can feel it.

I go to release my seat belt, but I can't move my left arm. That's when the pain in my body starts to register. My right leg is throbbing with blinding pain. I look down at my arm and it's totally fucked. Twisted at an odd angle.

I fight not to pass out as my body starts to tremble. I try to release the belt with my right hand, but something feels off with that arm too. I can move it, but something's not right.

I jump as the door beside me whines in protest. Someone on the other side is tugging to get it open. When it opens, the pretty chick fits her body into the overturned car. Blood is dripping from her forehead.

"I'm going to get you out of here. I saw him coming. Fucking jerk. I can't believe you did that for me. Oh God. I have to get you out," she says.

I start to smell smoke. It's too near for me to pretend it's not coming from my car. "Go, get out of here."

"No, I have to help you."

"Get back," someone outside the car demands.

She bites her lip as tears well, but she backs out of the car. I close my eyes. I'm going to die in here for some pussy I'll never have. What the fuck was I thinking?

Determined not to die like this, I open my eyes and start for the seat belt again. Suddenly, the smoke turns into flames. I'm on fire. My leg is on fire.

"My leg, my fucking leg."

Pitman ducks inside the car and I've never been more grateful to see his ass. He's around my size. He has a better chance of helping me out of here. I'm still trying to free myself of the harness.

"Dude, I need you to relax. I'm going to get you out," Pitman says.

I swallow hard and nod, moving my hand out of the way so he can try to get me out. He tries, but the shit won't budge. Tears spill from my eyes. I'm in so much fucking pain. I try to choke back my screams.

Luke Reynolds appears and tries to throw some blankets over the flames around my legs. It's not enough. I can't hold my cries back anymore. I feel like I'm dying. My skin is searing. I've never known pain like this.

"Fuck, fuck, I'm on fire," I yell out as Pitman finally cuts me free.

"Help me get him out," he barks to someone.

They drag me from the wreck as I scream my fucking head off. My entire right side feels like it's on fire. Someone pats my body.

"Help, fucking help," I think I cry out.

There's so much pain I'm not sure if my mouth is even moving. It's overpowering my will to help them get me the fuck away from this car. Something explodes, and just like that, it all goes black.

CHAPTER THREE

In the Silence

Shawna

A month and two weeks later...

"What are you looking at?" I say to Ven as I walk into her room. "Oh, who's that? He's gorgeous."

I don't tell her I already know he's the model from that race. I've been following him for a while. That crash was devastating to all his fans.

He has so much promise and he's breathtaking. I loved him more with his natural dark hair and when it was longer. He had this sexy thing going on where one side was cut shorter, kind of like a fauxhawk or mullet.

Just not too close to his scalp, which brought something pretty to his features. I can't explain it. His hair was so thick and lush. It stood out against those blue-gray eyes and long, thick lashes. His face is perfection—from his lips to his nose to his brows. I've often wondered why he went blond? It takes away from that perfect face.

My favorite picture of him is from that underwear ad with the black angel wings on his back as he rises from the water. His body is one thing, chiseled to perfection and underwear-ad worthy. However, it was the way his eyes popped as he stared intensely into the camera, with all that dark hair falling into his face, almost covering his left eye, that drew you in. Every time I look at it, I feel like he's looking through me.

"This is my new best friend. He just doesn't know it yet," Skittles sings and turns to face me.

Her scar comes into view, causing me to reach up to touch mine. It's insane that she would end up with one in almost the exact same spot. However, I was lucky enough to have a plastic surgeon see to mine.

If not for Ven, I don't know what I would have done when I got this scar. She's always been my hero. I smile because it would take more than a little scar to take away from her beauty.

"Really? You know him?"

"Sort of." She shrugs. "Anyway, what brings you by?"

"Oh, you forgot," I whisper.

"Oh shoot. Camera shopping. I didn't forget, love. I just have a lot on my mind."

"We don't have to go. It's fine."

She stands from her desk and places her hands on her hips. I look down at her and smile. I wish I were as short as she is. Mayven has always been so pretty.

Tiny and curvy. I have the curves, but they don't look the same in the tall package I come in. However, I'd never tell her that. Mayven has always made it her business to tell me to be proud of the skin I'm in.

I just don't have her confidence. She and Lex have always had this thing I'm lacking. No matter how hard I try to be like them, it never works.

"Are you crazy? I'm so proud of you. You graduated with honors. I'm buying you that camera.

"I want to be able to say I bought you your first professional camera and I was a part of you becoming an award-winning photographer. Come on, let me get this wig on and I'm ready."

"Okay, thanks. Um, your new bestie. He's that model from that crash, right?"

"Yeah."

"Did they let him out of the hospital?"

"No, they just woke him from the coma. He's a bit grumpy when he's lucid. It will be a few more weeks though, because of the break in his leg. I think that's causing him more pain and discomfort."

"Oh my God, that has to be insane."

"Yeah, a broken arm and leg, fractured hand and burns are all a lot to deal with. He's getting the best care, so I'm hopeful for him."

"I hope he's okay too."

I would love to have him in front of my camera someday. Those eyes, they'd be everything to look at through a lens. I want to ask so many more questions, but I clamp my mouth shut.

Kelex

I have no sense of time or where the fuck I am. Just pain, a whole lot of pain. The morphine wears off faster than I can savor the brief moments of relief.

I'd rather be placed back in a fucking coma. Four weeks of silence and no thought of how fucked up my life has become. Now, all I have is thoughts. Thoughts and pain.

It's better to sleep. That's all I want is sleep. However, every time I try, I'm thrown back into that car, and the pain doesn't help. It's like it's all happening again.

At the moment, I'd take being trapped over having this prick in my room. I feel him. He's here as if he cares.

I told him to get the fuck out and stay out. It's not like he gives a shit about me. He's just here to make sure I'm still breathing so he can get what he's wanted all my life.

No me, no Vander. I should kick the bucket just to spite his ass. It's not like my life will be the same.

Just as I'm about to black out again, someone else enters the room. I fight to keep conscious. Searing pain racks my body, making it an easy task.

"Why have you called me here?" It's the same guy from my father's office that morning.

"This is a safe place to talk. We need to have a conversation," my father replies coldly.

"We have nothing to talk about."

"Ah, but we do. I hear you think you're leaving Bridge Lake and Vander behind."

"What do I have left here? Why should I stay?"

"I've made you an offer. It wouldn't be wise to ignore it."

"Or what? You should stop underestimating m—"

"Shut your fucking mouth."

"Fuck you, Ulysses. I've given my all. You have no right to ask me for anything more."

"I will ask for whatever I need. I'm not done with you. You're not going anywhere," my dad snarls.

"Well, I'm done with you. You know, you're some piece of work. You still have your world. I…I have nothing.

"William is going to be released. They're sweeping all of this under the rug. There will be no justice. Vander kids are just like their parents. They never have to face the repercussions of their actions."

"You sound like a whiny bitch. What did you think would happen?"

"Are you fucking kidding me? I've lost my license for less, and the only family I have is gone. Yet, these kids are walking away with not even a slap on the wrist. And you…you are the worse part of it all."

There's a beat of silence.

"Don't shrug your shoulders at me, you son of a bitch. Every time I look at you, I'm reminded why I should have left this place behind years ago. Here your son is, alive. Don't talk to me about not being done because, as far as you all are concerned, I am."

"Are you sure about that? I can turn this all around in your favor. Let's say I'm offering up reparations for all you've been through."

"Fuck you."

"I'll hand them all over. The Castros, Lester, Marvin, Blake, Zoe and anyone else you feel owes you. All you have to do is be patient. Allow me to get Basil where I need him—"

"You don't know, do you?"

"Know what?"

"All this time, I thought you knew. I thought that was why you kept reaching out… You know what? Never mind.

"This won't bring my life back. She's gone for good. It won't bring him back either," the guy seethes.

"What are you two doing in here?" That's Jeff.

Thank God. Someone I can trust to get these two the hell out of here. My father is forever at something. *Asshole*. I want to open my eyes to see who this guy is, but I start to lose consciousness.

CHAPTER FOUR

The One to Watch

Kelex

Present...

"So you never found out who the guy was?" Blake asks, pulling me from the past.

"No, I never heard that voice again after that. I have no idea who he was," I reply. I then look to Pit as he rubs his tired-looking eyes. "Do you think you have what you need?"

He bares his teeth. "No—"

"Josh, oh my God, are you okay? You didn't do this. There's no way you could have done this," Shawna breathes as she rushes into the back room.

"I'm not saying that he did, but how are you so sure he didn't?" Ven asks as she lifts her head from the table to look at Shawna.

"I've been watching the news updates. They said Ulysses was dead for at least twenty-four hours. Josh wasn't here. I know because we've been together for the last week," Shawna murmurs.

"No, you said *you* were in Italy for a shoot."

"But I wasn't. I was with Josh."

I tug her into my lap before she can say another word. Cupping the back of her head, I take her lips and devour her mouth. I need this connection to calm my nerves.

When I break the kiss, I peck her nose and place my forehead to hers. Her lips are trembling. I know what happened in Greece changed everything for us, but I had planned to make things right this weekend.

"I'm sorry," she murmurs.

"This was on me. I'm the one who's sorry. Let's forget about it for now. Are they okay?"

"Yeah, I went to check on them. Achilles is still with them for the weekend. Jeff offered to take them, but Achilles had already fed them, and they seemed happy to be home," she replies.

"Thanks."

"It's late. We should call it a night and start over tomorrow," Skittles says.

Pit takes in a sharp breath. "She's right. I need you to tell me more, but my brain is on overload."

"Yeah, well, these two are chapping my ass with all the lies. I can't promise I'm not going to flip this table if we continue this shit tonight," Skittles says and rolls her eyes at us.

"I promise we'll tell you everything in the morning. It's time you know who I am and what that means to your family."

"I'm pregnant, not stupid. I've figured out a lot by saying nothing. I've been waiting on the two of you to be honest with yourselves, then me.

"If I didn't love you, Josh, my husband would be prying me off you. I know you know not to hurt her. If you do, I'm personally gonna bring you all the smoke and then some. We clear?"

I smile. I don't think it's one Skittles has ever witnessed. The way her eyes widen, I know she sees something she's never seen in me before. It's a smile Pit understands because he stiffens and sits up.

"One day, everyone in this room will understand how I feel about this woman. If anyone hurts her, they'll have to answer to me, not the Josh you know and love, but *me*.

"The one capable of what I'm being accused of. No one will ever hurt her again. It wouldn't have happened the first time if I had known.

"If I have to choose between who I want to be and who I need to be because of her. I will always be who I need to be."

With that, I stand, bringing Shawna with me. "Come on. We'll come back in the morning. We're heading to the condo for the night to be close if you need me. Happy birthday, Ox. Sorry about the drama, *xáderfi*," I say as we walk out.

"Did he just? Really?" Skittles huffs behind me.

"You're going to learn one of these days," I hear Lex snicker. "That one is the one we all need to watch out for."

Ox

"I'm so sorry your birthday weekend didn't turn out the way you wanted," Lex yarns as we walk into our home.

I tug her into me and give her a gentle squeeze. "I'm not sweating it. I'm just ready for all this bullshit to be over."

"I know what you mean. Who in the world would want to kill Ulysses and frame Josh?"

"May that motherfucker rest in piss. He was a son of a bitch and had it coming. He's lucky it wasn't me after the things I've learned in the last few weeks," I grumble.

Lex gasps. "Really?"

I tug her close and kiss the top of her head. "I want you to start carrying whenever you leave the house."

"I never leave home without it."

"Good. You'll have someone on you at all times from now on."

"Is Shawna safe?"

"I think you read the room. My cousin is more than some pretty boy. Something tells me all decisions are made or will be very soon."

"She's more to him than we think, isn't she?"

"Yeah, baby. A whole lot more. I get it now."

"But for how long? I've been thinking. Shouldn't Pit question where she was that day and night? I didn't know I was connected at first."

I sigh. "He'll know exactly what he needs by morning. For now, he needs sleep and so do we. Come on, I still have some celebrating I want to do," I say as I bury my face in her neck and palm her ass.

CHAPTER FIVE

Go Deeper

Kelex

The last few days have felt like the longest days of my life. However, I'm glad I followed my gut and sent Shawna ahead of me before I made that stop at my father's.

I lie here in bed with my thoughts racing. The things that were revealed before we left Greece gutted me. I didn't want to leave things that way, but I had to.

It seems something is always in the way when it comes to us. Like this morning, we need to head back to Fuck Off. I need to tell Skittles the truth and I need Pit to hear whatever will trigger him.

Then I need to call *Pappoús* and tell him what I've done. All this shit is forcing my hand. There's a problem we can no longer ignore within Vander and Bridge Lake.

Someone needs to step up soon to handle it. Who will that be? I have no idea, but this feeling in my stomach says it might have to be me.

All I've done to have a different outcome went out the window in the blink of an eye. What I've done leaves me with no choice. This rage inside that's been brewing since I was a boy got the best of me. I fucked up.

Then there's her and our world we're building. I don't want this for them. The look on her face is something I will never forget—she's seen the real monster I can become. My phone buzzes, pulling my attention.

Jeff: *You good?*

Me: *No, where were you?*

Jeff: *I came. You were gone. What are you going to do?*

I frown and toss my phone. I'm not having this conversation over text. He knows better. I can't afford stupid shit right now. One wrong move and I could go down for this bullshit.

Shawna comes out of the bathroom, looking sleepy. My heart swells. She's gorgeous. Her big brown expressive eyes, that cute button nose—everything about her draws me in.

She's tall, curvy, and made just for me. She took my breath away when I finally laid eyes on her for the first time. Truth is, she had me before I ever met her in person.

The things I've been willing to do for her in the last twelve years say it all. I don't know how to take away what she's learned about me. I can only hope she learns to see beyond it to the man I've shown her first.

The man who adores her. I don't know if she truly knows how much she means to me, but I want to remind her. We have to reconnect.

She slides beneath the sheets and rests on her side with her back to me. I turn and move closer to her, wrapping my arm around her to tug her back into my heat. Her lush ass presses into my erection. I reach beneath the sheet to push her silky nightgown up and glide my hand across her smooth skin to palm her fat pussy.

"Good morning," I murmur into her ear.

"Good morning. Should I get up and get ready to head out?"

"No," I reply as I part her folds with my fingers. "I want to make you scream my name and remind you why you're mine. Everything I do, I do to keep you all safe. You should've run when I told you to."

She laughs. "I can't run if your hand is between my legs."

"The time to run has long passed. You belong with me now. Come here. I need you."

She turns onto her back and pushes a hand into my hair. I crush her lips with mine for a deep, passionate kiss. I groan as she moans into my mouth. I settle between her legs as she cradles me with those thick thighs.

Breaking the kiss, I stare into her eyes. She searches my face with her gaze—the trust I see calms my thoughts. I don't think I've lost her, or reality just hasn't set in.

I bite down on my lip as I palm and knead her ass. She always feels so good in my hands. There isn't a moment when I don't want her.

"Josh," she whimpers as I pulse against her thigh.

I swallow her cries with another deep kiss. She sucks my lip this time. I love when she does that.

I've never been insecure about my fleshy lips. They've been a draw for modeling gigs in the past, but with Shawna and the way she kisses, I appreciate them all the more. I grasp her throat and deepen the kiss, nearly consuming her face.

Finding her wet for me, I begin to descend her body. I worship her skin with open-mouthed kisses. Once at the apex of her thighs, I turn my head and kiss her inner thigh.

"Babe," she breathes.

"I've got you, baby. Give your body to me. I promise to give it just what it needs. Relax," I say into her core as she has a death grip on my hair.

I smile when she loosens her grasp. Without a thought of the world outside of this room, I dive in and make her tight pussy rain for me. When I look up through my lashes, she's watching me and panting.

"*Mm*," I hum and push in deeper, lifting her hips off the bed.

I have her bracing on her toes as I climb in close and hold her to my face. Her juices fill my mouth, causing me to suck her lips clean. I'll never get tired of making her come.

She tries to cover her sex from me, but I knock her hands away and hold her hips up as I lift to my knees and push into her tight heat. A deep groan comes from me as she keens beneath me. Clawing my fingers up her sides, I rock into her slowly, allowing her to adjust.

"Shawna," I groan as I cover her hands with mine and pin them above her head.

She wraps her long legs around me and holds on tight. Her eyes roll back in her head as she calls my name. This feels amazing, but she's using her legs and tight hold to keep me at bay.

"Oh no, baby. I need you to take this," I breathe in her ear.

"Josh," she whimpers.

I take her mouth and roll onto my back. With her on top, I grasp her ass and guide her as she gushes all over me. I can't help but look into her eyes as I sit up.

I want to hear those words slip from her lips. She hasn't said them since.... I squeeze my eyes shut.

I'll never forgive myself if I've broken us. I knew, I knew from the beginning I couldn't have both. It's her or the darkness, but I still need and want her.

Shawna

I love him like this. I feel him everywhere—his hands on my ass, his thick length inside me, his tongue in my mouth. He's giving me all of him and I still want more.

I run my hands through his thick dark hair as I ride him. He's so hard. I'm trying not to sink all the way down, but he's not having it. He grabs my ass and guides me up and down, pushing all his length inside.

"Josh, oh my God," I scream.

He groans. "Look at me, baby."

I realize I've thrown my head back and I'm staring at the ceiling. I drop my gaze to his and lock eyes with those intense blue grays of his. He's so gorgeous.

Tightening my hold on his hair, I get lost in him. We're breathing each other in as I rock my hips against him. When he claws his blunt nails across my back, then holds me in a tight embrace, I shiver.

"Babe, oh my God, you feel so good," I whimper.

"I'm crazy about you, baby. You know that?"

I do my best not to let my thoughts slip free and almost fail. Instead of talking, I bury my face into his long locks. It's all I can do not to allow my real thoughts to fall out. I inhale his citrusy shampoo.

"Ah," I moan.

"Answer me, baby. You know how I feel about you, don't you?"

I wrap my arms around his head and kiss him. I can't tell him I know he cares about me. I'm afraid. I'm afraid of what all this means for us.

I'm afraid of the walls crumbling down around us. I'm scared shitless that the fairy tale is over and I'm about to lose it all. I'm afraid to breathe those words because they feel like a trigger waiting to end it all.

It's not like I haven't said them before, but that was before. I think I'm still in shock. Three days later and I'm in disbelief.

I haven't processed what this all means to us—if anything. Then there's what that says about me. I'm not ready to look at that. So I keep kissing him and start to ride him harder.

That is until he flips me on my back and really begins to drill into me. Breaking the kiss, he looks into my eyes. I see his worry and concern—I can't say what happened isn't a big deal, but I don't know how I feel about it either. Burying my head in the sand has always worked, so that's what I'm doing.

We can deal with one thing at a time. We have enough on our plates for now. I want to leave Greece in Greece. However, his gaze says he's not doing the same.

I hate that for him. I try to show him with my body I'm here with him. He sucks his lip into his mouth and rolls his hips into me as if steering something within me. He's going deeper than he's ever gone before. My eyes cross and tears leak back into my ears.

I cling to his back and go along for the ride. The strongest sensation fills my belly, blooming with each stroke. He shifts angles and growls as he plows into me.

"Shawna, baby. *Fuck*. I—" He snaps his head up as banging and the doorbell rings out through the condo. "Fuck."

He palms my ass and keeps going as he buries his sweaty face in my neck and sucks on my skin. I feel him spill into me seconds after I go over. He kisses my face and takes a second to catch his breath.

"I'll get it. Shower and get dressed. The sooner this is all over, the better."

"Okay."

He searches my face once more. I take him in as he does. He's so beautiful.

His features are so pixie-like. Sharp, but soft at the same time. As if molded and sculpted to perfection.

The way his dark brows sit over his gorgeous blue-gray eyes, the hard angles of his jawline to the sharp yet soft point of his nose, all complementing his soft bee-stung-looking lips. I hold my breath as he looks like he might say more. Instead, he pecks my lips and climbs from the bed.

All I see is perfection as he walks naked over to his robe. I love everything about him, including his scars. He has a body any model or swimmer would kill for.

"All right already, I'm coming," he hollers as he exits the bedroom.

Kelex

"What in the entire fuck?" I growl as I open the front door of my condo.

"I'm up. Things are starting to jump out at me. I need you to finish. Where's Shawna? She's next. She has a piece I need too. I almost have this shit. I know it."

"Bro, we were coming to you."

"Not fast enough. I'll drive you in. Go wash your ass. You smell like sex."

"Probably because I was having sex before you started banging down my door."

"Yo, about that. Skittles knows and she's hurt like I said she'd be."

"*Fuck*," I groan and pull a hand down my face. "How?"

"Turn the news on. Someone's spilling all your shit. Your wife, the kids, all your charities, and the businesses. They've been airing all your shit out all morning."

"Isn't that a good thing? It all paints me in a good light. A picture-perfect, upstanding member of the community."

"Not if they've also been showing all the shit your father was doing to you and your world, giving a very strong motive. So you want to get dressed and do this or sit here and allow whoever this is to get ahead of us?"

"Fuck, give me forty."

He snorts. "It's the hair, isn't it? Takes forever to get that shit all pretty again, doesn't it?"

I toss him the finger and head back into my bedroom. A smile comes to my lips as I run my hand through the longer side of my sweaty hair. I'd do anything for her.

Anything? My thoughts taunt. *Yeah, anything. Haven't I made that clear?*

CHAPTER SIX

Mr. Vander

Kelex

About Thirteen and a half years ago...

The bitter cold chomps my face as I stand out on the upper deck of the cabin we're staying at. This place has been peaceful for the most part when the house isn't lively with pranks and jokes. These guys have made me sharpen my skills. You have to come quick with your clapbacks around here.

I inhale deeply as I allow the atmosphere to swallow my thoughts. My phone goes off in my pocket. I pull it out, thinking it's Jeff. He's been going back and forth on joining us.

I get his reluctance to come up. His father is ill. I'm not even in the right state of mind to be there for him, although I want to be. Unlike me and mine, he and his dad have always been close. Also, unlike me, Jeff wants to walk in his father's footsteps.

I frown when I find it's not Jeff but my father sending me a text. I read it twice because I know my dad can't be this stupid. This shit doesn't even deserve a reply.

I'm still boiling over his words from earlier. The reason I needed to come out here in the first place was to breathe. The man disgusts me on a new level.

"Your career as an entertainer is definitely over. Your focus should be on the family business. I made sure you had the best care, but you know those people.

"They'll never see pasts those burns. Why bother with all that when you don't have to?"

"Because it's what I want," I seethed.

"Well, it's no longer an option. By the time you heal, you'll be forgotten. That is, if you heal fully. On camera, it will all look much worse than it is. Do you really think you have the balls to take that?"

"I'll be fine."

"You're my son. I'm looking out for you. It wasn't just your face they wanted. It was your face and your body. You are useless to them now. Focus, Joshua. Come to Greece with me. Let's show your *pappoús* you are ready."

"Ready for what?" I bark into the phone.

My head pounds as my pressure rises. My accident wasn't some sign for me to say yes to that life. I will find a way to do things on my own. It will be my life and my decisions.

"Whatever," I bite out as I look at the text, hating that he might be right.

I shove the phone back into my pocket. My father is riding my last nerve. Apparently, he has some people in Greece he wants me to meet to solidify his ambitions.

The only reason I have any intentions of going to Greece is to see my grandfather. He's the only one who's ever cared and asked me what I want.

He was the one to encourage me to start modeling and performing. He told me if I was going to do something outside of the family business, I needed to be the best at it—choose something I'd make a difference at.

I can't honestly say I was making a difference. However, I was one of the best. Doors were opening. I was proving myself and making a name. Once I dyed and cut my dark hair for a gig or two, my agent had gone crazy.

I landed my second huge modeling contract and was in talks for a few movie deals. A contract I lost and movies that fell through while I was laid up in a hospital bed with a broken arm, fractured wrist, and burns down my right side. One of many contracts I lost—unable to show up, they had to replace me.

"Here you are?" Skittles sings when she finds me out on the deck.

"Hey, what's up?"

She walks over with two steaming cups in her hands and a smile on her pretty face. Everything is so easy with her. Too bad I think she has a major thing for Pit. I haven't called her on it yet, but I plan to.

"I thought you'd like some hot chocolate. You missed breakfast."

"Thanks. I ate before anyone else was up."

"Is everything okay?" She frowns and her little nose wrinkles. It's adorable.

I swallow. Her concern for me always tugs at my heart. She doesn't know me. If she did, she'd be more cautious about becoming friends with me.

Now that I know who her father is, I know more, so I have to keep who I am hidden from her. I don't know if I'll ever be able to share that part of myself with her. Another reason it's a good thing she's not interested in me.

"I'm fine. Just a lot on my mind."

"Care to share? I'm all ears if you need me."

I sigh and think it over. I know things about Skittles's family I don't believe she knows. The soon-to-be mayor has distanced himself from so much of his and his wife's past, only reaching back when convenient.

However, you have to be on a different kind of level to know this. Things that happen inside Vander and Bridge Lake have a way of being washed away.

"Everything in my life is changing. Things I had control over before are so out of my control now. I hate having to answer to anyone. Now I have no way to make my own path and it's like I'm drowning."

"I can understand needing control. I also know that sometimes what you think you have no control over, you just might if you look deeper. Pull the right string and you'll find yourself back on top," she replies.

"You make it sound so easy."

"It's not, but in my book, you have to at least try."

I scoff. "For all intents and purposes, Skittles. Let's not forget I'm a living, breathing Two-Face. Including the dual personalities," I seethe, knowing I've said too much.

She looks at me with eyes full of concern. Placing her cup down on the banister, she then reaches out to touch my arm.

Bouncing her gaze across my face, it's as if she's seeing me for the first time.

"Two-Face? Josh, your burns stop on your torso. Why? How do you see yourself as Two-Face? Your personality is nothing like that."

I hold my snort in. *Baby, you have no idea.* Jeff and I witnessed my father brutally murdering a man when we were little boys. That summer, I was sent to Greece and learned who we are as the Nikolaou-Kylix family.

It's because of that murder I've never wanted to become the man my family wants me to be. I'd rather strip butt-ass naked and pose in front of a camera than become the monster my father is.

Before I can give her an answer, her phone rings. Good, I can avoid this conversation altogether.

"Go ahead and take your call. I'm fine."

She looks at me with concern as if considering my words. The phone stops ringing. I sigh. She's not going to let this one go so easily.

However, her phone rings again and her shoulders slump. Whoever is calling is determined to get to her. She holds up a finger.

"This is Shawna. I need to make sure she's okay. Don't move," she warns.

Shawna, the little cousin. Not the one who's two years younger. That's Lex. The three are closer than close, but neither Shawna nor Lex are related to each other by blood, only Mayven.

She's the glue between them. From what I've learned, they're from three different worlds. Mayven is the one who bridges the gap.

"Hey, Shawnnie. What's up?" Skittles says into the phone.

After listening for a few beats, Skittles growls into the phone. "Well, fuck them. You're amazing. I see I'm going to have to come see that bitch. I warned her to stay out your face."

I shake my head and smile. She's always ready to step up to the plate for those she loves. I honestly almost spilled the truth.

I turn back toward the view as she walks back into the house, tossing more threats around. I'm lost in thought as the door closes behind her.

We've been here for three days and I'm trying my best to be normal, to be a part of the group. No one has made me feel self-conscious about my burns. However, I skipped the hot tub gathering after the first night of strip poker.

Although they weren't, I felt like everyone was staring at me that night. It's early, but I need a drink. My mind is heavy with so much. So much that I don't realize someone else has joined me until Pit speaks.

"Does she know how dangerous hanging with you can be for her?"

I turn to look him in his green eyes. Oh, yes, Mr. Vander. William Pitman knows everyone's secrets. I learned this a few weeks ago.

Blake knows more about this guy than I do. My godfather warned me to keep hidden anything I didn't want used against me later on when it's convenient for this motherfucker's use. Pit holds up his hands as I narrow my gaze at him.

"I come in peace. I'm only looking out for her. Here's what I know about you.

"You model under the name Kelex, but that's bullshit. You are a part of the Kylix family. K-Y-L-I-X," he spells out loud. "You guys have reach all the way from Crete, where y'all have several fronts. It looks like you may run shit someday, but that's all shit that's being sorted out in Greece, outside my reach for now.

"However, I do know your family has some dirty-ass hands and she could be in a shit ton of trouble by being around you," he says.

"Well, let me clear some shit up for you. Yes, I am a Kylix. My family holds power in Vander and Greece. I, however, earned everything I have, including respect.

"Don't ever come at me like I won't set your shit straight in a heartbeat. I may not want this shit, but it's in my blood and it comes out whenever needed."

I inhale and look away from him to stare at the mountains as I tamp down my anger and think more clearly. Skittles has been a lifeline to me whether she knows it or not. She's not a part of that world and she's always willing to allow me to just be.

I need that. When I'm calm enough, I continue. "I care about her. She's the only one keeping me sane through all of this. So you don't have to worry about her safety.

"I'll end a motherfucker for even thinking about hurting her. She'll always be safe as long as I'm breathing, and she doesn't have to be none the wiser about it. You just worry about the bed your ass is climbing in.

"Blake Knight is just as bad as my dad. You know he and my grandfather are very good friends, right? Birds of a feather. You don't want this world, Pit. Find another way if you can; I'm trying my best to."

I respect my godfather and love him, but I know who he is. He keeps his distance from me for a reason. I've known all my life he's watching out for me, but our time together isn't frequent, especially after my mother's death.

"How's that working for you?" he grunts.

"Not good. Right now, I hate my dad. I don't think he likes my ass much either. You would think I set myself on fire just to ruin his perfect life and family. I know it's deeper than that, but sometimes it doesn't feel like it."

"Sounds like you need her more than I do," he grumbles.

"What?"

"Nothing," he replies and slaps me on the back. "Your secret is safe with me. Just keep your promise. That shit doesn't touch her door. Otherwise, I have a cure for your Mr. Hyde."

I snort. "Yeah, I got it. She was right. We're more alike than you think. Come on, I need a drink."

CHAPTER SEVEN

Heartbroken

Kelex

A year later...

I can't even pretend to imagine the pain Mayven is in. My heart aches for her. The way she screamed the night her mother died will always stick with me.

The call came in while we were hanging out. All I could do was hug her and be there. She's been a wreck since.

I'm very close to my grandfather, but I don't think I can even begin to understand losing someone you love so completely. I believe I would be devastated too. I was too young to remember the loss of my mother, at least not entirely.

"This can't be real," Mayven murmurs beside me.

Deacon reaches to place a hand on her shoulder from the pew behind us. I lean into her ear to whisper. "Hang in there. Breathe."

She exhales a deep breath and turns to peek over her shoulder. I think I know who she's looking for. When Pit hands over his handkerchief and a sad smile comes to her lips, I know I'm right.

I'm not going to be the one to betray her crush, but I'm positive, at this point, that she has a thing for him. I wonder how she would feel if she knew he once threatened me over her. I shrug the thought off and turn to look down the row at Skittles's family.

Her father looks like he's warring between holding it together and losing it completely. I look past him and notice the chubby-faced girl next to him.

Her eyes are filled with tears and her face is wet. What draws my attention to her is how much she looks like a lighter-skinned, younger version of Skittles. Almost as if they could be sisters, if not twins.

"And now, the family will come up to pay their final respects and have their final viewing before we head over to the cemetery."

With that announcement, our row stands. I can't help wondering how Mayven is so small. Her entire family is pushing six feet and over. However, she's the smallest in our row. The girl pops up and stands aside to wait for Skittles. I hang back, allowing the family to have their moment. Feeling awkward, I circle around the row to sit with the guys.

"Do you think she's going to be all right?" Tak asks.

I shake my head. I don't know. She has her moments. I look down into my palms.

I have my own shit going on, but I can still visit the few people I love and hug them. Reality hits. I need to go to Greece to see my grandfather. Maybe time with him will help me pull my head together.

I decide, in this moment, I'm going to head to Greece as soon as I know my friend will be okay. Skittles needs me now, but I'm not going to ignore the madness going on in my head. I need to fix my shit too.

I look up as Skittles and the girl hug. She towers over her. In the back of my mind, I note how gorgeous the women in this family are.

I shake my thoughts away. It's not even my mom and this day seems like a blur of emotions and events. Trying to focus is challenging.

There's no one for me to confront about this on Skittles's behalf. I can't make this go away for her. There's no one to destroy, no favor to call in.

I'm really starting to hate this feeling-powerless shit.

CHAPTER EIGHT

Not Ready

Kelex

Six months later…

I officially hate my life. I went from being a top-booked VIP model to having to beg for gigs that are headshots only. The clients who used to book me want more than my face.

That is, until they see my body. I tried. I truly did for about three months. Skittles, my new conscience, talked me into still going on shoots.

"See what they say. You're still hot as fuck. If they don't want you, then it's their loss," she'd said when I tried to avoid bookings.

When my agent called to encourage me to give it one more go, I gave it one last shot because I hated the look of pity on Skittles's face. Apparently, the photographer wanted me. The company the ad is for had no idea of the angle he was going for with me and the shoot.

"This isn't what we had in mind. He's a gorgeous model, but those burns are going to be a turnoff—"

"This is why I'm the photographer *you hired*. I have the vision. *You* have the money. Yes?" the photographer interrupts.

"Too much money if you ask me. Especially for this. What happened to him? I was so excited when you told me who the model would be."

"Clearly, he was burned. I believe he's more beautiful than ever. A true work of art. He was too perfect before."

"Hmm, to each their own. He's not for our target market. Fashion models are hangers. He's now a damaged hanger."

Those are the words that send me into a rage. "Are you fucking kidding me?" I hiss.

"Kelex—"

"Fuck you both and fuck this shoot."

I end up tossing their entire fucking studio. I feel so hurt and out of control. After flipping shit over and destroying the set, I storm out—not caring about the fact my career is possibly officially over now.

I pull my phone out and text Jeff and Skittles to meet up with me. I need to clear my head. I have so much going on in my thoughts.

After a bit of back and forth, Skittles tells me she's on her way to pick me up and we'll all go to her place. Jeff replies he'll meet me there—I won't hold my breath.

He hasn't been himself and I haven't had the strength to call him on it. It took some time to get him to open up to the idea of Skittles—he's still not there. I think he likes that she's sassy and smart and she doesn't take his shit.

That's what I love about her too. However, Jeff has never been good at sharing me as a friend. It'll take a while, but he'll come around.

She's the one person in my life I allow to put me in my place. I'm well aware I've become a bigger asshole since the accident. I already know I could have left the shoot without tearing the place up.

In all honesty, it was a jeans ad. Most of my burns were covered. I'll admit when I look at myself, I know they look worse to me than they truly are. However, it's people like that exec and my father who make me feel like a living, breathing Freddy Krueger.

I used to be confident to the point of arrogance. If this is Karma, fuck her and this bullshit life she's handed me. This was my way out.

I was going to make my own way. My old modeling contracts allowed me to tell my father to shove his traditions and expectations. I swear my father has gone from looking at me with pride to looking at me like a nightmare.

The shit that has come out of his mouth. I'm no longer his perfect son. His words have been harsher than those I overheard.

I can't look into a mirror without hearing him in my head. It makes me see the worst when I undress and look down at my body or at my reflection.

"All that money for nothing. I thought this would be healed by now. I can't look at you. The cameras will make this ten times worse.

"You can forget all about that career. They won't want you now. Don't disgrace our family with this...this Wicker Man portrayal."

"*Grr*," I growl and punch my head. Shoving my hands in my hair, I tug the short strands to hold the tears back. "Shut up, shut the fuck up."

There's a part of me that knows he keeps saying shit like that to seal my fate as a Nikolaou-Kylix. However, I may have to become that man. If I don't figure out what's next, I won't have a choice.

Right on time to keep me from spiraling, Skittles pulls up in her BMW SUV. I smile. Her car collection rivals my own untouched one.

Every time I try to drive one of my cars, I freak out behind the wheel. It's like I relive that night all over again.

She rolls down the window and dips her head to peek out at me. I love this wig she's wearing today. It falls in layered waves across her face, her right eye barely peeking out from under it. It falls right below her chin at its longest length.

"Hey, you. Are you all right?" she calls out.

I open the door and slide in. The tightness in my chest loosens a bit. The scent of coconut fills my nostrils. Every single one of her cars smells so good, each having its own aroma. Then there's her delicious scent.

I try to reel in the scowl on my face before I turn to her. When I do look at her, she searches my gaze. I don't know what she sees, but she reads me well enough not to ask if I'm okay again. With sadness in her eyes, she turns and places the truck in gear.

Another thing I love about her, she doesn't push me when I'm not ready. There are so many things I haven't told her about my life, but she's never forced me to give more than I'm willing to. Our friendship is one of mutual respect.

"One day, you're going to look back on all of this and you're going to realize it was all for your good. It may not seem that way today, but someday it will come full circle."

I snort. "Yeah, sure."

All of that is easy for her to say. She's not on the verge of becoming a monster. God, I was destined to be a monster, no matter what.

Maybe I should finally take that trip to Greece to see my grandfather. He'll listen to me. Maybe he'll give me some start-up cash to do something new.

My advances for the gigs I've missed have been returned and I'm not about to piss away my savings just yet. Not without knowing my next move.

Jeff has offered plenty of times to let me in on one of his new ventures or to front me some start-up cash. I love him for it, but I could never. With my grandfather, he'd only be giving me money out of my trust I don't have access to yet.

I'll gain full access after a few stipulations I'm nowhere near ready for. When I do cross those finish lines, I'll be set for life.

For most of the ride, Skittles falls silent as if she's thinking. I feel bad after a while and try to come up with something to talk about to bring life back into the vehicle. The tight space has become suffocating.

"You still planning that trip to Cancun? I'm looking forward to some Flyboarding. Have you talked to Lex? Is she still thinking of going?"

That does it. A huge smile comes to her lips. I love the way she is with her cousins. Lex and Shawna mean the world to her. She'll talk about them for hours.

She said Shawna was at the funeral, although Lex wasn't able to make it. However, I don't remember much from that day other than committing to a tat that hurt like hell. The shit we do for this woman.

"Yeah, I have a great place I'm looking at. It will fit us all. I talked to Lex before you called."

"She's thinking about coming, but she's crazy busy. It seems like everyone's busy for the weekend I was thinking of. Unfortunately, Shawna won't be around. She'll be traveling for an internship.

"Deacon is like you, all in, but Pit said he's heading out of town that weekend. Luke has a fight he's training for, and Tak's in the middle of writing a new album."

"You see, I told you I'm the only one you need. Why do you continue to cling to those other assholes?" I croon, making her smile more.

She turns to look at me and sticks her tongue out. I shoot her a wink. She laughs that crazy laugh I love. My day has turned for the better just from being in her presence.

"Lex will love you."

"I'll be glad to finally put a face to the name. Too bad I still haven't met Shawna. She sounds nice."

"Too nice for you. I'm almost nervous to put you two in the same room."

I place a hand over my chest. "Me? I'm harmless. Besides, you know I'm not going to fuck over your family. You've told me how shy she is."

While Shawna is the shy one, Lex seems more outgoing. Lex had a harder life than Skittles and Shawna. From what I gather, her father had a drug problem. At least, that's what Skittles has been told.

Being who I am, I know a little more about her Uncle Lester and the real reason the mayor may not want that connection known. However, those aren't my secrets to tell. I do often wonder how much Lex knows.

I believe the distance she's creating that Skittles has been so upset about is because she knows a lot more than Mayven. Shawna, on the other hand, is a sweet college student. As Mayven tells it, she's the most sensitive of the three.

My thoughts are broken into as the ringing of Mayven's phone fills the car speakers. The name Shawnnie appears on the screen. Skittles picks up and answers.

"Hey, Shawnnie," she sings the way she always does when her little cousin calls.

"Hey, Ven," she says almost sadly.

I suck in a breath as my groin tightens at the sound of her voice. It's like soft liquid smoke. Not too deep and heavy, but not high pitched either. It's the right blend of the in-between.

"What's wrong?" Skittles asks, seemingly picking up on the same sadness I overhear.

"I feel so out of place. We went to the pool today to lounge around. I thought I looked cute. I wore the black two-piece you convinced me to buy."

"Okay, you look great in that suit. What's the problem?"

"You know Amy and Skylar are almost a foot shorter than me. They make me look so much taller when I walk with them."

"Who the fuck cares? You're gorgeous, hon. Inside and out."

"Yeah, but when we got to the pool, this guy said, 'Damn, get rid of the tall, fat one and you guys are welcome to join us. Drinks on me.' then he snickered like he told some funny-ass joke," she replies, mocking the guy's voice.

"And you should have told him his mom will be a better man than he'll ever be," I bite out without thinking.

I should keep my mouth shut. This sounds kind of personal. Skittles didn't get to tell her I was in the car. I'm just so fucking pissed.

Even though I don't remember seeing her, Skittles has told me her curves run on both sides of her family. I'm assuming Shawna has a body like Skittles, and in that case, she's hot as fuck. Thick and tall, she's probably gorgeous.

Skittles laughs. "That was Kelex. He's in the car with me. He's right though. Although, I would have added that he could choke on those drinks and his boys' dicks since that's the only action he'll get for the weekend."

"Um, I'm not you. I would never say something like that. Hi, Kelex. I've heard so much about you."

"Hey, sweetheart. If you look as gorgeous as you sound. It's totally his loss. I'm six-two. I always find taller women sexy. Own that shit, baby girl. Hold your head high and own that shit. Never let anyone take that from you."

"Oh, hell nah. You keep that slick-ass mouth to yourself. This is my baby cousin. I'm not having it, Kelex. Shawnnie, he's right though.

"They don't make ugly or unattractive genes in our family. Your mom was a pageant queen. You're as tall and beautiful as she is. Maybe you should stop hiding behind the camera and let it show you what we see."

Shawna sighs through the line. "That's so easy for you to say. You've never been called the Jolly Green Giant. Your locker was never broken into, so the other girls could replace your basketball shorts and jersey with ones that were two sizes too small. After removing all your clothes."

"Sometimes, I wish we were in the same grade. I wish they would have tried all that with you while I was there. Shawnnie, one of these days, you're going to stop letting people shit on you. I hope I have a front-row seat because if they all knew what I know…"

"We're not the same."

"But you're no one's chump. Period. You're amazing. Try to enjoy yourself, hon. If you have any problems you need me to handle, you call. I love you."

"I love you too," she replies. Then in a shy tone, she says. "Thanks, Kelex. Nice talking to you."

She hangs up and Skittles punches me in the arm. "Don't be flirting with my cousin. She's not ready for a guy like you."

"Trust me, I'm not ready for anything more than some dry humping."

She pulls into her driveway and turns to me with a gasp. "You still haven't had sex?"

I look away as my chest starts to become tight again. I reach for the handle to get out.

"Kelex?" she says softly.

"No, I'm not ready."

CHAPTER NINE

Pappoús

Kelex

A month later…

I'm in a shit mood because of this man sitting before me. My father thinks I'm making this trip for business when it's anything but. I wish I could slap the smug look off his face.

"Everything will be fine when you get to Crete," he says as we sit at his favorite table at the country club, the waitress he's been fucking brings him a drink.

He sips the brown liquor and grimaces. I remain silent. I had planned to make this trip without him knowing. It's time I finally take a moment to clear my head and spend time with my *pappoús*.

However, Pappoús called my father to ask about my arrival and *Baba* took it upon himself to stick his nose in my business.

"You will see. While you are there, you can take time to meet up with your little friend. The model, yes?"

"Yeah," I murmur.

One of the things that attracted me to Phoebe was that she was Greek. For the past four years, while getting her modeling career going, she's been traveling back and forth for work.

The distance has worked for me, especially in the last two years. When I asked her if she wanted to hook up, she let me know she was in the States and would fly in with me.

"Good, you spend some time with her and forget about all this other shit. Phoebe is Greek and beautiful. I'm sure she'll help you to get your head on straight. Get to know her better. She might make for a good wife," he continues.

Sure, because it's okay for Phoebe to be a model, but I'm committing a cardinal sin. If only he knew. I've gotten to know Phoebe Argyros quite well. I know Phoebe on her knees. My fingers know her pussy, hell, I know her asshole very well—because God forbid we fuck before marriage.

Not that I would marry her. Phoebe wants the world to think she's a sweet, innocent girl. I call bullshit.

She's working the business for all she can get, however she can get it. I haven't fooled myself into thinking this is a love match.

She's been a whole slut for me as long as I didn't penetrate her vagina and she could book the same gigs I did. Don't get me wrong, she's gorgeous. Her dark hair and hazel eyes complement her olive skin.

We would be a picture-perfect couple, but Phoebe has never given me that feeling. The feeling you get when you're with the one.

The only feeling I get is that of her wanting to raise to the top of the modeling food chain. I swear, she'd spit back down on me like all the rest if not for the money I already have. My agent, my manager, all the other actors and models I used to run with—they've all stopped taking my calls.

"I'm going to see *Pappoús*. That's all I plan to focus on," I grumble.

"Your grandfather has babied you. We all have. Josh, you will meet with your grandfather and listen to the next steps you need to take to solidify your position."

I clench my fist and clamp my mouth shut. I've never wanted this position and I'm not going to roll over to take it now. At times, I feel like he's demanding this as punishment for what I saw when I was younger.

Jeff and I were told not to go out in the field and to stay away from the shed. However, we never listened and walked right in on the truth of who my baba is.

"I've prepared you for this because I see me and this life in your eyes. You were meant for this," he says as if reading my mind.

"Adrian will fall in line. He wants this."

It's the truth. My younger cousin wants a title, a name for himself. He's in Pappoús' face every chance he gets.

"Adrian isn't my son. It isn't his right. You, Josh, are my son and you are right for this. You're calculating. You have the instinct."

"What you mean is I don't want what you're after. You can run things and you never have to watch your back with me. Adrian or Constantine will have your head as soon as the opportunity arises," I reply.

"I fear no man. Especially not my nephews."

"You should," I mutter under my breath.

"*Ti ítan aftó?*" he questions.

"Nothing, Baba. I'm tired. I'm going home to get some rest before my flight."

***

"Wow, this place is gorgeous," Phoebe marvels as we walk into my grandfather's Crete home.

"I used to love coming here."

"Why stay at a hotel when we could be in all this opulence?"

"I don't allow just anyone to stay in my grandfather's home."

She frowns and looks me in the eyes. Let's not get this fucked up. We mess around, but she's not my girl.

"*Tzósoua*," my grandfather croons as he walks over to me. He pats my cheek before pulling me into a tight hug.

"Pappoús, you look well. It will be good to spend time with you. It's so good to see you."

"Who do we have here?"

"This is Phoebe, the friend I told you about. We've worked together a lot in the past."

"Ah, yes, it's nice to meet you. Helena, come. Take *Tzósoua's* friend on the tour of the gardens, so I can talk to my grandson for a bit," he says, waving his assistant over.

"I'll find you when I'm done," I say.

Phoebe nods and tucks her hair behind her ear. To be honest, her vibes have been off since she arrived for the flight. I almost left her behind. I'm not in the mood for bullshit.

"How's the modeling?" Pappoús says, turning his focus back on me.

I smile sadly. "I had to give it up. The burns and scarring weren't for everyone."

His blue eyes grow sad. He searches my face. "This accident, it has changed you." He points at my chest. "In here and here." He taps my temple. "No matter what, you are always a Nikolaou. Don't lose who you are. They don't want you. You model for yourself and show them what they gave up."

"I wish it were that simple, Pappoús."

"It is. Say the word. I will make sure you have anything you want. You have so much time to live, Josh. Do you know what your name means, *Tzósoua mou*? Yehoshua."

"God is Salvation."

"Yes, you survived that wreck for a reason. Don't mistake a gift from God. I get the final say on who takes my place. You don't have to do anything you don't want. I will name my next successor and the one after if need be."

He winks at me as his words sink in. My mother had three sisters. The two I know each had a son after I was born. They're still here in Greece. Both my cousins are spoiled and my grandfather doesn't care much for either of them, but everyone thinks he'll pick from the two of them to run everything in his place.

I know better. My grandfather has never intended to leave either of them a thing. Greek families can get vicious for power.

At least this one can. To this day, I don't think my mother's death was a true accident. I wouldn't put it past either of her remaining siblings or their husbands.

Blake Knight is the one person outside of my grandfather who I trust these days. I trust him because my grandfather trusts him, and for as long as I can remember, Blake doesn't fuck with my father or my aunts. There's something to be said for that.

"I see the wheels turning, *Tzósoua*. This is still a decision you will make. I will not rush it and I won't push you either. I think you should spend more time with Blake when you return to the US. It will be good for you," Pappoús says, breaking into my musing.

"Yeah, maybe I will."

"For tonight, take your pretty friend out. Let her show you who she is," he says and winks at me.

Um, he picked up on it too. I was hoping he would. It might be time to part ways with Phoebe. There's nothing there.

But who else will fuck you, Freddy?

At this point, I'm not even sure she will. The hand job on the plane was under a blanket. Besides, she was too busy getting off as I fingered her.

Betrayal

Kelex

I should have thought twice about having Phoebe join me. We've only been here for eight hours and I'm ready to send her ass back to LA or wherever she was before coming here. Dinner was a disaster. She spent most of her time taking photos of us or the food whenever she wasn't giggling at her phone.

I almost did book her a commercial flight to send her on her way. However, it's been so long since I've had sex. Besides, some head and her little tight ass are better than nothing.

Phoebe pounces as soon as we get to the suite I booked for her. I know this is a mistake from the moment we walk through the door. I'll be honest with myself. As horny as I am, I'm not ready to be intimate with anyone.

What if she's totally grossed out by me? What then? How do I recover from that?

Since the accident, it's been rejection, on top of rejection, on top of rejection. I've never been one to allow people in. However, everyone I've made a connection with to further my career has shit on me.

I know I'm asking for another dagger to the chest. With these thoughts running through my head, I can't even get it up.

"Should I order some champagne? Maybe this will get you in the mood," she says through her heavy Greek accent.

I shrug. "Why not?"

I head over to the minibar. Maybe some alcohol will loosen me up. It doesn't work when I hang out with the assholes and we're surrounded by hot, willing ass. However, with Phoebe being who she is, I might get in the mood and decide to finally get my dick wet.

We both make ourselves comfortable. I sit on the couch and kick my long legs out. Phoebe kicks off her shoes and wiggles out of her tight dress.

She walks around the suite in her red panties and bra. She does look hot. Two years ago, I would have let her suck me off in a heartbeat.

Tonight, I'm apprehensive. I could take her in the ass and just push my pants down a little. However, I know she's a grabber.

She likes to push at my thighs when I'm driving into her. She's also one to drop to her knees to suck the cum out of me without warning.

There's a knock on the door. I stand from the couch and head to open it. After collecting the champagne and glasses, I then head back to my seat and pour myself another glass of whiskey.

"I have music," Phoebe says when I return to the living area. "I can dance for you."

"Whatever," I say and knock back a tumbler of whiskey.

"Do you not like my body?" She pouts and cups her breasts. "I did for more jobs and you."

"You shouldn't have," I murmur and wave a hand. "You look fine. My head is just on other things."

"Things like your accident? Will you show me? Surely, this is not that bad? You are still gorgeous man with biggest dick I've ever seen."

I lift a brow. How many has she seen? Not that I believe for a minute she's been waiting on me while I've been in the States healing.

"I'm not there yet, give me a bit and keep the drinks coming."

A wide smile takes over her face. I want to see if she remains this eager once my clothes come off. Here's the thing, I've tried to get head once since the accident. The chick barfed two minutes in.

I can't say if it was because she was so drunk off her ass or if it was because the burns were too much. She begged off while apologizing before I could find out. Since then, I've been too fucked up in the head to try again.

Phoebe plays some music and starts to gyrate around the room. Soon I'm too drunk to think about how corny and goofy she looks. After a few more drinks, I actually come out of my head enough to get hard.

She removes her bra and I notice how her once-perfect nipples now look strange on her newly inflated breasts. I've seen better work. I shrug the thought off and focus on her bare pussy she exposes as she sits on the coffee table and spreads her legs. She starts to rub herself while she bites her lip.

The alcohol must be kicking in. I'm hard and trapped between my slacks and my leg. I'm not a boaster. I'm a doer. Which is how I end up on my knees between her legs, taking what she's offering.

"Josh," she moans as I lick and finger fuck her tight pussy.

I try to ignore the sight of her well-used asshole. No surprises there. I reach for one of her unnatural breasts. She squeals as she rides my face and calls out my name. I start to lose my erection as I think about whether this will be my only option.

Some Greek chick my father chooses for me because she fits the life. Someone who has allowed every guy with a smile to fuck her in the ass. Should I resign myself to this life?

I won't fool myself into thinking my father won't have me get my hands dirty. Avoiding the savage it seems I'm destined to become goes out the window once I agree to that marriage.

I'm no dummy. My father will have my grandfather erased as soon as I have it all in my hands. I'll sentence us all to death if my father thinks he finally has the power he's after.

Phoebe represents a portal to a way of life I've never wanted—hence my father wanting me to spend time with her. I've watched my friend adapt to this life after losing his father and having to take his spot. I'm not Jeff, though, and the power I'm on the other end of is far greater.

"Josh, baby, please," Phoebe pleads as if she is trying to reel my attention back in.

When I don't snap back into focus right away, she scoots back to toss her leg over in order to get off the table and get to her knees. Her eyes are filled with lust. I stand. Finally drunk enough not to give a fuck.

"I've wanted to suck your cock since we met on the flight. It has been torture waiting to see you again. I've had your portfolio sent to me to masturbate. My friends are all jealous that we've been dating," she purrs.

"Nothing lasts forever and nothing is promised," I say.

She looks up at me and frowns but doesn't stop pulling my zipper down. She reaches in to pull me out, not once looking down. It's as if I'm holding my breath, waiting for her to look. When she does, she pulls in a sharp intake of air. I purse my lips and go to zip back up, slapping her hands away.

"No, no," she says.

She licks her lips and closes her eyes before wrapping her mouth around me. I groan and try to focus on the feel of her mouth. I need this release, to be honest.

My hand hasn't been what I need it to be. However, the suctioning of Phoebe's warm mouth has my toes curling. The girl has upgraded her game. Although it's not lost on me that she won't open her eyes.

Frustration starts to grow, killing the pleasure that had started to build. A million thoughts race through my head. Phoebe used to give me eye contact while on her knees.

I cup her chin and squeeze her face. "Look at me," I hiss.

She opens her hazel eyes. I don't miss the wrinkling of her nose as she moves her gaze from my eyes to my torso, which is revealed as I hold my dress shirt out of the way. She looks lower.

I believe the gagging is either from me pushing her head or her taking me deep. Still, she closes her eyes tightly and rage fills me. I'm going to come because I need to, not because I want to continue this torture.

I screw my own eyes shut and grind my teeth. I try to think of anyone other than Phoebe. Skittles pops into my head and guilt consumes me. I shake the image off and think of the flight attendant from the trip here.

She was pretty, with golden-brown skin and hazel eyes. Her breasts fit nicely into her uniform shirt, and she had a nice ass. I imagine her full lips wrapped around me and roar. I pull out of Phoebe's mouth and bust on her face.

She looks shocked for a few beats. I tuck myself away and turn for the en suite in the bedroom of the suite. My buzz has already started to fade. I close the bathroom door and turn for the sink.

Turning on the faucet, I stare at myself in the mirror. Rage and bitterness swirl within me. I don't know what I'm angrier about. The fact she seemed disgusted by me, or the fact this is now my life.

I splash water on my face and clean myself up before putting myself back together so I can return to the main area. However, I don't get out of the bathroom before Phoebe's tear-filled voice reaches my ears.

"I don't think I can do this. It's not worth the money or people he knows." She sniffles. "No, it's not his face. He's still gorgeous above the waist." She pauses as the person on the other end speaks. "No, I don't think I can go through with it. It's disgusting to look at and my face was so close. What will happen this week when we hit the beach?

"He can't walk around in swim trunks looking like that. I think it goes down his leg." She's quiet again. "God, no. I'm never going to get to have that big cock inside me. It's still beautiful, but I couldn't look at it without seeing those burns out the corner of my eye."

I have such a tight grip on the bathroom door handle I might break it. Then she places the nail in the coffin.

"No, I'm not being shallow. Let me get a picture for you. I'll brave blowing him one more time as a pity blow and I'll sneak a pic."

I can no longer see reason. I storm out of the bathroom to the main area, whip out my dick, and piss on her dress and shoes that are tossed on the floor.

"You're not even the hottest option I had. Fuck your pity. What you should pity is your ass. You should lay off the anal. You're too young for diapers, but you're well on your way there, Sweetheart. Get your shit and get the fuck out," I bellow.

"How am I supposed to get home?"

"Do I look like I give a fuck? Ask your friend on the phone for a ride."

"Oh my God, Stavros, I think he's lost his mind."

"Are you fucking kidding me? You're talking to your ex? Get the fuck out, now."

"In what? You just pissed on my things."

"Next time, I'll aim for you. Get out."

Would I really piss on her? The old me wouldn't, but at this point, I might. I feel crazy.

As if I'm losing everything. Fuck this bullshit. My grandfather is right. I still have options. Phoebe scrambles for her things as I show some decency and toss her a robe.

She sniffles as if her feelings are hurt and she hasn't just crashed mine. If she can think this way, what will other women think? My life is over.

However, when I think of the life I saved to end up this way, I want nothing more than to hear her voice. It should be around three in the morning back home. I ignore the time and pull my phone out. The call is picked up on the fourth ring.

"Hey, Kelex."

I pull the phone from my ear to look at the number I dialed as my groin tightens from the voice. I know right away this isn't Skittles.

Although, like Skittles, her voice brings me a sense of calm. I amble over to the accent chair and flop down into it, leaning forward to place my elbows on my knees and take a calming breath.

"You there? It's me, Shawna."

"Yeah, I'm here, baby girl. Where's Skittles?"

"Drunk and talking shit to Pit on my phone since he hung up on her on hers. Is everything okay? You don't sound the same."

I snort and realize my face is wet. I haven't cried since waking up in casts, rigged up in that hospital bed. I shake my head as if she can see me.

"I'm having a really fucked-up day," I say.

"Oh, can I help? Mayven's pretty wasted, but I'm a good listener."

I don't want to hang up and be alone. It hits me. All I want is to feel human again. I want to be treated like a man. Not some freak.

"How have you been?" I go for a casual conversation because it's what I need.

"I'm great. I was hoping to get to talk to you. I'm going on my first date because of you."

"Because of me?"

"Yeah, your voice has been playing in my head. When I walk into a room now, I hold my head high and own my shit. I was asked out on a date. He's a nice guy," she replies.

I lean back in my seat and slump down. I have no right to be jealous, but I rub at the ball of jealousy that burns my chest.

"How old are you, Shawna?"

"I'm three years younger than Mayven. I'm twenty," she whispers shyly.

"And this is your first date?"

"Yeah, I don't go out much. I have school and assignments. Mayven's going to help me pick something to wear. Can I ask you something?"

"Yeah, go ahead."

"Are you and Skittles the same age?"

"Yeah, I'm older by a few months. I was born in July."

"Oh," she says sadly.

I smile. Skittles will kick my ass for this, but I know nothing will ever come from it. I just need that old feeling back.

"Shawna?"

"Yes, Kelex?"

"Joshua. Call me Josh or Joshua. And sweetheart, if we ever meet, run... I'm an asshole. You can do better than me, but I promise if I get the chance. I'm going to ruin you for life."

Her audible gasp makes me hard. I laugh to myself and shake my head. Fuck Phoebe. I'm Joshua Kylix. I'm the prize.

CHAPTER ELEVEN

Interception

Shawna

Two months later…

I look into the mirror with a huge smile on my face. My makeup and hair look perfect. This silk press is giving me life. The waves and layers are ridiculously lush. I can't stop running my hands through it to watch it fall back into my face.

I'm pulling off confidence I know I don't have and it's all because of *him*. As soon as Mayven told me Joshua was on his way back from Greece and she was throwing him a party at Pit's bar, I knew I was going to attend, and I never go out.

My phone rings, and I turn to float over to my bed, where I had tossed it after my last call with Skylar. My smile grows wide when Skittles's name and a pic of us light my screen. My heart swells at the sight of the picture. From the neck up, we really could pass for twins or sisters, at the least.

"Hey, you," I answer and sit on the bed.

"You sound like you're in a good mood. You're not bailing on tonight, are you?"

"No." I roll my eyes as if she can see me. "I'm still coming." I bite my lips and think of the best way to ask my next question. "So, am I going to get to meet your assholes for sure this time?"

"It looks like it. Luke is in town already. Tak's tour bus will pull in sometime tonight. Deacon says he has one large piece to finish, but he'll be there and it's Pit's bar. I told him I'll cut his balls off if he tries to skip out."

I laugh. Those two argue like a married couple. I wish Mayven could see how much I think Pit likes her. As a matter of fact, I think she's crazy about him too. She just tries to hide it.

I chew on my lip before I ask. "What about Kelex?"

"He called me when his plane landed. He got in from Greece early this morning. All is well so far. I can't wait. I miss him. Things haven't been the same without him."

I release a relieved breath. Good, he'll be there. I stand and walk back over to the mirror. My light blue jeans hug my thick curves to a *T*. I went with the high-waisted ones Skittles suggested. The half leather, half sheer peplum top hides my FUPA—I've been battling back and forth with over the last few months—and complements my breasts with the sheer wrap top and leather peplum overlay.

I haven't decided on shoes yet. Josh said he's six-two. I think I should go with my black thigh-high rider boots. Those will make my booty look amazing but won't leave me to tower over him.

"Shawnnie, are you listening?"

"Oh, yeah, I'm here."

"So, I'll pick you up after I pick up Kelex," she says.

My heart races. I can't wait to meet him. "Of course, that's fine. Thanks for giving me a ride."

"You know I have you. I want you to have a good time without having to think about how you'll get home. Hey, listen. That's Kelex on the other line. I'll call you back."

"Okay."

She hangs up. I zip my boot and do a spin on my toes in front of the mirror, clutching my phone to my chest. I sigh like a schoolgirl.

He told me to run, but he didn't say in which direction. I think I have a thing for assholes—if they're anything like Joshua. When I look at old photos of him, I think I fall in love every time.

I remembered him from my aunt's funeral. He was the one who sat beside Mayven and held her hand. She had all those handsome guys with her that day.

If my cousin had been my hero before, she became a goddess in my eyes that day. At first, I thought he was her boyfriend. After learning they're only friends, I've tried subtly to find out more about him.

When she mentioned he was a former model. I had to bite my tongue to keep from telling her I already knew that and used to stalk him and his profiles.

I don't know why he hasn't returned to modeling. He's perfect.

Kelex

"Hey, something has come up," I say to Skittles as my world reels. I look out the car window as Jeff and I ride in the back seat of his SUV.

"Do you need me to come get you now?"

"No, I'm with Jeff. He's trying to help me get out of here," I reply.

"Josh, what's going on?"

"I'll tell you when I wrap my head around it. I need to get back to Greece before my father makes that impossible."

"Is there anything I can do?"

"Thank everyone for the party and give my excuses. I'll call you when I get to Crete."

"Okay," she says, sounding so disappointed.

I'm just as upset. I was looking forward to spending time with my friends. I could use some time with real people.

"But are you sure you're okay?"

"Yes, Skittles, I'll be fine."

I say the words and can taste the lie they are as they roll around in my mouth. She sighs into the phone. I want to share the truth with her, but I don't know what to say. I'd also be exposing myself.

"I'll talk to you later," she says and we end the call.

"So you're disowned. What now? You want to burn the place down?"

I look at Jeff and raise a brow. I actually mull the thought over before shaking my head clear. I'm pissed, but I haven't reached that level yet.

"First, I need to get to Greece or at least find out why my calls aren't getting through to my grandfather. I spoke to him when I landed. He was my first call before I checked in with you and Skittles. Why won't my calls go through now?"

"We'll find out, but you do know you don't have to leave? I'll help you in any way I can. You need money. I have you. You need a place to stay. I have that covered. Name it. I got you, bro."

"Thanks, Jeff, but if I can get to my grandfather, he'll release my trust to me. I know he will. I can get my life straight from there."

"What will you do?"

"I'll find something."

"Remember our lemonade stand in elementary school?"

I smile and laugh. "Yeah."

"You made a fucking killing charging for kisses on the side."

"Dude, I took that shit to a new level in high school."

Jeff barks out a laugh. "I almost passed out when that mom slid you a hundred dollars to come over and help her garden." He rubs his chin. "If your other investments don't work out, you can always go back to mommy fucking."

I snort. "I never fucked her. She wanted to talk. Her son was being bullied. She paid me an extra grand to help him stop the bullying."

"You're shitting me."

"Nope, remember Achilles Makris?"

"The dork who started following you around senior year?"

"He was actually pretty cool, but yeah. I taught him a few moves to defend himself and I beat the shit out of those guys when I caught them trying him," I reply.

"Fuck, I remember walking into the locker room that day. I didn't ask questions. I just made sure your ass didn't get caught. You really are a motherfucking hero. The whole pun intended."

I fall silent and turn back to the window. I'm a peaceful guy for the most part. However, seeing what they did to Achilles and hearing him say he wanted to end his life over it—I had to do something.

"Do you still speak to him or his mom? She was from deep pockets if I remember right."

"Yeah, his mom was pretty cool. I still see her around. She's a member of the country club and Achilles is into tech or something. You wouldn't recognize him now if you saw him."

I keep to myself how connected I am to Achilles and his mom. It's something Blake Knight taught me. Not everyone needs to know everything. Not even "best friends." This happens to be one of those things.

"What the fuck?" Jeff says as he reaches for the safety handle above the back passenger door and leans forward to duck and look out of the windshield.

The private air hangar is swarming with cops and the FBI. I grind my teeth as we get closer. When we pull up, an agent raps his knuckles against the back window on Jeff's side.

The window is rolled down and the agent shoves his arm inside. The warrant is for you, Mr. Harrington, and this is for you, Joshua," he says, shoving a phone across to me.

I frown and take the device. "Hello?"

"I told you not to go running to Basil. He can't help you. I'll make trouble for everyone you know if they try to help you.

"I've had you placed on a travel ban list for every island in Greece. You want to be your own man, here's your start. Don't say I never did anything for you," my father snarls.

"I promise you, I will make you regret this. You've just made me a problem you never had."

I hang up the phone and roar. I toss the stupid phone out the window at the agent. My mind spirals out as I realize I have nothing but the clothes on my back.

I need to figure this out and my pride won't allow me to ask my friends for help. There has to be another way.

"*Fuck*," I bellow.

CHAPTER TWELVE

Guidance

Kelex

"You sure you don't need my help?"

"Yeah, I'm good. Thanks for letting me crash at your place last night. I'll catch up with you later," I say as I go to step out of Jeff's SUV.

"Josh?"

"Yeah."

"You don't have to do this on your own. I know my family isn't where it used to be, but I'm here to help if you need me."

"Some things you have to do on your own. I feel like this is one of them."

"Then what are you doing here?"

I shrug. "She helps me to think. What she's done in the last eight months is amazing. I can stand to be around that."

"Must be nice having Daddy's money to pull it all off," he mumbles.

I frown. "She didn't use his money. She's a lot smarter than you think."

"Does she feel the same way about you?"

"I don't give a shit if she does."

"I'm just asking. I've never heard her say much about you the way you talk about her. I don't think she sees you the same."

"Jeff, I'm here to be her friend, not get her into my bed. She can think what she wants about me. I like having her around," I say and close the door on whatever else he plans to say.

I've come to the one place I know will allow me to get my head on straight. Skittles's apartment. She's renting this place until her shop opens and gets going.

I'm a bit peeved with Jeff. I thought he was finally getting used to the fact that I've bonded with Skittles and the Assholes. I guess two months away has placed us at square one all over again.

I pull out my phone and go to dial Skittles to let her know I'm here. However, instead of making a call, my phone rings. I purse my lips and pick up the call.

"Hello."

"Joshua, get into the car. It's time you come see me. We have a lot to discuss."

"Blake, this isn't a good time."

"Sure it is. Your father has blocked you from your grandfather and cut you off. I have your options and a line that will reach Basil."

"Motherfucker," I say under my breath. I turn and look across the street. Sure enough, there's a black car with one of

Blake's guys standing outside of it. "Does this have to happen now? I need a minute to think."

"You need to remember who you are. Ulysses needs you, not the other way around, like he's made it seem. Your mother would want me to step in. Come to me. We're here to help."

I sigh, turning to look back at the building once more. My shoulders sag. A few drinks and laughs will have to wait.

"I'm on my way."

"Good."

***

I sit in the private room at one of Blake Knight's establishments. It's an art gallery. The one run by his longtime girlfriend, Zoe Gataki. Interestingly enough, this is only a hobby of hers.

I take a sip of water and look down at the text that just came in from Skittles. I love her concern for me. I grow annoyed as I think of Jeff's words about her.

Skittles: *Are you all right? Call me when you get a sec.*

Suddenly, the air is sucked out of the room. I hold my breath as I look up to see Zoe Gataki walk in like the boss she is. The white skirt suit she has on makes a statement against her olive-brown skin. The tight white skirt says, *yeah, I've still got it.*

The suit jacket with its wide lapels screams Cruella de Vil confidence. Her short silky androgens haircut that's pushed back off her face reminds me she told me her mother is Black while her father was from Greece.

I stand before she reaches the table. "Hey, Zoe," I croon as I pull her in for a hug.

Zoe Gataki is smart and gorgeous. She's a full-time attorney and runs this place on the side. Her father was big shit here in Bridge Lake and Vander back in the day. Zoe came from an affair he had with an attorney on his payroll. However, he never treated her like his illegitimate child. He raised her and his other daughter right alongside each other.

Rumor has it her husband Atlas Novack lost his life beating on her. I'm still not clear on when she and Blake started things, before or after she was widowed.

"Look at how gorgeous you are," she says as she squeezes my face. "Come, Blake is waiting for you. You boys have grown up so fast. I don't know what to do with either of you."

"How is Achilles?"

"He is here. *Éla tha íthele na se dei. Aftós kai o Bléik periménoun sto grafeío mou,*" she says in Greek.

I smile. I wasn't expecting Achilles to be here, but I'd love to see him too. He was a good kid and had become a friend. I follow her to her office, where Blake and Achilles are waiting.

When we step inside, Blake and some big-ass dude stand. Blake pulls me into a hug. When he releases me, the big dude beams at me. I look him in his eyes and my mouth falls open.

"Achilles? Get the fuck out of here."

"Josh, bro. It's good to see you," he croons and pulls me into a hug.

I'm swallowed in his one-armed embrace. This isn't the little shit I taught to fight and stick up for himself. Heck, he had filled out some the last time I saw him, but this, this is something else. I pat him on the back and squeeze a little. It broke my heart when he wanted to give up on life.

Kids can be so cruel. They only teased him because he was new and spoke Greek but looked Black. He spent a lot of time with his pappoús back then—that's who he lived with until coming to Vander to live with his mom.

Although lighter than his mom, you can still tell he has African American heritage. Greek was the language he was most comfortable with. It was all we spoke to each other when we met. Zoe loved that.

"How have you been, man?"

"I'm great. Just moved back. We should hang sometime."

"Come, Joshua. Have a seat. I'm glad Achilles is here. He's part of the proposal I have for you. Actually, he and Zoe will play a part in what I have to offer."

I sit down, my mind spinning a thousand miles a minute. How are these two supposed to help me and my situation? I need money and Achilles looks like he's more than capable of taking care of himself.

"*Nonós*, I'm going to need you to explain."

"Ah, yes, it's been a while since you've seen Achilles. He's made quite the name for himself in tech. However, he's still a bit shy.

"You, Josh, are charismatic. You can be the mouthpiece and face of the company I'm about to sponsor for Achilles. You will be his partner.

"You boys can split it fifty-fifty, but as far as the public and Ulysses will know for now, you are only the CEO, no vested financial interest," Blake explains.

"So you will be a silent investor. That way, he doesn't know of your involvement and I'm just a face. He won't know how deep my pockets go."

"And I'm going to make us millions," Achilles says with a huge grin. "Not just in tech. I have friends lined up to run a few restaurants, a couple of nonprofits, and festivals—all things my tech ideas and innovations will expand and make lucrative."

"Okay, but where do you fit in?" I say, looking at Zoe.

"Blake is the money, Achilles is the brains, I'm the legal representation and the doors to Vander and Bridge Lake."

My face clouds over. I know who Blake and Zoe are. They move Bridge Lake. Zoe snaps her fingers and heads roll.

I've heard she eats them for breakfast in the courtroom. One thing is for sure, our contracts will always be ironclad. I'll admit my interest has been piqued.

"I see that look, Josh. I'm not here to shove you into a decision. I'm here to show you what it entails. How you can be the man your pappoús wants you to be without becoming the man your father is," Blake says.

"And I'm going to show you the humane side of things. How to seduce your way through life with more than your face. When I'm done, every woman in Bridge Lake will offer you her husband's secrets because you're the smooth entertainer you've always dreamed of being," Zoe says.

"And when it's all said and done, the day will come when you'll see the man we know you will be. When that day comes, you will make your own decision."

"And if that decision is to walk away from it all?"

"Trust me, it won't be. You have a lot to learn about your family's past and how this place connects it all. Others want your crown, but their necks would break under the weight. You will rise, Joshua. The table is already set," Blake replies.

"Allow me to show you what you should have seen first," Zoe adds.

"But the decision will still be mine. Pappoús isn't taking back his promise?"

"It has always been yours to make. Just how your mother always wanted," Blake says as he looks me in the eyes, saying so much more.

I think their words over. I already know how smart Achilles is. I have no doubt he'll pull this off. I think of Pit and smirk. If Zoe can get me secrets from the wives of Bridge Lake, I can become as dangerous as he's become.

That's not such a bad idea. I know for a fact he keeps his hands clean. Now that Ulysses has made me his enemy, I'm going to take all the ammo I can get.

What was it that Skittles once said? Pit and I have a lot more in common than we think. I know Blake isn't innocent and will destroy someone for fucking with him, but can I do this and not become that guy?

I guess we're all going to find out.

"Looks like you have a partner, Ac," I say with a smile.

"Joshua, I think it's understood without saying, this is one of those things—"

"I'll keep it to my chest. This one is family only. Point me where you need me, when you need me and I'm there. You guys and Pappoús are the only family I have left that I trust."

Zoe looks at me sadly. "I know the first place you and I need to go. Blake is right. You need to remember."

I sit with my brows knitted, but her words carry a sense of truth. I'm so tired of being lost and angry. I'm going to trust them to help me help myself.

Shawna

Ugh, why won't that phone stop ringing? Where the heck is Ven? That's her phone, not mine.

I crack an eye open to find her hanging off the couch with drool running out of her mouth. I stifle a laugh and shake my head. I guess we did party pretty hard the other night, and she stayed up for as long as she could, waiting for a call from Joshua.

I feel bad that he never called. She's worried about him. I'm learning just how much the guys mean to her. She has a thing for Pit, but Josh and the others are like brothers to her.

I know my cousin. She'd do anything for them. It's one of the things that makes it hard not to love her.

Ven doesn't do things for you to give her anything back. She does it because she loves to help.

"All right already," I groan and move to pick up her phone. I grab it from the coffee table to see it's Joshua calling.

I smile as the name Kelex flashes across the screen. I was so disappointed when he never showed up to his own party. I had asked Ven to spend the weekend with her, thinking he might turn up there.

I can't wait to meet him in person. Knowing Ven has been waiting on his call, I answer before it goes to voice mail. I would hate for them to keep missing each other—at least, that's what I tell myself as I answer her phone.

"Hello."

"Hey, gorgeous. What are you doing answering Skittles's phone?"

I try not to gasp. I didn't think he would know it was me without me telling him. My face hurts from smiling so hard.

"She's knocked out. We had some drinks. I don't think she's going to answer anyone for a few hours."

He laughs. "She does sleep like the dead after a night of drinking."

"I know, right?" I laugh back. "Do you want me to tell her anything when she wakes?"

"No. I'll catch up to her. How have you been?" he asks smoothly.

"I'm good. Looking for a full-time job."

"You're a photographer, right?"

"Yeah."

"I could give you some numbers."

"I don't do a lot of fashion stuff. I want to do some photojournalism, maybe some documentary stuff."

"Ah, I've got you. I'll still pass along some numbers and you can see what comes up. How about that?"

"That would be awesome. If I don't figure it out soon, I'll be following my mom around for her campaign. So far from what I want."

"I hear you do some pretty impressive work. I'm sure you'll land something soon. How's the dating going?"

I bite my lip and shake my head as if he can see me. "That date was a total bust."

"Really? What happened?"

"He was shier than me. Can you believe he was texting me while he sat right across from me?"

"Wow," he scoffs.

"How are things with you? Did you enjoy your trip to Greece?"

"I did. I got to spend time with my grandfather. He always keeps me grounded. I wish I could head back there now."

"I hear it's gorgeous. I'd love to go with my camera. I'd people-watch through my lens," I gush before I can stop myself.

"So no fashion photography, but you're not against taking pictures of people. Got it. I'll take you and your camera to Crete someday," he says in his sexy voice.

"Really?"

"Of course, why not?"

"I don't know. You don't know me."

"I know I like talking to you. Every time you answer Ven's phone, you're on the other side of a shit day. Taking you home would be like a thank-you for being you.

"Besides, we're going to get to know each other. This is my number. Save it to your phone. I'm your new person. Call when you need me."

"Are you joking?"

"No, why would I joke?"

I bite my lip again. "Ven says you guys joke a lot. I don't know. I wasn't expecting you to want to talk to me."

"You're intelligent. There's something calming about you. And I'm less dangerous over the phone. You should still avoid ever meeting me, but for now, call me when you want to talk. You might just be saving me in the process, gorgeous."

"You don't know what I look like, why keep calling me that?"

"Something tells me I'm right. Didn't you hear?"

"Hear what?"

"I'm always right," he says through a deep laugh. "Later, Shawna. And baby girl?"

"Yeah?"

"Run."

CHAPTER THIRTEEN

Humanity

Kelex

I look down at the address on my phone and then back up at the building in front of me. Zoe asked me to meet her here. I twist my lips and start for the front door.

It's been two weeks since going to see Blake and talking to my grandfather on the phone. He had a lot to say and agreed with Blake's plan. My father hasn't stopped shit.

I'm going to meet up with Achilles after this. He's already put things in motion. I have a few docs to sign and I'll get my first payout. We fly out this weekend to look at a few of the restaurants. Knowing they will be steak houses, I've been reading up on the business, learning what I can on my own.

"Joshua, over here, love." I turn to find Zoe with an older woman next to her.

Zoe is dressed to the nines as usual, with gray slacks that flare at the bottom and a black leather blazer with an asymmetrical cut. If I had a woman like her, I'd keep it to myself as well.

"Good afternoon, handsome," she says after kissing both of my cheeks. "This is Minerva. She's the director of the program."

"Program? What program?"

"The program we're going to hit the elite up to fund. I find when you have the right motivation, rubbing elbows isn't so bad."

"It's nice to meet you, Joshua. Ms. Gataki has spoken so highly of you."

"It's nice to meet you as well. Can you tell me more about what you guys do here?"

"I can show you better than I can tell you. Follow me."

I spend the next two hours in awe. This is a place for young adults who have nothing and no one. Girls who have become pregnant and have been disowned. Young girls who no one wants to give a shot.

My bullshit seems so small against all they're facing. Some of them just need a place to hang to stay out of trouble. However, the resources are running low and the staffing sucks.

I've stepped in when asked. The best part was getting to hold a newborn who had just made it here after being released with his mom. I didn't worry about my scars as I took my shirt off and placed him on my chest. Knowing I could help the exhausted sixteen-year-old trumped my own shit.

"Humanity," Zoe murmurs with a smile in her voice.

"What's that?" I whisper, not wanting to wake the little guy.

"Humanity, it's what your father has never had. Your mother was too good for him. Doing what's necessary is one thing. Becoming a tyrant is another. Basil and your *nonos* Blake walk the right side of the line because they've kept their humanity.

"Not to mention, charity is always a way to work a room and be at the center of the right conversations. The money will come to you. One, maybe two charities of your own will be great to start with."

"Wait, I thought we were going to raise money for this place. What are you talking about?"

"I see your heart, Joshua. You are your mother's son. Trust me, you will feel better once this is done. And sitting on the board will be a gift. The wives will become curious."

"So we're after the wives of Bridge Lake?" I say and lift a brow.

"And Vander. They are the real power. Just like you listened to these kids today, you will listen to every woman. Hear her, show her you hear her and I promise you will have your father by the throat."

"I'm all ears."

***

Zoe was right. I'm on a high from helping out. I want to do more. For the first time, I'm thinking of more than myself and how things affect me.

My mind goes to Shawna as I ride in the back of the car, heading to see Achilles. I wish I would have asked for her number. I'd love to talk to her about this. I already sent Skittles a text. She wants to know how she can help.

"I don't know what I want to do yet," I mutter out loud as I return her text.

I plan to start a charity like Zoe suggested, but I don't know who needs my help most. I want to do something meaningful. Something that will make a real impact.

Skittles: *I'm here when you decide. I'd love to go to that place though. I'm all for helping the kids.*

I grin to myself. I should've known she'd want to get involved. Taking care of people is what she does.

Maybe when we all go on our trip, we can brainstorm about the charities I can start. Zoe has given me some time to think and come up with something.

Lex had to decline the trip, but I'm hoping Shawna is still game now that the dates have changed. I want to put a face to the name. I frown.

Just keep your promise. That shit doesn't touch her door.

Pit's warning comes back to me. I would never bring my shit to Skittles, but wouldn't I be doing so if I got involved with her little cousin?

Little Cousin. I have her by three years. It's not a lot, but I know my friend, in Skittles's head, that's like ten years, but I can't ignore this pull.

"The endgame hasn't changed. Keep your fucking distance, Harvey Dent," I mutter to myself.

I look out of the window as the car stops in front of Achilles's house. Blake has provided me with a driver and a car since that asshole father of mine sold all mine off.

It's cool. I'm over it. If you have something once, you can always come by it again. I'll get my collection back and more.

I smile as the kids playing out in front of the house next door come into view. This is a nice little neighborhood. Or at least it seems like it. I did notice it bumps up against a few rougher-looking blocks.

I step out and start for the door of Achilles's home. The little boy is fixing the chain on the little pink bike while the little girl eyes me walking up her neighbor's driveway.

"Hey, Mr. Makris," the tiny little girl sings and waves at Achilles as he steps out of his front door to greet me.

"Hey, Cat. What's up, True? You guys good?"

"Yeah, we're fine," the little toothless boy says and nods.

"Who's that man?" Cat asks, pointing at me.

"This is my friend Josh."

I give the two a small wave and they wave back. A dark-skinned woman with a huge swollen belly comes out of the house, wiping her hands on a dish towel.

"True, if you can't fix that thing, wait for your father to come home and do it," she calls.

"I got it, Mom. He'll just say he's tired. Cat wants to ride with me. I'll fix it."

I hold a hand up to Achilles. "You want some help?" I offer.

"That's nice of you. We don't want to put you out," the mother says.

"It's fine. It will only take me a sec," I reply.

"Oh, thank you so much. Cat, come on inside. We'll make the nice man some lemonade."

I give her a smile as she holds her hand out for her daughter and rubs her belly with the other hand. Cat follows her mother inside and I get to work on the bike with the boy.

"You're a cool big brother," I say to him as I get the chain on.

"It's my job to look after her and when my new little sister gets here, I'll take care of her too."

"They're lucky to have you."

"Thanks." He gives me a smile that fades as a white BMW pulls up. "I've got it from here. Thanks, mister."

"Anytime. You can call me Josh or J."

I stand, seeing he's a little nervous all of a sudden. A man steps from the car and starts for the house. I don't miss the glare he gives me and the kid.

"What's up, Roger? How's it going?" Achilles says, seeming to catch the tension.

The dude grunts and loosens his tie. He comes over and places a hand on the top of the kid's head. "Did you clean that room?" he says to the kid.

"Yeah."

"Why don't you head into the house and stop bothering Mr. Makris?"

"He's not bothering me. My friend was giving him some help with Cat's bike."

The dude pulls out his wallet and takes out a few bills to hand to me. I hold my hands up and take a step back. "No, I'm good. Thanks though."

"I insist," he says smugly, with a fake smile on his thin lips.

I look into his brown eyes. I see so much of my father as I look at this man. He's a real piece of work.

I can tell in True's body language this dude is going to give him a hard time. He shoves the money at me again. Achilles takes it. I look at him and narrow my eyes. He gives me a small shake of his head.

Roger turns for their house and starts for the door. True looks at me and gives a sad smile. I take the money from Achilles and beckon True to come closer.

"Here, you take this and get some candy or something for you and your sister," I whisper.

His smile grows as he takes it quickly and shoves it into his pocket. He wraps my waist in a quick hug and takes off for home.

"Ignore him. He's a douche. Mary, the mom, is a nice lady and True and Cat are good kids. Dude is crazy jealous. I think it's because he's the one cheating," Achilles snorts.

I shrug. "I'm not worried about him. Let him fuck around. I'll have a new pretty wife and kids. I still haven't found a place to live. That house looks nice."

"Same old Kelex. You know, I laughed my ass off when I found your profile and saw what name you were going by. Remember homeroom with Miss McGregor?"

"How could I forget? They fucked up all our names that year, but she refused to make them correct mine," I scoff.

"And you pissed her off every day by crossing the wrong spelling out on her bubble sheet to correct it yourself," he laughs.

"That's how I know she made sure they didn't fix it. I think I fucked her niece or something. That was the one time my dad made me proud," I muse.

"I heard about that. School's Open House night, right?"

"Yeah, he blew his lid, seeing our last name spelled K-E-L-E-X. He spent ten minutes berating her. And I quote… 'How the fuck can you live in this town and not know how to spell *my* son's last name? Do you not know who you're dealing with? I'm one breath from being the one to sign your damn paychecks, you cunt.'"

"I tried to calm him down and tell him she wasn't more than our homeroom teacher. That didn't mean shit. I bet my name was right the next day when she handed me my new schedule."

"Can I get you something to drink?"

"If you have water, that would be great."

"I was going to order in something to eat. Thai sound good?"

"I'm cool with whatever."

"I heard what you said about finding a place to stay. My home is your home for as long as you want. Although after we get these docs taken care of, I don't think you're going to have a problem finding a place. The advance is going to carry you through more than a few months comfortably," he says with a proud grin.

I clap my hands together. "Let's get this show on the road then."

He heads into the kitchen for a beat. I can hear him calling in our food while I wait. I look around the house. It's nice. Quickly, I weigh my options.

Not wanting to put Skittles out or drag her into my shit, staying with Achilles might be the right thing to do until I get a place. Staying with Jeff is out. We couldn't live together.

"Here you go."

Coming out of my thoughts, I look up as Achilles returns with a glass of water. I'm still in awe of how big this guy has gotten. He's three years younger than me, but right now, he's making me feel small.

That's not easy to do. I may not have as large and bulky a frame as Pit, but I'm no small guy. In high school, Achilles was a lanky kid, barely pushing five-two. Now, he has to be my height, maybe an inch or two taller and he's built like a linebacker.

"Bro, tell me what's been going on with you. Where have you been?"

"I thought I'd do some traveling for a bit before going to college," he starts before taking a seat on the couch next to me.

"My first stop was Greece. Mama asked me to go see some friends of hers while there. These guys were some heavy hitters. I decided to hang around and they pulled me in, taught me a few skills and got me into lifting.

"When it came time to decide what was next, I decided to come home. It just felt like it was time," he says.

I nod and empty my glass. That sounds about right. He's always been a fast learner. I'm sure Blake had something to do with his return.

We fall into talk of old times and continue to catch up. I'm reminded of our old friendship. I've always thought he was cool despite how others felt. Shy, but cool as fuck once you get to know him.

"Hey, I've always wanted to ask you something."

"Go ahead, shoot."

"Did you know Blake was the one who sent my mom to pay you to be my friend?"

I draw my brow and stare at him as my mouth hangs open. I didn't think he knew about that. Zoe had wanted me to keep it to myself.

"Come on, bro. I've known she paid you for years. One day, you were all I could talk about. The next day, you were talking to me at lunch."

"Okay, but what makes you think Blake put her up to it?"

"He'll do anything to protect me."

The doorbell rings before he can say another word. I'm starving and more than happy the food has arrived. I'm glad when he brings it right over for us to tear into it. Digging in, I bank my questions for later.

"Hey, do you know any hot girls or someplace to hang to meet some?"

I chuckle. "Yeah, I've got you. My friend owns a bar. We can head over tonight."

"Cool. Cool. It's been a while since I've had a good fuck buddy."

CHAPTER FOURTEEN

Dreams

Shawna

Two months later...

Darn it, I need to find a job. If I don't, my mother is going to drive me crazy. I don't want to work for her. I love my mom, but that's not what I want.

I've applied for a few traveling jobs, then called the contacts Joshua gave me and have been holding my breath since. I rush to the basket at the front of the house and grab my stack of mail before I head out the front door. This job thing has been a huge topic of interest for my parents.

Personally, I'm tired of talking about it. My mother thinks I'm too shy to land a job and my father wants to call in favors to keep me from having to work for what I want. I want to do this on my own.

"I'm tired of being babied," I murmur to myself as I place my car in drive.

My dream job would be to go on safari and take photos of the lands and wildlife. One of Josh's connections had a gig where I'd get to live with a tribe and do just that.

It's been a month. I don't think I'll hear from them. Since I'm going to Cancun with Ven and her assholes, I can at least avoid my parents for a week while I figure something out.

"Hello," I say as I answer the call coming in as I drive.

"Hey," Ven sings back. "Where are you? What are you up to?"

"I'm on my way to the mall to pick some things up for the trip. What's up?"

"Wait, you're going shopping without me?"

"I figured you were busy. I didn't want to be a bother."

"You're kidding, right? Where are you going to shop? I'll meet you there."

I laugh. My cousin can shut a store down with her shopping. I should have known she'd want to shop with me.

"I'm pulling into Vander Mall now."

"Cool, I'll be there in ten."

"Okay, I'll wait in my car. I'm in aisle *C*."

"Got it. See you soon."

She hangs up as I place my car in park. I reach for my mail to sift through. My hands start to shake when I get to the big navy-blue envelope with silver writing on it. The name of the company for the job in Africa is printed boldly in the top left-hand corner.

I toss all the other mail aside and open this one. Pulling the folder from inside and opening it, I squeal. It's a job offer. They want me to be one of their photographers. I look at the salary offer and nearly pass out.

"Oh my God," I breathe.

I pick up my phone, ready to call Josh to thank him. I wouldn't have had this opportunity without him. I go to dial but jump out of my skin when a tap comes at the window.

"What's up with you, scaredy-cat?" Ven says as she opens my driver's side door.

I place a hand over my chest as I look back at her. I guess it's better if I don't call Josh. I promised myself not to get in my head about having his number.

Nothing will ever happen between us. He's way out of my league. He's nice to me because of Ven. That's all.

"I got a job," I squeal.

"*Yes*, I knew you would," she says and does a little dance for me.

I laugh and step out of the car. She wraps her arms around my waist. I embrace her to squeeze her back. I wouldn't have had this opportunity without her friend's help. It was only a phone number, but a phone number I wouldn't have had.

"Let's get you some new work outfits."

"Oh, wait," I say and pout.

"What?"

"This means I can't go to Cancun. I'll be in Africa."

"Girl, forget about me and my crazy friends. You take your butt to Africa and get your bag. We're good."

"I love you, Ven."

"I adore you, Shawnnie. I'm so freaking proud of you."

Kelex

"This is the house you want to buy? In this neighborhood? Come on, you can't be serious. I have shoes from better zip codes. Why are you looking at this place?" Jeff gripes as he looks around like he sees something nasty.

"Dude." I laugh. "It's not as bad as you're making it. It's nothing like the estate I grew up in, but it's a nice place for now."

A For Sale sign went up a few houses down from Achilles's place and I decided to jump on it. It's a nice house with way more room than I need. It's located close enough to the airport for me to travel in and out without stress.

Something I'll be doing a lot of with the business. I go to explain this to him, but he's focused on his phone, so I don't bother. This is what I want. I don't have to explain myself anyway.

"Look, I can't even find a Starbucks around here. There isn't one for fifteen miles. You know what that means, don't you?"

"Fuck off," I scoff.

"I don't understand you. Take the gift your grandfather is placing in your hands and kill your father. Boom, all your problems solved, and I won't have to come visit you in this hole."

"Whatever." I wave him off.

"On second thought, there isn't one piece of ass who will want to come here. Go on, buy it. Heather, Holly, Helen." He snaps as he tries to remember my realtor's name. "Can you put in an offer for my boy?"

My realtor appears with a smile on her face. She reminds me of my third-grade teacher. She was always so nice to me. Mrs. Berk, I'll never forget her.

"Harmony, actually. I have a few places I still want to look at. I'll give you a call by the end of the day tomorrow."

"Okay, no problem. Let me know if you have any further questions. I wouldn't wait too long. This one is going to have a bidding war if we don't act fast."

Jeff snorts. "Like they'd be able to outbid him. He's lucky, but not that damn lucky. He'll buy this shithole if he wants it."

I ignore him as he murmurs under his breath. It's not a shithole at all. Everything is new. There are five bedrooms, four baths, and a nice basement for a massive man cave—or other extracurricular activities—if I wanted.

The truffled ceilings and built-ins add charm and character to the common area and the open floor plan is nice. It's a lot more than I was expecting.

"Being that they knocked down the former structure to create this larger new build, it's a hot find and in such a nice up-and-coming neighborhood," Harmony says. "You'll have the newest and biggest lot and house on the block."

"Then you buy it," Jeff mutters.

I roll my eyes and shake my head. I have no idea what his problem is today. He's acting like a brat who needs to be fed and put down for a nap.

"Thank you for your time, Harmony. I'll get back to you as soon as I make a decision."

I like the place, but I don't want to come off as too eager. It's the perfect home for a middle-class family. I'll be proud to say I bought it on my own, with my own money.

Since it's my own money, I do need to think about the cost for once in my life. I've always dreamed of someday being able to do this. Buying a home of my own and my father having nothing to do with it.

We walk out to Jeff's waiting SUV and climb in. I check my phone for missed calls. I've been hoping to hear from Shawna.

"This place, a trip to Cancun, and you're looking at a new car. Basil must have come through. Does that mean you're taking the lead too?"

"My grandfather has nothing to do with any of it. I'm a grown man. I know how to take care of myself. I've figured it out. I'll be fine."

He holds his hands up. "Fine, say no more. It's good to see you back. Lunch is on you."

CHAPTER FIFTEEN

Asshole's Retreat

Kelex

Three weeks later...

These Asshole trips are starting to grow on me. I've laughed more than I have in months. Skittles is great at booking the best spots.

However, I'm not going to lie. I was happy to hear Shawna got a job but disappointed big-time that she couldn't make the trip. I should've asked for her number. I thought she would've called by now.

"Decorating your new place is going to be so much fun," Skittles says as she comes out with two drinks in her hands.

"Yeah, I'm kind of excited," I admit.

I take a glass and sip at it. The bartender we hired has a heavy hand. We're all going to be lit within the hour.

Tak zips by on an ATV as Pit and Deacon chase after him. I guarantee he's done something to one of them. The pranks have been A1 so far.

Luke is still stewing over his missing eyebrows. Pit was so drunk last night he now has painted toes and fingernails. My favorite by far was Skittles getting Tak to wet the bed.

I'm never shutting my eyes around this woman. She's a little evil genius. It's the crazy laugh for me.

She laughs and it makes you want to laugh too. You can't stay mad at her for long. She sucks you right in.

"I like the neighborhood and that's a sick house. It's huge and so spacious inside. I can totally see that neighborhood turning into a baby Heart's Way," she muses.

"I was thinking the same thing."

Heart's Way is an elite community in Bridge Lake. While my home is now in Vander, it has the potential to grow into something quaint and homey like Bridge Lake's premium location.

"I'm proud of you. You haven't allowed anything to stop you. This is what I wanted for you. I know you don't like talking about your family situation, but I understand it's not ideal and you're building your life up on your own.

"Savor that, babe. That's some big-dick shit. Don't laugh at me. I mean it," she says.

I laugh and finish my drink. I know she has my back. She drove me to the closing and had a gift waiting for me after.

"So, who's our victim tonight, and what do we have planned?"

She gives me an evil little grin. "Did you know Tak can't sleep without music in his ears? I have his headphones," she says.

I burst into laughter as she wiggles her brows. I can see it now. He's going to be up all night tearing the place apart looking for them and getting on Pit, Luke, and Deacon's damn nerves while doing it.

"Perfect," I croon and rub my hands together.

Skittles's phone rings on the table in front of us. Her smile grows wider. I know right away it's either Lex or Shawna.

"Hey, Shawnnie," she sings into the phone.

I hop up and snatch the device from her hand and take off. I can't help smiling to myself as I jog away, my long legs creating the distance I need. I inhale deeply. I remember thinking I'd never run again—those first few weeks of therapy felt like torture.

I sure as fuck didn't think I'd be out here on the beach in shorts and shirtless. I still have days where I look at myself and see the worst, no matter how much I've healed. The healing that's happened physically hasn't happened mentally just yet.

"Hey, gorgeous," I croon into the phone as I laugh at Ven chasing after me and yelling. "Congratulations on the job."

"Hey, Joshua."

My smile grows. I love hearing her say my name. She sounds happy. That makes me happy.

"Hey, sweetheart. Why haven't you called me?"

"I, um. I guess I've been busy, and I sort of wasn't sure you really meant it."

"Let this be your first lesson in Josh. I don't say shit I don't mean, baby girl."

"I'm sorry. I'll make sure to call you soon."

"Don't be sorry. You never have to be sorry."

"Kelex, come back here with my phone," Skittles calls.

"Hold on," I say to Shawna.

I turn to jog backward and send Ven a wink. I pull the phone from my ear and send myself a quick text with Shawna's number.

"Okay, I'm back. They treating you well?"

"Yeah, I guess."

I frown. "What does that mean?"

"One of the other photographers is sort of a dick to me all the time."

"What's his name," I bite out darkly.

"Ivan. It's cool. I do my best to stay away from him. The village women don't like him either."

"You have pepper spray with you?"

"Yeah, Ven and Mom both gave me some."

"Good, keep it on you. Don't allow anyone to feel comfortable with making you uncomfortable. That's never okay."

"Thanks, Joshua. You don't know how much I needed to hear that. I think I'm homesick already."

"How long is the assignment?"

"Another two months, but I've been asked to sign on to go to Australia."

I place my fist in my mouth to bite down. I'm stoked for her, but this means it will be that much longer before I get to meet her face to face. Things are taking off for the business and my time is about to become supertight.

"I'm proud of you, gorgeous. Very proud."

"Josh, this is all thanks to you. Thank you so much. This is my dream job. Now if I could get you to sit for a shoot for me, my life would be perfect."

I groan. Not because I don't want to pose for her, but because she's so fucking cute. I know I would pose in a heartbeat for her and her alone.

"You let me know when and where you want me. I'll be all yours," I say, feeling the smile on my lips.

I'm caught off guard as Skittles jumps on my back. I clench the phone in one hand and reach to secure Skittles on my back with the other.

She bites my ear, then snatches her phone. I roar with laughter as she pants while catching her breath. I reach for her other leg to make sure she doesn't fall.

"Shawnnie, what's up? What was this asshole talking about?"

I laugh as I stop and place her on her feet. Turning, I look down at her as she listens. She searches my eyes, then a mischievous smile comes to her face.

"No, I didn't know he helped you get the job," she says.

She then covers the phone with her hand. "I forgive you and thank you but stop trying to get in my little cousin's pants, asshole."

There's no real bite to her words, so I wink at her and tug her into my arms for a hug. She places her head against my chest and returns the embrace as she talks on the phone. I walk us back to the table we were sitting at as the sun beats down on my back.

Ivan, huh? Pack your fucking bags. Today is your last day, motherfucker.

Shawna

They sound like they're having so much fun in Cancun. I wish I could be there. It was good to hear Joshua's voice.

I love my new job, but this guy Ivan really has been making it uncomfortable for me. He creeps all the women out. I do my best never to be alone with him.

What I didn't tell Josh is that he groped me last night. If my supervisor's laugh hadn't alerted Ivan that someone was on the way, I'd hate to think of what would have happened. My supervisor looked concerned when he found me, but I just rushed off, embarrassed that I'd gotten myself into such a situation.

"Shawna, we need you to ride out with us," Terry, my supervisor, calls into my hut.

"Okay, I'm on my way."

I check my camera bag and go to head out. I was supposed to have off this evening. Ivan was supposed to be shooting. That's why I was making my calls back home and trying to catch up on emails.

"I'm here," I say as I walk up to the Jeep the crew is waiting in.

I turn to see Ivan with his bags climbing into another vehicle. I knit my brows in confusion. He has all his gear and the luggage he came in with.

"Is everything okay?" I ask as I get into the Jeep.

"That guy pissed someone off. He got canned," Arty, one of the other crew members, replies.

My mind goes back to the dark sound of Joshua's voice when he had asked for the name of the guy giving me trouble. I shake the thought away. There's no way he could have done this. He's in Cancun with friends. We only spoke a few hours ago at most.

"Oh, that's sad," I mutter.

Not really, but I say it to be nice anyway. Everyone falls silent. I get the feeling I'm not the only one happy to see him go.

CHAPTER SIXTEEN

Wrong Girl

Kelex

As I sit in the dark in Ivan Welsh's home, I take a deep, calming breath. I'm not one to take your head off for no reason. You have to do something to provoke me. However, make no mistake. If you try me, if you poke the bear, I will erase you.

I've had to force myself from that truly dark place. The one that's telling me to string this bastard up by his balls and filet his ass. That's the type of rage I keep hidden. Instead, I'm going to make sure he dies slowly but painfully.

"What the fuck?"

Ivan gets his hand on the switch to turn on the lights and I pull the trigger. The light from the window behind me gives me all the illumination I need to hit my target just where I want.

Closing my eyes, I savor the sound of the bullets leaving my silencer. I stand, holster my gun, and fix my cuffs. Walking across the room to where Ivan is now gasping for air, I squat beside him once there.

"I had only planned for you to be fired. That was going to be as far as this went. That's the call I made... to make that happen."

I reach to slap his cheek as he tries to fill his lungs with air. I shouldn't take as much joy in this as I am. No matter how much this disgusting piece of shit deserves this.

"You feel that? You're about to die. You want to know why? Let me tell you why you're going to hell, Ivan. I received a call and was told you touched not only what's mine, but some of the others came forward once you were gone.

"You fucked with the wrong girl, Ivan. Your last two days were a gift. I needed that long to keep myself from peeling your skin from your body while you screamed for mercy. Now be good and allow me to listen to you take your last breath," I say as I look him in his eyes.

About fifteen minutes go by as he struggles for air. Then I watch as the lights go off and he takes his last gasp. A sinister smile comes to my lips. I stand and leave the way I came, whistling as I go. See, I can keep the monster at bay.

CHAPTER SEVENTEEN

Meet the Bags

Kelex

Two months later...

"Nice tan," Zoe says as she fixes my tie as we stand in the foyer of the banquet hall. "This fundraiser will be a test of your skills. Do everything I've taught you and you will do just fine."

"Turn on the charm enough to bring a smile, listen, show I'm listening, and never rush from a conversation. Be dismissed, not dismissive. I've got it," I reply.

"I think you just might. What do you think of Blake's date?"

"Who, Gia?"

"Yes, pretty, no?"

"*Ísos allá óchi o týpos mou.*"

"What is your type, Joshua?"

"You and *Nonos* shouldn't worry about that. Oh yes, I know he's put you up to this. Pappoús is probably in on it too. My love life, sex life, or whatever has nothing to do with the three of you."

"I know, but you're so young and handsome. Achilles says you don't date and he hasn't seen you hook up with anyone. I was just—"

"Meddling. I'm glad I moved out of his place. Had no idea he was spying on me."

"Not spying, just unable to keep the truth from his mother. How is the new place? Do you need help decorating?"

"No, I have a friend helping."

"Ah, Mayven Jennings. Her father will be here tonight. Can I assume that's more than a friendship after all?"

"You can assume anything you like, but remember what they say," I reply, lifting a brow.

"*Ypothétontas óti vgázeis énan kólo apó eséna kai eména.*"

"Yes, that it does. I don't know about you, but I'm no one's ass and I'd hate to see you make an ass out of yourself."

She laughs. "Your humor will get you far, Joshua."

"We can only hope. Although, in this room, I think the face will pull more checks."

"Yes, well, we're about to find out." She drops her voice to a whisper. "This is Annaliese. Her husband is a billionaire. They vacation here in Bridge Lake but are looking to become permanent residents. She's lonely and loves to talk. Good luck."

The statuesque blonde makes a beeline straight for us. She pulls Zoe into a hug with a fake kiss to each cheek. The game is officially on.

"Annaliese, I want you to meet Joshua. He's a good friend of the family. Joshua, this is one of my dear friends Annaliese."

I turn up my smile and take the hand she offers me to kiss the back. When I lift my head and straighten, she has a look of awe on her face. I smile deeper.

"It's nice to make your acquaintance, Annaliese. Such a beautiful name for such an exquisite woman."

"Oh my, it's nice to meet you as well, Joshua. You do look familiar."

"Ah, yes, Joshua used to model. You may have seen some of his work," Zoe says.

"Yes, that would certainly make sense. My husband decided to sit this one out. Would you mind if I burrow Joshua for a spin around the dance floor?"

"No, of course not."

I stick my elbow out. "It would be my pleasure."

I spend the next twenty minutes spinning this woman around the floor as she tells me about her failing marriage and badass kids. I offer sage advice and keep a smile on her face.

"Joshua, you are such a delight. I've wanted to get all that off my chest, but I could never tell my girlfriends or anyone else any of this. My therapist has become so judgy lately. I think Henry is fucking her if you want the truth."

"His loss." I wink. "Your secrets are safe with me. Didn't you say you needed to get over to the donation table before Mrs. Garcia leaves? It looks like she's about to take off."

I smoothly turn so she has a view of the table as the older woman makes a move. Instantly, I can tell she's torn. I give her waist a gentle squeeze.

"I'll walk you over. Maybe I can match your donation."

Her breathing hitches and she flutters her eyelashes. I can tell she's totally flustered. Maybe even a bit caught off guard.

"You don't have to do that. It was a pleasure. Thank you for the dance and your time. I hope to see you again at one of these. You're so charming."

I give a bow and take her hand to kiss the back once again. The blush that comes to her face speaks volumes. She turns and rushes off for Mrs. Garcia.

"Very well done."

I turn to find Zoe watching me. I pull her into my embrace and begin to dance her around. She looks into my eyes with a smile on her lips.

I glance around and find Blake and Gia spinning around the dance floor as well. I get how this has worked for them for so long. You would never think the two had any intimate connection. I haven't seen them interact all night.

"What did you learn?"

"They're getting divorced. She's buying the house here for her and the kids. He's staying in Texas. Her lawyers have him by the balls in the divorce settlement."

"Nice, you're a natural."

"Did you ever doubt me?"

"Not at all. I can't wait to see what you can really do. Now, let's get our charity some money."

***

I'm talking up a group of women Zoe has introduced me to when I take notice of Mayor Jennings watching me. I lift my champagne glass and tilt it toward him as I smile.

I already know he's not fond of me and the other assholes. I'm sure this situation doesn't look too favorable at the moment. I shoot him a wink anyway. I know the sharks when I see them.

Mayor Jennings is in familiar water, no matter what he has the rest of the world thinking. I snap my wrist out to check the time. I wonder what Shawna's doing?

Shawna

I'm freaking the fuck out. My camera bag was right here before I left to take a walk with some of the younger women in the village. Word came in this morning that Ivan was murdered a few months back, not long after he was fired.

A few of the girls wanted to talk about what happened when he was here. We've never had a problem with theft, so I didn't think twice about leaving my bag behind. I can't even imagine someone stealing from me.

I have to find my bag. If I don't, I can't go to Australia. I can't believe this is happening to me.

I flop down on my cot and bury my face in my hands. "We leave in two days. What am I going to do?" I murmur to myself.

My phone rings, startling me. I grab it and answer, trying not to burst into tears like a baby. I feel so stupid. I'm self-sabotaging my career.

"Hello," I sniffle.

"Hey, what's wrong?" Joshua rushes out over the phone.

"I'm so stupid. I left my camera bag in my hut and it's gone. I should just come home. Clearly, this is too much for me. I'm ruining my career."

"First, I need you to calm down. You're not stupid, baby. You're trusting. Big difference. You belong there as much as anyone else."

"I should give up. My mom sounds worried all the time, I miss Ven. Everyone here is so much more experienced. This has to be a sign."

"A sign that what doesn't break you will make you stronger. You're gaining experience. Your mom is a mom. She's momming.

"There's nothing that will change that. Ven misses you too, but she's busy getting her business off the ground. I need you to focus on you. You're growing, learning, and living. You've got this, gorgeous. It's a camera. It can be replaced."

"Ven bought me that camera. I owe her more than this."

"She'll understand. Things happen, sweetheart. I promise this isn't as bad as it feels in this moment."

"My mom isn't going to help. She already wants me to come home. I can't ask her for a new one.

"I have savings, but I have no idea where or how to get another one. I can't order one online. It wouldn't arrive here in time.

"I don't have the address of where we'll be staying yet. What if they fire me because I don't have a camera and can't get one by the time we get to Australia?" I ramble in a panic.

"I was calling to see when you guys head out," he says.

"We leave in two days. I'm so fucked," I huff.

He chuckles. "It's going to be fine. Act like nothing is amiss. Enjoy your last two days in Africa. Fly with the crew to Australia and I promise it will all be okay by your first day of work there. Do you trust me?"

"Yeah," I reply without thinking.

"Good, then believe me when I say this is nothing. It's going to work out."

"Okay."

"I bet you look cute as a button all worried and stressed over nothing."

"It's not nothing. Wait, you still don't know what I look like?"

"It is nothing and no. I want to see you for the first time in person. I want the living, breathing, real deal."

"Sorry to disappoint you," I murmur sarcastically.

"Stop that. Remember, hold your head high and own that shit. Life is yours for the taking. You can have anything you want."

"We're not talking about a thing. We're talking about a person," I say and bite my lip.

"Oh, baby. You don't want me. I promise you, I'm not what you want. You can do so much better than me. I'm fucked up in ways no one can redeem."

"Why are you allowed to say that about yourself, but I can't speak the same of me?"

He's silent for a few beats, leaving me to think I said too much. I drop my gaze to my lap. I should've kept my mouth shut.

"I'll make you a deal. You won't talk shit about you and I won't talk shit about me, deal?"

"Okay."

"But I'm going to warn you one more time. When we meet, run. Run away as fast as you can."

"Joshua," I giggle.

"You laugh. I mean it, gorgeous."

My face hurts from smiling. I feel so much better. I don't know how this will all work out, but I have this gut feeling that it will.

CHAPTER EIGHTEEN

All Better

Shawna

Three days later...

Why is it so hard for people to understand that I just flew twelve hours and spent another four getting settled into my apartment? I'm so freaking tired, but my phone won't stop ringing and someone is ringing the doorbell insistently.

"*Grr*," I growl into my pillow. "*Why?*"

I nearly sob as I drag my exhausted body from the bed and head for the door, continuing to ignore my phone. I don't have it in me to talk to anyone right now.

Mom wanted me to call as soon as I got into my new place, but I was so tired and overwhelmed. I still don't have a camera, so I might be headed back home soon anyway.

"Good day, love. Shawna Norris?" The carrier guy asks as I open the door.

"Yeah."

"Great, I just need your signature here."

I take the pen from him and sign off. He takes the pen and paperwork back, then steps back and grabs a huge box to hand to me. My brows shoot up to my hairline.

I'm not expecting anything. No one even knows my address yet. I take the box over to the table and set it down.

A smile comes to my face when I read who it's from. Joshua Nikolaou. I can't help wondering why he doesn't go by his real last name Kylix. Even when he used to model, although he spelled it differently, he still used it.

"Oh, my freaking God," I scream when I finally get the box open. "I think I love him."

I hug the new camera to my chest as I smile down into the box filled with a camera bag, new lens, and little odds and ends I really don't need but appreciate just the same. I can't believe he did this.

I rush to find my phone. When I find it, it rings again. It's one of my friends from back home. I ignore the call and pull up Josh's number.

"Hey, gorgeous. How was the trip? Did you get settled in?"

"Yes," I say with a huge smile on my face. "You bought me a new camera. You're my favorite person in the world right now."

"It's nothing. Now you can stick to being amazing and live out your dream."

"This means so much to me. Thank you."

"Don't mention it. By the way, your other camera was found and it's on its way back to the States. I figured since it has sentimental value, you'd want to keep it safe at home. This one you don't have to worry about. It's meant to explore and experience things with you."

"Are you kidding? This one has just as much sentimental value. I'm never losing it. I'll keep it safe and with me everywhere I go."

He chuckles. "There is a promise I want you to make me."

"Oh?"

"Never let anything cause you to give up, Shawna. No matter what's going on, never give up. Remember, I'm here waiting to talk to you and help you figure it out. There's no need to give up."

"I promise. Thanks again."

"Anytime. Looks like we better start planning that trip to Crete. You have a new camera to shoot me with," he says with a smile in his deep voice.

"You're really going to pose for me?"

"I said I would."

"Skittles says all you guys are assholes. I don't get that from you."

He scoffs. "You haven't interacted with me on the right day. I live up to my part when provoked. Trust me."

"Well, today, you're my hero."

"Well, the Bat-Signal just went up. I have to go, baby girl. Be safe, have fun, and knock 'em dead. I'll talk to you soon."

Kelex

I hang up the phone with a huge smile on my face. I'm tempted to look up a picture of Shawna just to get a peek at that face. I wonder if the smile in my head matches the real deal.

I pull up Google on my laptop and type in the daughter of Councilwoman Monica Norris. Before the results pop up, the doorbell rings. I quickly change my mind and close the window.

Instead, I head to my front door to answer it. I laugh to myself as I find none other than Jeff on my doorstep. For someone who hated this place, he's here an awful lot.

"What's up?" I say as I pull the door open.

"Your dad has fucked me out of a deal again," he gripes and moves past me to walk into the house.

I roll my shoulders back. My father and I haven't crossed paths just yet. I think that's for the best.

"He and my dad were friends. I thought he'd give me the courtesy of backing the fuck off those contracts."

"Are you taking a real hit? Is there anything I can do?"

"Take your rightful spot so he'll disappear," he bites out.

"Sorry to tell you. If I do, he's not going anywhere. He'll be my problem then, hovering to snake his way into shit."

"Do you really think your grandfather will allow that?"

I shrug. "I don't care either way. I'm doing well for myself. He can do whatever he wants."

"Yeah, I see you've found your way into some great investments. How's the restaurant business going? You think you'll survive the three to five years? It's not an easy business. You're taking on three to start. That's such a high risk."

"No risk, no reward. I've got this. There's no room for failure."

"I love that about you. I'm not taking on anything I can't guarantee a win at," he replies.

"Then you're not living. I'm not saying I'm not working my ass off, but I can't be afraid to learn and apply what I'm learning. If things are handed to me, where's the reward?"

He shrugs. "He asked about you."

"And?"

"I told him you were your own man. Doing your own thing."

"That's more than enough for him to know."

"He didn't even bother to ask about my dad or how I'm holding up after... I swear, he's heartless."

"Tell me something I don't know. You want to come with me to the track?"

"Why do you go there all the time? You won't get into a car to drive. I used to think you were trying to fuck Skittles, but I don't think you are. She's just a friend, so what's the deal?"

I roll my eyes. "You don't have to fuck every girl you're cool with."

"The hell I don't. Speaking of which, you mind if I have a go at Skittles?"

I scoff. "Good luck with that."

He frowns at me. "What's that supposed to mean?"

"Bro, relax. I mean nothing by it. She's just into someone. None of us have a shot until she admits that truth to herself."

"Whatever, come on. I could blow off some steam."

"Cool. I'll text and let her know we're coming over."

CHAPTER NINETEEN

House of Friends

Kelex

A month later...

"I love this place. Whoever decorated did an awesome job," a girl in a tight green dress says.

"I paid to do this room and two more upstairs," Jeff says.

I frown and turn to look over at him. He's plastered. No wonder he's talking shit. He purchased the lamps in this room and two of the rooms upstairs as gifts.

Skittles and Pit were the ones to pay for entire rooms behind my back as housewarming gifts. I was totally taken off guard, not by Skittles, but Pit. Yeah, that threw me.

I shrug it off as I look the girl over. Okay, she's totally his type. Shaking my head, I turn for the kitchen to get another beer. This housewarming turned into a much bigger party than I'd planned for.

The assholes are here and Jeff seems to have invited our entire senior class from high school. I don't mind. I just don't really care for a few of the people here.

"Hey, you," Skittles sings as I find her with a drink in her hand.

"Hey," I croon and tug her in with an arm around her head.

I kiss her forehead and hold her against my side. She looks up at me with a wide smile on her lips. She's tipsy too.

"What's the deal with that Achilles guy? I don't know how I feel about him yet. He's super shy, but really nice. I think it's cute when he gets tongue-tied."

"He's a good guy. Smart as fuck."

"Cool. It's a good thing you have me, though. Half these people are here to be nosy."

I laugh. "You picked up on that too?"

"Oh yeah, and the other half are groupies trying to spend the night or go home with one of your friends. Pit has told that skank over there it ain't happening ten times already and she's still trying," she says bitterly.

"You know, that would all stop if you'd tell him you want him."

She freezes and pulls away from me slowly. Her mouth is open as she looks back at me as if in shock. I smile at her and look her right in the eyes.

"Come on, you didn't think I knew?"

"Knew what?"

"Whatever, Mayven."

"Stop playing with me, Joshua."

I chuckle, then taunt. "You want me to hold your hand while you tell him how you feel?"

"Oh, shut up."

"You know he's into you too. It's crazy that neither of you sees it. You're both going to look back one of these days and see all the time you've wasted."

"Okay, my dear kettle. I see your face when you're texting that girl."

"What girl?" I say, feigning innocence.

"Whoever the girl is who makes your face light up every time she texts. Who is she?"

"I have no clue what you're talking about."

"Sure you don't. I like it when she's texting you. It's when I see you the happiest."

"Yo," Pit calls as he comes over with an arm around Kid's neck.

She works at his bar, but they seem to be good friends. I don't think he's fucking her. From the way that one chick is staring over at Pit, I think Kid's throwing him a lifeline.

"What's up? You heading out?"

"Nah, just needed to get away from that nutjob. Her breath smells like shit and she won't take no for an answer. She has two options at this point. Leave me the fuck alone or I'm going to spend the next hour flaming her ass," he replies.

"Dude, I'm always game for a good cracking session. The way those shoes are leaning, we can take shifts," I chuckle.

"Poor thing," Kid snickers.

"Poor thing, my ass. That's the same one I caught being nasty to some other girls for no reason earlier. I should've put her out then. I have no mercy for that shit."

Pit snorts. "The nerve, breath smelling like the crack of a bum's ass and she was nasty to someone. Yeah, I'm going in if she comes over here again."

"I'm here for it," I croon.

"Hey, guys," Achilles says as he joins our group.

I note that his attention is on Kid. I smile. She's a pretty one. I caught him checking her out at the bar a few times.

"Yo, I wanted to thank you for the update on my POS system. You saved me some cash and things have been running a lot smoother," Pit says to Achilles.

"No problem. Let Josh know if you ever need anything else. I'll be happy to help."

"I'm going to take you up on that. I want to put in a system to watch and run the entire place from one screen in the back. The front of house, the card room, everything."

"I can set that up for you. That's simple," he says.

"Kid, have you met my boy Achilles?" I ask.

"No, I don't think I officially have."

"It's nice to meet you," he says, holding out his hand.

"Your name is really Kid?" Jeff asks as he enters the conversation.

"No, but it's what I go by."

"Did you go to our high school? I know you from somewhere," he says as he narrows his eyes.

She shrugs her shoulders and turns back to Achilles. Just when I go to pull Jeff's coattails so my boy Achilles has a shot, the chick with the leaning shoes brings her ass over. I grin as I see Pit home in.

She comes closer and shoves Kid and Skittles out of the way to get next to him. Oh yeah. It's roasting time.

Shawna

"Hold on, baby," Joshua says into the phone. "Now, back to you, dead gums."

"What the fuck did you eat, the inside of a dog's ass? Your breath smells like three-week-old garbage and your hair looks like you were rolling under your bed right before you walked out of the house tonight."

I pull the phone from my ear to make sure I dialed the right number. I've never heard Josh talk to anyone like this before. I blink at the phone a few times as the roar of laughter comes through.

Good thing the device isn't next to my ear. They are all so loud. I forgot he was having a party tonight.

I press my ear back to the phone right as a girl replies. "You're both assholes."

"And you're thirsty as fuck, Garbage Pail Mouth," another guy says. "How many ways do you want me to say I'm not interested?"

"This party blows anyway," the girl huffs.

"That's cool, but you can take them turnover shoes and skate your ass right out of my house, Kickstand Feet."

"Oh," the crowd roars.

"Oh shit, look at her shoes," someone in the background says, causing more laughter.

"Gorgeous, you there?"

"Um, yeah. Is everything all right?"

"Yeah, just had to put out the trash."

"I forgot about your party. I was only calling to say hi before I call it a night."

"Don't worry about it. This has been pretty lame anyway. I'd much rather talk to you," he says.

"You have guests. I can call back later."

"Hang up and I'm coming to Australia. You put a smile on my face, so I'm told. I need to smile right now. Talk to me, baby girl. How are you?"

I bite my lip. I'm so tempted to hang up, so he'll show up here, although I wouldn't know what to do if he did. Not wanting to embarrass myself, I burrow under my covers and answer him.

"I'm great. This week has been awesome. I can't believe it will be over soon."

"Where to next?"

"How do you know I'm not coming home?"

"I see you. You're on fire. They're not letting you go this soon."

"Japan," I sigh. "Can you believe that?"

"Yeah, I can. You're amazing and so talented. You're just getting started."

"Thanks to you."

"Nah, this one is all on you. Be proud of that. You're making this happen."

CHAPTER TWENTY

Good Day

Kelex

I jog my way out of Achilles's house with my head down as I read a text from Shawna. She'll be free to talk in about twenty minutes. I smirk and shoot a text back to let her know I'll be waiting.

"Got you, Mr. Josh."

The words come from a tiny voice right as my ass feels wet. I turn to find Cat with a water gun almost half as big as she is as she grins up at me. Thank God I still have on my basketball shorts from my run before I came to go over numbers with Achilles.

I'm heading home to dress for a meeting, but I have an hour to waste. Looking at the tiny monster who just shot me with her water gun, I smile. She looks cute and innocent with her braids hanging down around her face and shoulders with clear beads hanging from them.

However, I'm not fooled. The pink shorts and T-shirt with the cute hairstyle are an illusion. The fabric that's starting to cling to my skin proves that.

"You're in trouble now," I say and go to run after her.

She squeals and drops her weapon as she takes off. I laugh and grab up the water gun as I follow. Just as I thought, True comes around the corner and jumps between me and his sister.

I spray them both until I run out of water. Cat stands behind her brother, giggling, and True sprays me back with a determined look on his face. I laugh my ass off because I know they've been waiting for me to come back out to do this.

These two have grown on me. They're one of my favorite parts of living on this block. When I have free time, I make sure to check in on them.

"We got you good, Mr. Josh," Cat sings.

"You guys did," I reply as I sit on the grass.

They each take a seat on either side of me. True bumps his shoulder against my side. I look down at him and return the smile he gives me.

"What happened to your leg?" Cat asks.

I turn to look at her. She's staring at my scarred leg. She reaches out as if she's going to touch it but pulls her hand back.

"I was in a car fire."

"Does it hurt?"

"Not anymore. When it happened, it did."

"I'm glad you're okay. We like you. You're nice to us, not like some of the other white people moving here. You don't yell at us for nothing or get nasty when we say hi."

I frown. "Who does that?"

"Nobody," True says quickly.

I draw my brows as I look at him. I can't help but wonder what he's thinking. He searches my gaze as I look at him. Then he smiles.

"Why are you so protective of us? I know what you did to Mr. Lewis after he ran over my bike," he whispers the last part.

Mr. Lewis is lucky all I did was cut up his rose bushes. I watched him intentionally run over True's bike. I was pissed when True got in trouble with his dad over it.

People can be cruel, but they have no right to be cruel to the young and helpless. Let them pick on me, someone who can fight back. Mr. Lewis watched as I butchered those roses and didn't move an inch to stop me.

I stared into his eyes, daring him to do something as I chopped them up. That fucker pissed his pants. It was that night I realized how close I could come to being just like my father.

"You're my friends. Adults shouldn't treat you guys like that. If someone does something to you. I want you to tell me. I'll make them stop," I say.

"See, that's why we like you and you have brown friends like us," Cat says.

I smile. Skittles likes them too. She's been wanting to give them toy cars they can drive, but I told her about their dad. I don't think it would be a good idea. He hated the fact that I got True a new bike.

"We hate it here sometimes. The new people moving here are mean and when we go down to the park…"

"Those kids are bad. They always want to start trouble and they think we're punks. Me and True always have to fight our way home or flame their butts and then they want to fight us 'cause they're not as funny as we are," Cat finishes.

"Yeah, it's best if we don't go down there. We like when you and Mr. Achilles hang with us, but you're grown-ups and have grown-up stuff to do. My mom doesn't want us in your hair all the time," True adds.

"You're never a bother to me. If you need something, come on down the block and get me. I mean it. Anytime. I'm here to help, promise."

My phone rings, reminding me I've been waiting on a call from Shawna. I pull it out and answer before I miss the call, placing the phone on speaker.

"Hey, gorgeous, I'm hanging with True and Cat. Say hi."

"Hey guys, how are you?"

"Hi, Shawna," they sing.

This is what I love about her. Just her voice brings calm and a smile to everyone's face. If these kids take to you, you're a good person. I've seen them shut down around others.

"Are you his girlfriend?" Cat says quickly.

"Um, no. We're friends," Shawna replies softly.

I don't acknowledge how much I hate hearing her say that. She is a friend, and for her safety, I need to keep it that way. I know all the flirting should stop, but I can't say I want it to.

"Oh, okay. Are you pretty?" Cat asks.

"She's gorgeous and one of my best friends," I say.

"Then why isn't she your girlfriend?"

"*Cat*," True drags out.

"I'm not his type," Shawna replies.

"Oh, okay. My bad."

"Cat, True, come on inside for lunch," Mary calls from the front door. "Hey Josh, how are you?"

"Hey, Mary. I'm good," I say. "I'll see you guys later. Thanks for the water fight. That was fun."

"See you later, Mr. Josh," they sing.

"Bye, Miss Shawna," Cat says and waves as if she can see her.

"Bye, guys."

Shawna

My stomach is twisting and turning. That little girl caught me off guard. I wish I hadn't said anything.

"What makes you think you're not my type?" Josh's voice comes through the line, pulling me from my spiral.

"Oh, um, I used to follow you when you were getting started. I...you...all the girls you dated looked nothing like me."

He tsks at me. "All an illusion. None of that was real. I couldn't tell you two thoughts from any of their heads. I never took time to get to know them because they weren't my type."

"You still don't know what I look like."

"And? Shawna, what's keeping me from you has nothing to do with my type."

"Oh, right. Mayven is your friend. I get it."

"No, baby, you don't, but that's why I like you."

I knit my brows in confusion. I always get the sense he's holding me at arm's length. A part of me thinks it's because he doesn't know what I look like. Then I wonder if it's because of Ven. Now I don't know what it is. I just know I'm drawn to him.

"I'm not going to run, you know."

"Yeah, I figured that, but I can't say I know how to walk away now."

"Then we'll pretend we don't know each other when we meet. Ven will never know."

He gives a chuckle that warms my belly. "Your cousin is the least of the things you should worry about when it comes to me, but enough about me. Have you finished your list?"

"Almost. I can email it to you when I'm done."

"Text it. I want to always have it handy. I'm going to make sure you live out your dreams, Shawna. Your happiness is my happiness. You have freedom I'll never have. I think that's why I'm ob—" he cuts off, leaving me hanging on his words.

"Damn, I have to go. I'll text you later when I have some free time."

"Yeah, okay. I have some proofs to look through. I'll be around."

"I need you to start living. Go hang out, gorgeous. Talk to you later."

I hang up and stare at my phone. I have so many questions running through my head. Why wouldn't he feel free? He's been building his own empire and doing great at it.

As much as I know about Joshua, he's still a conundrum to me. I sigh and look around my apartment. The others asked me to go out for drinks, but I didn't want to.

Why not?

I don't really know. I try to tell myself it's not because of Joshua, but I know deep down inside that it is.

CHAPTER TWENTY-ONE

Need Help

Kelex

A month later…

"Welcome home, Mr. Nikolaou," my driver says as I stand at the back door of my car after stepping off the jet.

"Thanks. I want a shower and my bed. No stops necessary," I murmur.

I'm so fucking tired, I could face-plant right where I stand. Being the voice and handler for our operation has been daunting. We've grown faster than I ever thought we could.

Between learning through books and research, Achilles's mentorship, and hands-on experience, I'm becoming an extension of him, which is what we need for the brand. No one expected me to be so good at this, but I know every inch of our business as if I built it all by myself.

The travel is tearing me apart, but I'm determined to keep going. My grandfather sounds so proud whenever we talk. I've learned from Jeff that my father hates that I'm doing so well.

That and that alone causes me to wake and push harder each day. The fundraisers are placing me in all the right rooms. Other than the lack of sleep, I couldn't be happier.

I lean my head back and close my eyes once I'm seated in the back of the Bentley. I grin to myself as the seat invites me in. This is only one of three in my new collection. My life hasn't missed a step, my father can go fuck himself.

"We're here, sir."

I open my eyes and look around. The first thing to grab my attention is the small child sitting on my front step. I haven't seen True and Cat in a few weeks.

I rush from the car to make sure he's okay. His tearstained face sets my blood on fire. I look around to see if I can deduce what's going on. Nothing seems amiss.

"Hey, buddy. What's up? What's going on?"

He launches himself at me and wraps his arms around my waist. He's shaking with his tears. "I can't do this. I can't do this on my own," he sobs.

"Do what?"

"Mommy is sick. My dad left. It's my job to help take care of us now, but it's too much. I've been trying. I've been doing my best."

"Wait, what's going on? Your mom is sick?"

"Yeah, she's been going for treatments, but they make her so tired. If they find out she can't take care of us and our dad is gone, they're going to take us.

"I can't let them take us. I've been keeping Cat clean for school and making sure she has lunch. I stay to myself, so no one asks questions and Cat promised not to tell.

"We've been fine. I've been getting us to school and Mommy has been getting to treatments. I pack Vernice's bag for her on the mornings they have to go out, but today, today I couldn't do it. It was too much," he cries.

I rub a hand against his back. My mind is reeling. I had no idea all of this was going on. Now that I think of it, Mary has looked tired the last few times I've seen her. Vernice is only a few months old. I thought she was tired from dealing with a newborn.

"What happened today?" I ask, trying to get my thoughts together.

"I woke up tired. I tried to make our lunch for school, but the bread started to rip when I put the peanut butter on. I got frustrated and knocked over the orange juice I poured for Cat.

"I was cleaning it up when Vernice started crying. When she wouldn't stop, I knew something was wrong. I got to the baby's room and...and there was poop everywhere. Vernice was covered in it.

"I couldn't clean her up and get us to school. My mom can barely move today." He lifts his head and looks at me. "I can't lose my mom. She can't lose us. She needs us to fight. She's fighting for us, but I can't do this on my own. I can't help her by myself. I need your help. You said you'd help me.

"Please help me. I need to be there to fight because she needs me, but I know I can't do this on my own. My dad doesn't care and Cat is still a baby. Don't let them take us, don't let me lose my mom. Help me," he sobs.

I'm speechless. He's a baby. True is six and Cat is four. I wasn't much older than them when I lost my mom. I can't imagine the fear and hopelessness he must be feeling.

However, my mom was taken from me in the blink of an eye. I didn't have to watch her die. I wasn't given time to fight with her, for her. This isn't a hurt I'd wish on anyone, especially not these kids.

"Little bro, I promise you're not alone. I'm here. I'm going to do this with you and if you can't do it with me, with her, I'll do it for you. You have help."

"Thanks, Mr. Josh."

"You can drop the mister. Call me Josh or J. We're family. Come on, let's go take care of your mom."

We stand and he places his small hand in mine. As tired as I am, everything else is forgotten. I nod for my driver to place my bags in the house and walk down the block with True.

When we get there, I note the empty driveway. It's still early, so I'm giving his douchebag father the benefit of the doubt. He better show up before the end of the day.

We step into the house and it's clear things have gotten out of hand. There are toys and clothes all over the place. I shrug off my suit jacket and begin to pick things up.

"Um, Josh," True says softly.

"Yeah, buddy?"

"I never did get Vernice and her room clean. Sorry, but can you help me?"

"Wait, you didn't get her changed? Dude, where is she?"

I look down at my watch. I guess it hasn't been that long. He must have just run to my place. I bite down on my anger. What if I hadn't come home? These kids would have been here with a sick mother and a baby.

I follow him to the baby's room. When I step inside, my eyes go wide. There's shit everywhere. The whole crib is trashed.

I go to call Skittles for help, but True is right. They will take him and his sisters if anyone finds out about this. I can't let that happen.

I made him a promise. With a sigh, I take off my cuff links and roll my sleeves up. Vernice is the first thing I attend to. She looks up at me from the crib as if nothing in the world is wrong.

"Come on, my little stinky princess. Let's get you cleaned up. True, can you show me where her bath is and then check on your mom. Make sure she's good and see if she needs anything. I've got this."

"Okay, and Josh?"

"What's up?"

"Thanks. People say things all the time, but they never stick to them. Thanks for doing what you say."

"Always, kid."

"Oh, you got help. Thank God," Cat says as she peeks into the room.

"Just get him the baby tub and anything else he needs. I'm going to take care of Mommy."

"Okay," Cat says, her lips trembling.

"Come on, sweetheart. We have a baby to wash. It's going to be okay from here. I've got you guys," I say to Cat.

She runs over to hug my leg. "Thank you."

Tears burn the backs of my eyes. Four and six, this is some bullshit. Roger Davis better bring his ass home. If he doesn't, I'm going to fuck up his existence.

CHAPTER TWENTY-TWO

A Real Man

Shawna

I've been trying to reach Joshua all day. I waited until afternoon because I knew his flight was an early morning one. I'm in North Carolina for a few days, not really close to Bridge Lake, but I wanted to let him know we're in the States.

"Hello," Josh breathes into the phone.

"Hey, did you get home?"

The sound of glass smashing and panting greets my ears. Right away, I know something is wrong. More smashing and panting ring out.

"I'll call you back," he pants and the call cuts off.

I sit, looking down at my phone. My heart starts to race. I hope he's okay.

Kelex

I keep swinging my bat, fucking this BMW up. Shawna has been calling all day, but I've been busy with Mary and the kids. Mary could hardly move.

She spent most of the day over the toilet. I stayed with the kids and fed them while keeping them busy as she tried to rest. I got their lunches for school ready and put their clothes out for the morning before I stepped out.

I'll check in again before I call it a night and in the morning, I'll see True and Cat off before I spend the day with Vernice and get Mary to her appointments. I'll have things under control before the week is out.

The kids will be taken care of and Mary will be able to focus on getting well. This asshole she's married to left when he found out how aggressive the treatment would be. Now I'm here to show him real aggression. I'm beating the shit out of this car.

True and Cat mentioned how much he loves this thing. I want him to feel this shit in his soul. His wife is fighting for her life and he's here with some woman. When I'm done with this dude, he's going to hate breathing.

"Hey, hey," someone growls.

I turn as Roger Davis runs at me in only his boxers. I rotate my wrist with the bat just before I swing it at his ribs. He gasps and falls back on his ass.

"You son of a bitch. You're going to pay for this."

I laugh and walk off, not bothering to look back. He's the one who will pay. A real man would never pull some bullshit like this. Three kids and a loving wife with cancer, he's less than shit under Mary's shoe.

I get to my car a block away and climb inside. "We can go," I say to the driver.

I pull out my phone as he drives off. I'm not done. This bastard gets no breaks.

"Hello."

"Fuck his life up. I want her and the kids to get a nice stipend. Everything else, bleed him dry. He gets no comfort."

"Got it," Achilles replies.

Shawna

"Hey, Ven. What's up?"

"Hey, Shawnnie," she sings. "Where are you? Your phone sounds so much better."

"I'm in North Carolina."

"Oh my God, are you coming home?"

"No," I say sadly. "Not yet. We'll be here for a few days and then I'm going to Grenada."

"I miss you, but I'm so proud of you."

"Thanks. I miss you too. How're your assholes?"

"They're fine. Kelex has been busy and traveling. Pit's having something at the bar. I'm probably going to head to that. Hold on a sec." She pauses on the other end for a few beats. "What the fuck?" she breathes, moving away from the phone.

"What? What is it?"

"I know the way he moves. This is Kelex," she says.

"What?"

"There's a video that just popped up of some guy with a mask on beating the shit out of some dude's white BMW. The asshole the car belongs to is one of Josh's neighbors. The guy beating the shit out of the car... I think it's Josh."

"No, really?"

"Yeah, Batting Rage, that's the title of the video."

I grab my laptop and search for the video. I watch with my mouth hanging open. The sounds in the background when I called him come back to me. Oh my God, it was him.

Why would he do something like this? I watch as he swings and hits some guy who runs out in his underwear. I have a hard time reconciling this video with the sweet guy I know.

"Wow," I breathe as I watch the video once more.

"Hey, I have to go," Ven says, pulling me back to the call.

"Later."

I hang up and watch the video again. His face is covered, but Ven is right. The body frame is right. There's no doubt it's him. I can't help wondering what happened to cause this. Josh is such a sweetheart.

CHAPTER TWENTY-THREE

Wait, Hold On

Shawna

Present...

"Wait, hold on," Skittles says, interrupting as we recount what happened all those years ago.

I remember most of it differently from Joshua. This is placing so much into perspective for me. I feel so naive. Joshua had so much going on.

I didn't see it from his side. I only saw things from the end, never the beginning. Greece shouldn't have shocked me so much. It's always been in my face, just covered in misunderstanding and lack of knowledge.

"Why didn't you ever tell me that's why you started the foundation? You were helping that family. That's when you went all secretive on me. I would have helped. You could have trusted me," Ven says through her hurt.

"I made a promise. I couldn't take the risk. I needed to get them help, not break their trust. The way things looked, you would have wanted to call someone," Josh says.

He drops his head and swallows. "You also didn't know me, the real me. I knew if anything happened to Mary, I was going to reveal myself when I took care of her husband," he continues darkly.

I start to bounce my knee nervously. I know how that all ends. Sadly, Ven doesn't need to know any of that. I'm still in shock about Ivan. I can't be the only one who caught that.

"You keep saying that. What do you mean I don't know the real you?"

"Ven, think about it. Where do you think I disappear to all the time? Why do you think Jeff called me when you entered Castro's race club? It wasn't to sit on the hood of your car and take pictures. Come on, what did you joke about when you met my grandfather?"

"He reminded me of an old Greek version of a mob boss," Ven gasps and turns to look at Lex. "This is what you meant. It's been right in my face."

Lex pulls a face at her. "Bing bong." She then turns to me. "I hope you got the message."

Joshua looks to me and frowns. He reaches to cover my still-bouncing knee. I lock eyes with him and see the same worry as this morning.

"Unfortunately, she has. I wish I could change that, but I can't. Just like I can't change who I am."

He pauses and looks down into his lap. His brows scrunch in the center of his forehead as if he's coming to some realization. I've watched him have this look before.

Then it's like he speaks his thoughts. "You guys know me as this sweet guy, sometimes an asshole, mostly the wiseass. You all know who I want to be, not who I am."

Luke snorts. "I know an asshole when I see one."

"You took the words right out of my mouth," Deacon adds.

I turn, remembering the others that are here as we relive our past. At the end of the day, each of these men has shown me kindness. However, I get Joshua's words.

I've seen his dark side. Not the asshole, but the man who has no mercy. What did Lex call him?

A savage, a killer. Right, I've met the savage who lives within this man. I know that face firsthand.

"Listen, I think we can all use something to eat. Have either of you checked in on those kids?" Pit says.

"I'll call Achilles," I reply.

"I need to get out of here for a bit," Skittles murmurs.

I hate the pain I see on her face. I lied to her. I've been lying to her for years. I went from living in a fairy tale to not knowing what I'd gotten myself into.

I still don't know what I'm doing. All I know is I'm in love with this man. Although I don't know if that's going to be enough when the smoke settles.

I stand to go call Achilles. Joshua catches me by the hand and stands to tug me to him. As if he can read my thoughts, he leans to whisper in my ear.

"I want to talk to you."

I lick my lips, look up into his eyes, and nod. The war playing out in his gaze hurts my heart. He searches my face and gives my hand a gentle squeeze.

"Pit, come take a walk with me," Blake says and stands.

Pit

Oh boy, here he goes. My brain is on fire, pulling at pieces and tying ends together. I don't know if I want to step out and talk to him now.

He walks over and places a hand on my shoulder. "You need to hear this. It fills in a gap you need. I get the feeling this is the right moment."

I look past Uncle Blake to see my wife heading through the secret door up to my private apartment over the bar. My heart aches for her. The news may have revealed Josh and Shawna's true relationship, but I think Mayven put together the pieces to know this started way before any of us knew.

I sort of feel responsible. If I had never told him to keep his shit from Skittles's door, maybe this wouldn't have turned out this way. I shake my head. Kelex knew when he was going to go after Shawna. There was never anything that could stop him.

I know him well enough to know this. I look into Uncle Blake's eyes. This motherfucker knew. I know he knew. Greece isn't outside of his reach.

Knowing this, I'm now curious as to what he thinks I should know now. I nod my head toward the door that leads out front and sigh.

"Fine," I mumble.

CHAPTER TWENTY-FOUR

From the Top

Blake

Ten years ago...

"Hello, Father," I said into the phone.

I'm still processing the news about Lester. My gut tells me it's all bullshit. Lester Smith isn't the type of man to commit suicide.

Why now? If he were going to do something like this, it would have been years ago. I can't make sense of it.

"Hello, Blake. How are my grandsons doing?"

"Anthony will be fine. I'm keeping an eye on him. William impresses me each day. The more I get to know him, the more he reminds me of Nicky, but sharper. He will fit the seat well."

"Good, I need to know these boys can handle this."

"Have you heard the news?"

I hold my breath. My father has always been fond of Lester. Allowing him to lose his hold on Vander and Bridge Lake has taken a toll on my father. It's been like allowing one of his sons to fall from grace.

I've dreaded sharing this news since I heard it. However, he needs to know. Our plan lies in knowing where all the players stand.

"Don't worry about this. Let things play out. I don't want Basil thinking I'm trying to push my grandson in over his."

A grin comes to my lips. I wasn't wrong. My father isn't who he is by luck. Vander and Bridge Lake are in our blood. We haven't lost Nicky for nothing.

"Very well," I say into the phone.

CHAPTER TWENTY-FIVE

I Am Who I Am

Kelex

Present...

"Come with me," I say to Shawna as I lead her down to the basement of Fuck Off.

"Should I call the house first?"

I shake my head and pull out my phone to shoot off a text to True. It only takes a few beats before he replies. I smile at his text.

True: *I got us. Take care of you. Don't let them take you from us.*

Me: *Never.*

I tug Shawna into the storeroom where Pit stocks the liquor, closing and locking the door behind us. Turning to Shawna, I look her over as she looks anywhere but at me. My heart sinks—could this be it—when she leaves me?

"True says they're fine," I murmur, waiting for her to make eye contact.

"That's good. I can run over and take them something to eat."

"That's not a bad idea. I'll go with you."

"Okay."

"Shawna, baby. You've been saying okay to everything since we left Greece. Look at me, please."

She turns to me and stares into my eyes. I move in close and cup her face. I can't keep myself from running my thumb across her full lips. Her brown skin has a bronze hue to it from all the time we spent in the sun while in Greece.

There's an unsure look in her eyes that's never been there like this before. I hate seeing it. However, I came to a realization upstairs.

This entire time I've been running from who I am. What happened in Greece happened because that's who I am. I didn't get that before.

All my life, my grandfather has given me a choice, but if I'm honest with myself. I can't change the core of who I am. What disturbed me as a child wasn't what I saw. It was the fact that I wanted to justify my father's actions.

I went from justifying to trying to figure out how I would have done it cleaner, better, smarter. As I answered those things, I found myself traumatized to know I could be so ruthless, evil, and calculated.

I blink my thoughts away and try to get to the bottom of this strain I feel. "We haven't been able to stop to talk about what happened. Are you okay? Are we still okay?"

Tears fill her eyes and her lips begin to tremble. Suddenly, desperation fills me. It's like I'm watching my world go up in smoke. It's all slipping through my fingers.

"Talk to me, Shawn. Tell me what's going on in your head," I plead.

"I don't know what to think, so I'm just not thinking," she says just above a whisper.

"And us?"

"I don't know, Joshua."

"What do you mean you don't know?"

Her nostrils flare in anger. "I don't know, babe. Let me think.

"I watched you kill a man with your bare hands, and in the next breath, we fucked like nothing happened and we haven't stopped to take a breath since. Only to return to you being accused of a murder we both know you didn't commit.

"I don't know how I feel about anything, Josh. I'm scared out of my mind. I don't know what's going to happen. We could lose everything we've been working for. All the lying I've been doing could've been for nothing.

"And that's the part that's about to make this all come crashing down. I hurt Ven. I see I did. I found everything I want but at what cost? I'm hurting people now," she says, the last part on a gasp.

These rooms are supposed to be soundproof, but I still move to the sound system Ox keeps down here to do inventory. I link my phone to the system and start to play "If You Let Me" by Sinead Harnett, then crank up the volume. This one means something to us.

Turning back to Shawna, I crowd her space and grab a handful of her hair to tug her head back and look down into her eyes. I swallow hard, trying to find the right words.

"None of what you just said is a lie, but I need you to trust me," I breathe against her lips. "I can't change who I am, but you have to know I did that for you. Just like I'm going to fix all of this for us. No matter what it takes."

"I don't want to lose you. I can't do this without you."

"You will never lose me and you won't have to," I say before I crush her lips with mine.

I deepen the kiss as I release her hair and roam my hands all over her body, settling with my palms on her ass as I lift her and walk her to the large wooden crate in the corner. It's just the right height to allow me to step between her legs and continue to devour her mouth.

She works on the buttons of my dress shirt as I claw my fingers up her thigh and beneath her dress. I continue to consume her mouth as I find her heat. I'm not surprised to find her wet as I drag the backs of my fingers against her weeping folds.

She sucks my lower lip into her mouth, pulling a groan from deep in my chest. I pull her panties down to get better access to her core. She sucks my tongue into her mouth.

I grin as I shove two fingers into her. She nearly jumps up off the crate. I still her with a hand on her waist, working her hot pussy with the other.

"I love you," I groan into her mouth.

"Oh, God, Joshua. I love you too."

Relief fills me. Hearing those words, I know I can make it all right. As long as I have her, I can do anything. She's become my everything.

She moves frantically to get her panties the rest of the way off while I continue to work her to orgasm. Her body begins to tremble and she gushes all over my hand. Lifting my soaked hand to my lips, I suck the digits clean, then reach to shove them into her mouth.

Shawna works to free me of my pants. Not removing my fingers from her mouth, I shove my tongue in and explore her cavern. Grabbing hold of her ass, I bring her to the edge of her perch.

"I love you so much," she says when I pull back to look into her eyes.

"You have no idea how much I love you, baby," I say as I thrust into her.

She gasps my name and throws her head back. This is it. This is the connection we've perfected. My skin hums with it. This is where I wanted to take us this morning.

She clings to my neck as I lift her from the crate and bounce her on my shaft. I'm so hard inside her. Her thick thighs have me wrapped in a warm embrace as her ass bounces with the force of our fucking.

She's dripping wet for me. I turn my face to take her lips. She meets me with that sweet smile of hers, pulling grunts and groans from me as I pound into her.

I squeeze her fat ass as I readjust her weight on my forearms, then lock my hands beneath her to hold her up as I move in and out of her wet pussy. The sound of her creamy center battles with the music and my pants and groans.

"Fuck, yes, Josh, fuck, babe. Yes, yes," she pants.

"There's nothing I wouldn't do for you, Shawna. I've got you, baby. I promise. I'll fix it all. I promise I'm going to fix it all," I breathe as I keep thrusting.

"I'm coming. I'm coming. Oh God, baby, I'm coming," she screams as her cream covers me and drips down my balls.

I bury my face in her neck and roar as I spill into her. I inhale her sweet-smelling skin and calm washes through me. I can make us right.

Shawna

I hold on to Joshua's arm with a smile on my lips as we go to step out of the storeroom. However, that smile falls and dread settles in the pit of my stomach once he opens the door. Blake is waiting right outside with a scowl on his face.

"When were you going to tell me about the mess you left in your grandfather's lap?" he bites out.

"I left nothing in his lap," Joshua says curtly.

Blake snorts. "That's not how it came back to me."

"My wife and I were having a nice day in when we were interrupted by banging on our hotel room door. We know nothing about the drama they were interrogating everyone about.

"I let them know we heard nothing and would be returning to the States as our vacation had ended. I gave a number to reach me. See... nothing for Pappoús to worry about.

"I'm calling bullshit."

I peek out into the hall to find Pit leaning with his head back against the wall, looking exhausted. He rubs his eyes and straightens. Joshua wraps his arm around my waist and tugs me into his side.

"Let me worry about that," he snarls.

Pit holds his hands up. "Listen, I'm not butting into your business. I'm just telling you, almost everything that's been happening to our circle involves us. Don't think anything is isolated at this point," Pit warns.

"In that case. You should know I was there that night. The night of the race. I had been there with friends."

Pit's brows shoot up into his hairline. "Why did I have a feeling you were going to say that? Come on, talk to me. Then you both can finish coming clean. Including what happened in Greece."

I sigh. Joshua gives my waist a gentle squeeze. I think I'm going to be sick.

CHAPTER TWENTY-SIX

Start with the Truth

Shawna

"So you're saying you watched the crash and followed Skittles after," Pit repeats as I finish retelling that night from my experience.

"Yeah, I followed Ven once my friends jumped in their cars and ran. I was outside the place she went into, trying to get the nerve up to go inside. My mom would have killed me if she knew where I really was.

"I was supposed to be at a friend's studying. One of my friends sent a text that the model Kelex was at the race, so we all hurried out to watch," I explain.

"That means every single one of us was there that night. Now things are starting to make more sense," Pit says.

"I'm glad it's making sense to you. I still don't see it," Tak says.

"Someone's trying to expose us," Joshua speaks up. "Maybe if you all know more about me, we can connect the dots."

"Why are you just now sharing? You know you can trust us," Luke says.

"It's not that simple," Ox replies.

"He's right. Vander, Bridge Lake, Pit, Ox, and I all have deeper ties than we could let on over the years. A lot had to fall into place. I had to hold my secrets close to the chest," Joshua says.

"Is that why you haven't told me you're married to my cousin? I've been waiting. I want to hear it from one of you.

"How long have you two really been seeing each other? I know it hasn't been since the cabin or my wedding. This started long before that.

"You were talking. I get that, but something changed. When? How did you end up with Danny if this was happening?"

I flinch as Joshua snarls at the mention of Danny's name. He's still pissed about that. It's one of my biggest regrets.

"That's complicated," I say. "I don't know where to start."

"Start with the truth. Neither of you has denied being married, not once. Be my family, be my friend. Tell me the truth," Ven almost sobs.

Joshua stands and moves to Ven's side. Deacon stands and allows Joshua to take the seat beside her. He wraps an arm around her and kisses the top of her head.

He murmurs something in her ear. She turns her head to sob against his shoulder. Although I know her pregnancy hormones are making this ten times worse, I couldn't feel any guiltier than I do in this moment.

"I'm sorry," I say in almost a whisper. "I never meant to hurt you. Danny was a mistake, but I love Joshua. Yeah, we haven't told anyone, but I love him."

"What?" Ven sobs.

"She's right, we were keeping secrets, but I'm in love with her," Joshua says. My heart swells hearing those words from him. I was so in denial when it came to his feelings for me in the beginning. "Let us try to explain."

CHAPTER TWENTY-SEVEN

Brokenhearted

Kelex

Five years ago…

I want a condo here in downtown Vander now that we've opened a new bar and grill. That way, I'll be closer to work when I need to be, but True is only eleven, Cat is nine and Vernice just turned five. I still worry about them. I want to stick close for a few more years.

Tonight, I wish I were in Bridge Lake. I stand before the floor-to-ceiling window of my office in my Vander headquarters with my phone in my hand as I text Shawna. She's home for the summer.

Me: *I'll try to come through to the race tonight.*

Shawna: *Cool. I'll try to see if Ven can get Mom to let me go with her.*

Me: *Your mom still not letting you out of her sight?*
Shawna: *Gah. No.*
Me: *Get there if you can.*
Me: *I can't promise I'll make it, but I'll try.*

"You know that race house? The one Marquis has brought into Vander," Jeff says, pulling my attention.

"Yeah, bad news all day. They run drugs through the drivers. I hope you're not thinking about getting in bed with that shit."

"Nah, just heard about it and was curious. Besides, I don't have two million sitting around to throw away for a team and that's just the buy-in. I'd still need cars and a team."

I shrug. "Cars wouldn't be a problem. I'm sure you could find a few guys from the old track, but again, those races are nothing but trouble."

"I hear you. Just thinking of my options. Some heavy hitters run some of the teams just for fun. Might be nice. I'd get to rub elbows with the real money around here. Something to keep in mind. You know?"

I grunt, my attention on my phone as I continue to text. It's crazy to know she's here for the summer. However, I'm not sure I'll be in town for much longer. I'm headed to Crete.

I could always take her with me. The thought brings a smile to my face. Pappoús would love her. He's already a Skittles fan.

"Who are you texting?" Jeff asks, looking over my shoulder.

"Nobody," I murmur and close the app.

I walk over to my desk and toss the phone down. Jeff called to remind me I promised to babysit his date's friend. That's the only reason why I haven't committed to meeting up with Shawna and Ven.

I owe him one for covering my ass. One of Vander's wives dropped in on me after reading too much into my interest. Jeff was happy to take her off my hands, and luckily, he didn't ask why or how I knew her.

"Doesn't look like nobody. Heart emojis for her name. Aw, shit. I think my boy is in love," he croons. "Come on, who is she?"

I'm not going to share, so he can let it go. One thing I'm learning from Zoe and Blake, they're a powerhouse because no one knows about them. I wish Shawna and I could be the legit version of them, so I'm keeping her to myself.

"You still thinking about joining me in Crete this year?" I ask to change the subject.

"I don't know. A business venture just came up. I'm considering my options."

"Cool, get to your bag. There's always next time."

My other phone I keep for calls from Greece rings. My thoughts turn to Achilles mentioning my younger cousin, Constantine, arriving in Vander and leaving almost as quickly as he arrived. I found it strange but thought little of it.

However, now it comes back to me because my grandfather doesn't call this line unless it's an emergency. I can't help but wonder if my father is up to something. I wouldn't put it past him.

"Mr. Nikolaou, your guests have arrived," my assistant says through the intercom.

"I'll take care of that," Jeff croons.

"Thanks, I need to take this."

I move to the hidden door in my office that leads to a secret room to take this away from prying ears. Once in the room, I answer the call and put the device to my ear.

"Hello."

"*Tzósoua*, I need you here now," Pappoús demands.

"Is everything okay?"

"I will tell you everything when you arrive. There is no time to spare."

"I'll see you soon. I'll leave right away."

Shawna

I'm buzzing with nervous, excited energy. I'm so happy to be back home. My mom has been hogging all my time, but tonight I finally broke free.

Ven is racing and I'm hoping Joshua will find time to come hang with us. He said he'd try, but I'm not giving up hope.

I spent so much time on my outfit, makeup, and hair. I want to look my best the first time he sees me. We've talked so much over the years; I feel like I know him.

I look at my watch and purse my lips. I wonder if he's free yet. I don't want to be a pain, but I don't know when I'll get away from my mom again.

I look up to see Ven talking with a few of the other drivers. I know a lot of these guys as the sons of lawyers and politicians I have to smile and be nice to during Mommy's campaigns. I wonder what their dads would think about these races.

I shrug and turn to find a quiet corner to make my call. If he can't make it, at least I can stop looking for him and hoping. He's never been annoyed with me calling, so what the heck. It won't hurt to try.

"Hello," a female voice comes through the line.

I pull the phone from my ear and frown at the device. My heart sinks as I see I dialed the right number. Joshua and I aren't dating officially, but I've never once thought about him seeing anyone else.

Maybe that's why he's always encouraging me to go out. I've always taken it as him wanting me to gain experience and make friends. He knows I'm shy.

"Hello?" the woman says again.

"Um, I'm looking for Joshua. Is he there?"

"He's a bit tied up at the moment. Who's this?"

"Um, nobody," I say as tears stream down my face.

I feel so stupid. What made me think he wanted me? I'm such a fool. I'm a twenty-seven-year-old virgin with a crush on a guy who was well on his way to being a freaking supermodel-movie star.

I hang up without another word and run my hand under my nose. Before I can think twice, I block him on social media and block his number. I'm not going to allow him to play with my feelings anymore.

I return to the track as Ven and the other drivers start to climb into their cars. I take a seat and drop my head, feeling sorry for myself. That's when the expensive shoes come into view.

"What's a pretty girl like you doing all by herself, looking so sad?"

I look up as the words come from the smooth voice. He's handsome in a mob movie, movie star way. I give him a cautious smile and sniffle.

"I'm not by myself. I'm here with one of the drivers," I say shyly.

"Where is he? If he's the one who made you cry, I'll handle him."

I smile. "I'm here with my cousin. She's a she, not a he."

"Oh, the pretty driver. Um, the looks run in the family. You mind if I have a seat? I'll keep you company while she's out there," he says and gives me a smile.

He's nice looking, but he's no…. I cut the thought off. I'm not mad that he's seeing someone. I'm upset because he never once made it seem like he was. I thought he wanted to meet as much as I did.

"Um, I guess so," I say and scoot over.

He sits and reaches out his hand. "The name's Danny. Danny Clavier. It's nice to meet you…"

"Shawna. Shawna Norris," I say and smile back.

He brings the back of my hand to his lips without taking his hazel eyes off me. I can feel my cheeks heat. Maybe this is a sign.

Joshua Kelex, you're not for me.

CHAPTER TWENTY-EIGHT

Summoned

Kelex

I'm usually more excited than this to be summoned by my grandfather. However, something feels off about this visit. For one, I'm leaving Mary and the kids for I don't know how long.

While Mary has been doing great, there are days when she gets a little overwhelmed and having me around to take a load off helps.

Zoe was right. Having someone other than myself to worry about has given me a sense of humanity. I'm slower to anger. I think things through more than I used to. Although now that Mary needs me less, I don't know if it's enough.

"Joshua," Helios croons with his deep voice and Greece accent as I step off the plane.

I move to him and allow him to pull me into a tight hug. I've known Helios since I was a boy. We're not that far apart in age. His father once worked for my grandfather.

When I'm in Crete, this is one person I can call a friend. I've been able to count on him throughout the years, so when I embrace him, it's with warmth and genuine happiness to see him.

"It's good to see you, my friend. Your pappoús has been anxious for your arrival. Let's go."

"Do you know what this is about?"

"Only that things have been changing for a while. I think you're here for the final changes," he replies.

"What was Constantine doing in Vander?"

Helios stops and turns to look at me in surprise. "He was in the States?"

"Yeah, what do you know?"

"I know nothing. However, I think I'm starting to understand what's going on. Come, we'll get you to the house for some answers."

We climb into the car and ride in silence. I have a million things running through my head. Wanting to clear my thoughts, I pull out my phone and text Shawna.

I frown when the message says not delivered. I shrug, thinking it's the reception. I close out of her contact and pull up Achilles's to shoot him a text. I left on short notice. He'll need to cover for me or move some things around.

I'm cool with either. My frown deepens as my text to him goes through right away. I back out to text Shawna again, not even bothering to pay attention to Achilles's reply.

Me: *Hey, I had to head out of town.*

Me: *Sorry. I'll make it up to you before the summer is out.*

Me: *If you have time, I have a minute to talk.*

All three messages post a red warning and say not delivered. "Did she block me?" I bite out. "What the fuck?"

Frustrated, I tuck the phone away as we pull up to the house. I push Shawna to the back of my mind so I can focus on what's going on around me.

"*Tzósoua*," Pappoús croons.

I lift a brow. I wasn't expecting to arrive to such a jovial mood. From his call, I anticipated seeing a bit more fire and ire. My curiosity goes through the roof.

"Pappoús, what's going on?"

"Ah, yes, there is much to discuss. My daughters and their sons, that father of yours, this business in Vander that is like an itch to my ass, the attempt on my life, and your awareness of those around you. Yes, much to discuss."

My nostrils flare. "Wait. Attempt on your life? What the fuck?"

"*Óloi éxo*," he barks. As everyone obeys and begins to exit the foyer, he waves for me to follow him.

"Pappoús, what's going on? When was an attempt made on your life? Do you know who's responsible?"

He moves out to the gardens in the back of the house. His stroll is thoughtful and leisurely. However, I know better. I can now see the restraint he's holding.

"Relax, we will get there. *Tzósoua,* there are two things to know in this life. Who your true family is and who your real friends are. Titles do not bare truths. People just mask themselves behind them, giving a false sense of security and comfort."

"What are you saying?"

"I want to ask you something and I need you to take the time to think about this. Do you know who your real friends are?"

I pause and think on his words. Skittles and Shawna are the first to come to mind. Then the assholes. I note Achilles and Jeff next. However, Achilles isn't necessarily in the friend category.

"I think I can say I do," I finally reply.

"Are you sure?"

Am I? Did Shawna really block me? That's not sitting so well with me.

"My crew. I know I can trust them. I don't give them all my secrets, but that's to protect them, not because I don't trust them."

"Ah, here. This is where I'll start. *Tzósoua mou*, listen to me closely." He has my attention the moment he calls me *his* Joshua in Greek.

"I have spent your entire life placing people into your life who would mold you into the man I know you can be. Some have made their way to you by fate, others I handpicked to give them to you," he goes on.

"What? Who have you placed in my life?"

"Blake isn't your *nonos* by accident. I'm well aware that your father despises him. We will get to why. It's time you know this too.

"Before your mother's untimely demise, I had planned for you boys to grow up together and become friends. William Pitman and Anthony Amato were always going to be connected to you.

"After your mother's death, I had decided to forget my plans. You were going to grow up and know nothing about this business. Then, your father, who has shit for brains, allowed you to walk right into this life.

"I asked him to send you to me. I wanted to see how you would react. Again, I made the decision not to immerse you in our way, but then you had your accident.

"Not long after, I found some things out. It was then that everything changed. You deserve to have that information before you make your decision. I've just been waiting for the right time," he finishes.

"What information? Sorry, Pappoús, I'm a little lost."

"I can see this. All of this is much like this maze we're walking through. Many twists and turns that lead us back to one thing, one place. I will do my best to unpack this for you to understand, yes?"

I nod for him to continue. These gardens always bring me a sense of peace. I take a deep breath and ready myself for what he's about to unload on me.

"I always wanted a son. I was going to hand him my seat in Bridge Lake. I like America and the money I've made there has been good to my family, but it is not my home.

"Many of us original families felt this way. The founders agreed we'd leave our legacy in the hands of the next generation. However, I had four girls and not one son.

"This didn't concern me. The families were accustomed to our old ways. I could just arrange a marriage with one of the other families. Our seat would then be secure.

"I loved Blake for your mother. They had grown up together. He and Nicky were good boys. Although it didn't take long for me to learn your mother and Blake would never be more than friends.

"Blake had fallen for Maria's best friend. Out of respect for your mother and Blake and, truthfully, the young woman who had Blake's heart, I decided to find Maria a different match."

"My father," I seethe.

Pappoús rolls his eyes. "*Nai, ilíthios o ídios.*"

A laugh bursts from my lips as he confirms and calls my father stupid. It's no secret Pappoús has always loathed my father to some degree. I've just never understood why.

"You see, I matched Maria with Ulysses with every intention of handing him my seat. Your father is just a greedy, stupid, jealous man. He could never get over the fact that I wanted to give my seat to Blake.

"Then Yannis Knight came to me. He was disheartened that we hadn't merged our families. He knew it was no slight against him.

"So we agreed to match Nicky and Willow. They, too, were friends. My other two daughters were not ready for America. I spoiled them. A world outside of Greece would have eaten them. They needed to remain here.

"Although if you ask your aunts, they believe I will allow one of their sons to run Vander and Bridge Lake. Like I would leave any part of my legacy in the hands of one of those idiots.

"They kiss my ass and dangle a dagger at my back as if I cannot see them." He pauses and looks into my eyes proudly. "I have left my treasures in the city that will belong to them. Four daughters, *Tzósoua*.

"Four daughters and four grandsons. You of which are the oldest. America belongs to you. All you have to do is take it."

I stand lost in thought for a moment. I list his grandsons in my head. Me, Adrian, and Constantine. I look into my grandfather's eyes as they light up.

"As I've said, I've been placing people in your life since you were a child. Anthony Amato is more than a friend. He's my second grandson. Willow and Nicky's son. Anthony Blake Knight."

My brows shoot into my hairline as the realization hits. "Ox?"

Pappoús pats my cheek. "You see. You are my smart one. I've been advised that you are the best fit for my seat and Anthony is better suited to take Blake's rule.

"However, if you decide what you learn isn't enough to sway your decision, I have my eye on William as my successor. He is not my blood, but he's as smart as you are. Anthony has the brains but not the necessary temperament."

I shake my head to clear it because right now, my thoughts are reeling. He's just said an entire mouthful and I haven't missed the part where he's trying to sway a decision from me.

"You've just said a whole lot. Yet you've avoided the topic of someone trying to kill you."

"Ah, *Tzósoua mou,* I have named the snakes after my life. Did you not listen to my words?"

I knit my brows in thought. "You're fucking kidding me, right?"

"Good boy. No, this isn't a lie I tell. They've been placing poison in my food for months." He winks at me. "Your pappoús is just a lot smarter than they are. However, I needed you here to see the entire picture and because I do believe an attempt on your life is next."

"Not if I get to them first. Listen, I need a shower and to think over all you have said. Hold the rest for tomorrow. We will talk then."

"Yes, you must be exhausted from your flight. I must see to Zeus's burial anyway."

"Zeus?"

"Yes, you know he ate what I ate. Odin always fed him first. Zeus stopped eating about two months ago and he wouldn't allow me to eat anything placed before me either. I started to feed us myself in the evenings when everyone went to sleep.

"Somehow, the poison was mixed into his food without him detecting it the day before yesterday. He whimpered throughout the day."

"How do you know it was poison?"

"I had Helios take his food to a lab. Odin has been on vacation for three months. His substitutes were sent by my youngest daughter.

"Let's just say Zeus's arrangements aren't the only things I'm going to tend to," he replies, causing me to fume even more.

Shawna

"Thanks for stopping by, Blake," my mother's voice carries from her office as I walk through the hall.

I move closer to her office. I hope this is the end of a meeting and not the beginning. I want her advice on what I should do about Joshua. Danny seems nice enough, he's been texting all day, but I can't help wondering if I overreacted last night.

"Thanks for seeing me, Monica. I wanted to check in in person. How are things coming along? Is there anything you need?"

I guess it's not the end. I back away and turn to head up to my room. Maybe I'll start looking at apartments. Joshua was supposed to tag along with me, but I'm an adult. I can do this on my own.

Or maybe I should find another travel assignment. Bridge Lake just doesn't feel like home like it used to. Home has been where my camera is.

My phone buzzes with a text. I pull it from my pocket and smile. It's Danny again.

Danny: *Have dinner with me. I would love to see that smile.*

I chew on my lip and debate on if I really want to entertain this guy. He seems nice enough. I don't think he's going to sit across from me texting the entire date.

I shrug.

Me: *Okay.*

CHAPTER TWENTY-NINE

Kalinýchta, Xadérfia

Kelex

I step from the shower and walk into the bedroom my grandfather keeps here for me. Every time I think of his dead dog Zeus, I see red. That rage that lives inside me starts to boil to the surface.

I grab my phone to call Shawna. I need to hear her voice so I can pull myself from where I know I'm headed. I dial her number, and this time, there's a single ring before it goes to voice mail.

"What the fuck? She did block me," I bite out and toss the phone down.

Moving to stand before the floor-length mirror, I take myself in. That darkness starts to seep through. All I see before me is a monster.

Looking into my eyes, all the blue has faded. They are completely gray. Reaching up, I push my wet locks back. The dark roots reveal my natural color while the blond ends expose the lie I'm trying so hard to hold on to.

The truth is, that possibility... that life is long gone. Standing before me is who I'm destined to be. I drop my gaze to my asshole tattoo.

The smoke and flames that billow up my chest and left side speak to this darkness that's always brewing and now has stoked a flame and is bellowing its way up through me.

Lowering my gaze to my burns, my vision blurs. I don't know what I see anymore. My skin could be completely healed, but I wouldn't know. All I see in my reflection is damage, inside and out.

"So be it," I say and dial a different number.

"Hello."

"Helios, I want to throw a party in my cousin's honor. Do you think you can get them there?"

"I'm sure I can."

"Good. You will arrive with me. I think we should fly in," I say coldly.

"Got it. See you tonight."

I've had time to think about what I plan to do. It's the fact that my idiot cousins thought it okay to try to off our grandfather and then turn around and try to target me that's caused this monster to wake.

Here's a fact about me, I don't wait for anyone to come to me. I bring that shit right to your door and make sure you find out. Adrian and Constantine want to see me. Here I am.

When in Crete, the world is at my fingertips, a fact I plan to prove. They want to be bosses. Let's see who rises to this occasion like one. I guarantee it won't be either of them.

Constantine

"What's this all about?" Adrian asks as we walk into the villa Joshua has invited us out to.

I look around and whistle. This is a nice setup. I grab a glass of champagne from the leggy blonde with the big boobs and sip it.

"Who cares? He's come to us. Once we kill him and get him out of the way, America is ours."

"You don't find this a bit strange? He wasn't supposed to be here for a few weeks."

I shrug him off and move out to the pool, where the party seems to be set up. Lights and music welcome us. The pool has my full attention. It's an infinity pool set before a gorgeous view of Mykonos, high up on a cliff that makes this place majestic in ambience.

"Look at our home. He will never have this, and now, we will run this and his home. Not the other way around," I croon, placing my glass down to take my shirt off.

I kick my shoes off and move to enter the pool. Adrian makes a sound in the back of his throat. He worries too much.

Instead of climbing into the pool with me, he takes a seat on one of the lounge chairs. I relax in the water with my arms propped up behind me.

"Well, where is he?" Adrian mumbles.

"I don't really care. When he arrives, the men know what to do."

I dive into the water and swim to the edge that flows over the cliff. I can't help wondering if this is one of Joshua's properties from Pappoús. I'll be happy to take this one.

As I'm having the thought, a gorgeous brunette exits the house. She hands a phone to Adrian and comes to hold another one out to me.

I move to take it from her as I look her over. Yes, I'll bed this one before the night ends. With that thought, I move back to look out at the view as I lean on the invisible edge.

"This is the life," I breathe to myself.

The phone in my hand rings. The one Adrian has does too. I lift a brow but answer.

"Hello," I say into the device.

"Hello," Adrian's voice comes through a moment after.

I turn to look at him while still wading in the pool. He shrugs and I pull a face. The sound of a helicopter catches my ear. Not uncommon around the islands, so I ignore it.

"How are the accommodations? Are they to your liking?" Joshua croons into the phone, pulling my attention.

I grin. "*Tzósoua.* Yes, this is very nice, but where are you? We're excited to see you."

"Is that right?" I frown and turn as the sound of the chopper gets louder, as if it's close by. I lean against the edge of the pool to look out for it. My mouth falls open as the helicopter rises right before me. As the vessel rises higher, Joshua comes into view. "Hello, cousins," he says darkly.

"Fuck," Adrian breathes into the phone.

Joshua looks me right in the eyes as he lifts a gun and pulls the trigger. I turn to see Adrian sprawled on the lounger with a hole in the center of his head. Turning back to Joshua, I go to plead for mercy. However, his gun is now pointed at me, his gaze still locked on me as well.

"Cousin, no, pl—"

CHAPTER THIRTY

Go Home

Kelex

I walk into the dining room for breakfast with a smile on my lips. I slept like a baby. This morning when I woke and thought of the pool of red I left in Mykonos, I couldn't be more satisfied.

"You did just what I expected," Pappoús says as I take my seat.

I tilt my head as I study him. "Were you expecting something else?"

He looks me in the eyes, his expression unyielding. A plate is placed before him. The young woman who brought it in takes the fork he hands her and cleans it in front of him before opening her mouth to show him she has swallowed.

"Thank you, that will be all," he says.

He then digs in himself. I'm pissed all over again to see he has to do this in his own home. My aunts and cousins have lost their fucking minds.

I can't say I'm surprised, but I'm still in awe of the audacity. At least two of them are handled. I have no doubt he will take care of his daughters.

Turning his attention back to me, he smiles. "It was how I would have handled it when I was your age. Not messy. This is good. You show restraint."

"But?"

"No, but. I want you to see we can be who we are without the brutality of Ulysses."

"You think the brutality is why I don't want this?"

"It has been my assumption."

"Pappoús, there are a number of reasons I don't think this is for me. The brutality is something I enjoy a bit too much. Which is why I refrain from going that far.

"The reason I don't want to take things over is because I want a normal life. I don't want to bathe myself in blood and greed. Your own daughters want to end your life and for what? Power? What happened to family, love, loyalty, honor?"

"You mistake the movies you wanted to act in for real life. There is no honor or loyalty in the real world. You either bathe in their blood, or they will bathe in yours." His voice rises as he drops his silverware to his plate.

"But, *Tzósoua mou*, it isn't always blood and greed. It can be family and love too. This is what I've been allowing you to learn. I can't make your decision for you but understand when you make it, it will be out of love," he finishes.

"You said there is something I need to know before I make my decision. What is it?"

He shakes his head. "I don't think you're ready. Go to Athens with Helios, have a good time. I have grieving guests coming. I wouldn't want you eating their food."

CHAPTER THIRTY-ONE

Changes

Kelex

Three years later…

I pull out my handkerchief and wipe my hands clean. I look the asshole in front of me over. I should kill him for making me have to come to Sunnyside to handle him.

"You're no longer welcome in Vander. If I hear your name, the next time we meet will be the day you take your last breath. Am I understood?"

"Yes," he gasps.

I turn and walk out of the room Helios has had my guys holding this prick in. Yes, Pappoús sent him with me. Someone he trusts.

I don't mind. No one knows my driver is muscle from Greece. I'm living my life as usual for the most part. Blake just asked me to handle this one since my name came up.

"Where to now?" Helios asks as we get to the car.

"Lunch with Jeff."

He frowns but nods. Sad to say, Jeff rubbed Helios wrong from day one. They don't get along at all.

I brush the thought off and climb into the car. My thoughts go to True and Mary. Mary had a checkup today. True was supposed to call me with an update. She's been in remission, but these visits always put us all on pins and needles.

Guilt rises. I haven't been around as much lately. I always feel like I'm living a lie when I'm around them. However, I can't seem to walk away. They are my family, my happy place.

My phone rings, pulling me from my thoughts. I pull it and see it's True. First, I roll up the partition. I don't realize I'm holding my breath until I answer.

"J, this can't be happening again," True sobs.

My heart squeezes, and I clench my shirt over my chest. I can feel his pain through the phone. He doesn't have to explain what he's talking about. It's our biggest fear.

Mary has become a friend to me over the years. Her children are my little buddies. This hurts so much, but I'm the adult. I need to be there for these kids.

"Hey, it's going to be okay. I'm here. We'll get through this again. We fight with her. We'll give her our strength, okay?"

"Yeah, okay."

"I love you, bro. I've got you."

I sit in the back of my car, reminding myself to breathe as I wipe my face. Right now, True is my main concern. I sit talking to him for another thirty minutes.

This couldn't be happening at a worse time. Pappoús has just called me to Crete for another visit. I'm going to have to figure out how to make this all work.

I won't break my promise.

***

"You all right?" Jeff asks as we sit across from each other in this Sunnyside restaurant.

I can't lie. I've been distracted since that call. I wasn't surprised to find Jeff on his way out of the restaurant as I arrived. I was late and moving lethargically.

"Just a lot on my mind," I reply.

"You still headed to Crete?"

"I'm supposed to be." I shrug.

"You taking the promotion?"

"I'm not sure about any of that right now."

He sits back in his seat. "Hold on, I thought you were ready. I've heard talk. You've been more involved."

"Don't listen to everything you hear. Things are never cut and dry. I have things here that need my attention more. Things more important than running a corrupt city."

"Your grandfather isn't going to wait forever," he says tightly.

"He'll wait as long as I need him to. If not, he can replace me. I don't give a fuck."

"Whoa. What's going on with you?"

"Nothing," I mumble.

We sit in silence for a few beats. I'm really not in the mood to be here. I want to head back to Vander to check on Mary.

"How are things with Achilles?" he asks, thankfully changing the subject.

"It's business as usual. Nothing to complain about."

"Is he going to back you to start that entertainment thing?"

"Yeah, I've been able to get a few kids into the music studio, but the real challenge is going to be producing the films for them."

Jeff still doesn't know that Achilles is my partner, not my investor. We've kept my role under wraps pretty well over the years.

"Is that really going to make you any money?"

I shrug. "Achilles asked the same thing. That's not why I'm doing it. Some of those kids have real talent. It's not their fault they got a shit hand at life. My goal is to give them the chance I once had."

I look down at my plate. The food tastes like nothing. I feel sick to my stomach.

Here I sit, about to drop at least two hundred dollars on a salad and a piece of fish. That's money that could go to one of those kids for books or something. Money Mary could use for medication.

"You done? I want to show you this storefront I'm looking at."

I lift my gaze and knit my brows. "Here? In Sunnyside?"

"Yeah, I'm thinking of doing a spa. There's a lot of money around here. Place it next to a yoga studio. You know?"

I knit my brows further. Yeah, I do know. Call me crazy, but he just sat with me and Skittles as we had this same conversation.

Only we talked about the local clinics around here and how we wanted to place the spa between the clinics and a yoga studio for wellness treatments. My foundation deals with helping single parents dealing with cancer cope with holding their families together.

For me, it's not a money grab. The families my foundation supports in the area will have full access. My phone rings and I shake the thought off.

"I need to take this and we can go," I say.

CHAPTER THIRTY-TWO

The Squeeze

Kelex

A month later…

"Bro, she's fighting. We just have to continue to be strong," I say to a sobbing True.

"What am I going to do if I lose my mom? Where will we go? My dad doesn't want us. All the rest of our family is gone or doesn't care. We're on our own."

My jaw nearly pops when he mentions his father. I've made that motherfucker's life a living, breathing hell. He's only alive because of his kids, although I've been second-guessing that decision lately.

"You guys have me. I'm not going anywhere."

"J, I love you, bro, but what are you going to do with three kids? We can't stay with you."

"Maria's House will take you guys in until we figure it out."

Or they can come live with me.

I've thought long and hard about this. It's not something I've brought up to Mary because I don't want to put more on her plate. It's my hope she'll pull through and I don't want to do anything to block that.

However, it's been weighing on my mind. I wonder if she should put in writing that she wants me to take the kids. I would be honored to do it.

True snorts. "So we become VIPs at your charity house. This isn't right. She's a good mom. Why her?"

"I can't answer that for you. I've been wondering the same thing."

I grind my teeth as I think of my mother and father. If it was a matter of keeping the better parent, I'd say I got the shit end of that stick too. He's right. Mary is an amazing person and an even better mom.

At fourteen, True should be out with friends drinking smoothies and checking out girls—his biggest worry getting his homework done. Not this, not what will happen to him and his little sisters when their mother is gone.

However, that's a question heavy on all our hearts. It's not looking good. Mary hasn't been responding well to the treatments this time.

"You should get out of here. You have that dinner, don't you?" True asks, bringing me out of my thoughts.

I look down at my watch. Zoe is expecting me. There have been new players entering Vander. They have Bridge Lake money, but they don't seem to understand the ecosystem here.

"That can wait," I reply.

Zoe and Blake want me to cozy up to the newcomers and find out all I can. Look for weaknesses in case they're needed in the future. I still haven't committed to taking over, but my connections have been helpful in doing all I can for these kids and others like them.

"We'll be fine. I'll call you if anything changes."

I cup the back of his head and kiss his forehead. I wish like hell there was more I could do. The one thing I do know—I can't be a guardian to these kids and take over Vander and Bridge Lake. I hope Mary doesn't make this sacrifice for my soul.

I'll happily fall into the darkness for these kids to keep their mother. My thoughts suddenly go to Shawna. I don't know what happened between us. I once thought she'd be my saving grace, the one to keep me from falling down the rabbit hole.

Then one day, in the blink of an eye, she was gone. I never made things official between us. I couldn't. However, I thought we were building toward more. I wanted more.

"Call me if you need me," I say, standing.

My mood has shifted from sad and melancholy to bitter and foul. I don't know how much good I'll be at charming anyone.

My phone rings as I make my way to my waiting car. I'm already dressed in my tux. Seeing it's Jeff, I answer.

"What's up?"

"I was wondering. You know that club we talked about, the one with the cars and things?"

"Yeah, I thought you were steering clear of that."

"I'm seeing some benefits. Besides, with the right team, I could win it all and return the money. All I need is the right investor. You know anyone with that type of cash to spare?"

"Not that I can think of at the moment, but I have a lot on my mind. Give me some time to think about it and I'll get back to you. You need some cash, bro?"

"Nah, I'm just trying to make a few moves to be like you when I grow up. Don't sweat it."

"You sure?"

"Yeah, it's nothing. I've got it. You going to see Basil anytime soon?"

"Pappoús has his hands full. I'm going, but I'll be in Athens most of the time. I'm not sure I even want to go to Crete."

"You know, all will be well for all of us when he promotes you here."

I snort. "That shit is so far from my mind. I'm not living out some mob fantasy, bro. All of that died for me as a boy. Listen, I have to go," I reply, my mind still heavy from my talk with True.

Shawna

"I want to talk to your cousin. You should do me a favor and invite her out to the races," Danny croons as he stands behind me.

He lifts a gift box in front of me, revealing a diamond bracelet. As if that would get me to drag my cousin into his world. I refuse.

I've messed up enough getting involved with him. I shut the box, not taking it from his hands. I don't want to get into it with him, but I'm not bending on this topic.

"She's busy. I don't want to bother her," I say.

"You know, you're really starting to irritate me. You won't let me fuck you, which would be a privilege for you, by the way. You have an answer for every fucking thing I say.

"I'm getting sick of this shit. Do what I say, Shawna. Get your cousin to come for a race. I'm not asking again," he growls.

"Okay, don't. As a matter of fact, don't bother calling me either," I snap back.

He grabs my face and pushes me back while he moves forward. I grab his wrist, and a little voice in the back of my head tells me to break it. However, I hesitate, and now he has me pinned to the wall, my face in one hand and my wrist in the other.

He gets right up in my face. "Do you even understand the shit I have on your mother and uncle? Keep playing with me, little girl. If I wasn't being told to keep you around…" he snarls in my face. "Just keep your fucking mouth shut and do as I say."

My mind races. Could he really harm my family? I know I've talked too much at times.

What the hell have I gotten myself into? I jumped out of the pan and into the fire. I'll keep my mouth shut, but I'm not bringing Ven around.

Fuck him.

CHAPTER THIRTY-THREE

Tame Who?

Kelex

"Is everything okay? You don't look like yourself," Zoe says as she joins me.

"Yeah, I'm good. Let's just do this."

"Aww, love, I thought you'd be in a better mood. I guess I'll have to enjoy this by myself."

"Enjoy what?"

"Pissing your father off."

"What?"

"He's here tonight. Seeing you with me is going to burn right through him."

Blake has mentioned in the past that my father isn't going to like the fact that Zoe Gataki is an active part of my life. Some old grudge or something. Knowing I get to piss him off brings a genuine smile to my lips.

"Oh great, we won't have to wait long," Zoe purrs.

My father is straight ahead of us with two women at his sides. One looks to be around my age and the other looks like she's fighting to hold on to her youth. Sorry to say she's failing.

"Joshua," My father croons.

"Ulysses," I mumble.

"This is how my son greets me?" he says with a false smile on his lips.

"Your son? Am I still considered that?" I lift a brow.

"Of course you are. You're my only child. I'm so proud of the man you've become. I've been following your endeavors. Very impressed. Collen, I'd like you to meet Joshua Kylix, my son."

"Joshua Nikolaou, I no longer go by Kylix," I say, widening my stance and lifting my head as I cross my hands before me to keep from punching him.

"Wait, aren't you that model?" The other younger woman he hasn't introduced says.

"Ah, yes. Joshua, this is Helen. I've told her all about you."

"Funny, how can you talk about someone you know nothing about?"

My father booms with a deep laugh as if I've told some fucking joke. He keeps smiling like the dick he is. I can't help but wonder what he's up to and why in the hell he's here.

Ulysses has never thought about anyone but himself. The only reason for him to attend a charity event is to advance his bullshit agenda.

Helen gives an annoying laugh. "Your father speaks very highly of you. I think he was hoping we'd get to know each other."

"For what? I'm not interested in anyone who would align themselves with this man."

"I see what you mean about needing to tame him a bit first," she says, then bites her lip as she eye fucks me.

I give a smug grin as I roll my shoulders back and settle into my stance. I don't know what game my father is playing, but I'll help him out and put an end to that shit right now.

"Helen? That's your name, right? Allow me to tell you something he hasn't."

"I'm a motherfucker. I don't respect shit that doesn't respect me. Even then, I'mma tell it to kiss my fucking ass. So tell me, you're gonna tame who?" I tilt my head to the side with my final words and grin with all my teeth.

I nearly burst into laughter as Collen gasps and Helen turns bright red as she clenches imaginary pearls. I turn to my father and lift a brow.

"Oh, where are my manners? Father, do you know my dear friend, Miss Zoe Gataki?"

"I heard you've been keeping suspicious antiquated company. Word of advice, my son. A snake will keep you comfortable in order to size you up before it strikes. Don't find yourself in the belly of the snake lying beside you to gauge your growth," he says as he eyes Zoe with disgust.

"Mm, sounds like you just described yourself. Glad I got away," I retort.

"It's been good to see you, Ulysses, as always. Joshua, I see some important people we should say hello to."

I toss my father a salute with my middle finger. Colleen sputters beside him, causing me to laugh as we walk off. I might be in a slightly better mood.

CHAPTER THIRTY-FOUR

Shattered

Kelex

A month later...

"Yo, pass me one of those," Pit says, pointing to one of the weed cupcakes Tak ordered in.

Deacon hands one over. Pit peels the wrapper back and goes to take a bite. He's so drunk and focused on the treat he doesn't see Skittles creeping up behind him.

"Ha, ha, ha." She releases that crazy laugh of hers after she shoves his face into the cupcake.

I force a grin and try to get into the moment. In truth, I should be a million other places than here—pretending life isn't falling apart all around me. My grandfather is still requesting my presence in Crete, my father has been trying to get me to meet with him, and Mary is hanging on by half a breath at this point.

I've exhausted all medical options. I've spared no expense to make sure I could do everything in my power to help them. Even expanding my empire faster and greater than I ever thought I could. Whatever happens, those kids will want for nothing.

But a mom.

I grimace at the thought. Coming out this weekend with the assholes was supposed to help me clear my head. However, it's been hours and my thoughts couldn't be more scattered.

"Get over here," Pit growls as he wipes icing off his face.

Skittles stands straight from where she's doubled over laughing and takes off running. They've both had a few drinks, so she manages to dodge him while tripping and still getting away.

I shake my head. I get ready to go back into the beach house we're renting when Skittles's phone rings on the table. I look at the screen and freeze.

It's been three years since I've spoken to Shawna. I've done my best to push her from my mind. However, her name is scrolling across the screen and the most gorgeous face I've ever seen stares back at me from the device.

Skittles is standing behind the gorgeous woman, with her chin on top of her head, while they both smile wide at the camera. I know the picture is recent because Skittles has on the sunglasses I gifted her a few weeks ago. My God, Shawna is so fucking pretty.

Anger and frustration fill me. I still don't know what happened between us. She blocked me and that was it. The only reason I left it alone is because I figured it was for the best.

So much has been going on since. I've become that other person. Mary and the kids are the only reason I've been able to push him back down in the last month.

Something deep inside tells me this is my chance to find out what went wrong. I get the sense I will forever regret not taking this call. Swiftly, I look around at the guys as they laugh and watch Pit chase after Skittles, tripping and fumbling drunkenly along the way.

Seeing no one's paying me any attention, I snatch up the phone quickly and turn to rush into the house. I jog up to my room for the night and shut the door behind me.

I stop to think about what I'm about to do for a split second. Just long enough to remind me how much I've missed her. Hitting the green button, I then bring the phone to my ear.

"Hello, Shawna."

She gasps before silence follows. A million asshole things cross my mind to say, but I swallow them down. I've never wanted to be that guy to her.

"What's wrong, baby girl? You don't miss me?"

"Hey, Kelex," she whispers.

"Nah-uh. You know better. That's not my name to you. What's up, gorgeous?"

"Is my cousin there?"

"She is, but I thought we could talk for a sec. At least long enough for you to tell me what happened between us."

"I wanted something you didn't."

"Says who?"

"Your actions."

"What actions?"

"Listen, this is a bad time for this. Please, I need to speak to Ven."

"What's wrong? Are you in some kind of trouble?"

"Listen, things have changed. I shouldn't be talking to you. Danny wouldn't like it."

I snort. "Who the fuck is Danny?"

"Um, he's my boyfriend," she says quietly.

"Danny who?"

"Danny Clavier. You wouldn't know him."

My mind races to place the name. When it clicks, my head nearly explodes. A sweet girl like Shawna has no business with a piece of shit like that.

"Baby girl. I know I told you you could do better than me, so why would you end up with someone the total opposite of better? Wait, is he the reason you sound off?"

"I can't really get into that much at the moment," she whispers.

"Listen to me. I don't know what you think I did, but... I'm still here for you. If you ever need me and I do mean ever, call. I'm still your person."

"Okay, I have to go."

"Shawna."

"Yeah?"

"I miss you. I'll be waiting."

She hangs up without another word. I stand with my jaw working. I don't like Danny Clavier. He's one of Julio Marquis's lap boys.

Blake has been keeping an eye on them both. Marquis has been smart in keeping his wife away from the elite circuit, so I haven't had access to her. However, Marquis's right hand, Javier, has allowed his bigmouthed wife to mingle happily and freely.

When she speaks of Danny, it makes my gums itch. Now that I know Shawna is the sad girlfriend who he cheats on, I'm sick to my stomach. The violent rage that rolls through me is all-consuming.

I dial the first person who pops into my head. I wanted to stay far away from Marquis and his races, but I know someone who's been salivating to get into them.

"Hello, ass face. What happened? Skittles had enough of your pretty ass. You want me to come pick you up?"

"Fuck you."

"Not interested, but I'd nail that new assistant you have. She's hot as fuck."

"Listen, do you still want into those races?"

"Marquis's? Hell yeah."

"I'll front you the cash. I just need some information."

"You do know Marquis is going to want to meet you? He'll know I don't have that type of cash to carry a team. The guy is thorough."

"Sitting down with him doesn't look good for your good-boy image. Hell, carrying my team could fall back on you. That's why I didn't ask you for the money. I'll find another way."

"You don't have to ask. Set it up," I say and hang up.

If that motherfucker has hurt her, I'm going to let out Mr. Hyde. He'll wish his mother were never born or that the bitch swallowed.

Baby, what have you gotten yourself into?

My phone rings, bringing me out of my thoughts. I look down and my entire body runs cold. I close my eyes and put the phone to my ear.

The sobbing is all I need to hear. I can't breathe. Words won't even come.

"What am I going to do, bro? What am I supposed to do? *Mama, Mama,* don't do this to us. What am I gonna do? She's gone, J. She's gone."

Shawna

"Can I get your car?" the valet asks as I stand outside the restaurant.

"No, thank you," I murmur.

I fight back tears as I hold my phone in my hands and stare down at it. Joshua was the last person I was expecting to answer Ven's phone tonight. Hearing his voice only made tonight hurt more.

Danny was going to hit me right in front of Javier and his wife in the middle of the restaurant. If Javier wouldn't have stopped him, I know he would have. This is it. I've reached my limit.

I need out before it's too late. I called Ven to talk about my options because I'm tired of this. I think I really wanted to say it out loud so it would click in my brain that this isn't for me. I want out.

I have so much regret now. I had no right to be angry with Joshua. We weren't in a relationship. If I could turn back time, I would.

I never would have gotten so upset. I would've waited to talk to him and asked what was going on before completely shutting him out of my life. I miss him too.

"Get your ass in the fucking car," Danny growls as he comes out of the restaurant and his car is pulled up.

I should have said something to Joshua, but what could he have done? Danny and the men he's tied up with could hurt him and then I really would never forgive myself.

CHAPTER THIRTY-FIVE

Broken

Shawna

Two months later...

"You've really been smelling yourself in the last two months. That fucking mouth," Danny snarls.

I lie balled up in the corner, trying not to shake, not to breathe, not to move. If I don't move, he'll stop. I need him to stop.

"You think you're so smart," he continues. "You always have to run your fucking mouth. Didn't I tell you not to speak?

"I don't give a fuck who asked you a question. Now look. Your smart mouth got you what you wanted. Always trying to make me look stupid."

I want to sob out a laugh. I don't have to try to make him look stupid. He does that all on his own.

I don't respond. He doesn't want me to. He never wants me to. I'm to take this beating and shut the fuck up.

I must be crazy. I've seen it in his eyes before. I know he wanted to do this so many times before, but I never thought he had the balls. He caught me off guard, and now here I am, unable to help myself.

"You know what, Shawna? One of these days, you're going to make me hurt you."

It takes everything in me not to laugh and cry at the same time. My eye is swollen shut. He's hurt me plenty enough. Usually, it's not with his hands but with his words.

Subtle comments started to become brittle blows to my self-esteem. It wasn't like this when we started. Danny was a different man.

Charming, a sweet talker, he said all the right things a shy girl like me needed to hear. I didn't know I was getting involved with the devil. A hazel-eyed devil with a smile that could fool a saint.

"Why do you stay with him?" My best friend Skylar's words ring in my head.

Skylar. I miss her. She never understood that it was not that simple. You don't walk away from Danny Clavier if he doesn't want you to walk away.

Leaving a man like him comes at a price. It always has a cost. However, tonight, I'm coming to realize staying with him comes with a price I'm no longer willing to pay.

Please, God. If you let me make it through tonight, I'll leave. I'll never come back. No matter what I have to do. I'll leave.

I brace for the kick coming for me, even as I silently plead for my life. Tears leak down my cheeks as the force of the blow knocks the wind from me. A gasp leaves my lips.

"Please," I plead, my lips chapped, busted, and sore.

"Shut up," he bellows. "Shut the fuck up. I treat your fat ass like a fucking queen, and you can't keep your mouth shut when I tell you."

I'm going to die tonight. As I lie in my torn dress, blood comes from my right ear, and at least two ribs are broken. I feel it in my bones. He's going to kill me.

God, please.

He goes to grab me by my hair, but his phone rings, halting his motion. He glares down at me as he pulls it from his pocket. Thank God, that phone is going to save my life.

"What?" he snarls at whoever is on the other end of the call. "No, that's not what I told you to do... What the fuck? No, he'll kill us both if I don't take care of it... Don't do anything. I'm on my way... No, asshat, I'm flying out."

Danny turns to head for the closet. I don't move an inch as he packs a bag and then returns to the bedroom. He heads for the door without a second glance at me.

He pauses at the door, his back still to me. "Clean yourself up. We have a lot to talk about when I get back. Don't even think about leaving, Shawna," he says coldly. "I own you."

Again, I don't reply. I remain still, not wanting to give him any reason to turn back around and come for me. I wait until he's out of the room and I hear the downstairs door close.

That's when I allow the sob I've been holding in to rip free. It echoes around the room and wrecks my already sore and battered body. I try to move for the first time and my lips tremble as I bite down from the pain that sears through me.

Yet, I don't stop moving. I try to breathe through my bleeding nose. It's not broken, but it hurts like hell.

My mind tries to tell me not to do what I intend to. Danny has warned me repeatedly that he'll kill me if I leave him. He promised to embarrass me and my family if I ever even thought about it.

Fuck that. Enough.

I drag my body to my phone that lies on the floor where I dropped it. When I reach it, the screen is broken. I'm still able to unlock it and call the one person I know who will do everything she can to get me out of this.

It's in her blood to get shit done and take care of her family. I can always count on Mayven.

"Hey, Shawnnie," she sings as she answers my call.

I can't help sobbing as I try to speak through my broken jaw. "I… I need you to get me out of here," I slur. "I need your help. Please."

"Shawna, what's going on? Why do you sound like that? Answer your FaceTime."

I don't want her to see me like this, but I answer. I need to get out of here. This is no time to be embarrassed by my circumstances. I inhale the best I can and open the camera on my phone. That's when I hear his footsteps on the stairs.

Oh God, no. Please no.

Kelex

"Why do I feel like you are running from me?" Pappoús says as he comes out to the gardens and finds me staring up at the moon.

"It's not you I'm running from. It's my thoughts," I scoff.

"Talk to me, *Tzósoua.*"

I blink away the tears blurring my eyes. I was able to stop child services from splitting the kids up, but they haven't granted me guardianship yet. I have to go through the process, which is why I shouldn't be here—I need to be home.

"All the money I have and I can't keep a simple fucking promise," I say to my grandfather.

"What have you promised?"

"I should've spoken up. I should've told her I'd take them. She could have given me rights before she…"

"Take who, *Tzósoua?* Rights?"

"The children. Pappoús, I shouldn't be here. I should be home with them. I don't think I can do this for you. I'm sorry, but I can't."

I wipe my nose and tell him everything from the beginning. I tell him why I don't think I'm a fit for what he wants and needs.

"You are a better man than you give yourself credit for. I knew you had something holding you back. Not even Blake was sure what. Out of respect for your life, I didn't allow him to dig.

"This, *Tzósoua*, this makes me proud. For now, they are safe, yes?"

"Yeah, but that's not official. I need the judge to grant me custody, but first, we have to get the social worker's approval and a few other things have to fall into place," I reply.

"Then this is what I want of you. Go through the process, and you will get them. However, I think it's time you started to date. I give you one year to find someone and get engaged."

My eyes widen. This isn't what I thought he would say. I sit dumbstruck for more than a minute.

"What?"

"Find a woman. We bury this life. You have your family. This is what I want for you.

"Vander and Bridge Lake will give me what they owe some other way. When was the last time you fell in love, *Tzósoua*?"

"I... I don't know that I have."

"*Um*, if this is what you believe, I think this is the best way I can help you. You will get the children. This, I am sure of.

"Your task will be to show me you deserve to be responsible for them. Sure, you have built an empire of your own, but have you learned to be a man? Show me you have. Find someone to carry this burden with, and I will give Vander to someone else."

"To Pit?"

"Or Anthony." He shrugs. "I've been watching. I know I have options. I like my original plan, but other arrangements can be made."

"Why won't you give it to *Baba*?"

"Um," he grunts. "You want this life with the children, yes?"

"Yeah."

"Then don't ask me about your father. Just know you are a better man."

"What about him? This is going to piss him off. I don't need him causing problems."

"Let him. Who cares? I will deal with Ulysses."

"I'll kill him if he takes this from me," I seethe.

"*Tzósoua*, this cannot happen. You need to pick one or the other. You are in, or you are out. You can't do things of our world from outside of our world. Do you understand this?"

I tighten my fists. Do I understand? I do, but that doesn't mean I have to like it. The last three years have awakened something in me.

I've allowed that darkness to roam free. However, for True and the girls, I'll push it back down. They need me more.

"I understand."

"If you change your mind for any reason, know that you are my first choice, but once you accept, there is no going back." He pats my cheek and stands. "Take some time to clear your head. Think about what I am offering. Then go home. You have an assignment to finish."

"Pappoús?"

"*Tzósoua.*"

I honestly can't say I'm angry with him for not handing this over to me. I know him and I understand he's asking me to work for my freedom. I can respect and honor that.

With every breath I have, I'll do all I can to make sure those kids are safe and happy. If I have to fake a relationship, I will. I have no clue where to start but one thing I do know… we're saving each other.

"I love you. Thanks."

"You are welcome. *Ki egó se agapó, Tzósoua.*"

CHAPTER THIRTY-SIX

Don't Give Up

Kelex

"You're packing?" Helios asks as he enters my room.

"Yeah, time to head back. You're welcome to come with me, but that's up to you. I'm not going into the family business."

"I think I will still come with you. I like America. You have become an honorable man. I enjoy working for you. It doesn't have to be in this business." He holds a hand up and circles a finger in the air.

I shrug. "We leave in the morning."

"Okay. I will be ready."

I turn back to my packing. I can't hide out here forever. It's time I go home.

I have a lot I need to get in order. I've been trying to think of someone I could ask to pose as my girlfriend until I get the green light from my grandfather to walk away. I'd give them some cash. All they have to do is keep the act up until the deal is done.

Shawna comes to mind. She would have been perfect. If she weren't dating that piece of shit, I would have asked.

"I still might," I scoff to myself.

As I have the thought, my phone rings. I check the time and then I grin when I see it's Jeff calling. This might be the universe telling me I'm on the right track.

"What's up?" I answer the phone.

"Tonight was the first night. The meet and greet. He wasn't there," he replies.

"He'll show up. I'm sure of it."

"Why the interest in him? Marquis is the real connection."

"This isn't about connections. I want eyes on Clavier. I have a feeling I'm going to need to see him about a friend."

I think of the deal I've made with Pappoús. I'm going to have to tread lightly if I do have to handle Clavier. Either way, I want to have eyes on him.

"Would that friend be Skittles?"

"No, what makes you ask that?"

"She asked to join my team."

"And you're just telling me this?" I seethe.

He sucks his teeth. "I called Pit to come get her, although I could have used her. This thing would have been a shoo-in."

"I thought you had a team that could handle it."

"They're okay. What I really could use is my old buddy behind the wheel. What do you say, come back and drive with me? You and I could take this whole thing."

I nearly burst into laughter. One, I never get behind the wheel. Two, Jeff is quite delusional about his driving skills. He's never won a race against me and has never placed in a race with or without me driving as competition.

He actually kind of sucks. After a while, he started to come up with all kinds of excuses for his cars. Then it got to the point where he'd just walk off and disappear before the race would start like he did the night of the crash. It's how I knew he wouldn't be back before the flags were dropped.

"I'll pass. Hey, you think you could set me up with someone?"

"Was that a joke?"

"No, you know what? Never mind."

"Are you feeling all right?"

I roll my eyes and toss down the jeans in my hands. Taking a seat on the bed, I fall back and look up at the ceiling. I want to get this all over with. Once the kids are under my roof permanently, I can breathe again.

"I'm fine. Pappoús made me a deal. I need to find someone and keep my nose clean."

"Keep your nose clean? What kind of deal?"

"He'll let me walk. I want to adopt my neighbors. If I can find someone to date and stay out of bullshit, Pappoús will back me and release me from my obligations."

"What the fuck? You're thirty-three. Why would you want to adopt three kids? What the fuck is going on with you?"

"Like I said, never mind."

"You're going to give it all up for those kids, aren't you?"

"I'm not giving anything up. Look, don't worry about it. Thanks for the call. I'll see you when I get back."

I hang up, wondering why I said so much. I'm just so anxious to make this work. Zoe is the one I need to talk to. Even Achilles and his fuck buddy would be more help.

Shawna

I lie in this bed, unable to move for fear of the pain that will radiate through my body with the slightest motion. I'm riddled with pain, but it's the shame that hurts the most. I've gotten Mayven in the middle of all of this.

For three years, Danny has weaponized my mother's and uncle's careers against me to keep me in check. My family shouldn't have to suffer because I was young, naive, and just plain stupid. I regret the night I met him. I wish it never happened.

I was so hurt after that call to Joshua. Joshua... I gasp as I think of him. It feels like I'm dying, but his voice has been the one thing to keep me hanging on.

Never let anything cause you to give up, Shawna. No matter what's going on, never give up. Remember, I'm here waiting to talk to you and help you figure it out. There's no need to give up.

I grab hold of his promise. I'd give anything to talk to him and hear his voice. I know one thing for sure, when I get out of here, I'm going to pull myself together. This will never happen to me again. No victims.

Aunt Celeste was right. You can't allow people to walk all over you and make you a victim. That's what I've done with Danny.

I thought I could share so much with him the way I did with Joshua. I learned I was so wrong. It was never safe to trust Danny. I know that now.

By the time I figured out the truth, it was too late. Tears burn my eyes and my jaw pulses with an ache that's blinding. I try to inhale deeply and my ribs holler in protest.

Don't give up, Shawna. Never give up. You're going to survive this.

As I lie here encouraging myself, Joshua's last words to me come to my head and I cling tightly to them.

I'm still here for you. If you ever need me and I do mean ever, call. I'm still your person... I miss you. I'll be waiting.

God, I hope he is waiting. I'm going to need my person. I miss him so much.

I won't give up, Joshua. I promise.

I know Ven is on her way. I just have to make it until she gets here. God, I hope I haven't done something that will get her hurt.

I did it again, didn't mean to. I'm so sorry, Ven.

CHAPTER THIRTY-SEVEN

Torn

Kelex

"*Fuck*," I roar and throw my glass across the room.

I feel like I'm going crazy. I stand in my office with my chest heaving. Dragging a hand through my hair, I move to the window and stare out, but my vision is blurred, causing me to see nothing.

"Josh, I know this looks bad, but I'm here to help. Tell me what happened," Zoe says calmly.

"It's all falling apart before I can even get a grasp on it," I say to my view of Vander. I turn from the window and look Zoe in the eyes. "Someone called the caseworker on some bullshit. She dropped in for a home visit," I seethe.

"Okay, I've walked through the house. You did a great job setting it up for the children."

I blow out a breath. "Fucking Jeff. I have no idea what he was thinking. He showed up at my place to throw a welcome home party for me. That's all fine and well, but I have three children under my roof."

Not to mention, I've been home for three days. He could've easily picked the bar or another night. Heck, I partied enough the other night for Leo's celebration, to be honest.

"Hold on. I need you to tell me exactly what happened. This doesn't sound like what the caseworker or Achilles said."

"The nanny knows Achilles. He's been helping out while I've been away. The kids know him.

"Apparently, once the kids were in bed, Jeff arrived with the party. Achilles said he tried to tell him it wasn't a good time, but Jeff insisted it was all right with me.

"I had spoken to him. He'd asked if he could introduce me to a friend of his. I said sure. I did not tell him to have a party in my place," I bite out.

"Okay, good. This wasn't your party. Essentially, he forced his way in and brought people into your home. The alcohol and nude women were all brought into the house without your knowledge, right?"

"My driver pulled into the garage at the same time the caseworker pulled up. I came in through the garage door to the kitchen while she entered through the front door. We saw that shit unfolding at the same exact time.

"And the children were all upstairs?"

"Yeah. You have to fix this."

"I'm going to take care of this, Josh. The caseworker may have put in her recommendation, but you still get a chance to refute the report. Lucky for us, the psychologist and ad litem are in favor of the children remaining with you.

"They will have to stay at Maria's house for a bit, but the foundation is better than them going into the system. All isn't lost. I'm more concerned with Roger Davis.

"While I'll get you guardianship, he's going to block the adoption. Any idea why he's so adamantly against you when he clearly doesn't want them?"

"You don't want the answer to that."

She looks me over for a moment as if she can see into my thoughts. I don't give a fuck about Roger. As long as I get the kids back in my home, I'll deal with the rest as it comes.

"Blake told me about your grandfather's offer."

"That's the last thing I can focus on right now."

"I can help if you want. I know a lot of nice young women who would love to get to know you."

"Or I could take someone's wife," I tease and grin.

"There is that. You'd have your pick there." She laughs, but I see she's not going to let this go.

I thought coming home would allow me to follow through for those kids. All that has happened since I've been back has been anger and frustration. I feel like I'm letting everyone down. The kids, Skittles, Shawna. Skittles's words from the other night come back to me.

I asked. I asked the one person who can help me. Pit is helping in the only way any of you can. I'm doing the best I can, Josh, I really am.

I work my jaw and clench my fists. She would believe that. I've never shown Skittles who I am, so she has a problem and she doesn't know to come to me.

Shawna.

"I see your thoughts. This isn't big enough for you to walk away from what you've always wanted. I can fix the situation with the kids. As for your pappoús's request, I think it's good for you," Zoe says, interrupting my thoughts.

"You're smart, attractive, and successful. You shouldn't have a problem finding someone. I know what your godfather and grandfather want for you, but this city will demand your soul. You have an out, take it," she adds.

"I couldn't find a genuine relationship before I became a freak show and I had all those things."

"How are you a freak show?"

I begin to unbutton my shirt and move across the room. Zoe lifts a brow at me. I stop before her and flip my shirttails back.

"Look at me. My leg is worse."

"You're kidding, right?"

"I don't see the joke."

"Josh, I've seen your leg. Honey, you can hardly see the damaged skin. It isn't as consistent in color in the trauma locations, but the textural differences are hardly noticeable.

"I can honestly tell you this is all in your head at this point. Besides, someone could set your *nonos* on fire tonight and I would still love that man and would remain by his side. Love sees no scars. The right person will fall for your heart," she says.

"And I'm to find that person in a year? When he said it, it sounded so easy. I lost myself in the hope he gave me.

"Now as reality hits, Zo, I haven't dated in years. I'm not always the nicest person to be around. What if he's asked me to do this because he knows I'll fail?"

"Sometimes, we allow our fear to talk us out of things. I think this is what's happening. For eight years, I've spent a lot of time getting to know you.

"You're a very charming young man. The mayor's daughter is a lovely young woman. Have you thought about her?"

"Mayven Jennings is taken. It's only a matter of time before those two catch on."

I shake my head as I think of Pit and Skittles. They are inevitable. I'm still surprised they haven't caught on. It's coming.

"Well, as you've said, you have a year. A lot can happen in a year. A few parties, some blind dates, we'll get this done."

I work to get my shirt buttoned back up. I'm not going to worry about this now. Push comes to shove. I'll find someone to pay. For now, I need to focus on getting the kids back.

My thoughts go to Skittles's words. Shawna is in some type of trouble. One call, and I can find out what's going on, but that will drag me back in.

You need to pick one or the other. You are in, or you are out. You can't do things of our world from outside of our world.

Pappoús was right. This is my chance. I can't step back in. Not to mention, if I don't know what the problem is, I can't do anything about it.

Yeah, I need to keep my head on straight for those who need and want my help. What looks like a simple fix will actually come back to burn me in the end.

"Believe me. If you go back on this deal now without trying, all your gains will be temporary."

I snort. "When did you become a mind reader?"

"Eight years is a long time to learn someone and you have a lot of your *Tou nonoú* mannerisms."

I release my first genuine laugh in months. When I was a boy, I wanted to be just like Blake, even as I watched him from a distance. When it comes to the life, he's the other side of the coin.

Shawna

"Shawna, are you going to send me your list?" Joshua said into the phone. His deep, sexy voice washed over me like warm honey.

"Um, I was going to text it tonight."

"There's no time like the present, baby girl."

"Okay. Fine, I'm sending it now. What do you want this for anyway?"

He asked me months ago for a list of my dream locations to visit and see through my lens. I've taken my time to really think about it. A shoot bucket list is something personal.

"Got it," he says with a smile in his voice. "I now have a guide to your dreams. We're going to make them happen."

"What?"

"When you want something, it's good to write it down and make a plan. This is the start of our plan."

"Are you serious?"

"Yeah. It's also a guide to making you happy. I do have selfish motives."

"When will you send me your list?"

"I'm simple. No list needed. If you're happy, I'm happy."

"Joshua?"

"Don't. Whatever you're going to say, hold on to it until you meet me."

I come awake with a groan. It dawns on me that a foot to my hip is what woke me. I turn slowly to find Danny glaring down at me.

"Get your ass up. We need to move," he snarls.

I hold back from giving him the finger. I can't help wondering if I'd be here if I were more like Ven or Lex. Tears burn the backs of my eyes, but I'm not going to allow them to fall. They're the one thing I have control over.

I sit up silently, that dream still clinging to my thoughts. I remember that day when we talked on the phone. I was so excited to get to meet Joshua in person. We'd grown so close, or so I thought.

As my face and ribs pulse with pain, I lock onto the dream and will myself to be strong. I'm going to get out of here and I'll live out my dreams. I'm not giving up.

"That mouth isn't so fucking smart with a broken jaw, is it?" Danny snorts.

I roll my eyes and give him the finger. He laughs and turns to walk back out of the room. I hate him so much.

CHAPTER THIRTY-EIGHT

Just Missed

Kelex

Six months later…

I stand in my bedroom getting ready for Skittles's birthday party at Fuck Off. Pit and Skittles have finally pulled it together. I'm happy for them.

I pull on a light-blue linen shirt and button it up, leaving the top three buttons open. Rolling the sleeves up, I then put a belt on my white slacks. I take a glance in the mirror before turning and going to sit in the accent chair to slip on my light-blue loafers.

I've just gotten my shoes on when my door creaks open. Vernice sticks her little head into the room, bringing a smile to my lips. That reminds me, I'll have to bring in that braider. Her cornbraids are starting to look fuzzy.

"Hey, you. I thought I put you down for the night," I say.

She pushes her way in and pads over in her footie pajamas. I lift her onto my lap and notice right away something isn't right. She settles in and tucks into my side.

"My tummy hurts," she whispers.

"*Um*, I wonder if those cookies you stole out of the pantry have anything to do with that."

I'll be honest. I couldn't even be mad at her when I found her cheeks full of chocolate chip cookies. Her little brown eyes sparkled with mischief as she tried to hide two more behind her back. I was going to place a lock on the door, but she may have learned her lesson.

I palm her forehead and kiss the top of her head. With a quick glance at my watch, I know I'm not going to make the party in time. True and Cat knocked out on the couch watching a movie the last time I saw them.

I could ask Rosy to get Vernice back to sleep for me, but I want to make sure she's okay before I leave. I stand and lift her in my arms to carry her back to her room. She places her head on my shoulder and wraps her arms around my neck.

"I'll get you back to bed and rub your tummy for you. How does that sound?"

"I love you, J," she whispers.

"I love you too, princess. No more cookies without asking first though, okay?"

"Okay, promise."

Yeah, her stomach must really hurt. I rub her back as I enter her room. This place is fit for a little princess, with pinks and purples all over the place. There are more toys in here than a toy store and I'd do it all over again if she wanted.

I place her back in the huge bed and pull the covers over her. She pats the space beside her with her little hand. Kicking off my shoes, I settle beside her and rub her little belly.

She reaches to cup my face and smiles up at me. I've known this little girl since she was a baby. Sometimes I think our bond is deeper because I'm the only father figure she's ever truly known.

"You're going outside?" she says.

"I'm going to see Miss Ven."

She gasps and her eyes light up. Skittles volunteers at Maria's house. The kids there love her. I've had guardianship of the kids for four months now, but they still spend a lot of time at the foundation for after-school programs and counseling.

"Can you tell her I said hi?"

"Of course."

"She's"—she yawns—"so pretty."

I know she's talking about Skittles, but Shawna's face pops into my head. I'm looking forward to meeting her tonight. I've been so focused on getting the kids back. I'm not sure what happened with her.

Jeff only told me Skittles resolved the issue and the races were done. He didn't win my money back and he doesn't think the races will happen again. I vowed not to stick my nose into that.

I'm out and if I can find someone in the next six months, then I'll be out for good. A grin comes to my lips as Vernice's little snores greet my ears. I kiss her forehead and go to leave quietly.

"There you are. Let's go," Jeff calls from below as I walk across the catwalk.

"Shh," I say, placing my finger over my lips.

The last thing I need is for him to wake everyone in the house. Rosy is here, but I'm sure she's gone to bed. If this wasn't for Skittles, I probably wouldn't bother.

Lies. You want to see Shawna.

***

I sit in the back of my car, staring at Fuck Off. I came with Jeff, but I called Helios to come pick me up. Overhearing Deacon saying that Tak had left to take Shawna up to the cabin soured my mood.

Once Skittles pulled me aside to tell me what all has been going on, I knew I couldn't stay and pretend to be fine. If Pit hadn't confirmed I wouldn't find Danny anywhere still breathing, I'd have his ass hanging from the top of the tallest building in Vander, ready to drop him.

I failed her. I wasn't there. That motherfucker put his hands on her. I'll never forgive myself for this.

I nod at Rosy's reply to my text. The kids are all safe and in bed. Decision made, I text Helios the cabin's address and settle back in my seat for the ride.

"Head to that address," I say to him.

Shawna

Tak was nice enough to allow me to stop at my place to pack a few things. After, he brought me to this gorgeous place. Ven was right. It does have a sense of peace about it.

After showering and changing into a pair of sweat shorts and a tank top, I pad barefoot down to the kitchen and, to my surprise, find food as if someone stocked this place for a visit.

I've been a bit jumpy lately, so I startle when the doorbell rings. I chew slowly on the piece of bread I just put into my mouth. My heart races as I move to the door, searching with my gaze for a weapon on the way.

I grab the glass figurine from the table under the mirror close to the door. When I get to the door, I tighten my grasp on the figurine and tug the front door open. I freeze in my tracks as my gaze is met by a blue-gray one.

"Joshua?" I breathe.

"Hey, gorgeous."

His voice is like a long hug I didn't know I needed. I turn back to the table and put the figurine down. When I turn back, he's at the threshold, watching me.

I don't feel alarmed. I'm just surprised to see him. In all honesty, I want to fling myself into his arms. However, I don't know where we stand. It's been so long and we've never been face to face.

"What are you doing here?" My words come out slurred because I'm still adjusting to having the wires out.

He knits his brows as he closes the distance between us. Tears well in my eyes, causing me to turn away from him. He cups my throat with his large hand, gently turning my face back to him with his thumb.

I go to pull away but freeze as I see his eyes mist up. His nostrils flare and his lower lip is trapped between his teeth and he's almost vibrating with… rage?

The look in his eyes is so intense. I freeze as I hold my breath. He places his forehead to mine.

I finally release a breath and reach to grasp his shirt. When he pulls back, he has that same intense look as he searches my face. He swallows hard, causing me to do the same.

"I'm so sorry, baby. I'm sorry I wasn't there to protect you," he chokes out.

"Oh my God, Josh. This wasn't your fault. And you were there. Because of you, I survived. It was your words I held on to," I say.

He tugs me into him, wrapping his arms around me. I fit right into him. His warm scent embraces me, causing me to inhale deeply.

My nipples tighten and my mouth waters. I can't believe I'm in his arms. I wrap my arms around him and clench the back of his shirt.

I don't know where it comes from, but the dams break and I release the tears I've been holding on to for months, three years even. I can't stop them. Joshua holds me tighter and rocks me gently.

"It's okay. I'm here now. I'm here."

Deep down, I know he's telling the truth. I've never felt safer in my life. It takes me a moment to process it all.

"Thanks, Joshua. I needed my person."

CHAPTER THIRTY-NINE

Need a Friend

Shawna

I can't believe I'm sitting out on the deck with Kelex, the model, sipping wine out of two mugs like old friends. After allowing me to cry myself out, he went in search of blankets for us to sit outdoors.

I found the bottle of wine and settled on the mugs after searching for glasses, to no avail. By the time he returned and pointed out where the glasses were, I had poured my mug. He only shrugged with that sexy grin and took the other mug to join me.

"I normally don't do this, but I need to know."

"Ut-oh," I say over the rim of my mug. "What don't you do?"

"I don't chase people. If you don't want to fuck with me, I don't fuck with you. I'm never interested in why and I'm not going to try to figure it out. It's their loss."

I drop my gaze into my cup. I already know what's coming next. My heart sinks. I wanted to forget all about this.

"What happened? Why'd you block me?" he asks.

I put down my mug and start to fidget with my blanket. I can't look at him as I say this. It hurts too much.

"I called you that night when you said you were coming to the race. A woman answered your phone. I felt stupid. Like you were leading me on.

"My feelings were hurt. I thought... I thought we had... I don't know," I whisper.

When I do peek up at him, he looks totally confused. I bite my lip and hold my breath. He puts his mug down and moves to the edge of his seat.

Reaching for my chin, he lifts my head. "I have no idea what you're talking about. We did have something. I don't know who you could have spoken to, but they weren't... I've only been yours.

"My life is complicated, but I've wanted to meet you since I heard your voice for the first time." He pauses and searches my face with his gaze. "You're more beautiful than I imagined. Can we start over?"

"I'm searching for something. I need to find myself again. Right now, I really need a friend. Is that okay?"

He drops his hand and nods. "Of course. I'm not the same person and I can see you've changed. Let's get to know each other. Like I said, I'm here. I'm not going anywhere."

"Thanks, Joshua. This really means a lot to me."

He kisses the tip of my nose. "Anytime."

CHAPTER FORTY

How I See You

Kelex

"Cat, if True isn't going, I don't think you should. He said those kids aren't cool," I say into the phone.

I woke feeling recharged this morning. As much as I wanted to kiss Shawna last night, I could see she wasn't ready. I racked my brain all night trying to think of who could've answered my phone that night.

I've been through so much since then I couldn't tell you what was going on at that time. My life is so different now. Now I have three kids, including a teenager and a preteen. A preteen who's hell-bent on driving me insane this morning.

"Come on, Josh, *please*," Cat whines into the phone.

"Cat, I said no."

"Ugh, you used to be so cool."

"You used to be little and cute. What happened?" I snap back.

She scoffs into the phone. "No, you didn't. Next time someone stops us and asks if we're okay because you have three little Black kids with you, I'm telling them you took us," she taunts.

I frown. I hate when that shit happens. People are crazy. However, I know she would never.

"I could drop you with a nice family you feel is more suitable now and save you the trouble, brat."

"You wouldn't dare," she gasps.

I chuckle. "I wouldn't because I love you. That's why you can't go. I'd lose it if something happened to you. Maybe next time, if the crowd is better."

"Fine. How long are you going to be away this time? Why didn't you take us with you?"

"It was short notice. I'll be a few days, but you text me if you need me. Be good for Rosy. Achilles said he's going to stop by to hang with you guys."

"I wish he didn't move away. I miss just going next door."

"I think he misses you guys too. Listen, I need to go, sweetheart. Stay out of trouble and no fighting with your brother."

"Okay, fine."

She hangs up and I turn my attention to Shawna, who just walked into the kitchen looking drop-dead gorgeous. No makeup, simple jeans and a T-shirt, but you would think she walked in dressed for a ball the way my heart is racing.

"You made me breakfast?" she asks with a smile.

"Yeah, come sit with me."

"I didn't think you'd be here this morning."

"I told you, I'm here for you. I'm taking a few days from work and the nanny has the kids."

Her brows shoot up into her hairline. Oh, yeah, I haven't gotten around to how much my life has changed. I guess I should come on out with it.

"Remember True and Cat?" I say as I place the plate of eggs and bacon in front of her.

"Yeah, the little sweethearts who lived up the block from you."

"Their mother passed away—"

"Oh, my God. I'm so sorry to hear that. Are they okay?"

"They have their good days and their bad. I'm their guardian. They live with me. Them and their little sister. It's an adjustment, but I wouldn't have it any other way."

"You are like the most awesome guy on the planet," she says and beams at me.

"Not sure if I'd go that far."

"How old are they now?"

"Fourteen, twelve, and six." I shrug.

"Six? You have a baby and two teens. Are you still traveling and things?"

"Yeah, they come with me most of the time. I have a team of tutors and nannies."

"Ven never told me any of that."

I blush a little. "Because she doesn't know. She's met them at the foundation, but I didn't have full custody then. She's had a lot going on in the last eight months. I didn't want to worry her with this."

She looks down at the table. "Oh."

I want to kick myself. Of course, Skittles had a lot going on. She's been dealing with a psycho kidnapping her cousin. The same cousin sitting across from me.

"I want to take them to Greece. You should come with us," I say to change the subject.

"I'd like to meet them. Maybe I could help out sometime."

"We'll make that happen. They'll love you."

She looks up and smiles at me. I can't stop staring at her. It's like I'm looking at Skittles, but there are subtle things that make Shawna unique.

Her lips are a bit fuller and so damn sexy. Her eyes, though sad, are a pretty brown and her hair frames her face in thick dark layers. She's a bit lighter than Skittles but still has a gorgeous brown complexion.

And that body, she has to be fucking kidding me with questioning how hot she is. She's tall, thick, and curvy, yet I still tower over her. I noticed that last night as I held her in the foyer.

"What?" she asks as I can't look away.

"I still can't get over how beautiful you are," I murmur.

She ducks her head and combs her hair forward. I noticed last night that she kept doing the same thing. As if trying to cover where her jaw was broken.

I've also noticed the slur in her speech at times. I've never wanted to kill someone so much in my life. Had I known what was going on, I would've broken my deal with Pappoús, no question.

"You used to hang with models and movie stars. I don't compare to them."

"Does your mouth taste like ass? Because you're talking shit," I deadpan.

She looks at me with wide eyes, then bursts into laughter. Her face lights up with it. I can't help but release my own smile.

"I thought Ven was the only one who could deliver like that with a straight face. You have her beat."

"I don't know how you don't see it. Do you look in the mirror?"

"Not really. Do you?"

I freeze and narrow my eyes at her. I've missed her calling me on my shit. Zoe was right. I still haven't come to grips with things in my head. A look in the mirror isn't the same for me.

I avoid it until my scars are covered. That's when my confidence returns. It's something I haven't addressed because I haven't needed to.

I wink at Shawna. "We have something to work on together."

"What's that?"

"Seeing the truth. I can't wait for you to see you like I see you."

"And you? Will you see what I see?"

"Someday." I wink again.

It's not a lie. I'm going to try to move forward because I think I've found the woman I want to take home to Pappoús. That means I'm going to have to put myself out there.

She's the one I want to see my scars. Let's hope she can love me through them.

Shawna

"I miss you too, princess," Joshua says, smiling into his phone.

"How long will you be gone?" The voice of a little girl comes through the speaker.

Joshua chuckles. "It will only be a few more sleeps. You can be a big girl until then for me, can't you?"

"I guess so. Can you bring me something?"

"Sure, I'll bring you something back. What should I bring you?"

"Um, I could always use a new princess dress. Oh, and a tiara. *Please*."

He laughs again. The smile on his face is breathtaking. I should be making our ice cream sundaes, but I can't tear my attention away from this amazing man.

"I've got you. Now be good for me and go to sleep."

"Okay, love you."

"Love you too, princess."

Oh my God, this man is really a father to those kids. I've witnessed him filling the role all day. First, he made an appointment for someone to go see the girls to wash and braid their hair, then he made one for a barber to visit the boy for a cut.

I couldn't help but smile as he went over the lessons for next week with the tutors. He wanted to make sure the kids were on track and being challenged. If I thought he was hot before, this man has now exceeded all my fantasies.

"Need some help?" he asks as he walks over to where I'm drooling and making our ice cream.

"Nope, I'm all done."

He lifts a brow and bites his lip. "Two? I thought we would share."

"I wasn't sure if you wanted to."

"Come on. Let's pick up where we left off."

I follow him back to the couch. We've been sort of playing twenty-one questions, trying to fill in some gaps. I'm not going to lie. The chemistry is there. The way he's been looking at me all day has kept my heart racing.

With each question, I'm starting to feel more and more connected to him. I love how at ease he makes me feel.

"Okay, so where were we?" I say as we settle in our seats.

"I think it was my turn to answer."

"Cool. Um, I have a question I've been dying to ask," I reply.

"Come on, let me have it," he says with a sexy groan.

"I always figured you dyed your hair for a gig. You haven't modeled in years. Why not go back to your natural color?"

His eyes grow distant for a moment. I bite my lip. Not sure I should've asked. Dropping my gaze to my bowl, I berate myself for being so stupid.

"I don't know, I think it's my way of holding on to the past. You know? When I went blond, things started to take off. I was in high demand.

"I guess I never let go of that. Or at least, I haven't wanted to. I knew where I was headed at that time in my life. I had a plan and I was sticking to it. Then it was all gone," he finishes, and his gaze grows distant again.

"I can't believe you got more work as a blond. You're gorgeous with your dark hair. I loved when it was long. That angel campaign was my all-time favorite. I knew then you were a star," I babble on before I can stop myself.

"Oh really? So you like the fauxhawk," he says and shoots me a smile. "I'll have to keep that in mind."

"My turn. What do you want to know?"

He puts his ice cream down and shifts on the couch until he has one knee bent, with his foot planted into the couch and his other long leg draped over the side. He pats the space between his legs for me to come to him.

My nipples tighten and my pulse picks up. It's like the air between us starts to sizzle. I take a calming breath and place my bowl beside his.

Slowly, I move to sit in the space where he pats. He wraps his arms around my shoulders as I settle into the space. I reach for his arms, but he takes my hands and laces our fingers together.

It feels like coming home. I melt right into him. He plays with my fingers as he rests his chin on the top of my head. My heart nearly leaps from my chest when he presses a kiss to the spot.

"How are you? Really. Is there anything I can do to make it better?"

I close my eyes, wanting to pinch myself to see if I'm dreaming. However, when he moves to kiss my neck and bury his face there, I know I'm not. This is real.

"I'm... getting there, I guess. I just wanted some time to think. I've been babied most of my life and that allowed me to act like one.

"I was so out of my depths with Danny. It wasn't what I wanted, and when I figured that out, it was too late. I get angry with myself because I could've fought him off, but he surprised me and I never got the chance.

"I don't want to be that person again. I don't want to be caught off guard, I don't want to accept less than I deserve, I don't want to be with someone just so I'm with someone," I say aloud, all my bottled-up feelings.

"You're doing more than you know, by the way," I add.

He tips my head back and looks into my eyes. I hold my breath, silently pleading for him to kiss me. Gently, he presses his lips to mine.

I close my eyes and savor the feeling. The kiss travels through my entire body. He's so gentle as he nips at my lips and caresses the side of my face.

He pulls away, causing me to open my eyes again. I stare into his blue grays and feel like I've found all my answers, yet I blurt out a question because I don't know what else to do.

"You really won't get behind the wheel of a car?" I ask after he made mention of the fact earlier.

"Nope. Haven't since that night."

"Do you think you ever will again?"

"There would have to be some extreme circumstances. Even then, I don't think I could bring myself to do it. So no. Not likely to happen in this lifetime."

"I admire that you know yourself so well."

"Keep talking. We can learn who you are together."

"But I'd rather you kiss me," I whisper shyly.

He leans in and takes my lips again. I forget all my questions and get lost in his soft, tender kisses. Now this is what making out should feel like.

I feel wanted and cherished, yet I don't feel any pressure as if he'll wait as long as I need. I like that.

CHAPTER FORTY-ONE

You're Not Ready

Shawna

Joshua has spent the last three days with me. While we've made out a lot, he's never pushed for more. I think that's making me respect and want him more.

It's crazy how we can sit in silence and still have this amazing connection. Like now, he's answering some work emails and I'm browsing on my phone. I'm thinking about taking an assignment to travel.

Something has come up in Italy and another position has opened in Spain. I'm keeping my options open. It could be time I stayed put. Lord knows that would make my mother happy.

"You hungry?" Josh asks, pulling my attention from my phone.

I open my mouth to say no, but my stomach speaks up for me. I guess I hadn't noticed how low I was on fuel. I smile and shrug instead.

"I guess."

He moves to stand over me and bends to peck my lips and then my nose. "Come on. We can cook together. Helios did some shopping for me," he says and gives me a gentle tug from my seat.

"You know he can stay here. There are plenty of rooms."

"He's good at the rental. I think he has a friend who's been coming in from Vander," he says with a smile.

Helios is handsome with his dark hair and hazel eyes. I might have a thing for Greek men. Josh pulls me in and places his forehead to mine.

Butterflies fill my belly. Nope, not Greek men, just this man.

"I like having you to myself," he breathes against my lips, then captures them in a searing kiss.

I'm a bit dazed when he releases me and laces his fingers with mine to lead me to the kitchen. We work together to get the things we need to make dinner.

"Lamb burgers and hand-cut fries sound good?"

"Yeah, perfect."

"Good, I know a recipe from one of the restaurants."

"How's business going? Are you still facing a learning curve?"

"Not really. I've been a lot more driven in the last few years. I couldn't afford *not* to know. It was learn or burn. Failing wasn't an option.

"I covered most of Mary's medical expenses. There was a lot even while she was in remission. True needed braces and it was easier to pull them from public school and place them in Vander Academy," he says.

"So you've been taking care of them since before they lost their mom?"

"Yeah, True asked for my help and I stepped in to do anything I could."

"What happened to their dad? I remember you saying he was a real jerk."

A dark look comes over his face. I almost take a step back. He shakes his head and cracks his knuckles at his sides.

"He doesn't give a shit about anyone but himself. I haven't adopted them yet because of him. He won't release his rights."

"That's sad. From what I've overheard, they really care about you, and you, them."

"Some people aren't worth the air they breathe," he says darkly. "Come, help me chop this up."

I move to where he is with the onions and herbs. He pulls me in front of him with my back to his front. Placing a kiss on my neck, he then guides my hand to chop.

I try not to close my eyes to bask in the feel and scent of him. Instead, I focus and breathe him in. His strength fills me and it's like with each chop, I'm healing.

Kelex

"Enough of this sad-ass music," I say and stand from the table where we've just finished dinner.

I allowed her to pick what we'd listen to, but I'm not about to sit here listening to her breakup playlist. I want to see her smile reach her eyes. It's happened a few times in the past few days, but not enough.

I move over to the dock and switch out her phone for mine. Sean Paul's "Like Glue" fills the house and I turn to pull her from her seat. Wrapping my arms around her waist, I start to sway her to the music.

She's shy at first, looking anywhere but at me. I spin her, bringing her thick, legging-covered ass into me. I bite my lip as I watch her start to wind her hips.

Pushing her forward, I then take a tight hold of her waist and grind into her. I grow hard instantly. She keeps dancing, looking back over her shoulder at me.

I'm trying my best to be careful with her when all I want is to grab hold of those thick locks and tug her back to me. I push those thoughts aside and focus on that smile that comes to her lips.

She places her hands on her knees and gets into it. For the next four minutes, we get lost in the music. I placed my phone on shuffle, so the next song to come on is "I Know What You Want" by Busta Rhymes and Mariah Carey.

She straightens and looks back over her shoulder at me. I spin her to face me and pull her in close. This time I do push my hand into the back of her hair and tug her head back.

I hover my lips over hers as I breathe her in and keep us swaying to the song. She's so fucking sexy. My restraint breaks and I take her lips.

I kiss her deeper than I have before. Before I can stop myself, I have a tight grasp on her ass. She moans into my mouth, pulling a deep-as-fuck groan from me.

I slide my hand into her leggings and knead her ass. I've never wanted anyone the way I want her. I know she feels how hard she has me.

When she sucks my bottom lip into her mouth, I lose all thought. She has her hands fisted in my hair. I slip my fingers into her from behind and find her soaked. Slowly, I slip my wet fingers from her sex and rub at her forbidden hole.

"Joshua," she gasps into my mouth. "Wait, I have something to tell you."

I pull away and look down into her eyes. The desire staring back at me makes my chest swell. This gorgeous woman wants me. It's been so long since I've wanted to be looked at like this.

Then she drops her head and breaks the connection. "I'm still a virgin," she says in almost a whisper.

Fire fills my veins. It takes everything in me not to lay her bare right here and now. However, as the words fully penetrate, I hear the words she doesn't say.

"You're not ready," I say and nod as I back off.

"Thank you."

"You don't have to thank me, baby. I'm always going to give you what you need. And when you're ready, I'll give you what you want and need."

CHAPTER FORTY-TWO

Not with Me

Shawna

I wake with a smile on my face. Last night was amazing. I think I'm falling for Joshua. The way he looked into my eyes to say I wasn't ready and he'd wait, I felt seen and understood.

It's not that I didn't want to. I just feel like I need to take my time. I don't want to jump into something and find myself lost again.

I squeal before I can stop myself. Covering my mouth, I pull myself together and throw the covers back to get out of bed and shower. I can't wait to spend the day with him.

I'm out of the shower and dressed when I go down to see if he's having breakfast. The house seems so still. As if no one is here with me.

The doorbell rings and I furrow my brow. My heart sinks. I know he's gone. I go to answer the door when the bell rings for the second time. When I open the door, there are two guys with roses in their arms.

"Shawna Norris?"

"Yes, that's me."

"Let's get these in and then we can work on the rest," he says to his partner.

I move out of the way to allow them in. They make about five trips. Soon the front of the house is filled with roses.

"Sign here, please," the guy says, holding out a clipboard.

I sign, then take the card he holds out to me. I close the door behind them and open the card to read it.

I'm sorry I couldn't wait to say goodbye. I had to get back to Vander. Something came up. I miss you already. I'll call you when I get a moment.

Josh

I try not to listen to the voice telling me he left because I didn't want to sleep with him. That would be a Danny move. Joshua cuddled on the couch with me and made me feel safe after our dance. I have no reason to doubt him.

Kelex

"Is this a joke? Does he think this will make me accept his invitation? How the fuck did this even happen?" I bellow at Zoe and Achilles while we're in my home office.

"It's one of our smaller entities. When you asked me to find a way to fund the film studio for the kids without giving anyone controlling interests in their PI, I decided to sell off shares.

"He purchased through a trust, so it wasn't a red flag at first. Jeff happened to call for a favor. When he came over to talk, he saw the name on a folder and informed me it was one of your father's," Achilles says.

"And you didn't pick up on this?" I say to Zoe.

"No, this isn't one I know of."

"Bro, this is a new one. I only know about it because he used the same one to fuck me over in a deal not too long ago," Jeff says.

"Thanks for bringing this to my attention, man."

"No problem," Jeff replies. "What about the ball? Are you going to go?"

"I think you should. It couldn't hurt," Zoe says.

"Why now? What the fuck is his problem? There's no way he could know about the deal," I seethe.

"We can't be sure of that. I've been wondering who made that call to the caseworker, now this. A lot has been going on in Crete. You still have an aunt left there. Her and her husband are still upset about your aunt and cousins."

"Why the fuck did he spare her?"

"She wasn't in on the attempts. They are still his children. That couldn't have been easy to execute."

I roll my eyes. He should've killed the bitch. If there's still someone in Greece who's feeding my father information, I want them gone.

"Dump the company. Sell off the rest," I bite out.

"What?" Achilles says in surprise.

"I said dump it."

"Josh, I said it was one of our smaller ones, but it's still worth about fifty million."

"So it's no loss. Dump it."

Jeff releases a low whistle. I ignore him. My mind is racing to figure out my father's angle. Why buy shares in one of my companies? What's his endgame?

"Are you for real?"

I stare at Achilles with a blank expression. I normally don't have to repeat myself. We've worked well together in the past.

"I don't wait for my enemies to take a win. Once you show me you want war, I show no mercy. This man left me for dead because he couldn't control me.

"Dump the company and sell it for half of what it's worth so he loses his fucking shirt," I growl.

"Isn't that going to bring you down bad?" Jeff asks.

"No, we're not going to lose any sleep," Achilles says.

"Must be nice," Jeff mutters.

"Back to the ball. It might be a good idea," Zoe says.

I frown. "Come, walk with me. I'll hear you out."

Zoe and I leave my office and walk through the house. The kids are in the living room watching TV. Once I'm done with all of this, I plan to join them for the day.

I walk out into the backyard and stand by the pool with Zoe. I turn to her and lift my head. She smiles and crosses her hands in front of her.

"Hear me out. It's a masquerade ball. He's throwing the event for the Jennings. You'll be surrounded by friends if you attend. In addition, this will be a room full of eligible women. Your clock is ticking."

I think her words over. Skittles and Pit will probably attend because of the governor-elect. I'm sure Zoe and Blake will make an appearance. Jeff sounds like he's interested in being in the room.

I pause in thought. "Does that mean Monica Norris will be there?"

"Of course, she's looking like a shoo-in as senator. This is an informal congratulations to them both. Marvin and Monica."

"I'll go."

Zoe lifts a brow. "What did I just miss?"

"I won't need to meet anyone. I've found someone and she'll be with the guests of honor."

Her brows knit in thought. I smile and wait. She then widens her eyes in realization.

"The councilwoman's daughter?"

I bite my lip and nod. "It's her or nothing. I'm not allowing her in that man's presence without me."

"Careful, Joshua. If he knows who she is and he does know about the deal, this is risky."

"I'd fucking kill him."

"And lose it all for sure."

"If something happened to her, it would all be for nothing anyway."

"Now I want to meet her."

"Good, I have a favor to ask."

CHAPTER FORTY-THREE

Demons

Shawna

"Mom, I said I'll be there. I'm getting ready to head out now."

"Shawna, I haven't seen you in weeks. Do you even have a mask or gown?"

"Mom, I have a ton of gowns in my closet. I'll come up with something for the mask."

"What's going on with you, Shawna? I've been by your place several times and you're never home. Your mailbox is full. It looks like you haven't been there in at least a week."

"Mommy, I'm away taking some me time. I promise I'll be there tonight. If you let me off the phone, I'll be able to be there with my hair and makeup done," I huff.

"Fine, your father and I will talk to you tonight."

I roll my eyes. How did I ever get away from her when I was dating Danny? The woman is impossible.

I shake my head as I end the call and grab my bag. I'm going to miss this place, but I don't think I can hide here much longer. It's time I face life again. Enough moping.

I open the door to wait outside for my ride. When I look up there's a beautiful woman standing there with her hand lifted toward the bell. I think I know her from somewhere.

"Hi, can I help you?"

"Hello, you must be Shawna. I'm Zoe Gataki. Joshua asked me to come and help you get ready for your date tonight."

I haven't seen Joshua in a week. We talked and texted, but we didn't talk about a date. I have no idea what she's talking about.

"I'm sorry. I can't go on a date tonight. I'll be at the masquerade ball in Bridge Lake. My mother is being honored."

"I know about the ball, love. Joshua would like you to be his plus-one."

"Oh," I say as my cheeks heat.

"Come along. I have a team waiting for us. You're going to make an exquisite date. He was right. You are tall and beautiful."

"Thank you."

My face is flaming now. I bite my lip and step out to lock up and follow her. My mind goes to Ven. I'm not sure how she will feel about me dating her friend.

We climb into the back of the car and settle into the seats. I stare into my lap, trying to figure out what this is all about. I decide to pull out my phone and text Joshua to ask.

Me: *Hey. Um, a date?*

Josh: *Ah, she has arrived.*

Josh: *Yes. A date. We'll see how well you know me.*

Josh: *Find me if you can.*

I can't help but smile. This is kind of romantic. I was dreading this event until now.

"Tell me more about yourself, Shawna," Zoe says beside me.

***

I look in the mirror and don't recognize myself. The woman staring back at me is breathtaking. I would never have picked this dress or thought to do this with my hair.

My face has a glow and glitters from my makeup. It goes perfectly with the pale-blue dress. The gown has a deep *V* and is sheer with stones that shimmer in the light, creating an illusion of being the only thing covering my intimate parts.

The mermaid style flows to the floor and pools at my feet and into a small train, making my height and curves look defined and alluring. The sequined shoes beneath are just as magnificent. Yet they probably won't be seen, shame.

"You're perfection. We tall women have to stick together. Our height makes us a display for gowns like these. You will turn every head in attendance tonight," Zoe says as she comes to stand beside me.

I smile at her through the mirror as she runs her hand down my sleek ponytail. She looks fabulous in the pink satin Roman-style gown she has on. Her peach-colored mask sets off her brown skin.

"Here, this will complete the look," she says, holding out a box to me.

I take the box as I start to feel giddy inside. When I open it, I find a pale-blue-and-silver mask covered in Swarovski crystals. It's a half mask and will only cover half my face.

"Here. Allow me. It has combs and will attach to your hair."

"Thank you," I say as she takes the mask from my hand and puts it in place for me.

When I look back into the mirror, my eyes mist up. I look like a real princess. My brown eyes sparkle from behind the gorgeous mask. I look like a work of art.

"Wow, you're a vision. Joshua won't remember to breathe. *Prinkípissa tou óntos.*"

"Huh?"

She waves a hand. "Forgive me. I'm just happy for my young friend."

Kelex

So far, so good. I haven't run into my father and that suits me just fine. I glance at my watch again, as I have a million times already. It's been two hours since I arrived and still no sign of Zoe or Shawna.

Although Shawna's parents have arrived. Growing impatient, I look around for them to see if I can get answers. That's when she comes into view.

I know it's her right away. The height, the curves, there's no mistaking her. However, I also notice exactly what I want for her. She has this air about her.

A confidence that exudes from her pores. It's like an aura around her and this is only from my view from behind. My feet are moving before I can tell them to.

I approach as her parents are called away for a photo op. Stopping behind her, I place a hand on her waist and lean into her ear.

"You take my breath away," I whisper.

She turns in my hold and looks into my eyes. I tighten my arm around her and tug her close. She searches my gaze beneath the mask, then smiles.

"I thought I was supposed to find you."

"I couldn't stay away. I got tired of waiting. Dance with me."

She nods and I lead her to the dance floor. It's not lost on me that the orchestra is playing a string version of Imagine Dragons' "Demons." This song couldn't say what I'm thinking more.

Instead of telling her this, I dance us around the room and hold her gaze for her to see it all herself. My heart swells when I note her smile has met her eyes. I squeeze her hand and bring her fingers to my lips.

"Your mask. It's the other half of mine," she says.

"Of course, like two peas in a pod. We fit, and so should our masks."

Her smile grows and she shakes her head as she smiles. I take the opportunity to dip her and kiss her neck. She smells delicious.

I would love nothing more than to devour her, but I know she's not ready. Her cheeks glow as I bring her back up.

"It's like I'm in a fairy tale. This ball is so beautiful. I feel like a princess, thank you."

"What if I'm the dark prince, baby? Do you still want me?"

"Yes," she answers almost instantly. "I think I'm ready to be more than friends. This feels right."

I grin. "You know you just fucked up, right?"

"Huh?"

"I'm never letting you go. You're mine now."

She laughs a gorgeous laugh and shrugs. "I'm okay with that."

"Good, because I don't think I could breathe if you weren't."

She smiles and places her head against my shoulder. I kiss the top of her head and smile with contentment. For now, my demons are at rest.

CHAPTER FORTY-FOUR

Help Me Understand

Kelex

Present...

"I remember that night. I didn't think you two met. Shawna, you were so happy and you wouldn't tell me why. Then you left before we had time to talk.

"Kelex, I never figured out if you were even there. Not until you told me you were the next day. You both left before dinner was served," Skittles says, breaking into my thoughts as I share them.

"But I still don't get it. Help me understand. Why did you both feel you couldn't tell me?"

"At first, I wasn't sure where things were going. Then you were busy with the wedding and then it was the house and the move. I didn't want to take away from any of that.

"I was supposed to tell you… I was going to tell you. It just never felt like the right time. This isn't on him. It was me. I think I was scared to tell the truth because it didn't feel real.

"I was living in a fantasy. The trips, the way Josh made me feel, the bond with the children. I guess I was scared if I said something out loud, it would all disappear," Shawna murmurs.

"It's not all her fault. I had people in my ear and other things going on. We thought it best to keep you out of it."

Skittles gasps and looks at Pit. "You knew." Her lips tremble as she looks at her husband.

He holds his hands up. "I just found out they were married yesterday before Kelex arrived. That was the text I got.

"Remember, I know Vander and Bridge Lake's business because of him." He tilts his head toward Blake.

"He's right. What I don't want him to know, he doesn't know," Blake says.

Pit turns to him slowly and narrows his gaze. Blake may be telling the truth, but I know for sure there isn't much he keeps from Pit. He was going to take over for me, after all.

Now, I'm not so sure. I may have blown that in one act of rage. Only time will tell.

"Maybe it's time we call it a night. We've been at it all day and Pit still hasn't found the answer we're looking for. Emotions are high and I'm beat, so I know you all are," Deacon says.

"He's right," Luke says.

"I know this feels like we were keeping this all from you, but we never intended to hurt you. Things happened so fast and so much had been going on. We wanted to protect you," Shawna tries again.

"I agree with Deacon and Luke. Let's call it a night. Shawna, you and Skittles can talk this out in private. I don't think having us all here to hover will do any good," Pit says.

Skittles shakes her head. "No, Shawna and Kelex need to go home to those babies. I can wait."

"Are you sure?" I say, staring at her.

She lifts her gaze and gives me a weak smile. I return the smile, knowing she'll be okay. This is a lot to process, and she's been more emotional than usual.

"Yeah, I'm sure. You know how I feel, but you... you and I are going to have a talk tonight," she says to Pit. "Good night, everyone. Get home safe."

My smile widens. This is the other reason I know this will all work out. The reason I wanted Shawna to be honest with her.

Thank you. I mouth.

She gives a shrug of her shoulders and gets up to leave. Pit looks at me and frowns. We both knew this day was coming. I don't envy him.

Shawna

We walk into the house and I'm so tired I could pass out right here and now. My emotions are everywhere. Josh was right. I shouldn't have held the truth back.

"You guys hungry?" True asks as he comes into the foyer.

"I could eat," Josh says. He then looks at me. "You?"

I shrug. I'm not particularly hungry, but I miss the kids. I want to spend some time with them before I call it a night.

Vernice comes running to wrap her arms around Josh's waist. He rubs a hand over her hair and rubs her back with his other hand. "Hey, princess."

"I missed you guys," she says, moving to wrap me in her embrace.

"Did you get your lessons done?"

"Oh, we going there already? Um, J, did your phone just ring? I think you guys need to handle some business or something. Yeah, look at that. Good to see you. Later."

I wrap my arms around her to keep her from taking off. Vernice is the cutest, smartest, most charismatic ten-year-old I know. I love this little girl so much and her bond with Josh is so heartwarming.

"Come on, I'll help you before we have dinner. I don't see why you always put things off when it only takes you a second to do them. You can't keep this up at your new school," Josh says.

Vernice pouts. "Why am I going to that place anyway? I like traveling with you."

"Now that Shawna will be here, you guys don't have to tag along with me all the time. You can stay home in your own beds and start having some type of normalcy."

"J, there's nothing normal about anyone around here. I'm ten and I've seen more places than most of the adults at that school. I'm more cultured, have better comprehension, and I'm sure I know more. It's a waste of time and money if you ask me."

"Whatever, mini brat. Let's go. I'm exhausted and hungry."

"See, let's forget all about my lessons. We need to get you fed and to bed."

Josh laughs. "Right, lessons. Now."

"Ugh," she growls, rolls her eyes, and walks away.

Josh turns to me and pulls me into him to kiss me. I lean my head on his shoulder and close my eyes. I try my best not to allow the world out there to come inside our bubble.

"It's going to be fine. Ven will forgive us. I think it's all a shock that it's been happening under her nose, but I know her. She's happy for us."

"I hope you're right. I love our life. I don't want it to be a problem."

"Baby, it's not. And if there is someone who has a problem with it, they'll have to deal with me."

"I love you."

"I love you more. Remember the first time I told you?"

"Yeah, Bali was a game changer. I'll never forget it."

"Me either. Greatest high of my life."

I smile and tighten my arms around him. That day made my heart race for so many reasons.

CHAPTER FORTY-FIVE

It'll Come

Pit

Skittles has been giving me the silent treatment all the way home. I probably should've stayed at the bar to close. I frown.

I'm not about to run from this. I've told her before there are some things I'm not going to involve her in. This time, I didn't feel it was necessary for her to know what was going on with Kelex.

We step into the house, and she heads to the bedroom, still not saying a word to me. I follow her because we're having this out tonight. I need my head clear if I'm going to pull the pieces we need.

She steps into the closet and starts to strip out of her clothes. I lean against the closet opening and watch her. Pulling her shirt over her head after placing her shoes on the shelf, she then pulls off her pants.

I roll my eyes. I'm not putting up with this. I know her stubborn ass will keep this going for days. I'm not having it. Not this time.

"Yo, you going to ignore me all night?" I say as I walk up behind her and wrap my arms around her waist.

I lean down and kiss the top of her head. She melts into me for a moment before she stiffens and turns to face me. Seeing the look in her eyes, I lean in to peck her lips.

"Why wouldn't you tell me they were seeing each other?"

"Mayven, I honestly didn't know for sure. I suspected, but I couldn't come out and tell you when it got this serious. Besides, if I told you what I thought, you would have gotten in the middle.

"What's that supposed to mean?"

"Baby, you love people so hard, you throw yourself at them. If you knew, you wouldn't have given them space to figure it out. Kelex had a lot of demons he was dealing with, but I could tell he cared about her.

"Shawna was so hurt behind that other bullshit. I knew she deserved this chance. Think about it, if you knew, what would you have done?"

She looks up at me with tears in her eyes. "How long did you know?"

"I figured something was going on around the wedding. That act, like they didn't know each other, was bullshit to me."

"So the cabin and all that was an act too?"

"I think they were having a fight. I really don't know for sure. Baby, it was speculation. I had nothing concrete to tell you. When they finish telling me what happened, I'll be learning the truth right along with everyone else. Blake really doesn't tell me much about Kelex."

"And why is that?"

"Because he's his godfather. And so you know. Kelex and Ox are cousins."

She buries her forehead in my chest. "What the fuck?"

"Baby, when this is all over, you're not going to see any of us the same way."

"Lex was right. I think my feelings are only hurt because I've been ignoring the truth. I've always known there was something different about you and Josh from everyone else.

"I also know Daddy and Aunt Monica aren't as clean as they lead everyone to believe. There are so many secrets in this place. Heck, I have a scar because the man you sent was someone I saw with my dad stitching up one of his guards."

"Really?"

"Yeah, it was clear Daddy didn't want whatever happened to get out. It was like a year before we met."

"Your father has a lot of skeletons. Let's leave those where they are. We have enough going on. Are we good?"

"Yeah, for now. I'm sure I'll be mad again tomorrow."

"Well, come here. Let me make it up to you in advance."

I lift her into my arms and turn to place her on the island in the center of her closet. She looks at me with a small smile as she reaches for the remote mounted on the side of the table and turns on the sound system.

Coco Jones's "ICU" fills the closet. I give a grin and nod. I've got it from here. Stepping between her legs, I then dip my head to take her lips.

I deepen the kiss and groan into her mouth. It killed me to see how hurt she was today. I want to erase all of that. With each sip from her lips, I do my best to.

She laces her fingers in my hair and holds me to her as I devour her mouth. Our tongues dance as I set the mood. The song demands I go slow and sensual.

"Will," she moans as I move my lips to her neck with slow, open-mouthed kisses.

Grasping her waist, I tilt her back until she lies back for me. Her chest heaves as I move down her body with more kisses. When I get to her core, I kiss the top of her mound before covering her with my mouth over her panties.

Wanting to taste her fully, I peel the fabric down her legs and toss it over my shoulder. Grasping the tops of her thighs, I pull her closer to the edge and feather kisses from her knee down the inside of her thigh until I get to the apex of her legs and pull the flesh into my mouth.

I suck as she writhes beneath me. She calls out my name and claws her nails through my scalp. I turn to blow on her sweet pussy before I pull her soaked lips into my mouth.

"Oh my God," she breathes. "So good. I love when you do it like that."

I grin and take things up a notch. Still fully clothed in jeans and a T-shirt, I devour her core like a man on a mission. My tongue action has her lifting off the tabletop while holding my hair tight like reins.

I eat her out until she's breathless. Reaching for her hands, I lace my fingers with hers. She rains all down my face and squeezes her thighs around my head.

I chuckle and pull free to tear my shirt over my head. Tossing it, I move to release my jeans and shove them down. I wipe my mouth, then hook my arms around her legs and guide my way into her tight pussy.

"Yes," she cries out.

I feed her a few inches at first, driving us both crazy. She starts to get really wet and I can't hold back anymore. I thrust in with deep strokes, then back off before starting it all over again.

"I'm always going to do what's best for you," I grind out through my teeth.

"I know, baby, I know," she cries.

"Good, don't forget it."

"Just keep fucking, Will. I'm about to come again."

I chuckle menacingly and proceed to give her what she wants. Crisis avoided. We'll live to fight again tomorrow.

Ox

I pull into the garage of our home and park. Lex seems to be lost in thought. She has been for a while.

I go to cut the truck off, but she covers my hand and halts me from shutting it all the way off. I turn to look at her and lift a brow. She has a little smile on her lips.

"What are you doing?" I ask.

"Come here. Scarlett has AJ. I need you."

Then she reaches for the radio and changes the song. Coco Jones's "ICU" comes on and she gets out and climbs into the back seat. I grin at her and turn to push my way out of the truck to get in the back with her.

Once inside, I close the door behind me and look her in the eyes. She looks worried and stressed out.

"You know this is going to work out, right? You don't have to worry. Pit will get to the bottom of it. It will come and I'll handle it."

"I love that you trust him so much. This is all a lot. I just want to take a moment to be. You know?

"I feel like since I've been back, my life has been consumed by all of this. Jenny, shootings, finding out my dad wasn't who I thought, and Zander. Come here, Ant. Let's be us."

"No, baby, you come here," I say and crook my finger for her to come to me.

A grin comes to my face as she climbs into my lap and cups my face. I grasp the back of her head and deepen the kiss, tugging her lip into my mouth. She smiles into the kiss as she starts to unbutton my shirt.

Reaching for her thighs, I push her skirt up and palm her ass. She begins to grind her hot pussy in my lap. I move my lips to her chin and nip it.

I drag my lips down her throat as I knead her ass. Lex reaches between us and unfastens my pants. I lift my ass as she tries to shove them down. She gets them down my legs and moves to peel her panties from under her skirt.

"Turn around," I say as I stroke myself.

Once her back is facing me, with my free hand, I grab her waist and guide her to slide down my length. I slide into her already wet pussy, her walls sucking me right in. I groan and throw my head back.

She starts to ride me. I tug her back against my chest and reach around her to rub her heat as she moans and finds purchase by planting her feet into the seat. She's fully open to me now.

I begin to thrust up into her as the song playing demands a sensual slow pace from us—one I'm not sure we'll be able to keep for long. I tug her face back as she twists around and looks over her shoulder. Taking her lips, I devour her, getting lost in the feel of her lips and tight sex.

When she starts to grind on me, I groan into her mouth and grasp her hips. I'm not going to last long like this. She feels too good and this is hot as fuck.

"Fuck, baby. I'm going to come. Keep riding me just like that," I grunt.

"I got you, Ant. You feel so good. It's so hard. *Damn.*"

I cup her throat and keep thrusting from beneath. All the world outside of us is forgotten. In this moment, it is her, me, and the air we breathe as one.

When I do spill into her, it's done knowing she's my forever. I've never loved anyone the way I love her and I never plan to try.

I get Josh. I understand him completely. I may not know all that happened, but I get loving someone so much you protect them with all you have.

Kelex

I lean in the doorjamb of my bedroom, watching my wife and kids. I don't know what I did to get this life. It seems like I've done more to fuck it up than keep it, but here they are.

True is sprawled across the foot of the bed as Vernice is tucked into Shawna's side, and Cat is on the other side, with her head resting on Shawna's arm. I find them like this a lot. They gravitate to her like I've become accustomed to doing.

Their laughter fills the room and my heart swells. Their happiness is what I live for. I hope Mary is happy with how I'm raising her kids.

True turns to find me watching them. He smiles and gets up. "Come on, guys. Let's go to bed."

"Aw, not yet," Vernice pleads.

"Stop stalling. I'll read your bedtime story," he says.

"Okay, fine, but you do the voices, or I'm going on bedtime strike."

I laugh to myself and shake my head. Cat kisses Shawna on the cheek and heads out. I tug her into my embrace and kiss her forehead before she passes me to exit the room.

"Good night," I murmur.

"Night, J."

Vernice runs over to hug me. "Night, J. We're having breakfast together in the morning.

"Aye, aye, captain. I'll be down waiting for you," I reply. "Good night, princess."

She beams up at me as I palm the top of her head and wink down at her. After another hug, she heads out of the room.

"We balling this weekend?" True asks.

"Yeah, I'll make time."

He leans in to whisper. "I'm cool with one of our midnight games. Those sandwiches and bowls of ice cream after be hitting."

I laugh. "A midnight game it is. You got any new music for me?"

"Yeah, I've got a ton. I'm getting better at using our studio. You think Lex might come over now that the news put our family on blast?"

I rub the back of my neck in thought. "I'll ask, but there's a lot going on."

"No worries, I understand. Just thought I'd ask."

"I've got you. I'll ask as soon as things cool down."

"Thanks, bro. Good night."

"Good night."

He gives me a pound and a one-arm hug before following after his sisters and closing the door behind him.

I tug off my shirt as I move toward the bed. I showered after dinner but had to go down to make a few calls. Now looking at my wife, all I want is to get lost in her.

"Everything okay?" she asks.

"Yeah, what's all this?"

She shrugs. "I'm finishing the photo album. I thought this way Ven would understand what I mean about living in a fantasy."

I lock eyes with her. "But you do know this is all real?"

"Yeah, I get that."

She looks away shyly and begins to put the pictures and album away. I watch her as she gets up and puts it all in the accent chair. The peach satin pajama set she has on captures my attention.

It makes her brown skin glow. I lick my lips, wanting to taste that skin. I shove my shorts down as she climbs back into bed.

"I don't know. You don't sound too convinced to me," I say and climb up the foot of the bed until I'm hovering over her to take her sweet lips in a searing kiss.

She pushes her hands into my hair and holds me to her. I grasp her throat and drink from her mouth. Taking my time, I nip and suck at her lips.

"Josh," she whimpers as I grab one of her breasts over her pajama top.

I move to release the buttons as I bury my face in her neck and suck on her flesh. She reaches for the remote and turns on the music. I grin.

I don't blame her. She knows she's not going to be able to keep quiet. Coco Jones's "ICU" fills the room.

The song sets the pace for me to make love to her. Challenge accepted. I move down her body leisurely, nipping and sucking as I go. When I peel her shorts from her body, I find a lacy pair of panties beneath. With a grin, I bring the shorts to my nose and inhale as I look her in the eyes.

She bites her lip and smiles as she looks back at me. I toss the shorts and flip her onto her front, lifting her hips in the air. She arches her back like a cat for me, causing me to groan as my gaze falls to her fat pussy.

The panties are a thong that her ass is swallowing up. Leaning in, I take a bite of her ass as I keep her pinned down with one hand in the center of her back.

"Josh," she moans.

I grin and move to the other cheek to bite it too. Looking up, I find her eyes on me. I run my finger beneath the string of her thong, finding it wet when I get to the thin fabric at her crotch.

The way she's watching me as I tear the thong to shreds has me so hard. Pushing two fingers into her, I begin to stroke myself. Then I dive in to take her core, feasting on her center until she's calling my name.

"Yes, Josh, yes."

My face is soaked when I pull back and turn her onto her back once again. I climb her body and settle between her legs.

Grasping a handful of her hair and tugging her head back as I dive in to kiss her neck while slowly thrusting inside her.

"Ah," she gasps.

I'm gentle with her, knowing this is our third time today. Instead of allowing me to be soft, she grabs my ass and rocks her hips, begging with her body for more.

I capture her lips in a deep kiss and give her what she wants. Her walls clench around me as I dive deep. She throws her head back into the pillow and cries out.

Gliding my hands down her sides, I then find her hands and lace our fingers together. She tightens her hold on mine. I drag our entwined hands up over her head and pin them in place.

I move my lips to her ear and groan. "I love you."

"Please," she says breathlessly.

She doesn't have to ask more than once. I take us both to the ecstasy she's pleading for. Just when I think it can't get any better, she pushes me onto my back and proves me wrong.

"I love you, Josh," she moans as she rides me and squeezes her breasts.

I stare up at her and my heart jumps into my throat. Remembering our talk before our world was turned upside down, I grab her waist and lock eyes with her. We nod at each other in understanding and give ourselves over to the moment.

"Yes," we breathe in unison as she tightens around me. I spill into her heat in the same breath.

No matter what comes our way, I will forever be owned by this woman. She's touched a place in my soul. All it took was hearing her voice for the first time and I knew.

CHAPTER FORTY-SIX

How It Changed

Kelex

Our car pulls up to Fuck Off and I notice five of the Asshole whips are here and a limo. It's early, so only our crew and Blake should be here. We climb from the car and I lead Shawna inside.

I squeeze her hand as we walk through the bar to get to the back room. There's something about her finally wearing her rings that has me full of pride. Now the world will know she's taken—she's mine.

"Finally," Pit says as we enter the back room.

"Did you come up with anything?"

"I have some things jumping out at me, but I'm not there yet. I'll know when I am."

"Okay, where were we?" I say and take the seat beside Shawna after I pull out a chair for her at the round table.

"Hold on," Shawna says, nodding for me to hand over the bag I have been holding with the photo album.

Placing the bag on the table, I slide it over to Skittles. I give Shawna's hand a gentle squeeze. Her nerves are rolling off her.

I know how much her cousin means to her. This bridge needs to be mended.

"What's this?" Skittles says.

"I wanted you to see our story for yourself. I've captured a lot of it on my camera. I had been making this for us and the kids, but I want you to see," Shawna says softly.

"I want to see this," Tak says and moves to sit on the other side of Skittles.

"Okay, where should I begin?" I ask again.

"Start with where it all changed. When did you two become more than friends?" Skittles says as she flips through the album.

I look to her and nod. "Okay. I think you're right. This will get us to what happened in Greece. You said you want to know about that."

"Yes, I've been waiting to hear that part," Blake says.

I pull a face and think back. This was when I started to piece my life together the way I wanted it.

CHAPTER FORTY-SEVEN

Miss?

Kelex

Three years ago…

I'm nervous as fuck. The kids are meeting Shawna in person today. She's going to stop by the center and hang with us for the day. There's a talent show tonight.

True and Cat will be performing. They might just be more nervous than I am. If they don't like Shawna, I don't know what the hell to do. Something tells me my grandfather knew this wouldn't be as easy a task as I thought.

The doorbell rings as I move in circles, trying to figure out what I'm doing. Man, I'm twisted today.

"Hey, did you find my doll?" Vernice comes and asks.

Right, I was looking for Miss Brownie. It's her favorite doll and she's not going to leave without her. Shit, the doorbell rings again.

I gave the staff the day. We'll be gone all day. It didn't make sense to waste their time.

"Come on," I say to Vernice and lift her onto my hip.

I start for the door and spot Miss Brownie in the hall. I scoop her up and hand her over to Vernice. She gives me a huge toothless smile.

"Thank you."

"You're welcome." I wink at her and reach to tug the door open.

I should've known it was Jeff. For someone who hated this house and didn't want me to take in the kids, his ass is always here. Sometimes, I have to wonder if childhood friends are meant to be just that, childhood friends.

Since Pappoús questioned me about my friends I've looked at all my relationships differently. In all honesty, sometimes I'm not even sure Jeff likes me.

However, he's been there when I needed him. He's had my back whenever it's been against the wall. That has always outweighed how much of an asshole he can be.

It's just the way he is. I shake my thoughts off and step back for him to come in. He looks at his watch and frowns. I know we were supposed to be out the door by now.

"Hello, Mr. Jeff," Vernice sings.

"Hello, Three," Jeff says.

"Her name is Vernice, bro," I snap.

"It's okay. He doesn't know my name because he doesn't like me. Newsflash, I don't like him either," Vernice deadpans.

Oh yeah, this one takes after me. My bad. I kiss her cheek and place her on her feet. We need to get going.

"Go get ready. We're leaving soon," I say.

She takes off for upstairs. I turn to face Jeff with a scowl on my face. I take another moment to think over our friendship. I once told Pit I trusted Jeff with my life. Now I find that, on some subconscious level, I wonder why.

It stands out to me that he can often do or say some questionable things. I've always written it off as his entitlement and laughed it off. He's always been this way.

However, now as I take a deeper look. I don't think I can place him on my solid friends list without an asterisk.

"She's seven, bro. Could you try not to be an asshole to her?" I seethe.

"I'm not the one who wanted to be Mary Poppins. Did you not just hear her? That's no seven-year-old," he says and shivers.

"Why did you even want to come to this? You clearly don't like kids."

"Oh, I like kids. The ones who go home at the end of the day. Besides, it's a talent show. Come on, I'm going to have so much fun watching them bomb. Your brats will probably be the only ones with talent and that alone is enough to make Uncle Jeff proud."

"I don't know whose uncle you think you are," Vernice says as she reappears with her little purse strapped across her body and Miss Brownie in her embrace.

"Oh, come on, Vern. I have lollipops. You want one?"

"First, my name is Vernice. Not three, not Vern. Vernice. Respect my name, respect my vibe. Second, I don't take candy from strangers. So no, I don't want one of your nasty old lollipops."

"Okay, Vernice, but just so you know. I might actually like you now."

"Woo-hoo. Lucky me. You see that, J. Your clown likes me," she murmurs.

I cover her mouth and try not to laugh. He asked for it. Jeff always has something slick to say to the kids and they aren't too shy to fire back.

"What did she just say to me?" He seethes, his face turning red.

"Get over it. You've said worse," I laugh. "True, Cat, come on. Let's go. We need to get to the center."

I release Vernice's mouth. She turns to glare at Jeff. He sticks his tongue out at her like a five-year-old. I shake my head at him.

"Hey, you dating anyone yet? Isn't your time running out?" Jeff asks.

"I have it covered. I'll be good."

"So you've found someone? Is it the chick you danced with at the ball? Is that going to work out for your grandfather? I mean, she wasn't Greek, you know what I mean. All that melanin isn't going to be a problem, is it?"

"This is why you need to allow me to handle this."

He holds his hands up. I look down at my watch. "Guys," I bark up the stairs.

"We're coming," True calls back.

***

"Thanks, Mr. Nikolaou," the little boy, Adam, says as I hand him his lanyard string after starting a snake for him.

"Oh, me next," Kennedy, one of Vernice's little friends, says and comes running over to take a seat next to me.

I look around for the millionth time to see if Shawna has arrived. She texted and said her mother needed her to make an appearance today. Zoe had to go to the same event.

I'm not mad, just frustrated. We've both been busy and haven't had a lot of time to spend together. Dating as a CEO and single father has been hard.

I pull out my phone to check for messages. Seeing none, I turn my attention back to Kennedy. She pushes her little glasses up her nose and blinks at me expectantly.

"How have you been, Kennedy?"

"I'm good. Mom's getting better. I think it's because I can come here while she gets rest. She doesn't have to worry about me."

"That's great. I'll send some flowers."

"She'd like that. She's going to be sad she didn't come today and missed you."

I laugh. A lot of the moms hang around to ogle me. I don't mind. It makes them happy. Most are dealing with so much. A smile on their faces is the least I can offer.

I look up from the lanyard in my hands and see the program's head counselor headed my way. I groan. We used to have a great HC, but she got engaged and moved away. This one isn't my favorite, but she'll do until I find a replacement.

She makes it halfway to the table I'm sitting at in the craft room when Shawna rushes in, looking around. A smile comes to my face. She looks amazing in a pair of nude brown heels and a black pencil skirt with a brown sheer puff top.

I love seeing the politician's daughter version versus the shy photographer version of her. I stand and saunter over. She locks eyes with me and sighs in relief.

"Josh," Tiana, the HC, calls and holds up a hand to get my attention.

I shake my head at her and continue to move to Shawna. I can't help myself. Her gloss-painted lips call to me. I dip my head and peck her lips.

"Miss Tiana, Miss Tiana, Ma'am," I hear Vernice call.

I close my eyes and groan. I turn to keep Shawna's first impression of this little girl from being some smart-mouthed shit. I find her with her hands on her hips, looking up at Tiana.

"Not now, Vernice," Tiana says in frustration.

"Yes, now. Ma'am, he's not worried about you. You need to do your job. Kennedy asked you for a snack twenty minutes ago.

"Clearly, her sugar is dropping. Billy peed his pants again and has been waiting for the change of pants you promised you were going to get, but I've watched you staring at Mr. J like you're stupid, trying to build up the courage to say something to him. Get it together. You have kids here who need you.

"Old musty butt. Need to be chasing soap, not men. Can we get that snack and them pants, please? We got enough problems in our lives. We don't need to deal with you."

"Vernice," I groan.

The kid hasn't told a single lie, but *damn*. I feel like I let Mary down because this kid is like a manifestation of my brain. However, she's more unfiltered than I am.

"I can help," Shawna says.

"Oh, thank God," Vernice says and comes to grab Shawna's hand to lead her to the cafeteria, where the snacks are. She tugs

Shawna over to Tiana and holds her hand out for the key to the pantry.

Tiana hands over the key as a look of shame comes to her face. Yeah, I'm making it a priority this week to find her replacement. Neither situation sits well with me. Kennedy's snacks are on a timer and Billy shouldn't be waiting for pants this long.

I turn to get him some pants and then find him in the bathroom to help him out, leaving Tiana looking lost. She knows what's coming. I don't play about any of these kids.

Shawna

"Oh, you left Miss Brownie," I say, turning back to grab the doll from under the auditorium seat.

All the kids were phenomenal. True and Cat were the stars of the show though. Cat can sing and True has the rap persona down to a *T*. I liked his lyrics too.

"Thank you," Vernice says and squeezes my hand, which she hasn't released.

Josh places a hand on top of her head and the other on the small of my back. I feel so overdressed, but I came straight from my mother's event. I had initially promised to volunteer here for the day.

Josh kisses my temple. "You want to have dinner with us?"

"Please," Vernice looks up to say.

"Oh, now you have to. This kid doesn't take to just anyone."

"Who do we have here?" A guy with dark hair and eyes says as he stops in front of me.

"Hi, I'm Shawna," I say with a smile.

"Jeff, nice to meet you," the guy replies with a smug grin on his lips.

"Oh, heck nah. You better back up—"

"Hey, Vernice," Josh says, cutting her off. "Can you take Shawna to find True and Cat? We need to go home."

"Okay," she mutters. "Come on, Miss Shawna. I can show you my artwork in the halls."

CHAPTER FORTY-EIGHT

A Little Push

Shawna

Two months later...

I was surprised when Zoe called to offer me an exhibit in her gallery. However, I was even more surprised when she offered to help me with a little problem I was having.

Zoe is probably the most confident woman I know outside of my family and she knows Josh. So I felt safe asking her if she knew anything I could do to get him to notice I was trying to advance our relationship.

I don't believe I'm doing a great job of flirting. It could be that he's always so tired when we do get to spend time together, but I wanted to at least try something different.

So here I am. I'm learning to pole dance and I have to admit, I'm finding a bit more confidence. The woman in the mirror before me looks strong, sexy, and ready to take on the world.

"Yes, Shawna, let it all out. You can't seduce a man until you can seduce yourself. Fall in love with you, honey. Own who you are," Zoe calls as I sweat my ass off and dance through the song.

My chest is heaving by the time she cuts the music off. I wipe the sweat from my brow with my forearm and stumble over to my towel.

"That was good, my love. I'm proud of you."

"Thanks."

"It takes a lot to find yourself after a man destroys your confidence, but it's not impossible to come back stronger than ever."

"You say that as if you know from experience."

She gets this look in her eyes. It fades quickly and the confidence I know her for returns. I've come to like this woman, but I know she has secrets.

"I haven't said this out loud in years. Come sit," she says, patting the space on the floor beside where she's sitting.

I sit beside her and pull my knees into my chest. Not wanting to rush her, I'm silent as she seems to gather her thoughts. She looks me in the eyes and gives me a sad smile.

"I graduated top of my class. I had big plans. Returning to Bridge Lake hadn't been one of them.

"However, my father had other plans for me. Plans I followed as a dutiful daughter. I married who he wanted, sat on the boards he wanted me to, and then one day, it all changed.

"My father passed away and my husband became this monster. I thought I was trapped. The only person who knew what was going on was my best friend. She saved my life.

"At first, when she tried to get me to leave, I didn't think I could. I didn't think I'd ever get out, but she never gave up. She stood by my side.

"She was the one to help me find an out. I was a shell of the woman I had been, but once I found my way out, I promised I'd never find myself in a situation like that again. I haven't looked back since."

"What happened to your husband?" I ask.

"I think he's dead. I asked for him to be spared, but I don't think he was. You want to know the truth?"

"Sure." I shrug.

"I wish I'd been the one to make it happen. That's my one regret. If I had it to do over, I would have killed him. I would have taken his soul for the one broken," she says.

"Anyway, enough talk of the past. My point is you deserve a man who cares about you and will cherish the amazing woman you are, but first, you have to own who you are. When you do, it will all fall into place."

"I hear you."

"Good," she says and gets up to go grab the bags she stashed in the corner earlier. "Now take this. Go shower off and come back here. We'll do it again."

I look up at her like she's crazy. I've been dancing for hours now. I think I got the point. Instead of saying so, I take the bags she hands me and clench them to my chest.

"Okay."

I mean, she's been taking this time out of her busy life to help me. The least I can do is dress up and do this one more time. I peek into one bag and groan at the stiletto heels inside.

Zoe looks down at her watch. "Come on, let's go. Timing is everything." She claps her hands together.

I inhale deeply and push up off the floor to go change. Once showered and in the changing room, I hold up the skimpy black outfit and lift a brow. Okay, Zoe is totally badass.

I was shocked as hell to find a strip pole and a room of mirrors in her basement. The tricks I've watched the older woman do on that pole and those she's taught me to do have blown my mind.

At first, I had no idea how any of this would help me with Josh, but one day, something just clicked. It was that day I understood what she was truly teaching me. Now I love the woman staring back at me.

"Let's go, Shawnnie," I say to myself and figure out how to get into these strings.

Kelex

"Joshua, you're right on time," Zoe sings with a bright smile as she opens her front door.

I smile and step inside, then turn to pull her into a hug. I was surprised when she called and asked me to make time to stop by. I'm a bit thrown when her scent throws me back in time.

"You smell like my mom," I murmur, caught completely off guard. "No, not her, but a memory of her."

She looks at me with wide eyes. "Yes, well, she gave me this fragrance. I can't believe you recognize it."

"It's one of the few things I remember about her. It was always around her."

"I can give you the name of it, if you like."

"What did you need me to stop by for?" I ask, changing the subject.

"Oh, yes, follow me. I have something I want you to see."

"All right."

I follow her to a door with a set of stairs behind it. She starts to descend them. I keep in step. When we get to the bottom, we don't enter the door straight ahead.

Instead, she leads me to another door and holds it open. I stop and look her over. She waves me inside.

"Step inside. This is my gift to you. Enjoy." I give her a pointed look. "It's fine, Joshua. I'd never bring harm to you. Go on in."

Stepping through the door, I realize I'm behind the glass, looking into another room. Suddenly, Shawna appears in a silk robe. I stand frozen, still close to the entrance I just walked through.

"Okay, love. Again. From the top and give it all you've got. Forget I'm here. It's you and the goddess within. Perform like you're showing Joshua all you've learned and want him to see."

Shawna only nods silently. I turn and find a throne chair in the room I'm in. I go and sit in it. For a brief moment, I wonder what Blake and Zoe are into.

I chuckle to myself and shake the thought off. That's when the music comes blaring through the speakers and I snap my head up. "Sweet Dreams" by Eurythmics pumps through the system and knocks through my chest, but what gets my blood flowing is the sight of Shawna.

She's facing the mirror in a pair of stripper heels and one of those tiny-ass swimsuits that crisscross and only cover her nipples and mound. I'm instantly hard as a rock and on my feet.

I move closer to the glass and take in the look in her eyes. There's a fire there I've never seen before. She begins to snap and rock her sexy-ass hips. Then it's like a switch is flipped and she starts to dance her way down the length of the room across the glass.

I follow like I'm being drawn on a string. My fingertips on the glass as if I can touch her as I go. She pauses at the end and whips her head before turning her back to the glass and pressing up against it.

Her fat ass comes into view. My pulse goes through the roof. The swimsuit is a thong. All that ass is on display for me.

"Damn," I breathe.

She pushes off the glass and dances over to the pole in the center of the room. Then she dances around it, keeping me mesmerized. I'm not expecting any of what happens next.

The way she mounts the pole and flips her body, then slides down and climbs up again, has me ready to break this glass and I don't think I'd need my hands to do so. It's not the outfit, the body, or the dancing. It's the newfound confidence that does it for me.

By the time she ends in a split with a triumphant smile on her lips, I know, without question, she's found a bit of herself again. I can't wait for her to introduce me to the goddess she's found within.

She gets up and struts over to snatch up her robe and saunters out of the room like a boss—ass giggling, hips swaying. *That's my baby.*

CHAPTER FORTY-NINE

Adventurous Love

Shawna

A week later...

I was so excited when Josh asked me to come with him and the kids to Bali. It's one of the places on that list I texted to him all those years ago. I can't wait to get my camera out and see it all through my lens.

"This place is so pretty," Vernice says as we all walk into the resort we're staying in for the next three weeks.

"Come, Miss Vernice. We'll wait over here," Rosy, the children's nanny, says.

"She's right. This place is breathtaking," I say to Josh as he leads me over to the desk with a hand on the small of my back.

He looks down at me. "You haven't seen anything yet."

I suck my lip into my mouth and look away from the heated look he's giving me. Something changed about a week ago. There's this sexual tension that wasn't there before. Yes, we've had chemistry and I know he's attracted to me.

It's just whereas I couldn't get him to get physical before, I've noticed when we do get to go on dates, he's been almost restraining himself from devouring me. Then he asked me on this trip. I'm hoping it's so he can put out these flames building between us.

"The kids are so excited," I say to change the subject.

"Yeah, this will be fun for them. I hope you guys can get to know each other more, but I'm looking forward to our week alone just as much," he says against my temple.

In three weeks, the children will be on their way back to Vander while Josh and I spend our final week at the Hanging Gardens Munduk. I have so many emotions running through me. It's like I've fallen into someone else's life.

It's not the money or the trips. I'm used to all of that. It's the romance of it all. I never thought going with a guy on a trip with his three wards could be so romantic, but Josh has made it so from the start.

The car that picked me up with flowers and a love note resting on the seat. The romantic breakfast we shared on the flight while the kids were on their e-readers or laptops. It all shows he's putting in an effort to bring me into his world.

"Here you go, Mr. Nikolaou. Please enjoy your stay."

"Thank you. Will our transportation be ready for this afternoon?"

"Of course. Everything is all set, and the children can join camp once they are settled. Their spa treatments are set for this evening."

I smile. Vernice did nothing but talk about the nature camp and True has been talking about his seaweed wrap since we left Vander. I love that Josh has planned things out not just for the kids to have fun but for them to enjoy the luxuries of a trip like this.

"Thanks. Come on, baby. Let's get showered and ready for our first date here."

Kelex

"You like my swimsuit, J?" Vernice asks as she runs out to the pool where I've been standing, staring out at the ocean view.

I turn and look down. She has a huge toothless smile on her face. I had her hair done before this trip and she insisted on getting clear-pink beads. They look adorable on her. The pink swimsuit is cute too, with its hearts and stars.

"*Téleio, panémorfo,*" I say in Greek.

"*Efcharistó,*" she replies, her smile growing.

"You're welcome. That was perfect." I hold up a hand to give her a high five.

I've been teaching them all Greek and had the tutors add it to their lessons. Vernice is catching on fast. Not that True and Cat can't understand me and reply. Vernice just seems to be taking to conversations faster.

I look down at my watch as True, Cat, and Rosy all come out to join Vernice at the pool. We should be leaving soon. I'm already sweating.

I should've put on shorts instead of these linen pants. However, Shawna still hasn't seen my burns. Something I know I can't avoid forever, but I want to try for as long as I can.

"I'm ready."

I look up and know I'm not going to stick to that plan. I want this woman so bad it hurts. She's fucking exquisite. The white dress she has on has a deep *V* front and slits up the sides.

Her pretty feet are encased in jeweled flat thong sandals, revealing her pretty pink toes. She had her hair braided for this trip and now they are pulled away from her face and hanging down her back in waves. She looks like a queen about to stand on an island above her subjects.

It's going to be hard to keep my hands off her. I move to her and place a hand on her hip.

"You look amazing." I place my nose against her skin. "And smell even better."

"Thank you, you look handsome as always."

"Come on, our transportation is waiting."

When we get to our ride and she climbs in, I have to rearrange myself before I climb in behind her. We fall into a relaxed conversation as usual.

I've thought about telling her about watching her through the glass at Zoe's, but I've seen that confidence in her since and don't want to ruin it. I love watching her blossom.

"Where are we going?"

"You'll see."

"Wait, you're one of Ven's friends. Josh, I'm so not into any of that extreme stuff. I'll shit my pants trying to jump off a cliff or something."

I laugh and lean in to peck her lips. "Don't worry. I've always got you. You'll thank me later."

"Oh no. Josh—"

I cut her words off with my lips. She melts into me. Gently, I place a hand on her thigh, easing it up her leg and under her dress. I stop right at the apex of her legs.

She breaks the kiss and looks me in the eyes. Biting down on her own lip, she nods for me to continue. Unfortunately, we arrive at our destination.

Shawna

"Oh, I'm sorry," I say and place my camera down on the table.

We're having a romantic lunch on a breathtaking cliff. It's just so beautiful up here. I couldn't help myself. I should be focused on our date, but I keep reaching for my camera instead.

"You're fine. I love watching you in your element. Your face lights up when your camera is in your hands."

"There's something magical about capturing the right moment, at the right angle, and immortalizing it forever."

"Come, sit on my lap and immortalize us," he says with a grin.

I grab my camera and stand. Rounding the table, I sit on his lap and hold my camera up. He wraps his arms around me and brushes my braids away from my neck to kiss it. I snap a few and then show him the viewing screen.

"I love this one," I say, looking at the pic of him looking up through his lashes as he kisses my neck. He looks like a true model, always finding the shot.

"I want that one. Can you send it to me?"

"Yeah, when I get to my laptop, I can."

I get up and go back to my seat. Our food comes and we eat while doing some small talk. I'm on the perfect date in the middle of paradise.

After an amazing lunch and some more talk, Josh stands and takes me by the hand. I have no idea where we're going until we get to the other side of the cliff and the giant swing comes into view.

"Josh," I gasp. "Oh no. Are you crazy? I'm not getting on that thing."

"Baby, trust me. Come on. It will be one of the greatest experiences of your life."

He looks at me with pleading eyes. I look at the swing and eye it. I don't know if I can do this.

I turn my attention back to him and he's unbuttoning his shirt. I stare as he reveals his tanned-looking skin. He shrugs the shirt off and drops it to the ground.

"I want to bare myself to you. That's a leap of faith for me. Take *this* leap of faith with me first," he says.

I place my hands on his waist. I don't touch the marred skin on his right side, unsure of how he will feel about it. Instead, I look him in the eyes.

"You're still perfect in my eyes," I say.

He wraps his arms around me and tucks his face into my neck, then kisses me softly. The sensation shoots to my core. I close my eyes and breathe him in.

"Do this with me. I want to feel this with you."

"What? You think that thing is going to hold us both?"

He lifts his head and pulls a face. "I know it is. Come on."

He lifts me onto his waist and heads for the swing seat. I close my eyes and start to pray. Josh kisses my temple and breathes a laugh against my skin.

"I can't, I can't, I can't," I say as I feel him sit and the swing is pulled back.

"Look at me, baby," he says.

I peek my eyes open and look into his blue-gray ones. He's smiling from ear to ear as he looks back at me. I search his face, in awe that this is the man I'm falling in love with.

"Put your hands on the ropes," he coaxes. He then places his hands right above mine. Still with his gaze locked on mine, he speaks to my thoughts right before we're released. "I love you."

I can't help but scream as we float out over the forest. The way my belly drops and my heart swells is a feeling I can't even describe.

He kisses my neck as we swing out. I've never felt more free in my life. I look into his eyes and smile.

"I love you too."

He leans in and kisses me hard. I'm so glad I did this. By the time we're back on the cliff, the adrenaline is still pumping, and I want to go again.

CHAPTER FIFTY

Come Together

Kelex

After getting back and checking on the gang in their room, we sat and listened to their excitement over their day. Vernice got to swim in the pool and ride the water slide.

Cat found some girls her age to hang with and had a blast. True made a few beats and wrote some songs. All in all, everyone had a great day.

As for Shawna and I, I think we're still on a high from that cliff-top swing. I wasn't sure I was going to get her to do it at first. However, I'm glad I did.

I meant what I said. I love her. With everything I am, I've fallen for Shawna. When she didn't make me feel some way as I revealed my scars, I tried not to get emotional. I'm so close to what I've always wanted I can't breathe.

"Do you need the lights?"

"No, the light from the laptop is enough."

I get a box of condoms from my bag and open them, pouring the packets onto the nightstand. Shawna looks up from her laptop and gives me a shy smile. "I'm going to jump in the shower," I say as I move to turn off all the lights and light some candles.

"Okay, I'm going to load these pictures and clear my SIM card."

I nod. She took a shower when we first came into the room. I warred with whether or not I should join her. Seeing my torso was one thing. What's going to happen when she sees the rest?

I hate this self-doubt. It's not like me. I never used to second-guess myself or be this in my head. Now I'm standing in the shower, letting my thoughts swallow me.

I'm so lost in thought I spin around in shock when my name is called. There she stands, completely naked, watching me. I hold my breath, waiting for her gaze to drop and her face to contort in disgust.

I reach to push my wet hair out of my eyes and watch her more closely. She enters the shower and comes to me. Then she places her trembling hands on my waist and looks up into my eyes.

"Can I touch you? Is this okay?"

I close my eyes, feeling like an asshole. She's trembling because she's just as nervous as I am, if not more. This is her first time.

I swallow my shit because this isn't about me. It's about her. I grab hold of her braids and tilt her head back.

"It's fine. Touch me any way you want," I say against her lips.

I search her face as I lean in closer to take her lips. She lifts on her toes to complete the kiss, running her hands up my back and into my wet hair.

I groan into her mouth and take over the kiss. Gliding my hands down her smooth skin, I palm her ass and pull her flush to my body. We kiss each other hungrily.

Without breaking the connection, I reach to shut off the water. Shawna sucks my lower lip into her mouth, breaking my restraint. Her confidence is seeping through again.

I lift her onto my waist and start out of the shower. I want her so bad; I almost place her on the countertop and take her right here in this bathroom. However, I force myself to keep going.

Her first time should be special, more than a fuck on a countertop. I slow my kisses as that reality hits. I need to take my time with her.

Gently, I place her on the foot of the king-size bed. She reaches to cover her breasts and bites her lip shily. I stand looking down at her sexy body, the glow of the candles dances across her skin.

Shaking my head at her, I say. "Don't do that. Never hide what's mine from me."

Her lips part in surprise, but she removes her hands, grasping the sheets beside her. Moving closer, I pin her to the bed with a hand on her waist and lean in to cup one of her breasts with the other and take the dark peak into my mouth. She writhes beneath me, calling my name.

Allowing her nipple to pop free from my mouth, I look her in the eyes as I lift my fingers to my lips and lick my fingertips. She squeals beneath me as I begin to rub her pussy. I go back to sucking on her breast.

Testing them both, I find her right one to be more sensitive and give it my full attention. I'm careful not to stick my fingers too deep inside her. I want my cock to be the one to pop her cherry.

I drop to my knees and push her legs back as I bury my face in her folds. My hands are all over her soft skin. Needing to relieve some of the pain, I reach to stroke my length.

"Josh," she pants. "Oh, God."

Her juices are all over my face, but I'm not ready to stop. I want her nice and wet for me. I don't let up until she has my head in a vise grip between her thick thighs.

I massage her ass until she loosens her grip and starts to come down from her orgasm. Wrapping my arm around her waist, I move her up the bed and climb over her. She looks up at me dreamily.

"You taste amazing," I breathe against her lips.

She cups my face, kissing and licking my lips. I reach for one of the packets on the nightstand. Pulling back, I bite into the wrapper, then roll the condom on.

Shawna eyes my length with her lips parted and a brow raised. I give a grin. My face isn't the only pretty thing about me. I'm on the thicker side and not too shy in inches either. Once the rubber is in place, I move over her and lean in her ear.

Nuzzling the skin behind it, I then suck her flesh into my mouth. "Josh, please."

"I need you to tell me if it's too much at any time. Can you do that for me?" I breathe into her ear.

"Yes," she replies.

"Are you ready?"

"Yes, I'm ready."

She reaches for my ass, tugging me into her. I capture her lips in a passionate kiss and push in slowly. I then pull out again.

She feels so good already and I've barely gotten the tip in. Grabbing the back of my neck, she moans into my mouth as I work into her gradually. Pulling back, I then snap my hips forward. My eyes roll back and I groan as her scream fills the room the moment I thrust into her.

I still, allowing her to adjust to me. Looking into her pretty eyes, I search to see if she's okay. She gives a small nod.

I kiss her nose and start to move again. The sound of her wet pussy fills the room as she begins to relax. She has me in a vise grip.

Grinding my teeth, I pause to keep from coming. I reach for her hands and bring them up over her head, caging her head in with my arms as I lean in and devour her lips.

"Mmm," I hum as she tightens around me.

Not able to help myself, I cup her face as I rock my body into hers. I'm doing my best not to go too deep, although I want nothing more. I've never felt this connection with anyone else.

"You feel so good, baby," I groan in her ear.

She shivers and wraps her arms around me. "You do too."

I can feel she's still hesitant, as if unsure of herself. However, she begins to claw her nails down my back and grinds her hips. I lift up and raise her hips off the bed. Shifting angles, I'm able to pump up into her.

"Josh, shit, Josh," she cries out.

I wipe the sweat from my face with the back of my hand, but I don't stop stroking. Her tits bouncing and those thick thighs locked around me has a deep rumble emitting from my chest.

Reaching for one of her breasts, I give it a squeeze and drop my gaze to our connection. I can see and hear how wet she is. I grab her hand and place it on her mound.

"Rub your pussy for me," I demand.

Her eyes grow wide but as I guide her to show her what I want that all changes. She bites her lip, her eyes roll back, and her pussy clenches around me. It's the O shape and soundless scream that breaks my restraint, causing me to spill into the barrier between us.

Shawna

I never thought it would be like this. Each time has been amazing and there have been several. He's pulled one condom off to roll another on within seconds.

I'm not complaining. I love sex with him. He makes me feel so cherished and cared for. He's not shy about showing me what he likes or how to learn what I like.

Now we're lying here in each other's arms and I don't want this to end. I run my hand over his muscled chest and smile to myself.

His hand on my ass flexes. "You need anything?" he says into my hair.

"No, I'm okay."

I glide my hand lower and run my fingers over his torso down to his leg. He flinches, causing me to pause and lift my head to look up at him. I search his face.

"Does it hurt? I'm sorry."

"No, it feels normal. I just wasn't expecting your touch."

"Why? I mean, if you don't like me touching you there. I won't."

"It's not that I don't want your touch, I just didn't think... Never mind."

"Josh, it isn't as bad as you described. I was expecting something different."

It's true. He made it seem like I'd find him totally repulsive. Although there is discoloration on his torso. It looks more like blood has rushed to the location.

His leg does seem to have a visual, textural difference, but not like swiss cheese as he described once. It's more like he leaned on a patterned mesh while sleeping, kind of like falling asleep on something and waking with the pattern on your face.

None of it took away from the view of his firm ass, strong-looking thighs, or muscular back when I walked in on him in the shower. I think the worst of it is on the outside of his right calf and foot. It's still not enough to take away from the man himself.

He looks me in the eyes. I can see his thoughts running across his face. I smile at him and reach to wrap my hand around his growing erection.

"Come here," he says as he grasps my face and tugs me toward him. "I don't deserve you. You know that?"

"Yes, you do," I breathe just before he crushes his lips to mine.

I smile into his kiss as I hear more than see the slap of his hand on the nightstand to grab another condom. He rolls me onto my stomach and straddles my thighs. I squeal in my head. Another position, I'm not sure which is my favorite yet.

I love them all.

I gasp loudly as he enters me from behind and grabs my hands beside my head. He laces his fingers with mine and starts to rock into me slowly.

"Josh," I moan and tighten my fingers against his.

"I love you so much. I can't get enough of you," he says in my ear.

I moan as he starts to kiss his way across my shoulder blades. He's so thick and long but isn't perfect. There's this pleasure mixed with pain that makes me crave him inside me.

Releasing my hands and grabs my hips, he pounds into me. His chest is pressed to my back as he used one of his legs for leverage to keep thrusting. I don't want this to stop.

It's so surreal. Even as I start to convulse—I don't know how much later—I'm in awe and can't believe this is happening to me. He pulls out and I still feel him as I throb in his absence.

"You okay?" he whispers in my ear.

"Mm-uh," I murmur, already half-asleep.

He laughs and kisses my shoulder. "I'll take that as a yes."

CHAPTER FIFTY-ONE

We Like You

Shawna

I wake with a smile on my face as I stretch my arms over my head. Despite Josh running me a bath to soak in in the middle of the night, there's a delicious bite of soreness between my legs.

My ass stings a little too from where Josh kept slapping as I rode him that one time. I roll over in bed, looking for his warm body and strong embrace.

I frown when I find cool sheets and no Josh. Sitting up, I look around and listen for him. Feeling alone in the room, I pull the sheet up to cover my body.

I look down into my lap and my thoughts take off all over the place. I feel so stupid. What was I thinking? All of my insecurities come to the surface.

My phone rings, grabbing my attention. I grab it and see it's Josh. Tucking my braids behind my ear, I then answer.

"Hello."

"Baby, I'm so sorry. Vernice slipped by the pool and cracked her chin. I've been dealing with getting her care for the last two hours. I'm just calling to check on you and say sorry," Josh says hurriedly into the phone.

"Is she okay?"

"She'll be fine. How are you?"

"I'm okay."

"Sounds like I need to do something about that. After last night, you should be more than okay."

I bite my lip, hearing the seduction in his deep voice.

"I'm great." I laugh.

"That's more like it. I'll be back soon. Why don't you order something to eat and take another bath? I'm sure another soak is needed after all that dancing we did."

"Dancing?" I say and lift a brow as if he can see it.

"You know what I'm talking about. Don't make me spell it out."

"Or you can show me your moves," I tease.

"I can do that. Trust me, I plan to do that. Take that bath, baby. You're going to wish you had."

I sigh and my smile returns. "I'm just glad everything is okay. I'll see you when you get back."

"Shawna?"

"Yeah."

"I love you. See you soon."

My heart nearly explodes. The smile on my face has my cheeks hurting. I feel like I'm in a dream.

Falling back on the bed, I squeal and kick my legs in the air. When did I get so lucky? The scent of his cologne surrounds me. I pull the sheets to my nose and inhale deeply.

I smile wider. He was such a gentleman about changing the sheets and taking care of me. Last night was perfect.

Kelex

I carry a sleeping Vernice back into the kids' room. She'll be fine. Although I freaked the fuck out when Rosy called to tell me what happened.

A smile comes to my lips as I find Shawna with True and Cat playing UNO. Something about seeing her with them fills my heart. She could have stayed to herself in our room. Instead, she's here looking like she wouldn't want to be anywhere else.

"Mr. Josh, I'm so sorry," Rosy says as she stands from where she'd been sitting, wringing her hands.

"She's fine. It wasn't your fault. We all know Vernice can be clumsy sometimes."

"Right," True says.

"Remember that one time when she walked into the kitchen cabinet?" Cat chimes in.

"Do I," True replies. "Miss Shawna, she was like five. I still don't know how it happened. I mean, it was right there. The next thing you know, she was on her butt crying."

I laugh. It really was crazy. I was stunned because I thought she would stop. I remember trying to help Mary with some paperwork or something, and the next thing we knew, we were all staring with our mouths open.

Shawna laughs. "You guys have some of the best stories."

"Our memories get us through," True says.

My heart sinks a little. I'm doing my best to help them make new memories, but I also want them to remember their mom. Sometimes, I wonder if I'm balancing it all. Now I have Shawna too.

"Thank you for allowing me to make new memories with you," Shawna says, pulling me from my thoughts.

"We like you. J could use someone to hold him down like he does everyone else. Besides, you're dope," True says.

"Yeah, come hang with us anytime you want," Cat adds with a huge smile.

Shawna looks up at me and I wink at her. The smile she gives me makes me feel like I might have this.

CHAPTER FIFTY-TWO

Anything for You

Shawna

A month later…

I love spending time with Josh. Although we don't get to do it often. I understand he has a lot of responsibilities. It's one of the things I admire about him. He gives his all to everything he does.

However, he seems more tense than usual. I've never seen him like this. He came over to my apartment to spend the night, but his focus has been on his laptop and his expression has been clouded over.

"Is everything okay?" I ask.

He looks up from his laptop and gives me a smile. "Yeah, I'm fine. Give me a minute and I'll give you all my attention."

"You're okay. I just wanted to see if there was anything I could do. You look stressed."

He rubs the back of his neck. "This deal is turning into a nightmare and I'm trying to figure out why," he replies, squinting at his screen.

I get up from the accent chair I'm sitting in and go to sit on the couch he's on. Shifting to my knees, I start to massage his neck and shoulders. He always works so hard.

He groans and rolls his neck. "Baby, you're a lifesaver. That feels so good."

"You're so tight. Let me work these knots out."

He closes the laptop and turns to me. There's a smile on his face. The stress from moments ago is now gone.

"I can get back to this later. I've missed you."

I laugh. "We were just in Chicago together."

"Baby, I was able to fly you in for a day before you had to get back to work. I've taken longer shits."

"Oh my God, really?" He shrugs. "I hope you've seen a doctor about that."

He laughs. "Whatever, you know what I mean. I spend more time missing you than getting to see you. It's driving me crazy."

He inhales sharply and pulls me to straddle his lap. I go willingly and settle. Placing my arms around his neck, I begin to massage his neck and shoulders again.

"This is all part of adulting, right?"

He groans and rolls his eyes. "You could always quit your job and travel with me."

I give him the side-eye. His smile grows and he reaches to push a lock of hair behind my ear. Shaking his head, he then pecks my lips.

"Right, I didn't think it was a real option, but the offer always stands. Are you going to do the exhibit at Zoe's gallery?"

"I don't know yet. I feel like that's for someone with so much more experience than me."

"She's seen your work and you impressed her. It's not every day she makes an offer like this. Think about what it would do for your career."

"Josh, did you put her up to making me this offer?"

"I would have if she hadn't, but this one is all on you," he says, rubbing my back.

"I still don't know."

"You work so hard. You deserve this."

"It's not the work. It's the attention and who am I to think I deserve my own exhibit?"

His face clouds over and his orbs turn gray right before my eyes. I suck in a breath and look down. He lifts my chin, so I'm looking back at him.

"You're Shawna Norris, a brilliant, talented, hardworking photographer who works her ass off on every assignment she gets. You're my woman, so even if you didn't have an ounce of talent, you would deserve this because I want you to have it and I can make it happen for you. And trust me, I dare a motherfucker to tell you otherwise and expect to keep breathing."

"Josh, that's just it. I don't want to feel like I got the opportunity because of you or my mom's connections. Because she's been hinting around at pulling favors just to keep me grounded."

"You amaze me. All my life, I've been surrounded by people who feel entitled to shit they have no right to and would jump at a situation like this, but you're worried about your privilege from dating me and having a successful mother."

"There's nothing wrong with working for what you want. When you truly earn something, no one can take it away, you know?"

He smiles and leans to bury his face in my neck. I hug my arms around his head and breathe him in. It's like he's pouring love into me.

"Believe me, I get it," he says into my neck. "I'm telling you the truth. Zoe loves your eye and your work. Take the offer. You earned it. I only emailed a few of your prints." He snickers into my skin.

"I knew it. Oh my God."

I push to get up, but he tightens his hold and kisses my neck while still laughing. I love this side of him. Josh is so down to earth. I never would have thought that before getting to know him, not back when he was a rising star.

"Baby, you do know I'd do anything for you? Even the shit you don't know you want or need me to do."

"Thank you. I appreciate it, I really do."

"I'm not the only one who misses you," he croons, changing the subject.

"I know. Cat has been texting me."

"You don't mind that I gave her your number, do you?"

"No, it's fine. She needed a woman to talk to. I didn't mind."

His gaze is focused on my lips as I run my hand through his hair. It's a bit longer these days. I think he's growing it out.

He still keeps it neat and combed in place, but it's just about two or three inches longer than it used to be on top. He reaches for my lips and runs his thumb across them. I love that his large hand can encompass my throat and the side of my face at the same time.

"Why are you so amazing?" he says, lifting his gaze to mine.

I shrug, not having an answer for him and knowing what he'll say if I deny his words. He tugs me forward until our foreheads are touching. That electricity that flows between us is still there. It travels through my entire body.

"Maybe if I spent the night fucking you, you'd be able to give me an answer," he says with a sexy grin on his lips.

I squirm in his lap. Forgetting what I was thinking or going to say. He crushes my lips with his and reaches to palm my breasts.

"I'm going to find your pussy wet for me, aren't I, baby? You miss me? You want me inside you?" he breathes into my ear.

"Yes, yes, yes to both. I need you."

"Good, because I need you too."

Kelex

I'd be lying if I said I haven't wanted to fuck the shit out of Shawna since she opened the door in those thin-ass leggings and tank top. Her long, thick legs were begging to be wrapped around my neck, that fat mound, begging me to pound it out.

And pound I did. We've just spent the last four hours making sure her neighbors know my name. Now I'm lying here staring at the ceiling, trying to figure out how to tell her about my grandfather's request without revealing who I am.

I'm going to need to be engaged soon and I have to tell her why. At least, as close to the truth as I can get because I'm sure he'll want to meet her. Things are going so good.

However, I know if I don't say something, it will come out and I don't think that will go over well. Sometimes, I get the feeling that Shawna still doesn't think this is real. As if... how could I not want her?

My phone rings on the nightstand. I roll my eyes. I'm not in the mood to talk to anyone. I let it go to voice mail, but a text comes through not too long after.

Jeff: *What's going on with you?*

Jeff: *You handle that request yet?*

Jeff: *If the black chick didn't work out. I might know someone.*

Jeff: *Or you could rule the world. We all benefit if you do.*

I snort and toss the phone back on the nightstand. I'm not in the mood to have this conversation. My friend has spent his whole life with this fantasy of becoming something I have no desire to become.

He's been fed the dream of me rising up and him rising with me. If I don't take the promotion, he can't have his. I don't owe anyone my life, so I'm not going to make decisions based on a false sense of loyalty.

"It's time to let that shit go," I mutter to myself.

"Um?" Shawna replies in her sleep.

"Nothing, baby. Go back to sleep."

She takes a deep breath and snuggles deeper into me. Kissing her forehead, I close my eyes to get some rest.

CHAPTER FIFTY-THREE

Vancouver

Kelex

Three months later...

With a lot of effort on my part, Shawna has fit into my life seamlessly. Although, I do feel guilty for not telling Skittles we're involved. My life has just been so busy and it's a conversation I want to sit down and have with her.

There's also the fact that I haven't officially been given my out. Keeping Shawna hidden has been hard enough. I'm not fool enough to think my enemies will go away because I want them to.

Since I can't go on a killing spree to keep my girl and her cousin out of harm's way, it's best we keep things to ourselves. Which is why I try to make it up to her with these trips.

"I'm so excited," Shawna says beside me as we ride from the airport to our rental for the week. "The Cap Bridge was on my list, specifically during the holiday season."

I lean to peck her lips. "I know. As soon as Achilles mentioned me taking this meeting, I thought of you."

Seeing this on her list was the first thing to come to mind. I try to fit as many of her destinations in as I can. Business has been booming, so it has been a challenge.

Work and dating are one of the reasons I've been missing out on more and more Asshole trips and get-togethers. I'm always on the go.

"We're only staying a week though. The lights aren't scheduled to start until the day after we leave," she says and her shoulders slump as she reads the information on her phone.

I place a hand on the back of her neck and massage it. She turns her gaze to me. I take her lips for a searing kiss, then lean into her ear while cupping her throat.

"You know I'd bend the world for you. You're going to see it. All you have to do is ask and I'll make anything happen for you. This is already done. Thank me later."

I pull away and her eyes are glazed over with lust. I smile and run my thumb over her now-swollen lip. She darts her tongue out, following the trail I make.

I lean in for another kiss. I can't wait to get her alone. Just the thought of watching her ride me has me hard. I'll never get enough of worshiping her body.

Shawna

He remained true to his word. I hold my camera up and snap another photo of the Canyon Lights. The Capilano Suspension Bridge Park is breathtaking. It's like a majestic winter wonderland. I don't know where to settle my camera.

I've taken so many photos already. However, as I go to see where Josh is, I freeze. As gorgeous as this park is, I think I find my money shot the moment I settle my gaze on him.

Standing among all these lights with a ball of light right above his head, he steals the moment. He's on his phone, gazing out into the distance, and he looks like he's posing without trying.

I smile as I lift my camera and take a few photos of him. He has on a beanie cap, so his dark roots are the only thing I can see. His peacoat accents his height and frames his face as his collar comes to his chin.

I gasp when he turns his gaze to me. The look in his eyes is so intense. There's a danger there I don't think I've ever picked up on before.

Through my lens, I can see his eyes are completely gray. I lower my camera, feeling like I'm intruding on his thoughts. Now I can't help wondering who was on his call. Whoever it was brought on a change in him.

"Sorry," I murmur.

"Would you like one with a smile?"

"Um, no, it's okay."

"Shawn."

A shiver runs through me. He's gotten into the habit of calling me the nickname. It always drops from his lips like warm honey.

I lift my head. "Yes."

"Take as many pictures of me as you like. Where do you want me?"

My thoughts go to something dirty, but my phone rings, pulling my attention. The spell and moment are broken as I see it's Ven.

Guilt settles in my stomach. I don't know how to tell her I'm dating her best friend. A part of me can't help fearing she won't be okay with it.

I'm not ready to give him up. I've been falling more and more in love with him. If Ven told me she didn't like this, I'd be heartbroken, but I'd walk away. My cousin is only ever out to protect me, so her words and advice mean everything.

I take a deep breath and pick up the call. "Hey, Ven. What's up?"

"Ugh, someone I can talk to," she breathes. "Why is it so hard to plan a wedding? I'll tell you why."

"My father is making this super difficult and my fiancé shrugs and tells me to do whatever I want. Men," she huffs.

I giggle into the phone. "It will work out."

"We should just elope in Vegas."

"Your father would kill you," I snort.

"Will you be back to go dress shopping with me? You got the dates, right?"

"I'll be there."

She goes silent for a moment. "Shawnnie, how are you? Is there anything I can do?"

"I'm fine, Ven. Thank you for asking."

"I love you. I only want to see you happy."

Tears fill my eyes. I close them as Josh walks up behind me and wraps his strong arms around me, kissing the top of my head. Guilt punches me in the chest, but I get the feeling he's not ready to tell her either.

"Ah, crap. My father drove me so crazy I forgot my cake appointment. Listen, I have to jet. Love you, babes. Call me if you need to talk. Later," she sings and hangs up.

I turn in Josh's arms. He kisses my nose. As if reading my mind, he speaks to my thoughts.

"We'll tell her. When the time is right. She has a lot going on."

"Yeah, I know."

He lifts my chin with his fingertips. "Come on, it's getting cold out here. I need to check on the kids and wait for my grandfather's call. Let's head back."

I lift on my toes and kiss him. He palms my ass and holds me to him. I break the kiss and lower back on my feet.

"I love you," I whisper.

His face lights up and he leans in to rub his nose to mine. "I was thinking the same thing. I love you too."

Kelex

I can't help watching Shawna in her sleep. How can you fall in love with someone while all they're doing is breathing? I brush a lock of hair from her forehead, knowing I'm completely gone for this woman.

The scar on her forehead comes into view, making me think of Ven. It's crazy that they have almost identical scars. Shawna's has healed more and looks faded, whereas Skittles's scar looks like Luke patched her up.

I wish I had been there to advise against that option. I've only noticed Shawna's scar when she sleeps or when we're having sex. Neither is an ideal time to ask where it came from.

"You're still perfect," I murmur as I brush my thumb across the scar. "I love you so much it hurts."

It's her heart. She spent an hour on the phone with the girls tonight because they wanted to hang out with her and hadn't seen her in a few weeks. I love that they love her.

I frown in thought. My heart begins to race. I have this deep fear that I could lose them all.

My phone lights up the dimly lit room. I turn and grab it to go into the other room. I've been waiting for this call.

"Hello, Pappoús," I croon into the phone.

"*Tzósoua mou*, you sound happy. Does this mean you've found someone?"

"I have."

"Good. When will you bring her to Crete?"

"Work has been busy, but soon."

"Good, bring the children as well."

I smile. "I will."

"Good, good. How's the adoption going?"

I frown. "The father still won't sign over his rights."

"Um, and you haven't done anything to change that?"

"No."

Not that I haven't wanted to. If I didn't think my grandfather would take it all back for my actions, I would have forced his ass to sign and then disposed of him. Especially after finding out he had been reaching out to Mary to gaslight her just to get me to back off.

I can't help wondering if she fell ill because of him. He's a fucking cancer, if there ever was one. I hate his guts.

"I'm proud of you, *Tzósoua.*"

"Thanks, Pappoús."

"We will talk soon."

I hang up with a smile on my face. I'm one more step away from being out from under this cloud. I'm going to live a normal life.

CHAPTER FIFTY-FOUR

This is the One

Shawna

Four months later...

"You have such a lovely home," I say to Basil, Josh's grandfather.

He seems to be a kind old man. He's very handsome and still looks good for his age. His eyes are sharp, like he sees more than you want him to.

"It is your home while you are here. This smile you bring to my Joshua's face, I never thought I'd see the day. *O Tzósoua mou eínai erotevménos*," Basil says with a wide smile.

Vernice giggles and says. "Yes, he is."

"*A, katalavaíneis ellliniká?*" Basil says and lifts a brow.

"*Nai, kai míla to ki esý.*"

"Very nice. I will only speak in Greek while you are here then," he says to Vernice.

"Actually, you can speak to all the kids in Greek," Josh says proudly.

"Is this so?"

"*Naí*," True and Cat say in unison.

"Well done, Joshua, well done. How about we have lunch? I would like to get to know you all better," Basil says in English.

I assume because of me. My nerves settle and I almost forget that I'm missing Ven's bachelorette party. I told her I wasn't ready to do something like that, which wasn't entirely a lie.

The truth is, my gut told me Josh needed me. I'm here because the look in his eyes when he asked me to come said this was something he needed to do. So here I am.

Kelex

This visit is bittersweet. I couldn't make time before now and Pappoús insisted I come right away. My time has run out.

I had no choice but to miss Pit and Skittles's bachelor and bachelorette weekend. You don't refuse my grandfather when he summons you.

"I like her," Pappoús says. "She's a sweet girl. I can see why you are so taken."

"She means everything to me."

"This is real? I know she's related to our little friend, the fireball. You wouldn't be trying to fool me, would you?"

"Not at all. Skittles still doesn't know about us. We've been keeping things private."

"This is good. Take a lesson from Blake. Don't be quick to let everyone into your business. Especially concerning your personal life. You understand?"

"Yeah, I hear you."

"Good. Then tell me, why haven't you proposed?"

I knew this was coming. I had planned to have a talk with Shawna and propose before this trip, but things didn't work out. I had to save that deal that's been falling apart for months and we've launched the film program for the kids.

"I haven't had time to find the perfect ring," I say.

He waves a hand at me. "This isn't a problem. We can fix this today."

My heart starts to race with excitement. If I had a ring, I would totally propose to Shawna. I would love nothing more than to have her under my roof and in my bed every night.

"Okay, let's make that happen. Greece couldn't be a better place to propose."

"That's my boy. I can't wait to see the gorgeous babies she will give you."

My smile grows. I'm going to love making those babies. I can't wait.

CHAPTER FIFTY-FIVE

Dream Come True

Kelex

"Are you sure your grandfather will be okay with the kids all by himself?" Shawna asks as we pack to head to Ios.

"He'll be fine. They're all old buddies now. Besides, Helios will be here with him."

The kids and Pappoús hit it off yesterday. It was like watching my grandfather with me when I was younger. They're good kids. They're not going to give him any trouble.

"Where are you taking me?" she asks with a bright smile.

I wrap my arms around her waist and pull her into my body. Thinking about our plans for the next few days, I take her lips in a passionate kiss. I think she's going to love what I have planned.

"It's a surprise. Bring a swimsuit and something to wear to dinner. We'll be back the day after tomorrow."

"That's not a lot to go on."

"You want me to pack for you?"

She laughs. "Really?"

I slap her ass playfully. "Go down to breakfast. I'll pack your bag. No worries."

She cups my face in her palms and looks into my eyes. Without a word, she places her forehead to my chin. I sway her in my arms.

"Sometimes, I think I'm dreaming. You're so good to me and…" She takes a deep breath. "I love you so much it scares me."

I reach to lift her face so I can look into her eyes. Placing a soft kiss on her lips, I then smile at her while running my finger across her lips. She reaches beneath my shirt and runs her warm palms up my chest.

"We're living the dream, not dreaming. Making you happy is my life's mission. The day I'm no longer good to you is the day I don't deserve you.

"Which will be never. I don't have words to describe how much I love you, but *with all I am… until my last breath…* and… *so much I'd dead for you* come up when I try to form the right ones," I say.

With tears in her eyes, she wraps her arms around my waist and holds me tight. I wrap my arms around her and kiss the top of her head. When she pulls away, I smile and run my hands down her two braids.

This look is sexy on her. I know I was hard as fuck when I had them wrapped around my hands while pounding into her from behind last night. We'll have to do that again later.

I peck her lips. "Go on. I'll pack what you need. I've got you. Enjoy breakfast."

"Thank you. See you downstairs."

Shawna

I loved the helicopter ride that brought us here. The sights were so beautiful. Josh kept me tucked into his side and I couldn't have been happier. I was wrapped in a cocoon of his delicious scent.

This place is so gorgeous. Our hotel room, the beach, the island. Ios, Greece, has taken my breath away. We're staying at the Calilo hotel.

When I say the place is absolutely romantic, it's so perfect I almost cried. The hanging bed and swing in our room remind me of Bali. I haven't been able to stop smiling.

"Are you ready?"

I turn at the sound of Josh's voice and my mouth falls open. He has on a pair of black board shorts. They hang low on his waist and hug his thighs and that sick bulge that I know to be a massive package when not concealed.

My mouth waters. He's so sexy. My fingers itch to grab my camera.

"Yes, um, what are we up to? Do I need anything?"

I wipe my palms on my bare thighs. I couldn't help but smile when I saw which swimsuit he had packed for me. It's a black one-piece, but the coverage is minimal. It's high-waisted with a deep *V* and crosses behind the neck. Sexy, but classy.

Josh eats me up with his gaze. It's like his eyes are caressing me. I cross my thighs and squeeze my legs.

"Get your camera, Shawna Norris. You have a photo shoot with—"

"Kelex," I breathe. "Do you know how bad I've always wanted to have you in front of my camera?"

"Today's the day, but I have one stipulation."

"Anything."

He gives me a wicked grin. "I get to take photos of you. It's time you see what I see. Show me how you see me and I'll show you what I see."

I look down at my toes and contemplate his words. I would love to show him what I see when I look at him, but I'm not sure I want to be on the other side of a camera. However, if it means I get to do this shoot, I'll do just about anything.

"Okay," I say and lift my head.

He lifts his hand and holds it out for me. Grabbing my camera and cover-up, I then go to join him. He dips his head and pecks my lips.

"There's plenty of sunlight still. How does a walk on the beach sound? "

"Great." I smile up at him.

He leads us out to the beach as he jokes around and keeps me laughing. When we get there, he releases my hand, runs to the water, and dives in. However, I'm not ready for the sight that emerges from the water.

I hold my camera up with a smile on my face as he begins to walk toward me. He looks up at the sky and it's the perfect angle. I take a few pictures before I have to take a deep breath to compose myself.

His shorts are soaked through and clinging to his skin. It's crazy how his imprint is so detailed as water drips down his legs. It looks like he has a forearm growing from his pelvis. I shake my head and bite my lip.

"Everything about him is beautiful," I breathe to myself. "Phew."

Refocusing, I find him staring straight at the camera with an intense look in his eyes. The power and BDE coming off him causes me to anticipate editing in Photoshop. These are going to be phenomenal.

I take a ton of pictures of him on the beach. Some of him lying on the sand. A few of him lying in it as the tide rolled in and splashed around him.

I didn't think it could get any better. Until we return to our room. To my surprise, he rinses off and rejoins me in a fresh pair of shorts.

"Ready to go again?" he asks, causing me to look up from my camera as I look through the shoots from the beach.

"If you're up to it, sure."

He drops his shorts and climbs onto the rose-petal-covered bed. I stand lost for a moment. I didn't know he meant nude.

He lies across the bed, angled to face me while lifting a leg to block the view of his privates. If I shoot from the right position, I might be able to keep from exposing him.

"Will this work?" he asks as he props his head up on his hand.

I lick my lips. A shiver runs through me as he gives me the most intense look. This feels so intimate and kind of dirty.

"Um, yeah. Hold on, let me get a new SIM card."

Once I have my camera ready and I'm all set up, I take advantage of the lighting that's still spilling into the room or alcove, if you will. Lifting the camera, I get lost in my subject.

"That's great. Can you turn your head for me? Look up."

He does as I request with ease. For the next thirty minutes, he opens up for me and my camera. Wanting to really show him what I see, I have him shift the other way to expose his right side.

"Perfect," I murmur to my camera after taking a few photos of him in the water surrounding our room. I have him place his shorts back on halfway through to take a few more before I'm fully satisfied.

"Let me see," he says as he comes up behind me.

I melt into his arms as he wraps them around me. My lip is trapped between my teeth as I move through the images to show him. I can't wait to get them loaded to enhance them.

They all look great and he looks superhot. Too bad no one else will ever see these. I'm not showing them to anyone.

"My turn," he says and kisses the top of my head.

"I'm not getting naked," I tease.

"You don't have to. You're beautiful just the way you are."

"Do you know how to use this?"

"I plan to use my phone. This is how I see you, remember?"

"Okay, where do you want me?"

"Wherever you feel comfortable. Take your camera and sit wherever you want."

I nod and go to sit on one of the rocks jutting out of the pool of water surrounding the room. I swipe my braids over one shoulder and look at Josh expectantly. He goes to get his phone and stares at me for a moment.

"Relax, take a few pics and act as if I'm not here."

"I can do that," I say nervously.

I point my camera at the gorgeous view and start to take pictures. Soon I'm so lost in the shots before me I'm not thinking about him taking photos of me.

I lower my camera, looking at the last shot I took. I'm swinging my legs in the water, carefree. That's when Josh's voice grabs my attention.

"You're the most beautiful woman I've ever seen. I would marry you today if you said yes."

I look up and laugh. However, after he takes one more shot, I realize he's not joking. He's on one knee with a ring in his hand.

"Joshua?" I say with trembling lips.

"Marry me, Shawn. Live this life with me. I'm happiest when you're in my arms. If you can see past all my damage and still love me, you're the one. The only one for me, marry me."

"Yes," I say and stand from my perch.

He enters the water and lifts me onto his waist. I wrap my legs around him and cup his face as he kisses me. I can't believe what's happening.

"In one day, you've made so many of my dreams come true," I say against his lips.

"I plan to spend the rest of my life giving you all the rest. I love you."

"I love you too."

"Good. Then you won't mind what I have planned tomorrow."

I pull back and look at him warily. The mischief in his eyes has me shaking my head. I already know what's coming.

"Josh," I pout. "The swing was a one-off. I don't know what you have planned, but my stomach isn't built for all of that."

He pecks my lips. "Trust me."

I roll my eyes. "Is it too late to change my mind?"

"Yup. You're mine. We're getting married, Mrs. Nikolaou."

"And?"

"And we're going cliff jumping," he croons and kisses me hard.

"No, no, no, no," I whimper into his neck.

He gives a deep belly laugh. "Trust me. We jump together and solidify our bond. It's going to be awesome."

"God, I must be crazy. I'm really going to do this with you."

"Crazy in love," he chuckles.

CHAPTER FIFTY-SIX

Adrenaline Rush

Shawna

I want to be a chicken and run, but Josh is asking me to take a leap of faith and I'm going to take it with him. I just refuse to look down over this cliff. I'm willing to go over if I don't see how far down it is.

I don't know how Ven does this shit. She's told me time and time again about the rush she gets from doing things like this. I guess getting engaged was a leap off a cliff I never thought I'd take.

"You ready?" Josh says in my ear as he walks up behind me after talking to the guy who brought us here.

"No," I snort.

He turns me to face him and palms the back of my neck to kiss me. "I'd never allow anything to happen to you," he breathes against my lips.

Lifting me onto his waist, he moves to the edge of the cliff. He turns his back to the edge and palms my ass. My head starts to spin.

"Josh, wait, I don't know," I blurt out.

"You don't know what? If you want to jump or if you want to get married before we return to Vander?"

"What?" I gasp.

"Marry me tomorrow. A small wedding in Crete. If you want something bigger, we can do that too. I just want you as my wife before we return," he says as he looks deeply into my eyes.

"Are you for real?"

"Yes."

"Okay." I nod.

He kisses me, then does a backflip off the cliff. As we free-fall, our entire relationship flashes before my eyes. I love this man so much.

My heart races with excitement. I can't believe I'm doing any of this. The laugh that bubbles up makes me feel crazy but happier than I've ever been.

"I'm getting married," I yell.

Josh takes my lips right before we hit the water. It's the most exhilarating feeling in the world. This day couldn't be more perfect.

***

"We're really going to do this?" I squeal as Josh lifts me into his arms after we make it back to dry land.

"Yeah, baby. We are. Pappoús is going to handle everything. He's been preparing since we arrived," he says with a big smile on his face.

"How did you know I'd say yes?"

"I was hoping you would. If you didn't, I was going to leave your ass on this island," he teases.

"You would never." I frown at him.

He kisses my nose. "No, I wouldn't. I couldn't breathe without you."

I wrap my arms around his neck and my legs around his waist. This day has been so surreal. My belly is full of butterflies. It feels like I'm about to be consumed by joy.

"How was it? Amazing, right?"

"Only because it was with you. By the way, you've totally been cheating. You keep throwing me curveballs just before the leap."

He laughs. "A master of distraction. You love me though. That's all that counts."

"Maybe I do, but I'm going to stop going with you when I realize you want to do something like this."

"Live, Shawn, live." He laughs and his eyes sparkle with it.

I look him over and smile. I have been living and it's because of him. I've never had so much confidence in myself.

"My mom is going to kill me," I murmur as the adrenaline begins to wear off.

"We can sit down for dinner with your parents when we get back."

"No." I shake my head and slide down his front to settle on my feet. "I don't want to take away from Ven's wedding. Do you think we're rushing things?"

"No, we both want this. We'll figure out the rest."

I scoff. "So what? We're going to pretend we don't know each other. I mean, come on, Josh. I show up with an engagement ring after I told Ven I couldn't make her bachelorette party? She's going to kill me."

"Then we don't tell her yet. The wedding is in three months. The best way to hide something is to stick to the truth. I told you to run. You didn't and now here we are.

"We stick to that. Make everyone think I'm just being an asshole to you. Once the wedding is over, we sit Skittles down and have a real talk with her."

"And say what?"

He cups my face and looks down into my eyes. "We say that I fell in love with you from that first call. We tell her that I almost lost you and I can't bear that again. We say that I'm nothing without you and because I have people counting on me, I need you by my side to breathe."

With that, he crushes his lips to mine and all thoughts of my parents, my cousin or anything else are swallowed by the emotions that take over me. I grasp his face and kiss him back feverishly. Breaking the kiss, he places his forehead to mine.

"Please don't take it back. Marry me before we go home. I promise it will all work out," he breathes against my lips.

I close my eyes and nod. I wait for the feeling of this being wrong to settle in, but it never comes. Truly, this is the happiest and most sure I've ever been about anything in my life.

"I'm not taking it back. I'm just thinking of the consequences."

"I've got you, no matter what. We're in this together, Shawn. When you breathe, I breathe. When you're happy, I'm happy. When you hurt, I hurt. I never want to see you hurt, so I'm going to make sure this doesn't hurt you. I love you."

I break into a face-splitting smile. "I love you too."

"Come on, we have dinner reservations."

Kelex

I work my jaw as I listen to Jeff on the other end of my phone. I'm supposed to be at dinner with my fiancée, but instead, I'm listening to how my father was the one behind that deal, and apparently, he's been fucking with Jeff's money as well.

"There's nothing I can do about that, Jeff," I seethe into the phone.

"What do you mean? You're just going to turn your back on him trying to fuck us over? How does he even have the power to do any of this?"

"I don't know and I don't care," I bite out.

"Right, your deal was saved, so it's fuck the rest of us."

"Are you fucking kidding me, bro? I worked my ass off to save that deal. I put in the hours, I lost the sleep, I missed the time with my family. If anyone should be pissed, it should be me.

"I'm telling you. I can't do anything about it. What you want me to do is off the table. I'm out. It's over, that's it," I roar.

"You're out?"

"I'm out."

"You mean you're engaged? You're getting married?"

I sigh and work my jaw. "Yeah, this is it. Hopefully he'll free me before we leave."

"But… it's only an engagement. Your grandfather's no dummy. You could break the engagement as soon as you're free. It's not over yet."

"Yeah, I think it is. Listen, when I get back, we'll talk. I'll look at your portfolio with you and see where we can get you some cash flow."

"Don't worry about it. I've been looking at those luxury grooming shops and salons. I might bite the bullet on that. It was one of my better ideas."

I narrow my eyes as if he's standing in front of me. That wasn't his fucking idea. It was something Kid shared with us while at Fuck Off. She asked Pit about it, hoping he'd put out feelers and maybe invest in her.

"Josh?"

"What?" I snarl.

"I love you, bro. Congrats. I thought that accident was going to take everything from you. I should have known. Nothing can keep Joshua fucking Kylix down."

"Not even the fires of hell, bro. Thanks. I love you too. I've got your back. My dad doesn't get to win. We'll get you right."

"I haven't been right since... Never mind. Call me when you're back on this side. We'll celebrate."

I shake my thoughts off. Maybe he did come up with something like Kid's idea on his own. I know for sure he never sticks to one thing. If it's hard work, he's on to the next.

One of the reasons I've never allowed him in on one of my ventures. Friends and business don't mix. Achilles is the exception. That's not just any friend.

CHAPTER FIFTY-SEVEN

Pappoús' Blessing

Shawna

"We're married," I say against Josh's lips as he holds me tight and looks down at me.

We're dancing at our little wedding reception. Basil outdid himself with this intimate affair. It's like a fairy-tale wedding you'd find in a snow globe or something.

"We are, Mrs. Nikolaou."

"You flew my parents in. This day has been almost perfect."

I wasn't expecting my mom to knock on the door while I was getting ready for my wedding, but the relief I felt when I opened the door and found her standing there took so much pressure off my chest.

I was happy to see Zoe too. My heart ached knowing Ven and Lex weren't with me, but every time I thought of Josh waiting for me, I told myself it was for the best.

"Why isn't it perfect?" he whispers in my ear as we dance and get lost in the music.

"You know why. If Mommy and Daddy know, how am I supposed to hide this when we get back?"

"I got the feeling you wanted them here. I gave Blake and Zoe a call to ask a favor. Your mom and dad agreed to keep our secret until we're ready. We don't need to know the details."

He caresses my forehead, then plants a kiss against the spot he just caressed. I go to ask him why I don't need to know the details, but his words halt mine.

"I've always wanted to ask. That scar, it's almost in the same spot as Mayven's. Where'd you get yours?"

I drop my gaze to his chest. "You know how I hate to fight?"

"Yeah," he says with a smile in his voice.

"It's not that I can't. I'm as skilled as Ven and Lex. I can operate a firearm as well. I just chose not to.

"Ven doesn't remember things the way I do. She passed out from her allergic reaction to the spiders. I think she lost bits of what happened right before.

"They were trying to separate us, but we weren't having it. I fought, I bit, I kicked, I did everything I could not to be taken away from her. I hurt one of the men and he got angry.

"That's when they put us in the room with the spiders. I freaked, tripped, and cracked my head. Mayven protected me. She's always protected me."

I pause as the tears start. "If I hadn't fought back, the spider wouldn't have bitten her. I thought she was going to die. I almost lost my best friend.

"Now, it's like I freeze. There's this voice telling me to fight, but I can't. Danny almost killed me and that shouldn't have happened because I can fight. I can protect myself. I'm just afraid of what I might cause if I do. That's stupid, right?"

He lifts my head and looks into my eyes. "No, it's not."

"Yeah, it is because I didn't fight back, and she ended up in danger because of me anyway. Joshua, I have eyes. Your family is different. You've been promising to take care of me. Does that mean you'll keep Ven from danger? I can't be the reason something happens to her. Not again."

He kisses my lips gently. "I promise. Nothing will ever happen to either of you. You both will always be safe. No one wants to see what will happen if I ever feel either of you aren't."

"I was stitched up while they saved her. That's why my scar is faded. I think it was a plastic surgeon. I remember Mom screaming something about getting me a plastic surgeon."

"I'm sorry. Forget I asked," he says and pulls me into a tight hug.

Kelex

"Thanks, Pappoús. Everything was amazing," I say as I walk with my grandfather along the beach.

"You are welcome, *Tzósoua mou*. I'm going to grant you your freedom as I promised. Just give me some time to choose who will replace you. Unless you've changed your mind?" he says with a small smile.

"Not at all. I still want out. I have my family. That's all I want."

"A few more months and then I will bury all of this. No one will know who you were born to be, but if you change your mind…"

"I won't."

"Fine." He shrugs. "Just remember. If you are out, you are out."

"I'm out. You don't have to worry about me."

"Then there is a different conversation we need to have. I have another offer. Your new life fits a vacancy I need filled. This is also why I've placed Zoe in your life."

"But I thought Zoe was to help with… You know what, never mind."

"Listen to me, *Tzósoua*. I've had all of you boys groomed for multiple outcomes. There are four important positions in Bridge Lake and Vander. The head of the family, the counselor, the enforcer, and the mayor. Yannis and I keep things running smoothly through these four.

"No drugs, no federal investigations, plenty of power and money. We have a mayoral vacancy with Marvin Jennings moving into the governor's mansion. I want you to be mayor.

"You don't have to decide now, but as you have decided to live a clean life, this is my offer to you. It removes you from all you don't want but allows you to be someone I trust to keep my hold firm in Bridge Lake and Vander."

"You want *me* to run for mayor?"

"*Naí*, you keep your hands clean; you will walk right into the office. I guarantee it."

I sigh and rub my forehead. I should have known it wasn't going to be as easy as I thought. Although this is a much better option.

"Think about it. For now, things are as they should be. Everyone is where we need them. Take your time. I'm proud of you. You are beyond the man I've always wanted you to be," he says with a smile.

"Thanks, Pappoús. I'll keep an open mind."

CHAPTER FIFTY-EIGHT

Walk Away

Kelex

Three months later…

I stand watching Skittles unknowingly laugh with my wife. Nothing about the secrets I've been keeping feels right, but I'm being forced to keep them because my father has lost his mind.

I wish Jeff would have kept all this to himself. In the last three months, I've learned enough to want to bury my baba right where he stands. However, if I do, it will all fall like a house of cards.

"She loves you. Not like she loves me, but she loves you," Pit says as he comes up beside me.

"I know, what's your point?"

"You think I don't see something's been going on with you? As far as I can dig up, it's not connected to Vander, but that doesn't mean it isn't happening."

"This is your wedding day. Walk away."

"It could be Christmas and you could be sitting in Santa's lap and I wouldn't give a fuck. I see you spiraling and I have this nasty feeling in my gut it's going to affect her in some way. So I want you to start talking now."

"You don't know everything. There's shit they don't want you to see and because of that, you need to mind your business," I snap. "Enjoy your wedding. There were sacrifices made to ensure you would. Say thank you and go dance with your wife."

"What do you need?"

"What?" I turn to look him in his eyes.

"What do you need? For as long as I've known you, you've kept us all at bay. You need something. What is it?"

"You're going to have the world on your shoulders in five seconds. Enjoy this freedom while you can. I'll figure my shit out."

"And Shawna?"

"What did you just say?"

"You look at her the way I look at my wife, not when I was pining after her and thinking you were fucking her. Nah, you look at her the way I look at my wife now that I am fucking her.

"I'm not stupid. You two didn't just meet last night. Your best friend isn't stupid either. She's going to home in on you two when she's not stressed out over planning a wedding."

"Then I suggest you buy her a house or start on those babies. Keep her busy because now is not the time for her to be involved in anything I have going on," I snarl.

"And I'm the one who'll be in the doghouse behind his secrets. She's going to be all in my shit for this," Pit mutters to himself. "Josh."

"What?"

"When you're done being an asshole. I'm here to help. You mean something to her and that girl means even more. So when you need me, I'm here."

I close my eyes and nod. "It was supposed to get better. I did what I was asked to do. He shouldn't be provoking me. This should be over," I choke out.

"Who?" Pit asks and places a hand on my shoulder.

I shrug him off and shake my head. "No one. Forget I said anything."

"Yo, talk to—"

"It's your wedding day. Go dance with your wife."

"Learn to tune that shit out, Kelex. If you want all of that to stay out there, you can't allow it to spill out in here." He taps my temple.

"How? You'd be doing me a favor if you told me how."

He shrugs. "I think you already know what works for you, but when I really need to shut everything down, music helps."

I give a nod and swallow. Closing my eyes, I think his words through. "Thanks, and Pit?"

"What?"

"Stay out of my business. Stop digging. They'll tell you what you need to know when they're ready."

"They who?"

"To have ears and not hear. To have eyes and not see. Today isn't the day. It's coming, but it's not today. Enjoy your wedding, Pit."

I turn and walk off. I need some fresh air. I catch Shawna's eyes and she follows as I exit the ballroom.

Shawna

"Is everything okay?" I ask as I find Josh in the parking lot of the reception hall.

"Pit knows. He doesn't know, know, but it's only a matter of time."

"So we tell them."

He shakes his head. "Now is not a good time."

I search his face. Something has been going on with him for the last few weeks. He's been irritable and short-tempered at times, not with me or the kids, but with everyone else.

"Why not? The wedding is over. We can come clean," I say.

"Baby, there's something else going on and it's just safer for us to keep this under wraps for now. I have a lot going on."

"Is that the reason Zoe gave me one of her guards?"

I was a little surprised when Zoe said Linus would be my new security. He was her wedding gift when we returned to the States. My husband is a very wealthy man, so I didn't find it too strange at the time.

"Linus is related to Helios. I know their family. I wanted someone I could trust to watch over you and the kids."

"That's not an answer to the question."

He sighs and pushes a hand through his hair. "Yes, but I don't want you to worry about any of that."

"Tell me what I can do. I hate seeing you like this."

He tugs me into a hug. I wrap my arms around him and hold on tight. It's been killing me to keep my distance this weekend.

"Go back inside. Find your cousin and have a good time. We'll worry about all this some other time."

"Josh, is she safe?"

"Yes."

"Then I don't want to tell her until all this blows over. If she's angry with me, I'll deal with it. I'd rather have her angry at me than in danger."

He pecks my lips. "Go inside. I'll be back in a bit."

I nod and head back into the hall. I walk past Jeff and give him a little wave. That's when I see Achilles. He's standing off to the side with his attention on his phone. I've been wanting to ask him about Vernice's laptop.

"Shawna," my mother calls my name, stopping me from making a beeline for Achilles.

I shrug it off and go to see what she wants. I guess since this is a wedding, I can ask him another time.

CHAPTER FIFTY-NINE

Birthday Season

Shawna

A month later...

"Don't move," Josh says as he holds me against his chest from behind.

My sex is throbbing. It's his birthday and we've been having birthday sex all morning. I spent the night here last night, something I don't do too often. Josh is so serious about keeping us a secret to keep me safe.

From what? I couldn't tell you because, as always, I've been burying my head in the sand. I love our routine. I spend my evenings at the center with the kids after school. If Josh is in town, he either comes to my place, or Linus escorts me here and back to mine.

"Fine, but I need a break," I laugh.

He kisses my shoulder. "No problem. I just want to hold you and talk. It feels like we haven't been spending enough time together. How are you, baby? You need anything?"

"I'm good. I'm going to buy a new laptop."

"What happened to yours?"

"I gave it to Vernice. Something is wrong with hers."

"You didn't have to do that. Why didn't you guys tell me?"

"You've had so much on your plate. It's no big deal."

He kisses the back of my head and gives me a squeeze. "I'll get you both new ones. From now on, I don't care what's going on. If you guys need something, tell me."

I smile and turn to face him. My smile grows as I reach to run a hand through his hair. It's so long now.

I've noticed he hasn't done anything about his roots in months. He keeps it in a man bun more often than not. This morning it's loose and all over the place.

"Have you decided what you're doing for True's birthday?" I ask.

"He wants to record in a New York City studio. You know, one where the legends have recorded before."

"That sounds so cool. We have to make that happen for him."

He runs a hand down my side and gives my butt a squeeze. "Happy to hear you say that. I want to make it a family trip. We're all going to New York. I've booked him a twenty-four-hour session and I have a songwriter coming in to do a few hooks for him."

"He's going to love that, babe."

"Yeah, I know. When we get back, his new car will be waiting."

"The BMW or the Mercedes?"

"I went with the Mercedes."

"Sweet. Have you heard anything else from their dad? Is he going to sign?"

He frowns. "No," he says curtly.

I still don't understand why the man won't just sign the papers. He doesn't want them. He's made that abundantly clear. I wish there was more I could do.

Josh's phone rings and he turns to reach for it. "Damn, I forgot I was supposed to meet up with Jeff."

"I think it's sweet that he's been teaching True how to drive."

"He's a good guy once you get to know him."

He shoots off a text and tosses his phone back down. I squeal when he pounces and tugs me back under him. He takes my lips in a deep kiss.

"I want to get lost in you one more time," he croons, his eyes sparkling.

"It's your birthday, do with me as you want, my love."

"Say a less."

Kelex

I open the gift Jeff hands me as True heads to the fitting room with a few pairs of jeans. The car and the studio are just part of his birthday gift. I plan to spoil him all week until his big day.

"I can't believe he's sixteen," Jeff says.

"I know. I remember the day we met. He was this cute toothless kid."

He's a great kid and I'm proud of him. His grades have been amazing, and he's been taking on more responsibilities, like volunteering at the center to help some of the younger kids.

"Yeah. Well, I bet you didn't think you were on your way to being Daddy Warbucks back then."

"Whatever, shut up." I shake my head and take the ring out of the gift box. I put on the gold two-finger ring and nod. It's nice.

"You know, that ring would look real sassy on anyone other than your pretty ass," he taunts.

"And yet, you just gave it to me."

"You haven't seen the best part." He reaches over and presses the side of the ring. A blade pops out. "I thought of you as soon as I saw this feature."

I lift a brow. "What made you think of me?"

He shrugs. "Your gladiator over there isn't always going to be around. Slitting throats and going about your business is the Kelex I know."

"That's my father, not me."

"It's a gift. You never know when it might come in handy."

"I doubt I'll use it as intended, but thanks."

"How are things going with the fiancée?"

"Good. We're happy."

"Nice. I'm happy for you, man. I hope your dad backs off and allows you some peace."

"You and me both. Hey, we've been talking about a skydiving trip. As always, the invitation is open. You in?"

"Mm, an asshole trip? If Tak is supplying the weed, I might go."

I laugh. "I'm not going to hold my breath."

"Nah, I mean it. I've been thinking about hanging with your peeps more. Vegas was fun."

"Vegas?"

"Yeah, the bachelor party."

"You went?"

He shrugs. "I knew you had to go see Basil. I figured I'd represent."

"Hey, guys. I'm done," True says as he comes over.

"I've got this one," Jeff says and pulls out his wallet.

CHAPTER SIXTY

New York

Shawna

I stare up at the ceiling in this hotel room, trying to fight back tears. Josh and I had our first real fight. It was after he excused himself to make a call.

I only wanted to check on him and let him know we needed to leave soon to join True at the studio. He snapped at me for no reason. I don't even know what made me lose it, but I did.

I was so mad at him for talking to me like that. Now I feel bad because I've seen that something has been bothering him. I should have been more patient. I'm almost grateful Vernice ended up with a stomachache.

She stirs in the bed next to me and opens her eyes. She wanted to sleep in my bed since the others would be at the studio all night. Twenty-four hours is a long time to be in the studio.

I didn't even know you could do that. I know True has to be in heaven. I can't wait to hear what he's done.

"How are you feeling, honey?" I reach to brush a hand over her hair. She gives me an adorable smile.

"I feel better. I wish we could go now," she replies.

"I know. Next time."

"Will they be back soon?"

"I don't think so. I haven't spoken to Josh yet."

Her face grows sad. She was bummed about not getting to go with the others. I was a little disappointed too, but she wasn't feeling well, and after the fight, I thought it best we stayed here at the hotel.

My phone rings and I see it's a FaceTime from Cat. I answer and she's smiling at me as she holds her finger up to her lips, then beckons me with her hand as if to tell me to follow her. The sound of an acoustic guitar fills the air as she walks through a door.

She starts to sing "If You Let Me" by Sinead Harnett. Cat has such a beautiful voice and tone. This song fits it perfectly. I run a hand through my hair and my mind goes to Josh.

I hate how we left things. Suddenly, Cat turns the camera, and Josh comes into view, playing the guitar. He takes over singing the hook of the song and flows right into the second verse.

My heart almost bursts. He's looking right into the camera as if looking into my eyes. My mouth falls open. I've never heard him sing like this. Yes, I knew he could sing, but this is so soulful and gritty. He's giving Cat and Sinead a run for their money.

My lips tremble as I listen to him finish the song. I get it. This is his way of saying sorry. It's the end for me when he sings my name as he says he'll love me like he's never, ever loved somebody. The tears I've been holding back all morning run down my cheeks.

"I love you, baby. I'm so sorry," he says after he sings the last note.

"I hate fighting with you. I love you too."

"Let me make it up to you. Helios is going to take the kids skating. Be ready to go on a date with your husband so he can make up for being an asshole to you."

I bite my lip and nod my head as I wipe away my tears. I'm still in awe of his voice and that he's just sang to me.

"I'll be ready," I say.

"How's Vernice?"

"I'm fine. I'm right here," she sings and moves so she can be seen. "Can Helios come get me now?"

Josh chuckles. "Get ready. I'll send him over, but you're going to miss the spa day I had planned for you two."

"Oh, um, nah. I'm fine here. Shawna needs me to pick her polish."

Josh laughs and winks at her. "That's what I thought. I'll see you guys later. I love you both."

"See you later, J," Vernice sings and jumps up to dash out of the room.

"I think you just made her day."

"I hope I can make yours too. I really am sorry."

"It's okay."

"No, it's not." He looks up as if someone grabs his attention. "Listen, I need to go. I love you. I'll see you later."

Kelex

I'm happy I was able to do this for True. Recording in New York in The Cutting Room is a big deal for him. Rap legends have recorded within these walls.

However, now that I've made one of his dreams come true, I need to fix things with my wife. I didn't mean to take my frustration out on her. She had no idea Achilles had called with news that had me ready to go back on my word to my grandfather.

Like I told my cousin Anthony, we all have decisions to make, but Pappoús may not get his mayor because my father is trying to make me kill him. If I weren't in New York, he'd be a dead man. I look over at Cat and True.

I can't go back on my word because of them.

I've been chanting those words to myself all night. I make myself focus on the task before me. I point to the picture on the device in my hand. I have a personal stylist showing me outfits for the date I have planned tonight.

"This one, she'll look great in this and this hair and makeup. You'll have to get the picture over to the spa ASAP. Make sure your team is done by eight. You can deliver my things to the front desk. I'll pick them up from there," I say.

"No problem, sir. Is there anything else I can do for you?"

"No, that will be all. Thank you."

"J, you ready?" True says expectantly.

"You and Cat head out with Helios. I have some things I need to take care of."

"Okay, cool. You all right?"

"I'm good. It's just time for me to let something go."

He shrugs and goes to leave with his sister. I pull the band from my hair and allow it to fall around my shoulders. I run a hand through it to push it out of my face. I almost forgot what it's like to have hair this long.

Holding the strands between my fingers, I look at the blond and purse my lips. It's more than True snapping on me last night about my roots and the blond hair.

I've been growing it out for a while. Actually, I've been growing it out since Shawna said she loved it dark and when I used to wear my fauxhawk. If I want a change, I have to make it happen.

"It's time," I mutter to myself.

CHAPTER SIXTY-ONE

Letting Go

Shawna

My husband doesn't half-ass an apology date. A makeup team showed up after my day at the spa and brought a garment bag with a cute black jumper inside for me. It's sort of an *I Dream of Jeannie* look.

Not something I would pick for myself, but it's cute on me. I can see why Josh chose it. The legs are slit up the sides and the front has a deep *V*.

The sleek ponytail with the braid around it that they put my hair in at the salon in the spa is perfect. I like the diamonds they placed on my eyelids like eyeliner. I can't help but smile in the mirror at my fresh, natural-looking makeup.

The strappy heels are sexy, but I don't think they're too high. I may come to eye level with Josh. It's all enough to give my confidence a boost.

"Shawna, J said he's on his way. We're heading out. Have fun," Cat calls into the room.

"Okay, thank you. You guys have fun too."

I turn for my clutch and check my things as I move out into the common area. Music starts to play. Cian Ducrot's vocal fills the room as "I'll Be Waiting" plays, causing me to lift my head.

I stop in my tracks and clench my bag to my chest. Josh lifts his head from fixing his cuff as his black suit jacket hangs from his fingertips. However, that's not what stops me and takes my breath away.

"You cut your hair," I gasp.

He gives me a panty-melting smile and pushes his free hand through the longer side of his thick, dark locks. It's almost exactly as I remember it used to be. I take in everything from his black suede loafers to his well-fitting black slacks to the black suspenders over his crisp black dress shirt with the top three buttons open.

"I did. I do remember you saying this is the way you like it."

He gives me a wink. I have to shake my shock away. Smoothly, he slips on his jacket and buttons it in place, then reaches to push his thick hair back once again.

It seems to have so much more movement and body now that the blond has been chopped away. I can't wait to run my hands through it. He looks so handsome. Scratch that. He looks so beautiful it hurts.

He lifts his hand and holds it out to me. "Come here, gorgeous."

I make my feet move forward and take his hand. He spins me in front of him and gives a low whistle. Slipping his hand into the opening of one side of my jumper, he grabs hold of my ass and tugs me into him.

"No panties?" he lifts a brow. "I don't think I thought this through. I knew you would kill this outfit, but now I want to keep you to myself."

He kisses my lips. "We need to leave before I bend you over and ruin our night."

"I have no problem with that. New York is overrated. We could come back another time."

"That's my girl," he says and kisses my neck.

"Josh," I whimper as he starts to knead my ass while kissing and nipping at my neck.

He pries my clutch from my hand and starts to walk me back into the room, tossing my bag down on a chair as we go by. Next thing I know, he has me lifted onto his waist as he devours my lips.

I can't hold back any longer. I push my hands into his hair and nearly squeal. It feels so silky and lush, just like I always imagined it would. I bury my fingers in it and tug, pulling a deep groan from him.

"You like that? Does that make you happy?" he says, nipping at my chin and grasping the back of my neck.

"Yes, I love it. It feels better than I dreamed."

"Good, I love when you're happy."

He allows me to slide down his front and turns my back to face him. I slide my ponytail out of the way as he unzips me. The front of the jumper falls to my waist and a thought comes to mind.

I want him happy too. With that thought, I push the jumper to the floor and turn to face him again. Josh cups my face in one hand and tugs me to his lips roughly.

He kisses me feverishly while I reach for his belt and release it. He pushes off his suspenders and tugs his belt off once I have it open. I work to get his pants open and drop down to my knees.

He looks down at me in confusion. Ignoring his expression, I reach into his pants and pull him out. Before I can lose my confidence, I take him into my mouth and look up into his eyes.

I smile around him as I start to work his length with my hands. No shame. I know I'm not getting that much into my mouth. Or so I thought. Josh is both thick and long. This is my first time.

He groans and cups the back of my head as he pumps his hips. I think fast and relax my mouth and throat.

I gag as he goes too far. "Fuck, baby," he hisses.

He pulls out and saliva drips from my mouth, hanging from his tip as he bobs before my face. I'm not going to quit. Instead, I place my hands on his thighs and find him with my mouth.

"Mm," I hum and try again.

Kelex

I throw my head back and close my eyes. Shawna has never gone down on me, but this is way worth the wait. Her mouth feels so good around me.

I've fantasized about this so many times. She totally has the mouth for it. I just wasn't going to pressure her into doing something she didn't want to. Now those fantasies seem so weak in comparison to the real deal.

"Fuck," I growl as I step out of my shoes.

This was not what I had planned for tonight, but seeing her dressed all sexy and the look in her eyes when she saw what I'd done. I would have cut the blond out of my hair months ago if I knew it would turn her on like this.

"Mm," a moan vibrates through me as she works my cock and slurps as she sucks and swirls her tongue around my tip.

I reach for one of her breasts and roll her nipple between my fingertips. She lifts her gaze to mine again. I give her a wink of reassurance.

"Just like that, baby. Lick the sides. Don't be shy. It's yours. I'm your personal popsicle. Get me wet and have fun."

"Mm," she moans around me.

Following my instructions, she tilts her head and licks the side before taking me back in her mouth to bob a few times and repeating on the other side. When she takes me in again, I hold her head in my palms and pump into her mouth. It feels so fucking good, but I can't wait to taste her and be inside her tight pussy.

She hollows her cheeks and hums. I lose all focus. Wrapping her ponytail around my hand, I tug her head back. She looks up at me in surprise. I grasp her face and bend to take her mouth.

"I want you," I say into her mouth.

Our tongues and teeth collide as I try to eat her face. I bring her to her feet, my grasp on her face still firm. Moving my lips to her neck, I kiss and suck. A hum leaves my lips as her sweet taste bursts in my mouth.

"Babe," she whimpers. "Oh my God, I'm on fire. Please."

"Patience," I tease.

I kick my way out of my pants as I grope her sexy body. I release her just long enough to retrieve a condom from my slacks. My baby is never the aggressor, so she takes me by surprise when she maneuvers our bodies for me to have my back to the foot of the bed.

She then pushes me down and takes the foil packet from my hand. I toss my head to get my hair out of my face, but before I can make a move, Shawna pounces, kissing her way up my abs.

I watch her ass lift in the air as she works her way up my body and pushes me back onto the mattress. Rolling the rubber onto my pulsing length, she then straddles my body and grabs a handful of my hair as she moves her lips to mine.

I take over the kiss, grabbing her ass with one hand and my shaft with the other to bring her down on it. She moans as she sinks down on me. I look up into her face and nip at her chin.

"Yes," she cries out.

"Easy, baby," I groan.

We set a relaxed pace, her riding me nice and easy. My gaze dances across her face as she enjoys herself. I wrap my hand around her throat and lift my other hand to her mouth to run my thumb across her lips.

She sucks my finger into her mouth and twirls her tongue around it. Her pussy ripples around me. I begin to roll my hips beneath her.

"Shit, Josh. *Ah.*" She gasps and places her hands on my shoulders.

I squeeze her throat gently. She looks into my eyes and grinds her waist. I suck my lip into my mouth and my eyes roll back.

"I feel you ready to come. Sit on my face. Let me finish you."

She whimpers and bounces on me a few more times. I lift her and shift to get her to climb over my face.

"Josh," she screams as I dance my tongue through her folds.

I hum and keep eating. Then she blows my mind for the second time tonight. She lifts, turns, and grabs my cock to remove the barrier and suck me into her mouth.

"*Fuck*," I drag out before I go back to bring her to climax.

I push two fingers into her and make her hum and sing for me. Her pussy joins in on the song, making that super wet sound. I know I can make her squirt, so I reach to rub her pussy while I suck on her swollen lips.

"That's it, I'm coming, I'm coming."

Shawna

"Are you hungry? Should I order something?"

Josh kisses my forehead. "I'll order us something in a bit. Sorry about our date."

I laugh. "That was my fault too. I'm not holding it against you."

"Good thing I told Helios to keep the kids out late."

"Right?" I snuggle into his side. "Have you heard anything more about adoption?"

"He's still refusing to sign. Baby, I'm in a good mood. Let's not talk about that."

"Sorry," I murmur.

I still don't know why he gets so irate when the subject comes up. Yes, it's frustrating and the adoption could have and should have been done by now, but the simple mention of it or the kids' father and it's like steam starts to come from his head. Not wanting to ruin the night, I change the subject.

"What made you change your hair? It wasn't really what I said, was it?"

"I'm ready to let go of my past. Looking at those pictures you took in Greece, it dawned on me that I wanted to be me again." He shrugs. "And you love me as me, so it was a no-brainer."

I sit up and hold the sheet up over my breasts. With the other hand, I cup the side of his head where the shorter side of his hair is.

"Do you not see this? How could I not love it and you?"

He laughs and tugs me down onto his broad chest. He then kisses me. "How could I not love you?"

CHAPTER SIXTY-TWO

Disrespect

Kelex

Seven months later...

"What should I pick up for Pit's birthday?"

"Get him something you think he'll like. I already took care of a gift from me," I say to Shawna on the other end of the phone.

"Oh, we're doing separate gifts."

"Baby—"

"No, it's okay."

I rub my tired eyes. It's frustrating not being able to give my wife an answer when she asks me when we can come clean about who we are to each other. My father has been quiet in the last month, but I'm not taking any risks.

"Pappoús wants us to come for a visit. I plan to discuss the situation with him then. Can you hold on until then for me?"

"Yeah, I guess. Are we going before or after our anniversary?"

"Right now, I don't know. I have some business I need to handle here. I guess we can go when I'm done with that."

I don't tell her that I've been meeting with campaign managers to run for mayor. If I'm going to do this, I want to know what all it will entail, Blake and Zoe have been instrumental in that. I know for sure Pappoús will want an answer when I arrive.

"Then how are we going to handle this weekend? Ven thinks I'm just crushing on you," she says, pulling me from my thoughts.

"Mr. Nikolaou, I have Bridge Lake Academy on line two," my assistant's voice comes through the intercom.

"Listen, we'll talk out what we plan to do tonight. That's Vernice's school on the line. Let me get that."

"Call me back if something is wrong," she says with concern.

I end the call with Shawna and pick up my office phone. "Hello?

"Mr. Nikolaou, this is Emily Frost from Bridge Lake Academy. Headmaster Bozeman would like for you to come in to speak with him. Would you be able to come in this afternoon?"

"What is this about? Is Vernice, okay?"

"She's fine. I believe I should allow Mr. Bozeman to inform you of the details."

I look at the time. I'm done with my meetings for the day. However, Helios is out running errands.

I shoot Jeff a quick text on my private line, hoping he can take me over to the school. We had plans to meet up later anyway. If not, I'll call for a car.

Jeff: *I'll be there in fifteen.*

Me: *Thanks.*

"I'll be there within the hour," I say into the phone.

"Thank you, Mr. Nikolaou. See you then."

I dial Shawna back. She picks up right away. Again, her concern comes through as she says hello.

"Hey," I reply.

"What's happening?"

"I don't know. They want me to come in, but they said she's fine."

"Would you like me to meet you? I'm wrapping up here. I can head there to meet you. I'll be there as soon as I can."

"I can handle it."

"I know you can. Let's just say I'm coming for moral support."

"I want to see you too."

"How did you know?" she says with a smile in her voice.

I chuckle. "I'll see you there. Be safe, gorgeous."

Jeff pops his head into my office right as we're about to end the call. I wave him in and stand so we can head out. The sooner I get to the school, the sooner I can find out what's going on.

"Love you, babe. See you soon," Shawna says sweetly.

"Yeah, me too." I frown because I hate not saying I love her, but with Jeff staring right at my mouth, something holds me back.

As far as Jeff knows, Shawna is still my fiancée, not my wife, and he doesn't think I have real feelings for her. Pappoús' words have stuck with me. When it comes to Shawna, the world is on a need-to-know basis.

"Oh, okay. Later." She hangs up before I can smooth things over.

"You ready?" Jeff asks.

"Yeah. Let's go."

"Is the kid okay?"

"Yeah, I'm not sure what this is about."

He snorts. "Twenty bucks says that little monster's mouth got her in trouble."

"Nah, I doubt that. She doesn't misbehave in school. She reserves all that for home." I laugh and shake my head.

***

Jeff gets me to Bridge Lake Academy in no time. I text Shawna and she lets me know she got held up, but she's on her way. Wanting to find out what's going on, I thank Jeff for the ride and head inside.

I can't imagine what's going on. I hope to God she didn't tell anyone off. Although it would be out of character if she did, which would mean they deserved it.

"Ah, Mr. Nikolaou. Thank you for coming in on such short notice. Please step into my office," the headmaster Mr. Bozeman says nervously.

There's a weird tension in the air. I also take notice of the old lady sitting with a smug look on her face. My curiosity is piqued.

She reeks of old money, old Bridge Lake money. Ignoring her, I step into the headmaster's office.

"Please, have a seat."

I release the button on my suit and take the seat he's offering in front of his desk. "Would you like to tell me what this is all about?"

"It was brought to my attention that we might have made a little mistake. We're going to have to move Vernice to the waiting list for the Rising Star program."

"Excuse me?" I seethe.

"There was only one seat available. Someone made a clerical mistake and placed Vernice in it. I'm very sorry, but—"

"You called me here to tell me you want to pull *my* child from the gifted program because of a clerical mistake. Do I look stupid to you?"

"Of course not, Mr. Nikolaou. I'm trying to explain—"

"Explain what?" I roar.

"Brian Douglas was the candidate who was supposed to get the spot. It was a slight oversight."

I start to see red. He's talking bullshit. It dawns on me where I know the old lady from. Josephine Douglas. The Douglas's are not a founding family but they get a pass and have run in the right circles.

I tilt my head to the side. "You do realize Vernice has been in this program for the last three months? Let me also remind you of the fact that you were there for her intake, and it came out of your mouth several times that Vernice was the most advanced student you'd seen in years.

"So tell me. How does *my* child go from being a top… no, let me correct myself… the top candidate for the program to losing her seat because of a clerical error?

"Let me tell you what I think happened. Someone greased your greedy little palms or promised you some type of donation and now you think you're going to take *my* little brown-faced child and remove her from a seat she has earned.

"How many languages does little Brian speak because *my* child speaks five. By next year, I'll have her fluent in seven. What reading level is Brian on? *My* child reads on an eleventh-grade level at the age of ten.

"I've challenged her to write a dissertation this summer because she wants to level up. Does Brian have that type of ambition? Don't play with me because this is a fight you won't win. *My* child will not be moving from the program, nor will you be able to keep your position if you ever try something like this again.

"Check your records, Vernice's tuition has been paid up for the next four years. Anything she participates in won't need to fundraise because I'll cover the entire program out of pocket. There's also one more thing you should know."

"What's that, sir?"

"Zoe Gataki. That's the name of our family's attorney. So tell me again, what's the issue here?"

"Mr. Nikolaou, I'm so sorry for wasting your time. There is no issue. I assure you it's taken care of. There won't be any further issues," he says, looking like he's about to shit his pants.

I stand and button my suit jacket. "I'm glad we could clear things up. Send for Vernice, I'll be taking her home with me today."

"Yes, sir. Right away."

Without another word, I walk out. As I walk by Mrs. Douglas, I return her smug grin. The audacity of these people.

I'm still fuming as I wait for Vernice to meet me in the front hall of the school. I look down at my watch and my gut tells me to double back. I'm just about to turn the corner when I hear the old bitch hissing.

"You, you little— Four generations of Douglases have been in the gifted program here. How dare they give you a seat because of affirmative action or whatever bullcrap your people have come up with now? My Brian should be in that program, not you."

"Lady, I don't know what you're talking about and your breath stinks. Get off my arm and get out of my face," Vernice snaps.

"Ma'am, get your hand off my child. I'm not going to repeat myself," I hiss.

Vernice yanks her arm away and comes running to me. I wrap an arm around her and start for the glass doors to exit. I hold the door for Vernice to step out ahead of me. Then I step out and hold the door for Mrs. Douglas.

She gives me a false smile as if she's embarrassed she got caught. I wait until she's about to step through the doorway and release the door, so it slams right in her face. I return her smile as her expression turns to one of shock as she stumbles back.

"Joshua," Shawna gasps, causing me to spin on my heels.

Shawna

I still can't believe my husband did that. That woman had to be about sixty years old. I can't get the stunned look on her face out of my head.

The worse part was the fact that he wouldn't even allow me to see if she was okay. He grabbed me by the arm and marched me to my car. I've been so heated with him.

I should have gone home to my place. I thought I'd be able to calm down to find out what happened with Vernice at school, but his lack of remorse has been driving me crazy and I can't cool off.

"Here," Jeff says, handing me a cup of tea.

"Thank you."

"It must be hard being engaged to someone you don't know that well."

"What?" I say and furrow my brow.

I take a calming breath and remember not everyone knows we're already married. That must be why Josh didn't say I love you back earlier. At least I can stop being mad about that.

"I'm just saying. You're doing him a favor, right?" Jeff continues.

"What do you mean?"

He shrugs. "He had to get engaged to pull off that deal with his grandfather. You came along at just the right time.

"That's why you agreed to the engagement, isn't it? To help him out. A year isn't a long time to make something like that happen, I'm glad you were there for him, but this has to be hard.

"I'm sure you're learning all types of things about him that might not be so pretty. Josh has more than one side. There're Josh, Joshua, and Kelex. You never know which you'll get. It's one of the things that has kept us close all these years."

"Um, Jeff, you'll have to excuse me."

I think I'm going to be sick. Basil was the one to put our wedding together. Was it all for some deal Josh never told me about?

I feel so stupid. It all makes sense now. How he insisted we get married right away. Him proposing out of the blue while we were in Greece.

"I need to talk to you," I demand as I storm into the bedroom where Josh is lying on the bed with his laptop.

"You're finally ready to talk to me?"

"Tell me the truth. Did you or did you not have a deal with your grandfather to get engaged within a year?"

"What? How do you know that?"

I bite my lip to hold back the tears. I don't need to hear anything else. I take the chain from around my neck that holds my rings and throw the chain and rings at him.

"We're done," I snarl and turn to rush from the house.

"Shawn, Shawna," Josh calls after me, but I don't stop until I'm in my car.

I make it to my parents' before I fall apart. I knew it was all too good to be true. Why am I so stupid?

CHAPTER SIXTY-THREE

What's up with You

Shawna

I never went into my parents' house. After I cried myself out, I realized that would be the second place Josh would come to look for me. I needed some space.

"No, Joshua, I still haven't heard from her," Zoe says into her phone.

I hate to drag her into the middle of this, but she's the first person I thought of. I glance over at Achilles. He's not too happy about his mom lying for me or at least I think that's what his problem is.

He's been scowling since he arrived and found me here. Zoe hangs up and looks at me. "There, that should buy you some more time," she says.

"Thank you. I'm so sorry about this."

"You do know he's not stupid, right? You've been hiding out here for what? Two days. It's only a matter of time before he shows up here," Achilles grumbles.

"I know. I'm sorry about all of this. I'm leaving today."

"You don't have to rush off. I think Joshua would rather you hide out here safe with me than be somewhere out there," Zoe says.

"Unfortunately, I have to face the music," I say.

"Pit's birthday weekend?" Achilles says.

"Yeah, if I don't go, my cousin is going to wring my neck."

My phone starts to ring for the millionth time. I look down to see it's Josh again. Ignoring the call as I've done all the others, I sigh and fight back the tears.

"I'm here if you need me," Zoe says gently.

"I'm fine. I'll be okay."

I've been chanting that lie in my head all day. If I can make it through this weekend, then I can ask for a divorce. I just need to make it through the weekend.

Kelex

"You want to tell me what's up with you?" Skittles says as she comes to join me in the car.

"Not really. Can we focus on whatever it is you're doing to help Ox?"

"I know how to multitask."

"I know you do," I murmur under my breath.

"All right, all joking aside. You sent me a text in the middle of the night to ask me if Shawna was coming this weekend. What's going on with you and my cousin?"

"At the moment, nothing. She's not talking to me."

"Ow," I say and grab my arm where she just punched me. "What was that for?"

"I knew it. I knew you were talking to her behind my back."

"It's more complicated than that."

"Josh, I'd be lying if I said I wasn't happy for you. You deserve to find someone to make you happy. However, this is Shawnnie.

"Don't play with her. Not because she's my little cousin and I'll hurt you if you ever hurt her, but because she's…"

"Sensitive, compassionate, at times unsure of herself and painfully shy despite being amazing, talented, caring and selfless?" I say.

"Well, damn. Yeah, all of that. I just want her happy. I wish I could take back what happened to her. I wish…"

"I'll make you a promise. I'll give everything I have to make her happy. No matter what it takes, she will always be happy and safe."

"Can you really promise me that?"

"I just did. Have I ever broken a promise to you?"

"No, you've been my best friend. I trust you."

"Then trust that I care about her and I've got her."

"I knew I should have kept your pretty ass away from her. It was Pit's idea to pair you two up in the wedding party. Ugh, now look," she teases.

I fall silent and swallow down my guilt. Shawna was mine way before the wedding. I could come clean, but I made Shawna a promise as well. Besides, I don't even know if there's anything to come clean about.

"Do you want me to help? You know, fix whatever's going on with you two?"

"No, I can work it out. I just need to see her."

"I think I like you for her. You have a big heart. Don't forget to show her that."

I smile. "You want to get involved in this so bad, don't you?" I laugh.

"I do. I really do. You'd be like her second boyfriend ever. I'm always so scared for her."

"I also worry about you. Are you sure you're ready?"

"I know I am. She's the one, Skittles. I'm not playing with her."

"Good, I love you, Kelex."

"I love you too."

"Oh, and one more thing."

"What's up?"

"Is she why you changed your hair?"

I laugh and shake my head. I know she's fishing for information. I just let it go.

CHAPTER SIXTY-FOUR

You and Me

Shawna

My car wouldn't start, which made no sense. Achilles was kind enough to bring me up to the cabin, although that was kind of awkward.

I didn't miss the look of longing on his face as he looked at the house. The music could be heard from out front and the house just seemed to be more lively than the last time I was here.

"Yo, you good, baby girl. You need anything?" Pit asks as he carries my bags upstairs for me.

"I'm fine. Thank you. Is Mayven here?"

"She and Kelex took off shopping. They should be back soon."

My heart skips a beat with the mention of Josh's name. I have no idea what I plan to say to him when I do see him. I know I can't avoid him.

"Here you go. This one is all yours. I put you next to Kelex and across from Leo since they're the only other single people in the house. You know, so y'all don't have to hear those other motherfuckers fucking all night," he says with a mischievous grin and a wink.

"Thanks."

"No problem. You need anything else, let me know."

"Happy birthday, Pit. Thanks again."

"Thank you. You make sure you have a good time tonight."

I sigh, knowing I'm going to be miserable all weekend. I go into my room and start to unpack my things for something to do.

"Hey."

I turn toward the door and gasp as I see Lex with her head popped in the room. I haven't seen my cousin in years. She's actually Ven's cousin but we've always seen each other as family.

"What are you doing here?"

"Long story," she says and rolls her eyes. "Get over here."

She opens her arms and I rush into them. Her warm embrace means everything in this moment. I squeeze a little tighter before I let her go.

"Come sit with me. You have to tell me everything that's going on with you," I say and tug her over to the bed.

"Well, I'm here with my husband," she starts.

"Your husband?"

"Yes, and our son AJ."

My brain races. I drop my mouth open as it clicks. Ven teased Ox the weekend of the wedding about that little guy. I have to admit, I had questions, but I never thought he belonged to Lex.

"Ox, your husband is Ox?"

"The one and only. Has been for about fourteen years."

"Oh my God. How did Ven take it?"

"She was going to kick my ass until she saw it was me, but overall, she seems to be okay with it."

"Oh, cool."

"So what's been going on with you?"

I wave her off. "Never mind me. I want to hear all about you and how you've been married to one of Ven's friends all this time and we've never known about it."

"You have that kind of time?"

"Sure do."

As long as she's talking, I don't have to think about my own situation. So I sit and listen. My mind is blown when she's done. I have so many questions.

"You hungry? I'm going to head down for something to drink."

"Um, I'm going to make a few calls. I'll meet you downstairs," I say.

"Cool, see you in a bit."

I call Zoe quickly to let her know I'm settled. Then I stand staring at my phone wondering if I should at least text Josh to warn him that I'm here. The sound of my door closing causes me to turn.

There Josh stands, staring back at me. I frown and go to leave the room. I get my hand on the handle, but he cages me in with his hands against the door, preventing me from opening it.

"We're not leaving this room until you talk to me," he breathes in my ear.

"We have nothing to say. I can't trust you."

"I have never lied to you. You're my wife. How can you not trust me?"

"You married me for some deal or something. It's not real."

He grasps the front of my throat and turns me to face him, pressing me up against the door. Before I can say a word, his lips are on mine. I whimper into his mouth and get angry with myself for melting into him.

"There are things you still don't know about me. Some I hope you never find out, but I've never lied to you. Ever.

"Did I have to get engaged? Yes. But I didn't have to get married. I married you because I love you. I'm staying married to you because I love you," he says against my mouth.

I look up at him and search his eyes. My heart still hurts. All the confidence I've been building feels false.

"Shawna, baby, this is real. I really love you."

"Why?"

"Why what?"

"Why do you love me? It doesn't make sen—"

He cuts my words off with a hard kiss. I lock my fingers in his hair and hold on tight as he devours me. There's something different about this kiss.

"I'm sorry. I shouldn't have rushed things. I thought you were ready. I thought you saw what I saw," he says and moves to kiss behind my ear.

As he kisses my neck and unfastens my jeans, I try not to make a sound. However, the moment he shoves his long fingers into my panties and pushes them into me, I lose the battle.

"Josh," I cry out.

"You're so gorgeous. I sit up at night watching you, wondering what I did to deserve you. You're amazing. You stepped right in and helped me create a family for children who aren't either of our blood, no questions."

"Oh my God, Joshua," I moan as I try to grab his wrist and slow the climax he's creating.

"You look at me and see me, a man, not my scars, not my demons. You have always seen me. Even when the darkness tries to peek through.

"That's it. Come for me. Stop fighting it, baby. Let me show you pleasure. All I want is to give you pleasure. If for no other reason than because it's what you deserve."

"Fuck," I gasp as my legs tremble as I lift up on my toes and gush all over his fingers.

I place my forehead to his chest. "I need to think," I whisper.

"You don't need me. You don't need anyone to prove you're beautiful, intelligent, sexy as fuck, and worth loving. When you allow yourself to see it, you'll understand why. You will never have to ask me or anyone else why.

"I love you, Shawn. I'm in love with you. I spent eight years waiting for you. That's why I rushed to marry you. Not because my grandfather put a clock on my head. I did it all because I love you."

"And if you didn't find me here that night? If we hadn't started dating. What would you have done?"

"I would have become a monster because there wasn't anyone else for me."

With that, he kisses me one last time before placing his fingers he pulls from my pants into his mouth. He locks gazes with me as he licks his fingers clean.

"This fight is over. Tonight, you're sleeping in my bed."

"But... what about Ven?" I whisper.

"I'll take care of that. You and me, Shawn. Focus on you and me."

Kelex

I'm sitting in bed with my back to the headboard as Shawna sits between my legs. I have my arms wrapped around her shoulders as I bury my face in her hair and inhale. It's good to have her back in my arms.

I thought the night would never end. Seeing Ox and Lex war it out musically with so much passion almost made me grab Shawna and call it a night. I was the first one to get up to leave when Ox mauled Lex's face.

"That was fun," Shawna says, breaking into my thoughts. "Are all of you guys' trips like this?"

"Usually there's a lot more pranking and crazy shit."

"Crazy shit like what?"

"Midnight snowmobile rides. Naked skiing. Name it, we've done it."

She snickers. "Really?"

"Yeah, we've done some crazy shit over the years."

"Why did almost everyone look so shocked that you could sing? Have you never sang for them before?"

"No."

"But you used to sing when you were modeling. I remember you posting a few videos."

I grin and move my face to the crook of her neck. "Not everyone stalked me back then."

"I didn't stalk you. I was just a follower. You were so talented."

"It's okay, baby. I picked up on the stalker vibes a long time ago."

"Shut up, Josh."

I laugh and suck her flesh into my mouth. "Honestly, none of us liked each other before... Ven brought us together. Before that, I didn't know her, even though we did run around some of the same circles.

"Once we became friends, all of that was over. I stopped singing and all of that," I say and shrug.

She reaches to lace her fingers with mine. I begin to play with her fingers as we fall silent for a moment. I get lost in my thoughts until her sweet voice pulls me back out.

"Maybe we should just come clean and fess up?"

I sigh. I had been hoping this wouldn't come up, but I'm not going to fight with her about it. I have no proof it's not a good time.

"If that's what you want."

She turns to look me in the face. "Really?"

"Yes, really. You want to do it together?"

"I don't know? Maybe I should tell her alone."

"I'll do whatever you want."

She sits silently for a beat. I can see her thoughts racing. I know my wife. This isn't what she wants. She's just not ready to ask for what she truly wants... the truth from me.

Because I'm a bastard still hiding my secrets, I don't press. I take her lips to change the subject instead. I'll step on those grenades when the time comes.

CHAPTER SIXTY-FIVE

Come Clean

Kelex

Three weeks later...

"Why am I here?" I say to Blake.

He's called me to his place at butt fuck o'clock in the morning. I'm cranky and I need him to spit it out so I can go back home and climb into my bed. It's bad enough I was up all night fielding calls about an incident at one of our festival locations.

At this point, I don't believe anything that's been happening in the last two weeks is a coincidence. I'm also annoyed with Blake and my grandfather. I feel like they're allowing this bullshit.

"I need to talk to you."

"Okay, I got that. What about?"

"I'm going to reveal who you are to Pit. It was brought to my attention that Ox already knows. Your pappoús has made his choice."

"Finally. It's about time," I say in relief.

"Hold on. I think there's something you should know. I'm choosing to tell you what your grandfather hasn't. I think it's become important for you to know."

I fold my arms over my chest. "Okay, I'm listening."

"Your mother wasn't hit by a drunk driver. That story Ulysses has been feeding you all these years has been bullshit. She and her friends were in a car accident, but it was because a device was placed on the car that incapacitated your mother's ability to operate the vehicle.

"That hit created a world of chaos. The women in that car were all connected to powerful families and or men with power.

"Your father stood to benefit from the type of confusion it caused because it turned the table against itself. Everything imploded from there. However, none of us wanted to believe he would do such a thing. Ulysses has done some crazy shit, but this...this was over the top."

"Are you standing here telling me my father is responsible for my mother's death?" I seethe.

"That I'm still not sure of. We tried to siphon out the truth but kept hitting a wall. Basil and my father grew tired and had planned to leave it alone.

"That was until a certain chain of events started. We knew that door was opening again. We also know that while your father is the one who keeps opening it, he's blind to the consequences and repercussions of his actions.

"Okay, so why should I know this now? What do you think will change?"

"Your mother and her friends were the consequences the last time your father wanted to make a power play. This time you and your friends seem to be the targets."

I sit up straight and roll my shoulders back. "What did you just say?"

"Basil and Yannis want to meet in Italy. I'm to make the trip with you, Anthony, and William."

"Leave them out of this."

"Joshua," Blake says in warning.

"Leave them out of this," I repeat.

I stand, vibrating with rage. I'm going to kill him. I never thought my father would stoop so low.

"Joshua, sit back down. I'm not done."

"What else could you possibly have to say?"

"I don't think he gets what he's doing. He doesn't know he's been betrayed and will be again."

"Well, aren't you forgiving. I'm not. In my father's case, stupidity is a choice. He's only blind when it serves him."

With that, I turn to leave, tasting my father's blood. He's going to pay for this. I don't care about the consequences.

"Josh, Josh, Joshua," Blake roars behind me.

I ignore him and keep walking. There's only one person I want to talk to, but I doubt there will be much talking.

Shawna

I came up to the cabin, hoping to get a chance to come clean with Ven. She's my cousin, so I feel this should come from me. I also knew I'd have Lex here to support me.

So why haven't I been able to spit the words out? I'm here hiding out in the bathroom, too chicken to look my cousin in the eye and tell her I'm married to her best friend.

"Grow up, Shawnnie. Go out there and tell the truth. Stop all the lying."

I've been lying since I got here. I could have just come clean when Ven asked what was going on with me and Josh. To be honest, I think I'm lying because if I speak the truth, the seams are going to start to burst.

I should've asked Josh why he needed to be engaged, but I've been dodging asking that question for three weeks now. I keep replaying the look on his face when he slammed the door in that woman's face over and over.

That wasn't my husband. Jeff's words have been playing on repeat in my head.

Josh has more than one side. There's Josh, Joshua, and Kelex. You never know which you'll get.

I'm thrown back in time to the night I called while he beat the crap out of that man's car. Then the way he nearly vibrated with rage when he first met me. As if holding himself back from turning to go find Danny.

What do I really know about him? Maybe the truth should stay hidden so I don't open Pandora's box. I shake my hands out in front of me.

"Shawnnie, you okay in there?"

I startle and turn to look at the closed door. "Yes, I'm fine. I'll be right out, Lex."

"Okay, I'm going to make AJ something to eat. Are you hungry?"

"Sure, I could eat something."

"Okay, see you downstairs."

I wash my hands and splash some water on my face. I guess I've been hiding long enough. When I go to step out, my phone rings.

"Hello," I answer.

"Please hold for Mr. Kylix," a male voice says on the other end of the line.

I stand with my brows drawn. Joshua never goes by that last name and he always calls me direct. It's not until I hear the voice on the other end that I know I'm not holding for my husband.

"Hello, am I speaking to Shawna Norris?"

"Yes, this is she."

"My name is Ulysses Kylix. I am—"

"Joshua's father. Yes, I know who you are."

Josh never talks about his father. I've always gotten the feeling it's a sore subject. Knowing my cousin Lex and how she was with her dad, I've always tried to respect that.

"And yet, I don't know you very well. Other than the fact that you're Monica Norris's daughter and you're seeing my son."

"How can I help you?"

"I'd like for you to have dinner with me. That way, we can get to know each other. You have become family, after all."

I chew on my lip. He knows I'm Josh's wife. I don't know if this is a good or a bad thing.

"I'll have to speak with Josh. Can I get back to you?"

"We really don't have to involve him just yet. It's one dinner. Just the two of us. Once you get to know me for yourself, then we can involve my son."

"Um, I don't think that's a good idea. Like I said, I'll think about it and speak to Josh first."

"Okay, my dear. I'll be in touch. I hope to get to meet you soon."

I hang up and stare off into space. I don't know if this is a good thing or not. I'll have to talk to Josh later.

CHAPTER SIXTY-SIX

Target

Shawna

Two weeks later...

"I'm sorry, but the answer is still no. Josh wouldn't like it. I can't," I say into the phone.

"Allow me to worry about my son. It's only dinner. Next week, yes? I've made reservations at Château Brione for Monday, seven o'clock."

"Mr. Kylix," I start, but he cuts me off.

"Call me Ulysses. Listen, Shawna, I have to go. I'll be waiting Monday evening. Have a good day."

I hang up the phone with Josh's father and sigh. He's been calling every day since that first call. I tried to mention the call, but as soon as I mentioned his father, he got that look and I changed my mind.

I don't like that side of Josh. It's so dark and scary. It's almost like a trigger for me. I'm always thrown back to the kidnappers who took me and Ven or my time with Danny.

I look in the rearview at the car behind me. Linus doesn't ride with me on weekends when I want to visit family and things like that. Josh agreed because having Linus with me would raise questions. Questions we don't need or want.

I shake off the call and my concerns and head to Lex's front door. Ox has a really nice house. It's fit for a family. I can't help but wonder if he bought it with Lex and their future in mind.

It's so clear to see how much he loves her. I ring the bell, still lost in thought. I'm going to have to tell Josh about the calls from his father.

If I keep it from him, it will be worse and I already feel like I'm lying to everyone. While I wait for the door to be answered, I send Josh a text. I smile when his reply comes through.

Josh: *We can talk about anything you want as long as you're in my home tonight.*

Josh: *I miss you in our bed.*

I've been staying at my place. I had some work things and given my place is in Bridge Lake, closer to work, it's just been easier.

"Hey, Shawnnie," Ven sings, pulling my attention.

I look up and everything happens so fast. I stumble forward into the house and Ven rushes by me. The next thing I know, shots are being fired. I drop to my knees and curl into a ball as glass and bullets fly everywhere.

I'm so confused. My heart is racing. I think I'm going to be sick.

I've done it again. I've brought harm to the ones I love. I did this.

"Are you guys okay?"

No, I'm not. I'm in shock. However, I fall back on what's become my coping mechanism. I start to lie because the truth doesn't make sense.

Why was Linus shooting at us?

"Yeah, that's that car that's been following me," I say.

"Someone has been following you?" Ven seethes.

"I thought so. I still get paranoid. I wasn't sure at first."

"How long?" Ven barks.

"Since my last date with Kelex. Two weeks?"

"Does Kelex know?" Lex asks.

Oh God. When I tell him this, he's going to be pissed. I begin to wring my arms.

None of this makes sense. Linus is supposed to be protecting me, not shooting at me, but that was his car.

"No, I didn't say anything. Like, what can he do?" I snort.

It's an honest question. I know Josh is going to be upset, but if I were in danger, what could he really do to protect me? He's a CEO, not Bryan Mills.

"If your new boyfriend is who I think he is, a whole fucking lot and you need to tell him."

Ven looks at Lex and pulls a face. I stare at my cousin as my eyes fill with tears. Not telling her the truth hasn't kept her out of harm's way. It seems to have made it worse.

I'll have to fix this. I'll find a way to fix this. My bad luck can't keep hurting those I love.

"He's not my boyfriend. I'm not his problem."

"What?" they say in unison.

"I think it's time you and I talk," Lex says.

"Where's your piece?" Ven demands.

"Home."

"Excuse me? You're the senator's daughter and you're seeing a guy who has enemies."

I stare at Lex, this time wondering what she's talking about. She just got to town. What could she know about Josh that I don't?

"Okay, what aren't you telling me about Kelex? What enemies?" Ven says and narrows her eyes.

"Read the room, Ven. You fuck with killers. Half of your friends, including your husband, are savages. The kid is the only one I might give a pass, but his wife is questionable in my book. The fighter, it's in him. Push comes to shove. He might pull a trigger or two."

My brain starts to glitch. I don't know the assholes well, but I can totally see Lex's point. They all carry an air of danger, but Pit, Ox, and Kelex are different. They wear that danger.

"Y'all been doing too much ballroom dancing. Y'all know what a savage looks like. Why do you think your panties get so wet for the guys you both chose?

"You both know in your hearts you gravitate to danger. I'm not the only one. Tell that man you're being followed, Shawn, and stop leaving the house unarmed."

The room is starting to spin. So much flashing before my eyes. Finding out that the photographer from my team in Africa was murdered after he made it back to the States. The car Josh destroyed. That look... Oh. My. God.

I think I really go into shock now that the realization hits me.

Kelex

"Are you fucking kidding me?" I roar.

Jeff shrugs. "Bro, he was dead when my guys got there. Someone slit his throat."

I had Jeff and his guys go to find Linus for me. I couldn't send Helios for his own cousin. If push came to shove, I could have used Jeff to handle the situation after I got my answers. I thought Jeff could make it happen quickly and quietly.

"This doesn't make sense. Why would he do this?" Helios says.

"Whoever killed him probably shut him up so we'd never get those answers. I bet if we did some digging, this would all lead back to one person," Jeff says.

"My father. He's been calling Shawna. Can you believe that shit?"

"What does he want?" Jeff sits up and asks. "What has she told him?"

"Nothing. She doesn't know anything to tell him. He wants to have dinner with her. Monday at Château Brione."

"You should go instead. I'll go with you. That would shock the shit out of him."

"If I go, I'm going to kill him."

"I think you should go. See if you can find out if he's connected to this. I still can't believe my cousin would do this."

I turn to Helios. "Maybe you should take some time. Head back home to be with family," I say.

"My duty is here with you. If Linus did this, I wouldn't be able to be there the way I should. This has brought our family shame. I'm not ready to look Basil in the eyes."

I nod. The Papadopoulos family has been loyal for years. This would be a hit to their pride.

"I think I will go to dinner in Shawna's place. It's time Baba and I have a talk."

CHAPTER SIXTY-SEVEN

Talk to Him

Shawna

It's been five days since the shooting and Josh doesn't allow me
to go anywhere by myself. He also won't allow me to sleep
anywhere but under his roof.

I can't shake Lex's words from my head. I'm married to a
man I really don't know. That look has been right beneath the
surface all week.

My thoughts have been racing with what all that means.
However, I freeze outside of True's room when I hear what
sounds like sniffles. The next thing I hear is the sound of a
phone ringing on speaker.

"Hello."

"Hey, Dad."

"Truman," a man replies stiffly. "How are you? How's Catherine?"

"We're fine. Vernice is doing well too."

I move closer to hear better. True takes a deep breath as if frustrated.

"What can I do for you, Truman?"

"Dad, I need you to sign the papers. It's been four years. We want to be adopted. I want that for my sisters. *Please*."

"Do you have any idea what that boy has done to my life? Why the hell would I sign my children over to him?"

"Because you don't want us," True bellows. "Stop being selfish. Stop punishing me and my sisters for your crimes. Don't do this to them.

"It was me. I saw you with your girlfriend, I told Mom. In two years, I'll be eighteen, but I'm not ready to take custody. Josh will take care of them, so I have a chance to be a proper man and start a life.

"Let him take care of them. Sign the papers, give up your rights. Let them have a father."

"What difference does it make? You were always a mama's boy, making things bigger than they needed to be," the man snarls.

"It makes a difference to us. To them, Vernice especially. Why can't you understand that? You've never wanted us, so what's the big deal?

"Mom got pregnant with me and you were stuck with your little Black girlfriend. Do you know how disgusting it was to keep hearing that?

"Better yet, to hear my own father repeatedly ask why we came out so dark? You've never wanted us because you've never believed we were yours. Just sign the fucking papers.

"You won't have to question anything else about us because we never want to see you again. I fucking hate you," True sobs into the phone. "Just let us go. Let someone love us, set us free."

"I'm not going to do that, Truman. If that boy doesn't restore all he's taken from me, I'm not going to lift a finger. My wife is gone. You children don't know me. He took everything from me."

"And yet, you won't do right by us. You're a narcissistic asshole. This has always been about you. How you will look, how you feel, what you get out of everything.

"You didn't even call me for my birthday. Do you know how old your daughters are? Do you know my mama died apologizing for you? Her last breath was wasted saying she was sorry about you," True snarls.

"You know what, forget it. I hope when you take your last breath, you're all alone, and you're in so much pain you beg for the end. You're already dead to me."

The sobs that come from the room after he hangs up tear a hole through my heart. True is such a sweet boy. I had no idea.

I move away from the door, wiping the tears from my eyes. There has to be something I can do. I know the girls have asked before when Josh can adopt them. It truly is something they want just as much as Josh does.

"Whoa, you all right?"

I look up as I run into Jeff. He and Josh are going to Château Brione instead of me. I'm glad Josh isn't going alone. He'll need someone to help with that temper.

I still haven't told him it was Jeff who told me about the fake engagement. He asked once, but we were interrupted before I could answer. I truly don't think Jeff meant any harm by it. He was just talking.

"I'm fine," I say and wipe my face.

He pulls out his handkerchief and hands it to me. I take it and give him a small smile. "Come take a walk with me. Tell me what's going on," he says, placing a hand on my back.

"It's nothing."

"You're in tears. If Josh sees you like this, he's going to assume it's his father's doing and that's going to set him off."

"It's not his father. It's the kids' father. Do you know much about him?"

"No, not really."

"He sounds like a piece of shit. Those kids want Josh to adopt them and he's blocking the way. I wish there was something I could do.

"Some way to get him to see reason. You know, maybe if it came from me and not Josh or the kids, he'd separate his anger with Josh from the situation.

"Sounds like he and Kelex are triggers for each other. I don't know much about him, but I've seen the look Kelex gets when he's mentioned."

I jerk my head back as he calls Josh Kelex. I think that's the version of Josh with the dark side. As that thought occurs, it sets into my belly that this is none of my business. I don't want to call that side out.

"You know what, never mind. I don't know what happened between him and Josh. It had to be something big for him to do this to his children. Forget I ever mentioned it."

Kelex

I walk into the restaurant, barely holding my anger in. I should've had him come to a private location where I could strangle him and watch the light disappear from his eyes.

"Joshua," my father croons. "I wasn't expecting you. Where's your lovely wife?"

"Wife?" Jeff says while standing beside me.

"Ah, you don't know? My son here is a married man. Come, sit."

"How do you know who she is or about our marriage?"

"I still have family in Greece and I'm a resourceful man. Please, Joshua, sit. We need to talk. You have a lovely wife and I want to get to know her. I brought a wedding gift for her."

I start to see red. There's no way I'm sitting through dinner with this man. Not knowing what I know.

"I'm going to say this once and only once," I hiss low, trying to hold on to my composure. That grip slips quickly. "You stay the fuck away from her, or I'll kill you. Why care about me now?

"I don't need shit from you. I never ask you for shit. You made it clear you wouldn't help me if I did.

"You're a selfish prick. You've never thought about anyone but yourself. All the lying and stealing.

"If you didn't stand to gain something from me, I don't think you would have ever tried to be a father to me. Not that you've been worth a shit at it, to begin with."

"Josh, just sit down. Come on, you're making a scene," Jeff says as he tries to tug me down into the seat next to him.

"No... you stay out of this," I bark, then turn back on my father. "I know what you want from me. I know what you've been waiting for. You're going to die waiting if I have anything to say about it.

"Or you'll have to kill me to get it like you did my mother, you son of a bitch." With that, I turn to leave.

I'm so pissed off my face is burning. I pace the front of the restaurant as I wait for my car to pull up. I'm surprised when Blake appears before me.

"Are you ready to listen?"

"To what?"

"There is more going on here. Information you need so you can be on guard. We need you to find the missing answers."

"Answers to what?" I bellow.

"To who's trying to take you down?"

"You always have the answers. Why do you need me for this?"

He pulls a hand down his face. "Because this one has been coming from outside of my reach. The more we dig, the more the strings tangle, but there's always one common thread."

"Oh really, and what would that be?"

"You. You and your friends. I can't leave them out of this because they're already involved. Come with me to Italy. Let's figure this out."

"What does this mean to my freedom?"

"My main goal is to cover you boys. We find answers and I'll cover you. If you find the answers and feel you need to take this into your own hands, I'll cover you. My job is always to cover you and that's what I'll do, no matter what." He shrugs. "Come with me to Italy, Joshua."

"Does he not own a phone?"

"Some things can't be said over a phone or within the parameters of Vander or Bridge Lake. Some things you need to see."

Frustrated, I run a hand through my hair. It feels like Blake is siding with that monster, ignoring that he's the problem. However, something tells me I should get to the bottom of this.

"Fine, but just me. Leave Pit and Ox out. When do we leave?"

"I can be ready within the hour. Meet me at my hangar."

Blake's car pulls up and he turns and climbs into it. I stand with my brows pinched. After all my father has done, I don't believe he's innocent.

If he could dig for information in Crete, he could have gotten to Linus and turned him. He's been pulling bullshit for years.

But would he really kill your mother?

For the power, I think he would. If he did, I'm not letting him off the hook. I pull out my phone and dial Shawna.

I'm not ready to drag her into this. It's best she stays here. I work my jaw while I wait for her to answer. She picks up on the second ring.

"Hey, is everything okay?"

"I need to take a trip. I'm headed to Italy."

"Oh, do you want us to come?"

"No. I don't want to pull them from school for this. When I get back, you and I are going on that anniversary trip. Greece is calling my name."

"Oh, okay, I love you. Call me when you get there."

"I love you too. I'm going to the condo to pack. Helios will stay behind with you guys."

"Be safe, Joshua."

"Always."

CHAPTER SIXTY-EIGHT

Yannis Knight

Kelex

"Blake, it's good to see you," the gray-haired man says as he enters the study we've been waiting in, followed by Pappoús.

"Hello, Father. You look very well," Blake says.

"I try. This must be Joshua." He cups the sides of my face and kisses both my cheeks. "Basil, you have a reason to be so very proud. He's grown into a fine young man."

"Yes, that he has," Pappoús says with a broad smile.

"Do you remember me?"

I narrow my eyes at this man. "Sorry, not really."

"Ah, don't worry about it." He pats my cheek. "I'm Yannis Knight. You were very young the last time I saw you, but I'm not who you came to see. Have a seat."

I unbutton my blazer and sit. I'm thoroughly confused. Blake said we needed to come see his father and Pappoús. Who am I here to see if not him?

The door opens again and in walks a Black man. I look between Pappoús and Yannis for answers. I sit back in my seat and steeple my fingers in front of my mouth, losing my patience.

"Hello, Joshua. My name is Lester Smith."

"Wait, you're the guy who committed suicide on the Bridge Lake Bridge. Lex's father."

"Yes, that I am."

"What do you have to do with my mother's death?"

"My wife was in the car with your mother. It was a hit. A hit that was sanctioned by the corrupt families we pushed out."

I hold up a hand. "Hold on. What?"

"Ah, yes. Let me fill you in. When you didn't want to take my place, I didn't bother you with these details." My grandfather interrupts. "Bridge Lake was founded by our family. Vander was founded by the Knights. After we came together, the other families joined us soon after to form the syndicate to protect our investments.

"There were five families when Bridge Lake and Vander united. The Nikolaous, Knights, Gatakis, Georgious, and Jennings. When the syndicate formed, eight others joined. The Novacks, Pudduses, Ravens, Bradshaws, Vespuccis, Castros, Harringtons, and Harrises.

"Orion Kylix was the last to join the table—although his seat wasn't one of any power. However, he was a worthy addition in other ways. I knew his family from home. I vouched for him," Pappoús says. "I couldn't know then who his son would become."

"Your father has a habit of making poor decisions. There had been a little buzz of a coup being staged once Yannis and Basil decided to return to their home countries. We ignored it for the most part," Lester begins again.

"Then the Pitman family entered the picture. They became pawns for the dirty work. It's our belief that while your father may have been a part of the coup, he did not know they were going to kill your mother. They were actually planning to frame him. However, something went wrong.

"I could never find out what. Or who was heading the plays, but I know I got close. I was about to stumble upon something the morning of that race.

"I still believe the race was used to distract me and it did for a while. In the beginning, Marvin didn't know who you boys were or who all was involved. I covered all your tracks until our opposition shut me down.

"I then turned my attention back to getting answers and I was closing in again. That's when I had to leave because I got too close. Yannis was able to pull me out," Lester says.

"Okay, and what does this have to do with me now?"

"Your father is about to be blindsided again. This time, you're the target. He's in bed with the enemy and doesn't know it," Lester says.

"It's in my best interest to protect you as well as my grandsons. The person, this marionette who's been dancing just outside our reach, is getting ready to cut the strings and I don't believe Ulysses sees it coming," Yannis says.

"In other words, your father is no longer useful," Lester finishes.

"And you had me come all the way here because…"

"Because five years ago someone tried to get my attention," Pappoús says.

"And nine years before that, they had mine," Lester says tightly. "You... you believe your crash was an accident. I have reason to believe it wasn't. You do know who I was to Vander, don't you?"

"The eyes and ears," I reply.

He nods. "You know how they say a criminal can't stand not receiving credit for their crimes, so they'll return to the scene of the crime?"

"Yeah, I've heard that."

"The person responsible for your mother and my wife's deaths returned and didn't receive the spotlight they were looking for. Now they're back to finish."

"We need to find them before they do," Blake says.

"Aren't you the see all of my era? Pit gets his information from you," I toss at him.

"Not this time. Again, it's outside my reach and I don't think I'm looking at all the pieces."

"Then I'll handle it," I bite out.

"How?" Yannis asks.

"What do you know about your oldest grandson?" I say with a grin.

CHAPTER SIXTY-NINE

Testing One, Two

Kelex

I've been thinking over all I've learned in the last twenty-four hours. There's something nagging at me. I don't want to believe it, but I'd be a fool to ignore this feeling.

I didn't mention it to Blake or the others because those men aren't playing. Pappoús might want me to keep my hands clean, but he's not going to hold back. I need to be sure before I set something in motion I can't change.

Sitting in the back of the car on the way to our flight back, I take a calming breath. Then I shoot off a text.

Me: *Time to celebrate.*

Me: *I'm thinking skydiving with the crew. You in?*

Jeff: *What are we celebrating?*

Me: *I'm free. That's it. Vander goes to someone else.*

Me: *That chapter is finally closed. Nothing can change my fate now.*

Me: *Nothing but me losing my shit and bringing it all down on my own head.*

Jeff: *Yeah. Skydiving sounds cool. I'm in.*

Jeff: *Has someone else been named?*

Me: *Nah. There's a vacancy, but who cares?*

He goes silent, but I wait. I know he's not done. There're two ways this can go. The way that tells me I'm wrong and the one that says Pappoús has been trying to show me something all along.

Jeff: *If you want something done. You do it yourself.*

Me: *What?*

Jeff: *Nothing.*

I grin and tap my phone against my lip. I'm ready to get back home. I have a lot to think about. Opening a different contact, I send another text.

Me: *I'm ready to call in that favor.*

Pit: *What do you need?*

Me: *Keep a seat open. I'm coming to see you.*

Pit: *I've got you.*

I drop my phone in my lap and look out of the window. *I'll have those answers soon.* I snort.

"Ut-oh," Blake says beside me. I turn to look at him. "I know that sound. What are you thinking?"

"I've been raised by kingmakers."

"Yes, you have. Now to watch the true kings rise," he says with a wide grin.

"From chaos comes clarity and order," I murmur and laugh to myself.

CHAPTER SEVENTY

Can We...

Shawna

"We're really going to have another wedding here?" I breathe against Josh's chest.

We've been making love all morning. I think he's trying to cheer me up from last night. I was sad to hear Kid still hasn't woken up.

It seemed like all hell broke loose when Josh returned from Italy. So much seems to be going on around us. A part of me couldn't wait to take off.

Although another part of me wanted to be there for my friends and family. I've been so worried. I'm grateful to Josh for taking my mind off it all.

However, I know we need to come up for air soon. He has to go out to meet Pappoús before we leave, and I need to get back to packing. We're going back home tonight.

"That's what you want, right?"

"Yes, it's going to be amazing. Everyone we love can come and the truth will be out there."

We plan to tell everyone the truth when we return to Vander. In a year, we're going to come back here to Greece for our wedding anniversary and a wedding with all our family and friends.

I inhale and smile. Josh kisses the top of my head and runs his fingers down my back. I run my hand across his abs and snuggle deeper into his side.

"Babe, can I ask you something?"

"Anything."

"Do you…" I pause and bite my lip. Taking a deep breath, I go to start again. "Um, do you think?"

He chuckles and rolls me onto my back. Looking deep into my eyes, he cups my face and runs his thumb across my lip. I love when he does that.

"What is it? You can ask me anything, anytime. Talk to me, baby."

"I was wondering, do you want babies? Can we have babies of our own?"

He crushes his lips to mine and slips into me for the first time without a condom. My eyes roll back. He feels so good.

"Yes, Shawna, I'm going to give you a baby. We're going to have more than one. Is that what you want?"

"Yes, yes, Josh, please."

"You feel so fucking good."

He pins my legs back and really works his body into mine. I'm so wet my juices start to roll back into my ass. I didn't know sex between us could get any better.

Kelex

I've been thinking about starting to expand our family. Now that we plan to tell everyone, I can't hold myself back. My eyes roll back as I dive into this wet pussy.

I groan long and hard. My first time being inside her raw is nothing short of amazing. I'm so hard and she's so wet. I cup her breast and dip my head to pull her nipple into my mouth.

She pushes a hand into the back of my hair and holds on tight. I couldn't tell you for how long we fuck as I worship this sexy body. All I know is her.

"Josh, babe. I'm so close," she cries as I shift angles and plow deeper.

I lift my head and look her in the eyes as she ripples around me. Leaning in, I ghost my mouth over her chin, then her lips.

"I want you to come with me," I demand.

I roll onto my back and hold her to me as she rocks her hips into me. Grasping her face, I take her lips in a passionate kiss. She sucks my lip into her mouth and moans.

My entire chest warms as I spill inside her for the first time. I wrap my arms around her and hold on tight. I just need to breathe her in for a bit.

"I love you," I rumble once I catch my breath.

CHAPTER SEVENTY-ONE

A Gift

Kelex

"You didn't have to come to Athens," I say to my grandfather.

"I wanted to see you. I have been thinking a lot about what we've asked of you."

"It needs to be done." I shrug.

"Yes, but I know you. What is to say you won't dip your toes back into our world when you learn the truth? This is your mother, my daughter, we are talking about."

"I'm confused. Why ask this of me if you don't want me to handle it my way?"

"That's not what I've said. This is why I wanted to talk to you face to face. I already know what you will do. I just wanted you to know it's your one pass. I'm not going to go back on my word when you do what you do.

"I will hand Vander over to your friend myself. This thing you say he can do. I think that's enough to trust him in my spot. You will be mayor, yes?"

"I'm still thinking about it."

I don't tell him I'm leaning toward a yes. I still haven't talked to Shawna about it. Growing up in a political family did take a toll on her. I'm not sure how she would feel being a mayor's wife.

"Good, don't hesitate to do what you have to do, but only what we're asking of you. *Eímaste xekátharoi*," he says.

"Yes, we're clear."

He pulls me into a hug and pats me on my back. "Kiss Shawna for me. It was good to see you."

"It was good to see you too, Pappoús."

***

"Yes, that will be perfect. My wife will love it. No, we return to the States this evening, but contact us with anything you need."

"Thank you, Mr. Nikolaou, I will. Again, it is an honor to plan this event for you," Cora, the wedding planner, says.

"Thank you. We'll be in touch," I say and hang up as I get out of the car to head into the hotel.

I haven't stopped smiling since this morning when we made the decision. I had to do something to get that sad look out of Shawna's eyes from last night. She's been calling back home to check in on Kid. We've all been worried about her.

Speaking of which, I want to beat Shawna to it today. I dial Pit and Ox. They are the only two I trust at the moment.

"Yo," Pit answers.

"Hello," Ox says next.

"I return tonight. How is she?"

"She's still not up. Lex went to see her this morning. Leo says they're hoping she'll wake in the next few days," Ox replies.

"Good. Do you have anything for me yet?"

"When it comes to that ghost. Not yet," Pit says. "As far as your boy. We know it was him. He's been moving weird and shit. Talking big shit and making promises he can't keep."

"You want me to handle him?" Ox offers.

"No, that's my problem. I just needed confirmation. I plan to turn that TV off myself."

"I'll keep digging and running through what I know," Pit says.

"Thanks. See you at the party."

"See you, bro," they say in unison and hang up.

Helios comes to my side and places a hand on my shoulder as he whispers in my ear. Fire fills my veins. Ignoring the conversation I just had with my grandfather, I pull out my phone and dial Achilles.

"What's up, Josh? I'm pulling into your driveway now."

"Good. I need you to shut down all and any eyes on my location ASAP. I'm talking blind birds and all. Then find me for the past"—I look down at my watch—"thirty minutes and make me disappear. Can you do that?"

"You know I can."

"Good. Send me a text as soon as you have that done."

"I'm on it. I'll text you in a minute," he replies.

I hang up and walk into the hotel. Helios follows silently. We ride up to my floor and the doors open. As they do, my phone pings.

Achilles: *Done*

"Head to your room. I haven't left mine all morning."

"Got it."

Shawna

I'm so confused, but I'm not going to miss out on this opportunity to make this happen for the kids. When this man appeared outside our hotel room door here in Greece, I had no idea who he was at first.

"Um, Mr. Davis. We can sit out here. Would you like a bottle of water?"

I lead him to the balcony where I've been sitting, finishing my breakfast and waiting for Josh to return so we can pack our things. This week has been awesome and so romantic, although I do miss the kids.

Especially now as I stand looking into their father's face. All three of them look like him. Just brown-faced versions.

"No, I'm fine."

"How did you know we were here? How can I help you?"

He reaches into his back pocket and pulls out some papers. Smoothing them out, he stares down at them. I glance over and see his signature already on them.

My heart begins to race. He's giving up his rights. About damn time. I look at him once a few beats of silence pass. Something crosses his face and he looks back up at me with a glare.

"Your friend had me sign, took care of my travel, and said if I came here, that boy would be willing to talk to me about restoring my life. It's been too long. Too much has happened. I shouldn't have bothered coming here. I don't think there's anything he can do to change my mind."

"Why is that? I know the kids would like for you to sign."

"Your boyfriend is an entitled piece of shit. I think he was fucking my wife and then he moved in on my family."

I want to laugh in his face. True told me, before we left, what really happened, and I believe every word he said.

"My husband is a kind man. He only wants the best for those children. I know, for a fact, he was never romantically involved with your wife."

"Listen, bitch," he roars and stands from his seat. Before I know it, he has my knife from breakfast clenched in his hand, pointing it at me. "I want my fucking life back. Those kids should be in a fucking home, not living better than I ever have. Truman doesn't need a fucking Mercedes. He's sixteen. I worked for that BMW your *boyfriend* destroyed."

"Mr. Davis—"

"Josh," I gasp as he rushes out onto the balcony and grabs Mr. Davis by the throat, the knife falling from his grasp. Josh backs him against the railing. I hold my breath as I watch Josh with his chest heaving.

"Are they signed?"

"Ye—"

Before I can get the word out fully, Josh throws his palm into Mr. Davis's throat, sending him over the glass rail of the balcony. We're nine stories up. That man isn't going to survive that fall.

I stand to rush to look over, but Josh grabs me. He places his hand over my mouth and presses his lips to my ear. I'm trembling, in a state of shock.

"I need you to do something for me. Can you do that?"

I nod my head as tears start to spill over. It just registers that music is playing in our suite. He kisses my forehead and backs me into a wall inside. I wrap my legs around his waist as he presses into me.

He moves his lips back to my ear and continues. "I killed that son of a bitch. He deserved it, but now I need to cover it up. I've had all the cameras wiped.

"Now we're going to make it look like I've been here with you all morning. I'm going to turn this music up and we're going to fuck loud and dirty. Don't hold back, be as loud as you want to be, just like this morning. Can you handle that?"

I nod again. He uncovers my mouth and kisses me. I focus on him so I don't freak out.

While he kisses me and holds me up against the wall, he pulls out his phone and changes the song, then turns it up. Tank's "Too Late" begins to play. It's not that loud, just loud enough to set a mood, I'm guessing that's his point.

When he breaks the kiss and looks into my eyes, I see the darkness he's been trying to hide. It's right on the surface. His eyes are completely gray and there's something else I can't pinpoint.

I yank his shirt up to pull it over his head and toss it aside. He removes my shirt next. Shoving his hand into my bra, he pulls my breast out and sucks my nipple into his mouth.

"Oh," I gasp when he tears my panties from my body and shoves into me.

I think I've lost my mind. I'm so wet for him, as if he just spent hours going down on me. We kiss frantically as he pumps inside me.

"Oh my God," I scream as he starts to bounce me on his length. "Josh, shit. Just like that, babe. Fuck, baby."

"Yes, Shawna, give me that tight pussy, baby," he groans.

"Josh, yes, yes, oh, yes, Joshua."

He pulls away from the wall and slaps my ass. I gush all over him. This has to be the best sex we've ever had. I force myself not to think about that.

He bites my lip and tugs. I get lost in the feel of him, clawing my nails down his back. I bury my face in his neck and hair.

With my nose, I push his hair out of the way and suck on his flesh. He hisses out a curse and digs his short nails into my ass. I switch to the other side of his neck where his hair isn't obstructing my access and latch on to his skin.

He releases a growl, causing me to lift my head and scream in pleasure as he bounces me harder. Pulling out, he steps out of his pants with me still in his arms. Then he moves over to the bed and tosses me onto it. I look at him and reach to cup my breasts over my bra.

"Come here," he says and grabs my ankle to pull me closer. Grabbing my skirt, he peels it from my body. Then he turns me.

My head is now hanging off the bed. He reaches to shove two fingers into me and pumps the long digits into my wet sex. I reach for his hard length as it comes close to my face.

"Fuck, yes, baby," he grunts as I take him into my mouth.

I hum around him as he starts to fuck my face. I suck my juices from his shaft happily as he builds me to climax. Pulling out of my mouth, he flips me over and lifts my hips in the air. The next thing I know, he has his face buried in my ass as he eats my pussy from behind and fingers my puckered hole with his thumb.

"Yes," he groans when I start to stroke him and find him with my mouth to start sucking him off again.

"Oh shit," I cry out as he pushes his thumb into my ass and I come like he just pulled a trigger.

My legs turn to jelly and I sink down onto my stomach in a trembling, convulsing mess. Josh unfastens my bra, then turns me around, this time climbing onto the bed beside me. Then he thrusts into me from behind. Holding my legs open, he pounds into me. It feels so good I can't help but cry out mindlessly.

He palms my throat and tugs my head back. Then he leans into my ear and starts talking dirty. He's so damn hard. I didn't think he could get any harder.

"That's it. That's my girl, fuck me. Fuck me like you know you own me." He slaps my ass. "Fuck me, Shawn, fuck your husband."

"Harder," I cry.

Sweat starts to cover my face and my heart is racing. However, I don't stop and neither does he. He devours my mouth as he pulls out and taps my pussy with this length. My eyes cross.

"So good," I keen.

He turns me onto my back and covers me with his body. Thrusting into me, he reaches for my ass and pumps into me. I claw at his ass and squeeze around him.

"Fuck, yes," he moans and licks from my collarbone to the center of my throat, then up to my chin. I open my legs wider and pull them back. He palms my thighs and really dives in.

We cycle through at least ten songs before the banging on our suite door starts. Josh keeps pumping into me on the bed.

His cheeks are flush and his hair is all sweaty. I'm convulsing like a madwoman beneath him. He grasps my face in his hand and moves to whisper in my ear.

"Put on a robe and come out in two minutes if they're still questioning me," he says.

I nod and look up at him in shock. My eyes widen when I see the purple marks I've left on each side of his neck. I furrow my brow.

This is really happening. He pulls out and goes to grab a towel to wrap around his waist. We've fucked our way out of the rest of our clothes, so we're both completely naked at this point.

Looking toward the balcony, I see the papers still out on the table. I wrap myself in the sheet quickly and go to grab them and shove them into my purse. Following Josh's instructions, I then wait two minutes.

Kelex

"Hello, we're sorry to bother you"—the guy, who I assume is the manager, looks down at his tablet—"Mr. Nikolaou. These officers would like to ask you a few questions. There was a man pushed from this side of the hotel and they're questioning all our guests on this side."

"Wow, that's terrible. How can I help you? Would you like to come inside?"

Both officers look me over. One leans in and whispers to the other. I reach to push my hair out of my face. The officer listening to the other widens his eyes and turns to his partner to say something and nods toward me.

The partner looks at me and they both grin. I look at them expectantly. They glance down at my towel. I'm still semihard beneath.

"No, I don't believe we need to come in," the whispering officer says.

"Are you here alone?" the other one asks.

"No, my wife is here."

Right on cue, Shawna walks up behind me. Placing a kiss on my shoulder, she wraps her arms around my waist. I turn to look back at her. She lifts onto her toes, and I peck her lips.

"Is everything okay?"

"They say someone jumped or was pushed from one of the rooms," I reply.

"He was pushed."

"Oh, sorry. It's a shock to hear either happened."

"Is there anything we can do?" Shawna asks.

"No, it seems you've been busy. We won't disturb you any further," one of the officers says as he eye fucks my wife.

"This is our last day here. We will be returning to the States this evening. Would you like my card?"

"Yes, we'll take your number," one says.

"Mr. Nikolaou. Are you related to Basil Nikolaou?" the other asks.

"*Nai, aftós eínai o pappoús mou,*" I reply.

"I don't think we'll have any further questions. Thank you. Have a safe trip back to America."

"Thank you."

I close the door and Shawna collapses against me. I hold her upright and lead her back to the room and pack our things to go.

CHAPTER SEVENTY-TWO

Taunting

The Real Problem

Present...

"What the fuck were you thinking? You were not supposed to kill Ulysses," I seethe.

"You weren't going to do it."

"Because I have half a brain, asshole."

"You said you needed him gone. He served his purpose. Josh wasn't biting and I need to trigger him. If I can't trigger him, then I need him out of the way. It's a win-win for me."

"No, it's not, you idiot. Do I have to spell this out for you?"

"Ulysses was the only reason we've been able to hide all this time. I had him bankrolling this operation because he wanted to take them all down. He didn't see it coming. I was going to take them all down and his son in the process. You just blew everything up."

"No, I didn't."

"Yes, you did and you don't even see how. You can't frame him for the murder. He wasn't in the fucking country. You know how I know he wasn't in the country?"

"How?"

"Because you gave me his fucking trigger. I pulled it, dipshit. All we had to do was sit back and snatch his freedom away. Basil was going to revoke his right to walk.

"Ulysses would have gone down with Joshua's rage. A month, two tops and I would have completed my life's mission. I would have avenged my sister, my career, and my nephew. Why do you keep fucking everything up?"

"Me?"

"Yes, you," I roar. "You had one job. Only one job.

"Every time it's just one and you still managed to fuck it up. He was your cousin. All you had to do was your job.

"You don't think through shit. You just blow shit up and take everyone around you down with you. Never an exit strategy, just boom." I throw my arms up in the air. "What you did to that girl was so fucking fucked up and stupid. What's wrong with you?"

"She was onto me," he mumbles like a big spoiled baby.

"You're a fucking liar. What you did was unnecessary, uncalled for. If she wakes, your name will be the first one out of her mouth.

"And the guard. All you had to do was let him do the job, then give him back his daughter and the cash. He should have been on his way back to one of the Greek islands to hide away for a bit. No, you go and kill him."

"I tied off a loose end," he snarls back at me.

"You know what? Get the fuck out. I'll handle this on my own from here."

"Good luck with that. I hope he burns your ass alive."

"Like you allowed them to do to my nephew? Fuck you. I hope he figures you out and puts a bullet in your head like his daddy should've done to yours."

My chest is heaving. I'm so pissed off. All the sacrifices and work I've done. All for nothing. It's all down the drain. Months… years of trying to provoke Joshua. I finally pulled the right trigger and this asshole kills his father while he's not even in the country.

"*Fuck*," I roar into the empty room.

CHAPTER SEVENTY-THREE

Pulling Threads

Pit

Present...

"I was on my way to my father's to confront him about Davis. I thought he was the one who sent him to Greece. He was dead when I got there," Kelex says, bringing us back to the present.

"What happened to Jeff? I thought he was your ride," Ox says.

"He never arrived. I called a car service. He texted me the morning after the arrest like I was the one who stood him up."

"I bet I can tell you why," Ox mutters.

I start to leave the room again. I'm looking down at the race this time. Not as if I'm there myself, but from the view all the stories have created.

I zero in on a bunch of high school kids a few cars over from mine. Shawna was there. I saw her before we lined up for the race. She stood out because she looked as if she was trying to hide from someone.

I turn my head and see Jeff talking to Jeremy. I frown. I didn't know Jeff that well back then, so I didn't think about what they were doing together. I didn't give it a second thought.

Suddenly, something else pulls my attention. The scene before me fades and is replaced with the night at the race party. Jeff's words come back to me.

This is no place for you, dollface. Besides, you're a distraction I don't need to be a part of. I have my own reasons for being in these races.

Kelex footed the bill for him to be there, but as I pull memories from back then, he never seemed too interested in where Danny was. I saw him in Marquis's face more than anything.

All that fades and I tug at a different thread. Kid… she spent most of her time talking to Achilles at that housewarming party, but as I left that night, I saw Jeff shooting his shot. I remember thinking she was out of his league.

"I got it," Tak shouts, snapping the thread I'm following. I'm back in the bar, looking around at everyone. "It's Achilles," he croons like he's so proud of himself.

"Were you dropped on your head, or did we do this to you?" Deacon says.

Luke sits back with his elbows on the back of his chair and his hands folded over his chest. "It's not Achilles."

"Why not?" Tak says like a pouty teenager.

"Were you paying attention? It's not him because he's one of them," Luke says.

I snort. I guess I wasn't the only one to pick up on that. I look to Uncle Blake and lift a brow. He nods for me to continue.

"My uncle once told me you never let them learn what's most important to you and you never leave what you love vulnerable.

"He's true to his rules. Achilles is his son. My and Ox's cousin, Josh's godbrother. Zoe Gataki's son." I pause as something about that tries to catch my attention.

"Jeff is a problem," Luke says, looking at Josh. "Not the problem, but a problem."

I nod. "He already knows this. Jeff isn't who I'm looking for here. Someone else is hidden in all of this."

I float out of the room again. This time I'm back in that room as a little boy as my mother walks in. The woman with her was Zoe Gataki.

I come back to the present and start to snap my fingers as my brain races faster than I can speak. Blake said once to pay attention to names. They're important.

"Uncle Blake, you've been with Zoe Gataki for years. Since we were little. She was married to Atlas Novack for a while. His sister Sofia Georgiou was killed in a car accident with Janice Smith and Maria Nikolaou-Kylix.

"Novack later lost his medical license. It was some bullshit and he swore he was being framed. Motherfucker.

"I'm the kid. I was working to get his license back before that race and getting locked up." I look to Kelex. "The dude talking to your dad at your house and in the hospital was Atlas Novack."

"But why is he after us?" Skittles says.

"Jeremy Harris was Atlas's nephew. He was Sofia's son. We buried Atlas for the shit he did to Zoe. He almost killed her.

"I had Marvin call him in to remove a bullet from one of his guard's shoulders. A bullet I placed there to lure Atlas in, then I used that to get his license revoked.

"He'd been threatening Zoe, after she had me spare his life. I made it so he was nobody and had nobody. His life was over before you guys started your engines. I would never have pinned him for this," Blake muses.

"Because we were looking for big money, but if Ulysses was footing the bill, it all makes sense," I say.

"Are you sure?" Kelex asks.

"I'm positive. Atlas was who I called to stitch Skittles up. I was calling in a favor because the firm I did my internship with wanted to drop his case. I kept working on it anyway until I got locked up.

"Oh my God, that's the man who stitched me up when I was little. I remember his eyes," Shawna says, looking up from her phone.

Skittles takes the phone from her to look at the picture she pulled up. "Yeah, that's him. The guy I recognized from helping Daddy."

"So he saw you guys that night and put it all together. Now it all makes sense. Atlas has an axe a mile long to grind with the families on both sides of the fence.

"He blamed us all even though we had nothing to do with Sofia's death. After the cover-up done to keep you guys out of trouble after Jeremy's death." Uncle Blake pauses and frowns. "That was fuel to the fire.

"Where do we find this motherfucker?" Ox says.

"Now that I'm sure of who we're looking for, I'll cast a wider net."

"I don't get it. Jeff is one of us. How is he involved with this guy?" Tak says sadly.

"Blake, what was Jeff's mother's maiden name?" Kelex asks darkly.

"Harris."

Kelex

We walk into our bedroom bone tired. I just want to climb in the bed and stay there for at least three days. Too bad that's not an option. Blake wants us to meet him back at the bar in the morning.

"This is all so crazy," Shawna says.

"I know." I tug her into my arms and give her a squeeze.

"I've learned so much about you in the last two days. Mayor, huh? Do you want to run?"

I exhale. "I don't know. Would you be mad if I did?"

"Not at all. You would be great, but I don't think that's what you want."

"What makes you say that?"

"You build things, you protect people, you handle shit without question. I can see why Pappoús wanted to hand things over to you. Pit works where he is. I think you would make a great gatekeeper of Vander and Bridge Lake," she says.

"That comes with that other side of me. I don't want to be that person."

"Do you really think you could be like your father? I mean, from what you've said, he was vicious, without boundaries."

I stand and think for a moment as I sway her in my arms. "I want to go to bed proud of what I've done, not wondering if I'm losing my soul. Does that make sense?"

"All the sense in the world." She pecks my lips.

I take over and sip deeply from her mouth. When I break the kiss, I take a sharp inhale of air. "Maybe I need to be mayor."

She smiles up at me. "I'll support and love you either way."

"I love you, baby. Our family is all that matters."

CHAPTER SEVENTY-FOUR

Flames and Fears

Kelex

We're all over at the track at Skittles's shop. After meeting with Blake, everyone needed to blow off some steam. Skittles, Luke, Deacon, and Tak are all on the track.

I'm sitting with Pit and Ox as we look on. Shawna stayed home today, she and the girls have plans and True is working on some music in the home studio.

"Thanks, Pit. I appreciate what you've done."

"It was nothing. All information just sitting there. I'm glad I could help."

"You know what doesn't make sense to me?" Ox says.

"What's that?" Pit asks.

"If Sofia was his sister, how was he involved in that accident?"

"You know, I've been wondering the same thing," I reply.

"She wasn't supposed to be in the car," Pit says. "I remember them saying that. Zoe was meant to be with them, but she was sick and Sofia went instead."

"You speak to Jeff yet?"

"We texted this morning. He's still on board with the trip. I don't think he suspects anything."

Jeff and I texted for about thirty minutes. It took everything in me not to go off. The entire time he acted as if everything was normal.

"Yeah, but how do you plan to make sure he comes? He's bailed on us millions of times."

"Don't worry about it. I'll get him there."

My phone rings in my pocket. I pull it out and answer, seeing it's True. I put it to my ear with a smile on my face. He probably has something new he wants me to hear.

"What's up, True?"

"J," he whispers. "They shot Helios."

The smile falls from my face as I stand. "Who shot who?"

"Some guys. I don't know who they are. I was down in the studio. I cut off the music and heard the shots coming from upstairs.

"When I crept up to the first floor, I found Helios bleeding out and some guys with guns holding Shawna, Miss Zoe, and my sisters hostage," he whispers again.

I'm already in motion. Ox and Pit are hot on my heels. "Is anyone else hurt? Where are you now?"

"They didn't see me, so I ran back down to the basement to call you. I think they shot more people. I just didn't come across them, but Miss Zoe had her guards today," True rushes out.

"Stay hidden. I'm on my way."

"Oh, shit," True says and there's a little scuffle.

"Hello, is this *the* Joshua Kylix?"

"Who the fuck is this?" I snarl.

"I'm a friend of a friend. Or at least I was. You can call me Atlas."

"What do you want?"

"I thought about putting a bullet in that bitch upstairs, but that's not enough. I want you. You will make them hurt. You're connected to enough of them to make them pay for all my losses.

"You have twenty minutes." I cover the phone with my hand and mouth. *I need the keys to my car.*

Pit nods and takes off for Skittles's office. I've been keeping the car she built for me here.

This asshole Atlas continues as I stand vibrating with rage. "If you're not here in twenty minutes, I'm going to start shooting people, starting with your pretty wife, then I'll move on to the cute kids. Twenty minutes," he snarls and hangs up.

"Give me the keys," I demand as Pit comes jogging back toward me.

"Bro, I can drive you."

My house is on the other side of Vander. It's a forty-five-minute drive. If I want to make it there in under twenty minutes, I need to drive.

"I have twenty minutes. Respectfully, no one here can make that drive faster than me."

"What's going on?" Skittles calls as she pulls into the garage and steps out of her car.

I catch the keys as Pit tosses them to me. I can tell he wants to say something, but I'm not in the mood to hear it. Instead, I race to jump in my car.

I start the engine and it growls beneath me. The tailpipes snarl and pop. I grip the steering wheel as I start to sweat. I can smell the smoke and feel the heat of the flames. The seat belt feels so tight across my chest. I tug at it as if that will help.

I'm losing my shit. In my brain, I know I'm not trapped, but I can't force myself to put the car in drive. The passenger doors open in the front and back.

Pit slides in beside me and Skittles climbs into the back.

"Okay, motherfucker. You may be the fastest driver here, but your ass has to drive and you're not while the clock is still ticking," Pit says.

"Pit," Skittles hisses. "Kelex, honey. This is my family. I'll get us there. Let me drive."

"*She's my wife*," I roar. Sweat mixes with tears. I can't let her down. After all I've done for her—for our family—I have to do this. "I promised."

"Then shut that shit out and let's go," Pit says as he turns on the radio.

"Radioactive" by Imagine Dragons starts to play and I close my eyes. The flames recede in my mind, and I ignore the smell of smoke. I step on the gas and let the engine rev.

Shawna means more to me than my fears. I can do this for her. I release a roar and throw the car in drive.

For the first time in fourteen years, I'm behind the wheel and I do one of the things I do best. I tear out of the garage and head for my wife and kids.

"That's what the fuck I'm talking about," Pit and Skittles say in unison.

I ignore them and focus on getting home. Skittles can build a ride. This car floats like a knife through butter. I'm moving through Vander like a man possessed. My heart is pounding and my blood is pumping.

"Looks like all the assholes are keeping up. Guess you're not the fastest after all," Pit taunts.

I glance in the rearview and see the others on my tail. I shift gears and push on the gas. That old feeling comes back, the thrill I used to get from being behind the wheel.

I don't have time to acknowledge that Pit's taunting was because I was driving scared. I suck it up and get it done. The others left in my dust, I turn into my neighborhood. Within seconds, I'm pulling into my driveway.

Shawna

"Tell me, Zoe. Have you missed me?"

"Not at all, Atlas. I hoped you were dead. The world would have been a better place."

Atlas snorts. "I've waited for years to get back at all of you. How does it feel? I'm going to take your golden boy from you."

"What are you talking about?"

"That bitch's son. If it weren't for Joshua and her...," Atlas bellows as his chest heaves. He pauses to wipe his mouth. "If it weren't for that christening, you wouldn't have reconnected with that piece-of-shit Blake. They would have stayed out of my business."

"Maria did that shit on purpose. Getting you into the same room as him. Basil, Yannis, and Blake all still sit on their thrones and watch us scramble. Taking whatever they want, when they want, while you and those other bastards do their bidding," he snarls.

"You've been jealous all this time of a child? Joshua was a baby. My godson didn't deserve for you to take his mother or for you to keep me and Blake at arm's length," Zoe almost sobs.

"She had everything and she still took you from me. I returned the favor."

"You're petty. You were always dangerous because you were secretly jealous of them all, even before I left you for Blake. You couldn't handle not being on the inside.

"You had to get involved with the enemy. That's how you made the list. That's how access was stripped from your family. You got Sofia killed."

"Shut up. She wasn't supposed to be in the car. I wasn't supposed to lose my sister."

"Cry me a river. You killed three women. Made widows and broken children."

"Shut up. You ruined my life," he yells.

"Are you fucking kidding me? You were beating my head in. You brought this all down on yourself."

"What happened in our home was our business. You had no right to run to them. You ran to the powers that be and tore my life apart to become a whore," he sneers.

I dart my gaze over to my bag. I just need to get across the room. Tiny fingers wrap around mine, pulling my attention. I look to Vernice and squeeze her hand.

She looks at me with tears in her eyes. *It's going to be okay,* I mouth.

She gives me a small nod. I look over to True and Cat. I have to shake my head at True. He looks like he's going to make a move.

"What do you think you will accomplish here, Atlas?" Zoe says.

He falls silent and looks as if he's truly contemplating her words. I glance at my bag again. He has two other guys with him. If I can distract all three.

No, that's how you get people hurt. Just wait for help.

I start to chew on my lip. That old fear creeping in. If I do nothing, everyone might be safe. Or I could end this now, but at what cost?

All the training my aunt did when we were children comes back to me. I see at least three options for defusing the situation and getting us to safety. However, I also see how each can go wrong and get someone I care about hurt.

"I don't know anymore," Atlas says, and the wavering in his voice catches my ear.

"At first, I wanted to be seen. If I had gotten the families to war, I would have risen up from the smoke, but Sofia wasn't supposed to be in the car. The other families, they double-crossed me.

"Ulysses promised me revenge, not knowing I took part in killing his wife. He bankrolled all of this. Once his son did what he wanted, I was supposed to get my revenge.

"Then he and everyone else started changing their minds and their plans. All of them useless. None of them thought about what I lost.

"Just taking the money and fucking things up. Each and every one of them. No one stuck to the plan. Now Ulysses is gone. I could have made things work, got him back on track, but he's gone."

Something outside catches one of Atlas's guy's attention. He turns as the other one is distracted by something he's reading on his phone.

In a split second, I make a decision and rush for my purse. I have the bag in my hand when everyone cries out. I look up to find Atlas with his gun trained on me.

Vernice rushes over to throw herself in front of me. I pull my gun and drop the bag to the floor. My stomach turns, I've made the wrong decision, but I'm going to die on this hill to save this baby.

"Mister, I don't know why you're here or what you want, but my ancestors don't play about me. Put your gun down. 'Cause I promise you if you take my mom from me or hurt her in any way, you're not going to make it out of this day breathing. On God."

"I'd listen to her if I were you." I glance out the corner of my eye to see Josh, Pit, and Ven all aiming for Atlas and his two men. "You wanted me, I'm here."

"Kids, I need you all to come upstairs with me," Ven says calmly.

"Go on, no one's going to harm you," Pit adds.

"This place, you people. All you do is take. Jeremy didn't deserve to die like that. You all shouldn't have walked away with no consequences."

Now I'm pissed. I lose my temper and growl, "No consequences? No consequences? Danny almost beat me to death.

"Two broken ribs, a broken jaw. Oh, but you were beating your wife's ass, so that's no big deal to you. Your nephew nearly killed my cousin and my husband—"

"It was only meant to be him," Atlas bellows.

"What?" I breathe.

"Jeremy and Jeff were supposed to get the device on his car. Jeff, the idiot, chickened out and didn't do what he was supposed to.

"Jeremy died being loyal to me. I owe him someone's blood. I owe him all of your freedom."

"Enough," Josh snarls.

I catch a glance of one of Atlas's guys going to pull the trigger as he aims at Josh. Before I can think about it, I aim and fire. He falls back with a bullet between his eyes.

"Go on, take the shot. Your grandfather would love to hear you killed someone. You'll be trapped in this life, in this grief I've had to live with. Your out will be gone. Do it," Atlas taunts Josh.

I look to Josh and see the anger on his face. My heart breaks as I think of his words last night. He doesn't want to do this.

He wants a different life. I turn my gun on Atlas and go to fire again, but he drops to the floor with a hole in his chest as a pool of blood forms on his shirt.

I look around and my gaze lands on Zoe. She drops the smoking gun in her hands and stumbles to the nearest chair. I jump as another shot is fired.

I turn to find Blake and Ox aiming at the last guy. However, it's Ox's gun that's smoking. Before I can register all that has happened, Josh has me in his arms.

He's holding me so tight I can't breathe. I wrap my arms around him and return his embrace. Pit starts to bark orders and the room buzzes with movement.

Ox comes to pry my gun from my fingers. I break down as the events of the last few months settle in.

"It's over. This is all over," Josh says into my hair. "I love you."

"I love you too," I sob.

CHAPTER SEVENTY-FIVE

Burning It All

Kelex

I walk into my study with the package that was just dropped off by a courier. I close the door and move to my desk. Looking at my watch, I see I have about two hours before I need to head out. Still plenty of time to check on Helios in the hospital.

I open the envelope and pull out the recorder inside. My curiosity is piqued. I look at the envelope and turn it over. It doesn't say where it's from.

I press play and the voice that comes through is unmistakably my father's. I sit back in my chair and stare up at the ceiling. Even in death, this man invades my life.

"Joshua, if you've received this, I was right. Atlas couldn't be trusted. He and his pets have turned on me. My son, I am sorry.

I was too hard on you and I made many mistakes and I've been trying to right them.

"I need you to know I've been trying for years to tell you, to show you I made a mistake. I lost my way. You're angry with me.

"I don't blame you. I shouldn't have cut you off, but I'm proud of what you've done with your life. You're a good man and very smart. Smarter than I've been.

"I thought Atlas would help me right the wrongs I created years ago, but I didn't see his anger and agenda until it was too late. I was young when I went to the other families. I didn't know they would destroy anything in their way. I picked the wrong side in my greed and jealousy.

"I... I just didn't want to believe your mother's death was my fault. My actions set that in the moment. I've regretted that all my life. I loved your mother. I love you.

"I lost myself in grief. Grief, pride, jealousy, and greed cost me everything. Basil was right in how he handled you. I was too stubborn to listen.

"I just wanted to say... sorry. I brought all of this into your life. You're a great man, Joshua. Continue to be who you want to be. I... I love you. Goodbye, my son," the recording stops and I work my jaw.

Blake and Zoe told me last night that they suspected that Jeff had been lying about all the deals and things my father supposedly botched and blocked. Even buying the company shares was a farce. My father wasn't in charge of that trust. It was one of the entities Atlas was given to accomplish their goals.

I pick up the recorder and throw it across the room. He was trying to tell me. He wanted me to know. My anger wouldn't allow me to listen.

"I'll handle it, Baba. I'll make it all right again. Goodbye," I murmur to myself.

***

"So this guy… did he say what all this was about?" Jeff asks after his harness is placed on him and we start for our skydiving flight.

"He didn't get to say much. He had my wife at gunpoint," I reply.

"How does your grandfather feel about this? I mean, you took a life, right? Are you back in? Can we celebrate in earnest?"

"I don't know if he's going to go back on his word. She's my wife and my best friend's cousin. I had to handle the situation."

"Wow, your best friend? I remember that once used to be my title. Does your best friend know about your little family?

"Does she know you're married to her cousin? Has she ever had your back when you needed it? Does she even know who you are?"

I whip around and glare at Jeff. Not wanting to jump the gun, I close the space between us but keep my cool. I'm barely holding on to my anger.

"I'd be very careful of what you say next. She knows what I need her to know. You all know what I want you to know." I tilt my head to the side. "You're getting familiar, Jeff. It's starting to feel like disrespect. You wouldn't be disrespecting me, would you?"

"No, I'm just saying I've done a whole lot more for you than these people. I was here first. I've been loyal to you all our lives."

I dip to look him in the face as he hangs his head. "You sure about that? Everyone changes to suit their needs, have you?"

"No disrespect," he says tightly. "I just don't want to see you lose yourself."

I take a step back and lift my head. I nod, pulling a hand down the corners of my mouth. "Then you don't know me. Not like you think you do."

He throws his hands in the air. "I'll back off. You won't hear a thing from me again."

I snort and start for the plane.

"Josh, I'm not going to go. I'm going home. I have some shit to do."

"Get on the plane, Jeff. I have my grandfather's ear. I can get you what you want. That is if it's still what you want."

Just as I thought, he breaks his fucking neck to get on the plane. Pit, Ox, Achilles, Lex, and Skittles are already on the plane, seated on the straddle benches, Achilles on the floor. Jeff turns to look at me.

"I thought this was an Asshole trip. Where are the others?"

"Have a seat. Everyone who needs to be here is here," I bite out.

He moves to take a seat on the floor, eyeing me as he buckles his seat belt. I take my seat and do the same. The door is closed and we take off. We all remain quiet for most of the ride.

It takes twenty minutes to get to altitude. With each second, my rage builds and bubbles to the surface. Five minutes out from the jump, I look at Jeff.

"Come, Jeff, you're jumping with me."

He gets up and moves to stand with me. Our years of friendship flash through my head. I treated his ass like family. He was like a brother.

Power is a funny thing. It's not meant to be placed in the hands of everyone. Some jump out the window, thinking they have a hold on it, only to find out they didn't close their hand around it.

Some claim to have it, but they're only talking to themselves. Others make a claim but know they don't have it, so they lie, steal, and cry victim toward true authority. I don't want to be any of those people.

It's the fact that I don't want it that makes it mine to wield. I was born for it. It's my birthright and because of that, I'll find my way and everything will fall into place.

I shake my head clear and pull out my phone. I dial my grandfather as I make a decision on what I truly want. Now is as good a time as any.

"What are you doing?" Jeff asks as I dial.

"I'm calling Pappoús. He has positions to fill."

Jeff gives me a smug grin. While the FaceTime rings, I look him in the eyes.

"You know what's crazy?" I say.

"What's that?"

"I'm going to have to send those kids to therapy after all of this. There's even a chance my wife is going to wake up in a few weeks and realize I've killed in front of her. My grandfather could go back on his promise, and I'll become someone I never wanted to be, but all you're worried about is rising in power in Vander," I say.

"Yeah, there's a part of me that really wants to be a friend and care about all that. I love you, Josh, truly I do, but then there's this part of me that needs to take my spot in Vander, so fuck all that."

I scoff. "Burn it all, right?"

He shrugs. I hold my hand up as Skittles looks like she's going to lunge at him. The instructor I've paid handsomely opens the door and moves aside as I previously told him to. Pappoús picks up right on time.

"*Tzósoua mou,* how are you?"

"I'm good, Pappoús. I have that decision for you. I don't think I can be mayor. Mayven would be a better fit. Give it to her. I want my crown," I say.

In the next breath, I push the button on the bar ring Jeff gave me, releasing the blade. Swiftly, I slice his throat. I then kick him in the chest, sending him flying backward from the plane.

Then, because I have so much rage in me, I pull my gun, step to the opening of the plane and shoot him in the chest seven times as his body falls, all while filming for Pappoús to see.

When I look at the screen and flip the view for Pappoús to see my face, he nods. "This is what you want?"

"It's who I am. No one is forcing me and I'm doing it my way. I just have one question. Why not tell me it was him I couldn't trust?"

"I wanted you to learn a lesson."

"And what's that?"

"Once you see a snake and it's attack, you will recognize it in the future before it gets close enough to strike."

"Lesson learned."

"Very well. All of you boys and my little friend come to see me. We will finalize the positions."

"See you soon."

CHAPTER SEVENTY-FOUR

Forever Mine

Kelex

A year later...

I smile to myself as I look in the mirror. I'm dressed in my tux with a blue tie on. I push a hand through my hair to get it out of my face, but it tumbles back into its layers.

I grin as Pappoús comes to pat me on my shoulder. When I turn to him, he reaches to fix my tie. His eyes are filled with so much peace and joy. A look I've never truly seen on him before.

"Now you look ready," he croons and pats my cheek.

"Thank you."

"You continue to make me proud, *Tzósoua mou*. You've exceeded my expectations."

"I've done what I felt was best."

I have. Back home, I've done what needed to be done. First order of business was to shut down the other families for good. My years of getting to know the Vander and Bridge Lake wives came in handy.

No more plotting, no more scheming from their husbands. Most were willing to move on and never return. Others I had to deal with more forcefully.

I'm glad to say that part of my life is over. This is the life I wanted. I'm married with three amazing kids I now call mine. I'm surrounded by true friends and I've made my own success.

"Happiness looks good on you. Come, let's go see our girl."

I smile broader. I love the relationship Pappoús has with Shawna. When we're in the States, he calls her almost every day.

Shawna

If I thought my first wedding was out of this world, I was mistaken. This has been beyond my wildest dreams. So many moments that have made my heart swell.

Starting with breakfast with my dad and uncles. Uncle Lester had such a big smile on his face. Almost as big as the day he returned to Vander and saw his first grandson for the first time.

Lex lost her shit. We were all in tears as they reunited. It's a day I'll never forget.

Like today. Seeing him play with AJ and Colten has been one of the highlights. It's good to be surrounded by family. No secrets, no lies.

Then there was the moment during the ceremony when Josh and I gave the kids glass shadow boxes with copies of their official adoption papers. We'd waited until then because we wanted them to feel like they were a part of our day.

Then there was the moment when my husband sang to me. I'll never forget that because he did it with wings on his back and a choir backing him. He sang "I'll Be Waiting," reminding me of when he cut the blond from his hair.

"What are you thinking?" Josh leans into my ear to whisper.

I look up at the chandeliers hanging over the long table as our family and friends laugh around us. Taking in the flowers and elegance, I smile. Then I take in the smiles on our kids' faces.

"I'm thinking about how lucky this baby will be." I cover my stomach as I speak the words.

Josh grabs my face and turns me to face him. He looks into my eyes, his own sparkling with joy. I give him a small nod and he takes my lips in a deep kiss.

"I love the fuck out of you," he breathes into my mouth.

"I love you too," I laugh.

Assholes for Life

Skittles

Fifteen years later...

I come out of the bathroom and walk through the house Josh had built for Shawna and their big-ass family. It's my best friend's birthday. Fifty-one years old. I can't believe we're so old and we're closer than ever. I now know all of Josh's secrets.

I often stop to think about how I wouldn't be here if it weren't for him. Josh saved my life. I gained a family that night.

My assholes have turned into a bunch of fine-ass silver foxes. Although my husband thinks I don't know that he's been having his hair dyed. I give him a pass because he's keeping that body intact.

I stop to look at the pictures hanging in the hall Shawna has made into a gallery. My face breaks into a smile as I look at the picture of Kelex with wings on his back.

Shawna loves that photo. She re-created the original shoot and made her own version. I turn my gaze to another picture. This is Josh with his youngest. Perseus is his father's twin.

It's like Kelex spit him out. It's no wonder at six, he's taking the modeling world by storm. That little smile is priceless. While Perseus is his father's shadow and wants to do everything his daddy does, Kelex has turned out to be a girl dad. His four little princesses have him wrapped around their fingers.

Not to mention the fact that Cat and Vernice are thirty and twenty-six and can still call their dad any time of the night and he'll go running. My friend is a great father to all his children.

Including his oldest, his little buddy turned grown man. True is such a talented young man. Young, black, and successful, that's how Forbes described him last month.

"Time flies," Shawna says as she walks up beside me.

"Tell me about it. I can't believe we're so old."

She laughs. "Speak for yourself."

"Um, you're right. You're still out here having babies."

"Perseus is six. We're not having any more babies."

"Did you not see your husband's face when he blew out the candles? I think his wish was to have one more baby. You better watch it tonight." I laugh and dance out of her reach.

We make our way outside to the rest of the party. Ox is in the pool with AJ and Leo. I can't believe AJ is going to be eighteen. He's so handsome. All my nephews are.

AJ is almost as tall as his dad now. At one point, I thought Ox and Kelex were in a baby-making competition. Every time

Shawna would announce she was pregnant, Lex would turn up knocked up next.

I'm not about that life. I had one more after our twins. Two boys and a girl. That was it for us. Nicky and Nina were first, then we had Ethan. The only reason Lex and Ox only have four is because when Ox found out she was pregnant with a girl the last time, he didn't want to try anymore.

He shut that shit down so fast I still laugh my ass off when I think about it. Although he's crazy about Kylie. That man will tear your head off for looking at his little girl wrong.

"Auntie Ven, look out," Colten croons as he and Bruce run by and dive into the pool.

Their older brother AJ frowns at them and splashes them with water as they come back up. I shake my head. These kids are something else. I still can't believe I have two sixteen-year-olds.

I move to sit on the edge of the pool between Kelex and Pit. Josh is holding Perseus in his arms as he's fast asleep.

"If it isn't Mayor Mayven," Josh murmurs.

"Shut up," I say and frown at him.

This has been a long-standing joke for the last sixteen years. Because of him, I've been the mayor of Bridge Lake for three terms and Vander for one. I can't remember the last time someone called me Skittles.

We've grown up. Will is a public advocate, Josh sits as controller, and Ox is a city council member and both Lex and Shawna lead community boards. I don't think we run Vander and Bridge Lake the way our parents and grandparents wanted us to, but we're doing a lot of things our way.

Although, don't get it fucked up. The savages still come out when needed. My Assholes are still assholes.

We still live life doing what makes us happy. However, I was surprised when Leo announced he'd be running for Bridge Lake's mayoral office.

I smile as I turn and look at Josh. "You know, you still owe me ten grand," I tease.

"For what?"

"You guys all married within five years and had kids. Where's my money, Josh?" I say in my best Stewie voice before bursting into laughter.

"I'll get right on that," he snorts. "You know, you were right about something else."

"Oh yeah, what was that?"

He turns to look me in the eyes. I see why Shawna loves his hair like this. Even with the streaks of gray, it's still so full and lush and brings something pretty yet dangerous to his features.

"I'm looking back and realizing it was all for my good. It all came full circle," he says, then dips to kiss Perseus's brow.

"Yeah, I guess it did," I say with a smile as Shawna comes and sits next to him, placing her head on his shoulder.

Laughter draws my attention back to the pool. Ox has Lex wrapped in his embrace from behind. The kids are splashing Leo. He has a huge smile on his face as he splashes them back.

It did come full circle for us all. I can't say I'd change a thing because it shaped who we are. All this love came from what we've been through.

"Yo, Ethan, leave your sister alone. She said she doesn't want to get her hair wet," Pit calls to our youngest son.

"Thanks, Daddy," Nina says and rolls her eyes at her little brother. "Ugh, you play too much."

"I've got you, baby girl," Pit croons. Then he looks at me. "That kid always has to take it too far."

"Um, wonder where he gets that from?" I tap at my lip.

"His mother."

"I wonder who this new baby will take after?" I muse, covering my stomach.

"Mayven, you know you're fucking lying. My knees can barely handle lifting your ass and tossing you around these days. Leave them change-of-life babies to pretty boy over there."

Kelex gives him the finger. I fall into Pit laughing. He wraps an arm around my head and kisses the top. "What would I do without that laugh?"

"You will never know."

"That laugh makes me miss the cabin," Josh says.

"Right, good times. You guys remember that one Christmas?" I say while looking at Leo with a smile.

Pit and Josh crack up. "Thank God it worked out. They probably wouldn't have talked to us ever again if it hadn't," Josh chuckles.

"You can say that again," Pit says through his laughter.

I smile at the memory. I still love my guys. No matter what's going on, they're still my Assholes for life.

ACKNOWLEDGMENTS

The goal from the beginning of this series was getting Kelex back behind the wheel for the love of his life. I did that. I am releasing this series from my life and finally moving on. It is done. Leo for Christmas will be a wave goodbye, the icing on the cake.

Thank you so much for your support and patience. This took a lot from me. I had to work through some things to get it done. In the end, I love Josh and Shawna and who they became. It's always my goal to write what makes me happy. If I can stand on my words with integrity and heart, I've done what I set out to do.

I write romance. The kind that is based on love and respect. I'm an author of words and love. I give escapes while creating an escape of my own. I give the gift of joy in words. I thank you for the emails, comments, posts, inboxes, and encouragement that confirms I'm in line with my mission.

Huge shout-out to my husband again. He talked me through this, encouraging me the whole way. When I was done and ready to say nah, next. He told me to keep going, do my thing.

As always, I will not take for granted the opportunity to say, *I thank you, God, for this gift.* I put my all into this. As God gives to me, I give to the world. To Him be all the glory. I thank God for covering me. I will repeat, anointings are God given and can never be stolen. Touch not His anointed, do His prophets no harm.

Next! *We're going back to the Legally Bound Universe. Trevor!*

Wait, there is more to come! You can stay updated with my latest releases, learn more about me, the author, and be a part of contests by subscribing to my newsletter at
www.BlueSaffire.com
If you enjoyed *Kelex*, I'd love to hear your thoughts and please feel free to leave a review. And when you do, please let me know by emailing me TheBlueSaffire@gmail.com or leave a comment on Facebook
https://www.facebook.com/BlueSaffireDiaries or Twitter @TheBlueSaffire

Other books by Blue Saffire
Placed in Best Reading Order
Also available....
Legally Bound

Legally Bound 2: Against the Law

Legally Bound 3: His Law

Perfect for Me

Hush 1: Family Secrets

Ballers: His Game

Brothers Black 1: Wyatt the Heartbreaker

Legally Bound 4: Allegations of Love

Hush 2: Slow Burn

Legally Bound 5.0: Sam

Coming Soon…

Wild Hearts: Lost Hearts Series
Pieces of Trevor's Heart: Lost Hearts Series
Ballers 3: His Team

Out Now and Complete Series
Work Husband Series

Unexpected Lovers
My Best Friend's Wish
The Ones Left Behind
The Last Ones Standing

The Blackhart Brothers Series

Calling on Quinn Book 1
In Deep: Kevin or Nothing Book 2 Coming 2023

The Lost Souls MC Series

Forever
Never
Always

Check out Blue Saffire exclusives on the
BlueSaffire.com website

Razor
Dane
Trip
Dom
The Fixer
Lost

Other books from Evei Lattimore Collection Books by Blue Saffire

Black Bella 1

Destiny 1: Life Decisions

Destiny 2: Decisions of the Next Generation
Destiny 3 coming soon…

Star

Other books from Royal Blue Gay Romance Collection written by Blue Saffire

Kyle's Reveal
Beau's Redemption

www.ingramcontent.com/pod-product-compliance
Lightning Source LLC
Chambersburg PA
CBHW061507020726
47502CB00006B/1971